The Best
AMERICAN
SPORTS
WRITING
1998

The Best AMERICAN SPORTS WRITING 1998

EDITED AND WITH
AN INTRODUCTION BY
Bill Littlefield

Glenn Stout, *Series Editor*

HOUGHTON MIFFLIN COMPANY
BOSTON • NEW YORK 1998

ISSN: 1056-8034   ISBN: 0-395-79764-0

Printed in the United States of America

QUM 10 9 8 7 6 5 4 3 2 1

(continued on page 400)

Contents

Foreword

I GET A LOT OF MAIL.

Each year I receive hundreds and hundreds of story submissions. Most are sent by writers and editors, but some are sent by their wives, husbands, parents, children, former roommates, current roommates, ex-lovers, current lovers, imprisoned acquaintances, or schizophrenic stalkers. On rare occasions, I've even received submissions from the well-meaning stranger who just wanted to make sure I didn't miss a story he or she really liked. In addition to these manila envelopes, I also receive hundreds of magazine subscriptions, resulting in thousands of individual issues, all of which make the circuitous trek from my P.O. box, to the floor of my car, to the kitchen table, to my room, to a box, then to the floor next to my chair, where they either go into a small box and occasionally whisper, "Read me again," or start a reverse trek which ends every second Wednesday in the plastic box of recyclables at the end of my driveway.

Don't get me wrong. I don't mind. Reading for a (partial) living is an exquisite and sort of perverse pleasure, one I particularly enjoy when I walk past sites of previous employment, like large holes in the earth full of mud and concrete. I enjoy getting all this mail, particularly when I send something into the small box that whispers back. Some of my best days are spent with the stories that make it into this book each year. There is little I enjoy more than gnawing on a great story while time slows and sometimes seems to stop.

The only drawback to serving as series editor is that I've ended up on every mailing list in use on the North American continent. I get so much residual junk mail that I'm tempted to start gluing it all together into bricks and building a house worthy of a profile in *Popular Mechanics* ("You Can Build a Postal Palace . . . for Pennies!"). I receive such items as catalogs for everything from collectible dolls to health aids to road signs, the expected barrage of offers for credit cards offering interest rates that rise from o to 39.9 percent after six minutes, and promotional materials for every magazine of every possible description ever published or even discussed in a conference room with air conditioning. As difficult as it is for a worthy example of writing to catch my attention, it's a hell of a lot harder for one of these disposables to catch my eye. In fact, in the eight years I've been doing this, it has happened once.

I open almost everything, because I don't want to send cellophane out with paper and thereby commit an eco-crime, so I do my best to separate envelope from contents. One day in the midst of last year's sports writing season, I happened across a scrap of promotional material for *New Magazine*.

Before I begin insulting the undoubtedly hardworking and talented writers who work for this what-will-remain-anonymous *New Magazine*, I have to say that I don't really believe any of the market-driven, hyperbole-ridden drivel contained in the promotional packet. I don't believe the writers for *New Magazine* do either. Some of them will probably be in this book someday. But I'm not going to allow that to stop me. For among the bulleted phrases that breathlessly touted the arrival of *New Magazine* was one that, well, just made me get over to my chair and sit right down.

Not only did New Magazine promise to be "BIGGER" (ooh!), "BOLDER!" (aah!), and "MORE EXCITING!" (as Grandma used to say, "Now my head's just a-whirling"), *New Magazine* also promised to be . . .

. . . "A MUCH FASTER READ."

Now that, as they say, is a thought.

In my experience I've found that much of the world's best literature has, in fact, been marred by just this defect, for being a "slow read." I'm telling ya', *Middlemarch* would have been one hell of a read if it only would have taken fifteen minutes. *Ulysses?* A dream in half an hour. Same goes for *The Iliad* and all those other books I've still got sitting around from college. Let's face it, even short books, like *Tao Te Ching*, shouldn't have taken more than a second or two. "Uh-huh" and "Uh-uh" just about sum it up, don't you think? And two pitches are plenty for a baseball game, too.

I don't know how, but that little nugget of a literary goal had escaped me, my seventeen years of education, and my near decade in reasonably full employ as a writer. It's no wonder I haven't gotten more accomplished, what with way too many not-so-fast reads clogging my mail box and cluttering up my house. Of all writer-stuff I've worried about over the years, from proper footnoting and "who" versus "whom" to the emergence of language poetry, this "fast-read" business somehow slipped right past me.

And I'd always thought that really good writing was timeless, and that time spent reading didn't detract from my life, but added to it. I guess I was mistaken.

But it's far too late for me to change. Call me a Luddite if you want, but here at the world headquarters of *The Best American Sports Writing*, we see things a little differently. We have a "bullet phrase" too, one which we quaintly refer to in the archaic form as a "slogan" or "shibboleth." Here it is . . .

"A MUCH SLOWER READ."

And I mean slow in the sense it's so good you don't want to rush through it, except perhaps, in anticipation of the next story. Because here at *TBASW*, we believe that writing is more than just the transmittal of information or an excuse to send advertising into your home every month. If I've done my job, this book will take you a while to read and will feel like time well spent.

What I look for in the mail each year is the best writing that happens to be about sports in some way. That's what this book is and that's what I try to provide, without prejudice in terms of the writer, the subject, or the source. I know this is a great comfort to some of the writers at *New Magazine*, because some have told me of their nefarious plans to slip "slow reads" in between its covers. Good writing simply can't be stopped. I believe writers are much too smart for that.

Those still seeking a fast read may wish to skip the next several paragraphs, which describe how to send me material for consideration for *The Best American Sports Writing 1999*. You will probably consider it a waste of time and won't want to appear in the book anyway. I'll let you know when *The Best American Faster Reads* is coming out.

Each year, I read every issue of some three hundred sports and general interest magazines in search of writing that might merit inclusion in *The Best American Sports Writing.* I also look at the Sunday magazines from about fifty daily newspapers and read as many newspapers as I can. I try not to miss anything, so each year I send requests to the editors of more than three hundred magazines and three hundred newspapers asking them to submit stories to me for consideration, or better yet, provide me with a complimentary subscription to their publication.

The subscriptions really help. I live in a small town and the post office is a big employer. Besides, individual submissions sometimes risk getting overlooked in the glut of material I receive each January. Writers and readers and any other interested parties are encouraged to send me stories they've written or read that they would like to see in this series. Writers should pay attention here, because your editor may not bother submitting anything, and let's face it, who knows your own work best — you, or that person with a title who is always messing up your lead to justify his or her salary?

Each year, I submit the best seventy-five stories or so to the guest editor, who makes the final selection. This year's guest editor, Bill Littlefield, set a new standard with his willingness to read additional material and entertain a dialogue over their merits, all of which have combined to make this year's *Best American Sports Writing* one of the strongest yet. Richard Ford, who will guest edit *The Best American Sports Writing 1999,* has his work cut out for him.

To be considered for inclusion in next year's volume, each nonfiction story must have been published in 1998 in either the United States or Canada and must be column length or longer. Reprints or book excerpts are not eligible. I must receive all stories by February 1, 1999. Due to a change in our publication date, this deadline is as firm as one can imagine.

All submissions must include author's name, date of publication, publication name and address. Photocopies, tearsheets, or clean copies are fine. Reductions to 8 ½ x 11 are best. Submissions from on-line publications must be made in hard copy. Submissions cannot be returned, and I don't feel it is appropriate for me to comment on, or critique, any submissions. Submit as many stories as you wish, but if you send me thirty stories, they all better be good, and if they are that good, you may want to put them in your own book. Publications that want to make 100 percent certain their contributions are considered should provide a complimentary subscription to the address listed below. Those that already do so should make sure to extend the subscription for another couple of years.

Please send subscriptions or submissions to this exact address:

Glenn Stout
Series Editor
The Best American Sports Writing
P.O. Box 381
Uxbridge, MA 01569

You may also contact me via E-mail at ChinMusic@compuserve.com. I'll try to answer, but I don't go there every day. However, *no submissions of material will be accepted electronically.* There is no way for me to make certain any such submissions were really published, so please respect this request.

Copies of previous editions of this book can be ordered through most bookstores. Earlier volumes may be available from out-of-print book dealers that you can find in the Yellow Pages. Unfortunately, I do not have copies of earlier editions, nor can I be of any assistance in helping you acquire any.

My thanks again go out to my editor Marnie Cochran, who doesn't mess with my leads, guest editor and friend Bill Littlefield, Siobhan, and Saorla, who is responsible for me doing most of my work at dawn, long before she wakes. Yet once again, I dedicate this book to the writers, and to all those who continue to produce the work that speaks to me — slowly — long after I have read it for the first time.

GLENN STOUT

Introduction

IN THE FINAL CHAPTER ("The Meaning of Life") of a remarkable book (*How the Mind Works*) Steven Pinker, the head of the Center for Cognitive Neuroscience at Massachusetts Institute of Technology, asks this question: "Why do we pursue the trivial and futile and experience them as sublime?"

Professor Pinker is not puzzling over the attractions of our games. He has in mind various pursuits which many folks regard as anything but "trivial and futile," and which they would certainly consider more significant than basketball, soccer, baseball, or even the Super Bowl. Professor Pinker has in mind art, literature, music, and philosophy.

But the question could as easily be asked about the kabillion-dollar industry of our games. As Damon Runyon (a great writer who, happily for sports, sometimes wrote about them) would have put it if he'd lived long enough, we value Michael Jordan, Tiger Woods, Mike Tyson, Monica Seles, and Nikki McCray "no little and quite some." The proof is in the paychecks they and others earn for doing what they do, and in the even larger paychecks some of them receive for pretending to be very enthusiastic about particular soft drinks, shampoos, and exhaust systems.

The standard answer to Professor Pinker's question as it applies to sports is that we value our best athletes because they do things we can't do. One sports writer of my acquaintance was asked how he felt about the elimination of the slam dunk contest at the NBA All-Star Game "because it had become dull."

"I don't get it," he said. "Since when is men flying dull?"

But the "they can do what we can't" answer isn't the only explanation, and the greatest athletes don't just fly. For years before anyone ever hears of them, they devote themselves to their crafts, often in solitude, sometimes to the exclusion of other pursuits most of us take for granted. (Literacy and the childhood opportunity to play at something pointlessly and without consequence are two common casualties.) They work themselves into extraordinary condition and stay there. They ignore all sorts of distractions and diversions and bring to their work great resources of concentration. The best of them get as good as they can possibly be at doing the thing they do, and the rest of us, watching them and leading our better-balanced lives, wonder about how good we might have gotten at something if we'd devoted ourselves to whatever we do as ferociously as the athletes have embraced running or hitting or shooting. In that respect and others, they bear our dreams. One day a friend and I were talking about that function of our athletes, and the friend suddenly smiled and said, "Maybe we don't pay them enough."

And athletes do more — or at least most of them do — when our games go as they're supposed to go, that is, when somebody at center stage in the drama of sport doesn't kick a cameraman, choke his coach, or bite his opponent's ear off. Absent buffoonery, the athletes give us images of spontaneous brilliance within a setting that is described precisely by boundaries and rules. They do exceptional, sometimes initially inexplicable things within a context that is apparently simple to understand and appreciate. Why the stock market will do whatever it will do next is beyond anyone's comprehension, never mind that the myriad analysts have to say something at the end of each weekday's action. You can't say with certainty whether the Bears or the Bulls will win on a given Saturday evening or Sunday afternoon either, but because of those obvious, dependable boundaries and the unmistakable distinction between a ball caught and a ball dropped, when it's over, if you've been paying attention, you can re-create the action, find turning points, and analyze strengths and weaknesses. Then, after dinner, you can take out your videotape and do it again, even more confident that you understand it all, since you've used the technology. This is as true of a grade-school basketball game or hockey game between squirts, mites, or midgets as it is of a tilt between millionaire pros, though anyone who spends much time studying the former should be grabbed by the ears and shaken until some of the BBs bounce into different slots.

The point here is that at all levels, our games appear to offer us what our personal relationships, our work lives, our court system, and our stubborn, feeble attempts to cure the culture's plagues and predict the weather rarely provide: final scores, irrefutable winners and losers, heroes and bums. Kurt Vonnegut called it "foma": the lies we need to be happy and free.

But in the hands of our best practitioners on their best days, the stories of our games also give us what Professor Pinker was asking his question about in the first place: art, literature, music, philosophy. I don't know many of the writers whose work appears in this collection. I've never asked the few whom I do know why they've chosen as their subjects games, the people who play them, and the people who watch them. But even in this single collection, some of the answers are evident. An observant soccer mom can see in the ambience of a kids' game the heartbreaking, impossible struggle to raise children without stunting them, endangering them, or abandoning them too early to their own devices. A fellow seeking to establish "bird-watching as a blood sport" can ask in that context questions which sound worthy of Professor Pinker's challenge: "How to see? How to see more clearly? We know so little of inner light sources, speak so little of them, sound so flaky when we do, yet our seeing illuminates so little of our world!"

If you want to write a great story involving sports, it isn't necessarily a bad idea to follow the crowd to the brightest lights. Consider history. Norman Mailer traveled to Africa for the Heavyweight Championship of the World. Roger Angell attended the '86 World Series. Hunter Thompson sort of went to a Super Bowl. We're grateful that these three were among the hundreds of writers at these large events.

But as numbers of the writers represented in this series have demonstrated, lining up for the big game isn't the only way to go after a great story. Consider rock lifting. Consider the delight the writer Tad Friend must have felt when he asked the Basque hero of this obscure competition to explain what had gone wrong when he'd failed to lift the rock, and this answer came back: "The stone was very heavy."

It's been said of great poets that they sometimes seem to be speaking to each other, even across centuries, worrying and reworking the same few, worthy themes. There's a bit of that going on in this collection as well. If you think too much can be said even about a phenomenon as brilliant and well financed as Tiger Woods, for you there is Bruce McCall's contention that "No game designed to be played with the aid of personal servants by right-handed men who can't even bring their dogs can be entirely good for the soul." If you cannot bear even one more story about how achieving expertise at a game can create character and lift one from poverty and despair, there is former football player Elwood Reid's chilling epitaph for his own career: "It left me with this clear-cut of a body, a burned-out village that I sacked for sport." If you don't quite buy Steve Marantz's earnest contention that men admire the greatest female athletes for reasons that have nothing to do with their looks, there is Tony Hendra's one-liner about the bullfighter with whom he is smitten: "Christina Sánchez just might be sex incarnate."

Nor are the comparisons and contrasts limited to duels between one-liners. One of the pleasures of choosing the stories for this collection came in the discovery that several of them side by side will ignite splendid debates. Which has the more powerful plot? The tale of a tennis player who may be on the edge of achieving all there is to achieve in sports? or the chronicle of a basketball player who managed, somehow, to sidestep the wealth and glory for which he seemed destined? or the portrait of the feisty hitter who's been through legal wrangles, jail, divorce — enough suffering, certainly, to have learned something — and who has apparently learned nothing?

Another question for debate suggested by what follows: where will the growing interest in women's sports at all levels take us? to a time more balanced and sane than the buy-this-buy-that sound and fury of the NCAA's March Madness, the NBA Championship, and the Super Bowl? or to a place where the inclination of men who have power to abuse women who don't will be even more thoroughly grafted onto all that's already wrong with our games?

And sometimes the questions (and invitations to debate) are more universal. Check Gary Smith's challenge in the middle of his piece about a family of high-wire performers and their most spectacular and dangerous stunt: "You keep watching and tell me what you think," Smith writes. "I can never decide if The Pyramid's a prayer to God, or a thumbing of the nose at Him."

In the best moments of the best of these stories, we think about such things and more. Maybe it's not possible to decide in the abstract which is more noble: to submit to age and declining powers with grace, or to rage against gravity's not-so-gradual triumph. But three cheers, minimum, for the writer who can bring the conflict into focus with the struggle of one man or woman trying to live through it each day while everybody's watching. (And a fourth cheer if he or she can make us laugh.) This is not, of course, a conflict limited to athletes, and that's another reason we pay so much attention to these stories. Whether consciously or not, the young man or woman who chooses to devote himself or herself to a sport chooses to die twice. It's been said lots of times, but the fact is no less a fact for that, even if the circumstances have changed for a lot of the athletes. A ballplayer at thirty-eight is an old man. His peers may be just beginning to excel in whatever professions they've chosen. It's no doubt easier to face retirement from your life's work if you've put a lot of money away, as many retired athletes today have done. But even if you're rich, waking up in the morning without the activity and purpose that have been the center of your day for, say, twenty-five years, is spooky. Even Magic Johnson kept coming back. It would not be accurate to say we feel compelled to watch athletes at the end of their careers in the same way and for the same reasons that we slow down when we pass a traffic accident. But there is, in each case, a chance to make mortality's acquaintance vicariously, temporarily, and with minimal risk.

We watch the games for the fun of them, too. Some of us paint our faces and some of us bet. Some of our best writers are drawn to the games for the fun as well, but in their work they do more than remind us of the sensational catch or the thirty-foot bucket at the buzzer. They stop, for a moment, the merry-go-round of games and lead us to what they've discovered in one career, or one contest, or one moment. And as good writers always do, no matter what they're writing about, they show us that whatever else is in the story they've found and built and rebuilt, we're in it, too.

BILL LITTLEFIELD

TONY HENDRA

Blonde and Sand

FROM GQ

I'VE ATTENDED QUITE A FEW BULLFIGHTS IN MY LIFE. I still
don't know exactly what it all means, nor, I think, does anyone else,
least of all the mad dogs of People for the Ethical Treatment of
Animals. But I've never been to a corrida where I didn't feel the
urge to cheer the death of the bull. There's relief on behalf of the
matador — that the guy hasn't had his innards unzipped — and
you feel an intensely visceral release from a spectacle that combines
athletics with blood, blades and mortal danger. So you always give
Ferdinand a big send-off.

But when I first saw Cristina Sánchez — the petite, shapely 25-
year-old blonde who in 1996 became the only woman in Spain's
long and machismo-drenched history to qualify as a full-fledged
matador — it was different. *I wanted to be the bull.*

I don't mean just that I identified with the bull. Sure, those
electrifying Picasso ink sketches in which naked Minotaurs couple
with naked Amazons were pixelating across my fantasy screen. But
what I had in mind was this: for a few moments, I actually wanted
to be a 1,200-pound mountain of mad, black muscle armed with
two-foot-long ice-pick horns and see — against all the odds — if I
couldn't tag her.

I know. Sick.

All I had to go on was a scratchy, shaky bootleg video of Christian's *alternativa*. (The *alternativa* is an initiation ceremony in which
a matador fights a full-grown, 4-year-old bull for the first time.) But
it was enough. She was something entirely new, something young

and — if you go for that high-cheeked, gypsyish look — beautiful. And on top of it all, deadly. A deadly goddess-babe.

Her first kill as an official matador was by the book. But even on the bumpy, jumpy tape, I found her hypnotizing. She wore a gold-and-sky blue *traje de luces* that broadened her shoulders and shrink-wrapped her belly, hips and thighs. Her thick blonde hair hung in a heavy French braid, oddly echoing the era one hundred years ago when the men who fought bulls advertised their calling with a distinctly unmanly pigtail.

Her nostrils flared white with tension, the classic Iberian profile, so taut it looked as though something along the line from her forehead to her throat might snap. At arm's length, her right hand held a razor-sharp three-foot sword. Sighting down the sword at the dark, panting mass before her, she lowered her left hand, gently waving a piece of red flannel to coax the huge Minotaur head toward the sand, so the bull would not lurch forward and bury its horn in her groin. Then she rose on tiptoe, froze for a long moment and, with one swift running lunge, thrust the sword over the bull's horns and deep into the back of its neck.

The bull died quickly. The crowd came to its feet. Cristina Sánchez had made the taurine history books and — more to the point — *ABC World News Saturday*. There was coverage across the globe, notably in animal-rights-conscious Britain and the United States. But for Cristina, the PETA principle seemed to have been suspended. Her right as a woman to breach this particular boys' club superseded the rights of the innocent animal brother.

For me, beast that I am, all I took away from the whole affair was . . . sex. I know, I know. Even sicker.

The sexuality of the bullring isn't something aficionados talk about much, perhaps because, from Homer to Hemingway, bulls have tended to be a guy thing. There are few more potent symbols of machismo than a fellow in spangled tights facing down what Tom Lehrer once called "a half-ton of angry pot roast" — and it's a very serious business. Bringing up sex in so rarefied a context is a bit like commenting to your Super Bowl buddies how thoroughly you admire the roundness and firmness of the wide receiver's buttocks.

Much preferred are grandiose statements about strength and courage, mortality and art. If there must be explanations of the hold bullfighting has on the collective id, they tend to expound on its ritual symbolism and atavistic roots. Paco Aguado, a correspondent for *Tendido Cero*, Spanish television's top bullfighting show, voices a common interpretation: *"El toro representa la naturaleza salvaje; el torero simboliza la victoria de la raza humana."* ("The bull represents the savagery of nature; the bullfighter symbolizes the victory of the human race.") Joseph Campbell, the mythologist, once explained the bullfight as a reenactment of the primordial rituals in which shamans of the sun symbolically overthrew the night: "The brave moon-bull with its crescent horns slain by the solar blade of the sparkling matador."

Well, O.K. But why does the late-twentieth-century public still bring such naked passion to the plaza? Defeating "the savagery of nature" for the umpteenth time doesn't seem like a priority when you have an Audi triple-parked outside. In the Age of Halogen, shamans of the sun draw a lot of unemployment.

The fact is, sexuality drives the frenzy of the bullfight and suffuses the image of the matador. Hemingway understood that in *The Sun Also Rises*, and not just its effect on Lady Brett. "He's a damned good-looking boy," says Jake Barnes. "When we were up in his room I never saw a better-looking kid." And Madonna grasped the bullfight's sexual symbolism in her "Take a Bow" video. In one respect, this sexuality is right up front. Every "sparkling matador" I've ever seen wears his unit bunched prominently on his inner left thigh with only skintight pants for protection. His basic stance to the bull is literally balls out, thrusting his crotch at the animal as he goads it into a charge. This is either courageous or stupid, depending on where you're coming from, but there's not a lot of symbolism going on. It's "my balls against yours, brave moon-bull." Most of the multiple, and often hideous, *cornadas* (horn wounds) that matadors suffer throughout their careers are in the area of the groin and lower abdomen.

The sexuality of the corrida has always had a profound hold on women. In Spain, a society largely unmoved by North American notions of gender roles, virility is still considered desirable, and demonstrating it in the very real danger of the bullring is much admired. Thanks in large part to television, bullfighting is going through a sustained boom, and the top rank of young toreros — almost all in their mid to late twenties — are treated a lot like rock stars. To the dismay of taurine graybeards, Gap-clad teenagers and young women flock to the rings, and the olés become ever more treble. The biggest heartthrob for this treble-olé set is a gangly 23-year-old sad sack named Jesulín (little Jesus), a poor boy from Andalusia who appalls purists by promoting corridas starring only himself, which only women can attend. They often throw their bras and panties onto the sand, along with the more traditional hats, flowers and wineskins.

Aficionados fear to tread in the sexual quagmire of the corrida; academics, however, rush in. Just as American eggheads troll the daytime soaps for metaphor and metonymy, their Iberian counterparts love to cogitate on the titillating allegory of the bullfight. The bull is an ancient symbol in Mediterranean civilization (bull worship has been documented as early as 4000 B.C., in the Halafian culture of Syria and Turkey) and, through its connection with the moon, is associated with female, as well as male, fertility. So there is considerable scholarly speculation about the sexual roles played in the ring. There are the crypto-Freudian theories: that the bull represents the id, whose dark chthonic forces must be tamed and overthrown by the superego (the matador); or that the bull represents patriarchal authority, the father who must be killed and replaced by the son. These notions embrace the obvious fact that the bull is masculine, but a more tendentious school claims that the role of the bull is actually feminine. The "seduction" of the bull by the matador's cape work prefigures its penetration by his sword. (Kenneth Tynan echoed this when he compared the bull to Othello and the matador to Iago.) The sword is supposed to enter the bull at only one spot — a small circle an inch or two in diameter between its shoulder blades. If the kill is perfect, the sword will penetrate up to the hilt. The symbolism here is obvious. (You could even think of the bull's horns as legs if your mind works that way.) One learned Spaniard, Professor Enrique Tierno Galván of the University of Seville, penned a monograph on similarities in the way Spanish men speak of bulls and women. There are several; the most striking is *"Los tiene muy bien puestos"* (literally, "He/she has them very well placed"). The phrase can refer to either horns or breasts.

Some of the most convoluted interpretations of taurine sexuality are, predictably, French. Professor Julian Pitt-Rivers, a prominent anthropologist from the Sorbonne and an expert in Mediterranean cultures, argues that a gradual role reversal occurs during the bullfight. The matador begins as *"feminino,"* teasing the bull with his large gold-and-magenta capote, flaring it seductively like a dress; the rampaging bull at this point is *"supermasculino."* Then, as the bullfighter begins to dominate the animal with a much smaller cape in the faena, the central part of the fight, the matador becomes progressively more male and the bull more female, until the climax — the moment of penetration — when the matador has become *"supermasculino"* and the bull *"ultrafeminizado."*

But what if the matador happens to be a woman? All this academic onanism evaporates. Freudians don't claim that women kill their fathers. The seducing-the-feminine-bull theory doesn't work either, unless the female matador happens to be a trifle bullish herself. And yet my tape of Cristina breathed sexuality — uncomplicated, unacademic sexuality. I began to ask myself why there aren't more women toreros. In fact, why aren't they all women? The spectacle is a lot easier on the eye, not to mention the libido. There she stood in pass after pass, scarlet cape inches above the sand, crotch thrown out with the best of them toward the bull. The beast was totally masculine. The beauty was totally feminine. The bull's job was to, well, penetrate her. Her job was to avoid that eventuality, then croak the sucker. Thelma-and-Louise time. One could understand why women around the world might identify with Cristina. Yet nothing excluded the guys. On the contrary. Watching Sheryl Swoopes hit the hoop from downtown can be inspiring, but it's not a turn-on. Cristina Sánchez just might be sex incarnate. She might be God. Can you have sex with God?

I took the next flight to Madrid.

Spain is bull crazy. The map of the peninsula, Spaniards point out, is shaped like the hide of a bull. All advertising is banned along the nation's superhighways except the logo of the Osborne Distillery, an extremely lifelike black fighting bull made of bolted metal, three stories high. (It is effective advertising: when one of these babies looms out of the morning mist at you after a night on the red-eye, you need a drink to calm your nerves.)

My first two days in Madrid deliver little but a dozen unreturned phone calls to one Simon Casas, Cristina's *apoderado* (manager). Like the entire taurine world, Casas lives on a cellular, but he's harder to get hold of than Rogers & Cowan. I discover that other reporters have encountered similar frustrations trying to do pieces on bullfighting. But perhaps I can show these guys a thing or two. I've done interviews with bullfighters before. There's a dance you have to do — gallop after them, prove you're real. I'll get her in the end.

Though mired in tradition, bullfighting is not an elitist pursuit. It has always been like boxing: a way for poor boys to make good. Cristina, I discover, fits the mold. She was born in 1972 to a poor family in Parla, a nowhere suburb of Madrid. Her father, Antonio, was a banderillero, one of the matador's ring team who plants banderillas, brightly colored sticks with harpoon points, in the bull's withers. Harpooning bulls didn't pay the bills, however, and Antonio had to double as a municipal fireman. The young Cristina adored her dad, but it was bulls, not backdrafts, that caught her fancy. At the age of 15, she did a couple of passes with a cow and, according to the official bio, "felt something strange" take hold of her, something she "liked." Her parents didn't like it, not one bit, and they did their best to dissuade her from what soon became an obsession. She was working in a beauty salon, training to be a hairdresser, but she spent all her spare time practicing in the bull-ring in Parla, the only girl in a crowd of hopeful teenage boys.

Something strange she liked that took hold of her? In the raging ocean of hormones teenagers surf, what one-of-a-kind wave was this? What must it have been like to date a teenager whose main interest was goading and stabbing large animals? And these days, what went through Cristina's mind when she stood in the ring in all her ball-less, balls-out splendor, taunting the mad mountain of muscle? Did this excite her? Compelling questions.

In 1989 Cristina finally persuaded her parents to let her enroll in Madrid's Escuela de Tauromaquia (bullfighting school). She graduated two years later, to much head-scratching amazement, first in her class. Between that time and 1996, she went on to fight well over a hundred secondary fights called *novilladas,* accumulating countless trophies, much critical acclaim and three substantial *cornadas* — one in the stomach. But her most difficult fight was penetrating the thick hide of the bullfighting fraternity.

Muriel Feiner, an American expatriate and the author of a definitive book about women and bullfighting, *La Mujer en el Mundo del*

Toro, had told me, "At every stage that Cristina succeeded, people would say, 'Sure, but just wait until she gets to the next level. She won't have the strength to deal with 3-year-old bulls; she won't have the strength for 4-year-old bulls.' But she's succeeded at every level." One blunt weapon of establishment resistance was the refusal of several of her fellow toreros to appear in the ring with her. Since Cristina's *alternativa*, though, the traditionalists have been softening. Fighting on the same card with Cristina in that all-important fight were two highly respected veterans, Curro Romero, a minor legend to many fans, and José Mari Manzanares, who might be described as the Eric Clapton of bullfighting. Their support provided a foundation on which her hard-earned experience could build. The only truly rancid reaction to Cristina came from Jesulín. Asked if he would appear with her in the ring, he said, "Never," adding that women belonged either in the stands or "in the kitchen, backing up men." Jesus, little Jesus, lighten up.

Most Spanish women I speak to — unlike their American counterparts — find nothing outrageous in his remarks. They laugh them off: "He's from Andalusia." Even if they have no intention of spending their own lives anywhere near a kitchen, they see Jesulín's comments as evidence of his admirable machismo, which only makes him more adorable. Little Jesus clearly knows his audience. And however much his grandstanding for female fans bugs the traditionalists, it makes sense. A guy facing down mortal danger in the ring has a particular appeal to women. It might also follow, as I suspected from my tape, that a woman facing down mortal danger ought to have a special appeal to men. Confusion and intellectual gymnastics arise when aficionados insist that a man facing down mortal danger ought to appeal primarily to men. Isn't there a homoerotic element to that formulation? No, say aficionados, there is nothing but valor and art involved. You can best appreciate the corrida when you rise above crass sexuality and think of the torero in the ring as neuter. Which in turn may explain the ickiness I sometimes feel around passionate aficionados (though never around aficionadas). It reminds me of the way I used to feel as a kid, getting the kiss of peace from a priest. Sexuality is icky only when it's denied.

Cristina doesn't see herself as a sex symbol. She's focused exclusively on wanting equality with men in the ring. She insists on being

called a "torero," not the more grammatically correct "torera."
(*Torero* is a powerfully virile word in Spanish, often used to compliment men with no connection to bullfighting.) And she's been
quoted as saying dismissively that men come to her fights only
because they "want to see my panties." She might be right about
that, but clearly she too aspires to the aficionados' higher, more
ascetic ideal: to be above crass sexuality, to be admired only for her
art and valor, to be thought of in the ring as neuter.

Hmm. There's one way to settle all this — see the goddess-babe
in action. Happily, she's scheduled to fight in Seville, the spiritual
capital of bullfighting. Here she'll have to pull out all the stops;
display her art and valor without reservations. Happily, too, I now
know from my sources that Casas, and Cristina herself, are aware of
my determination to interview her. The chase is on. I have their
attention. I'm circling the target. Pursue her to Seville, get in their
faces, and the prize will be mine.

La Maestranza, in Seville, is one of the top three bullrings in Spain
(the others are in Madrid and Bilbao) and easily the most beautiful. The inverted crown of its airy Moorish arches echoes the city's
ancient roots and its once colossal opulence. Three days into my
trip, in the blue-gold melancholy of a Spanish autumn twilight, I'm
sitting one row from the *callejón,* the circular corridor behind the
heavy wooden fence that encloses the sand. The *callejón* is where
the matadors hang during the action; I'll be close enough to
Cristina to count the spangles on her pants. Better yet, if Casas is
with her, I might be able, in the sea of olive-skinned Iberianity, to
register my big Celtic mug on her consciousness.

Three hours earlier, I had been briefly introduced to Casas by a
woman friend who is also a friend of Cristina's. Our rendezvous
took place at Seville's primo taurine hot spot, the Hotel Colón.
Casas, a hustling, chain-smoking psychopath whom at first blush I
wouldn't trust across the street with my toothbrush, was offhand
and hissy, preoccupied, he said, with the evening's fight. But later
— in the infuriatingly oblique way these things are handled — the
mutual friend assured me that Casas had given my quest his blessing; this evening, after the fight, I will get to meet the bull-whacking
beloved and work my magic. Yes!

In the ring, in the flesh, Cristina is stunning. She strides across the sand with a manly swagger that is utterly feminine. Many matadors strut, chests puffed out like angry pigeons, but with Cristina it's graceful, natural, balletic. She's wearing a green-and-gold *traje de luces*, and when the plaza's artificial lighting overthrows the night in the name of the sun, she bursts into flame, a wild, glittering beacon topped by thick golden hair under which you can just see tiny pearl stud earrings. The bull smashes out of the *toril* (bull pen) and crashes round the ring, ripping huge splinters of wood from the barrera as it tries to spear a human. Although they'd never admit it, there isn't a man in the plaza whose buttocks aren't clenching at the thought of those horns and Cristina's sparkling ass.

The fight proceeds down its well-worn path. Cristina passes the bull with the large cape, the capote. The passes seem somewhat perfunctory, but there is a lot of wind in the plaza — a source of considerable danger for a matador, since the cape and the bull are hard to control. In any case, the crowd is mightily enthused. Stately Seville loves Cristina. Why, I haven't figured out. It's not just the novelty of having a woman in the ring — there's some other emotion in the plaza I've never felt before.

It's not easy to assess her. The wind is making her nervous. When she is working as close to the bull as she is now, a flapping cape becomes even more dangerous. Her courage is unquestionable, her technique excellent, her stance — the line of her body and cape — often exquisite. Frankly, though, from an ascetic, asexual, objective, pure, priestly, saintly point of view, there's nothing going on down on the sand that will make taurine history.

But it doesn't matter! In supersophisticated, hypercritical Seville, no one cares. The closer the horns come to the fragile body, the more the excitement builds. The whole place — men and women, treble olé and graybeard — is with her. For once there are none of those sneaky second thoughts you usually have at a corrida: this is a contest? Do I enjoy seeing quarts of blood streaming down an animal's back? Why must these guys wear their pants so tight? The dynamic of this fight is plain and simple, its allegory crystal clear. There's this really tiny, really pretty, really clever woman. And there's this really big, really stupid, really dangerous animal. Who you gonna root for? The animal? Get outta here! Croak that sucker, goddess-babe!

And, yes! It's a turn-on. All danger in the theater is — and this theater happens to be live. This Pauline *is* lashed to the tracks, and the train *is* thundering toward her. Everyone can let go. In the dark anonymity of the plaza, all is hidden and there's nothing to hide. One competent *pase de pecho* (literally, a pass of the breast) and the horn slashes so close it almost rips a bauble from Cristina's bolero. The crowd goes nuts. She turns and extends her left leg in slow motion like a dance, smooth green thigh exposed to the bull. They go nuts again.

Then, in the inexorable drama of the sand, she croaks the sucker. It isn't perfect, but the sword slides in, and the bull is dead. The place erupts. Whew!

I haven't smoked a cigarette in twenty years, but I want one now.

Later, back at the Hotel Colón, all of taurine Seville is crammed into the lobby waiting for a glimpse of La Torero. The consensus is that the corrida sucked. Nevertheless, there's elation in the air. They haven't seen a great bullfight, but beauty and virtue have triumphed. When Cristina finally shows, she's mobbed. The mutual friend and I muscle through the crush; I'm right behind the goddess-babe, who's exquisitely small, clad in a close-fitting virginal white dress, blonde hair flowing down her back. She's turning. I ready my groveling Spanish phrases. . . .

And she's gone. Who knows why? Fans, cameras, drinks? Shit. I'm so furious with frustration, I repeatedly stamp on the floor. For the next hour, I press through the solid block of Sevillanity, trying to get to where the strobe lights hold Cristina or to find Casas. I give up. I go to bed. Four in the morning, the mutual friend wakes me. All is not lost. She's spoken to Cristina directly. Lunch or dinner is promised in Madrid the next day.

Absolutely rock solid. I'll have to cancel my flight back to New York. Do I mind? Kidding? I'm ecstatic.

The next morning, on the bullet train from Seville to Madrid, I plan my strategy. A few token journalistic questions, then my friend will fade discreetly. In my broken — charming — Spanish, I'll get more intimate. Work my way closer. Bullfighters tend to identify with Hollywood. So I'll talk movies. I'm a produced screenwriter. I'll talk remake of *Blood and Sand*, except Juan Gallardo, the tragic young bullfighter, becomes Juanita, the tragic young bullfighter.

Working title: *Blonde and Sand.* I'll talk an updated remake of *The Sun Also Rises,* with Pedro Romero as a woman. Jake Barnes falls in love this time, except he had his nuts blown off in Desert Storm. . . . Or perhaps there's a lesbian thing with Lady Brett. . . . I'll have to play it by ear. Working title: *The Daughter Also Rises.*

I check into a dingy hotel near Madrid's Atocha station that looks as though it had been transported brick by brick from turn-of-the-century Manila. Around noon I start waiting by the phone. One o'clock, two, three. . . . Don't give up yet — the Spanish eat lunch at three, dinner at eleven. Four o'clock comes, five. . . . The mutual friend calls. She's just spoken to Cristina. The torero is terribly sorry. She blew off the day to visit a bull ranch outside Seville. But lunch in Madrid tomorrow is double rock solid. I recancel my rebooked flight to New York.

To pass the time, I do more research on the object of my desire. One mildly depressing piece of intelligence is that Cristina's ambition is to become a television sportscaster. Seems a little meager. Seasons of triumph and glory, a taste of immortality, only to end up in some pokey studio in suburban Madrid doing *The Bulls at Nine?*

Here's Maribel, coming out for her second animal. Maribel is making history today — the first matador in Spanish history with an entirely female ring crew. Picadors, banderilleros, sword handlers — all women. And of course the bull is a woman. The men-only crowd is going wild. Maribel's wearing a gold-and-silver traje de luces by Galliano, the pants cut low in the back, a very revealing bustier top. . . .

I begin to wonder if I'm nuts — hanging around a foreign capital waiting for a phone call from a 25-year-old blonde. But she's the modern descendant of the Great Goddess who ruled the Neolithic Mediterranean for millennia, enthroned between the horns of a mighty bull, symbol of the lunar destiny of all things.

That's worth lunch.

The Great Goddess thing gets me thinking. What if Cristina is tapping into a race memory even older and more powerful than the fiercest apologists of bullfighting claim? Isn't it possible that Joseph Campbell was right, except that the shamans of the sun were women, not men? How old is the ritual of challenging the most dangerous beast in nature? No one knows. It could be that women, as shamans of light and fertility, fought the moon-bull for countless millennia until, a mere smidgen of time ago, men horned in on the action. That's why Cristina's role in the ring seems so obvious and natural, whereas with men there's always some moment of sexual confusion, when we're reluctantly confronted with their femininity.

The next day at noon, I again report for duty in my dingy hotel room. Twelve-thirty, one o'clock, two. . . . My friend calls. Change of plan. Cristina's back in Madrid, but she's having lunch with some bankers. She definitely wants to have coffee afterward, at four or five. Not to worry. Triple rock solid. To make absolutely sure, she'll leave her cell phone on all afternoon.

As the hours pass, I dip into some back issues of *¡Hola!*, Spain's premier gossip sheet, and come across some sobering information. She's carrying on with other men. There's El Cordobés, a matador with whom she often shares the fight card, who claims to be the bastard son of the original El Cordobés, who became an international superstar cavorting in the bullring in the sixties. (El Cordobés senior denies paternity.) But apparently this romance is a media invention. In real life, she's hot for a Mexican pop singer named Carlos Jimenez. Cristina, Cristina! No Spanish pop singers were available? No Americans?

Three o'clock, four o'clock. . . . They must be into appetizers by now, ice broken, the *blanco* flowing. . . . Five. . . . Can even the Spanish, with their loopy lifestyle, not be getting into the cheese course by 5:30? Six-thirty arrives; my friend calls: *¡DESASTRE!* She's beside herself. She's been calling Cristina incessantly since we last spoke, four and a half hours ago. Cristina's cell phone is turned off, her father Antonio's cell phone is turned off, Casas's cell phone is turned off — every cell phone with even the most tenuous connection to Cristina Sánchez is turned off.

It's as clear as the ice blue Spanish sky. *I've been stood up.* I fly 6,000 miles to write the article of my life about the passion of my life, and it's "Sorry, I'm washing my hair this month"? This hasn't happened to me since high school. Then, with all the clarity of a sword sliding up to the hilt between my shoulder blades, I GET IT!

This has all been a corrida! The opening seduction, Cristina's skillful moves gradually getting me closer, convincing me I was about to achieve my goal, then swiveling away at the last second.

Hell, when I failed to get to her at the Hotel Colón, I actually pawed the ground. For the last four days, I have been the bull — big, slow, stupid and trusting. I got my wish. With all the weaponry at my disposal — faxes, phones, experience, the vast resources of a big-time American magazine — I haven't even come close to tagging her. She's acknowledging the roar of the crowd, and I'm being dragged out of the ring by my hooves.

No question, goddess-babe. You're the best. Cut off my ears; cut off my tail. You win. But I'm joining PETA in the morning.

RICK TELANDER

Asphalt Legends

FROM SPORTS ILLUSTRATED

Booger, man. Booger the thing. Won't believe the handle on the dude. Booger make your butt look foolish. Yo, man, Booger be real.

It's always somebody. Once it was Herman the Helicopter. For a time it was the Hawk. Then it was the Goat. Then the Destroyer. When I first walked into the bubbling cauldron of New York City summer hoops almost a quarter century ago, gathering material for a book that would be called *Heaven Is a Playground*, it was the Fly. James (Fly) Williams, street player supreme. Six-foot-five, bowlegged, skinny as a rope. Missing a lot of teeth. Could do it.

Yo, man, check it out. The Fly is lighting boys up over at the Hole. He's shakin' and bakin' at Foster Park in Flatbush, doing his thing out at Coney Island. I seen him do a whirlybird from the top of the key at the Rucker, man, no lie. Saw him score 60 against the brothers in Bed-Stuy. Got an attitude, know what I'm sayin'? But the man can light it up. Better 'n the Doctor. Yo, man, the Fly be real.

They are legends of the asphalt city game, epic players in a pastime that is itself legendary, an offshoot of the indoor sport that Dr. James Naismith invented in a YMCA gymnasium in Springfield, Massachusetts, in 1891, with the purpose of providing, as he wrote, "recreation and the development of certain attributes that are peculiar to the game." Old Doc Jim listed those attributes in his book on the game: initiative, agility, accuracy, alertness, cooperation, skill, reflex judgment, speed, self-confidence, self-sacrifice, self-control, sportsmanship. He didn't list the ability to work the ball like a yo-yo on a string, to rise and throw down a monster uh-huh jam, to cross over faster than an eye twitch, to apply a

Wilson facial to the chump who's thinking maybe he can stop your ass from doing what it pleases out here on the nasty, steaming, melt-your-heart blacktop.

It's a fact that the city game is played when and where it was designed not to be played: outdoors, in the sweltering heat, when the gentler games of summer — baseball, tennis, golf, swimming — should rule. But the only thing that rules year-round in the canyons of the inner city is the rock-solid stuff beneath your feet. No country clubs here. No grassy outfields. No 50-meter, sky-blue swimming pools. No riding stables, white beaches, sandy bunkers, trout streams. Just the basketball courts. And the warriors who flock to them, flashing at times like laser beams, flaming to glorious heights, smoldering with hope, illuminating crazy dreams and then, too often, fading into the dark.

Just now the tiny, fence-enclosed court at West 4th Street in Greenwich Village is rocking. A tournament is under way, one of the dozens of outdoor hoops programs that run all summer long in New York City, from Staten Island to the Bronx, from Far Rockaway in Brooklyn to Harlem in Manhattan. In this game most of the players are grown men, some are quite skilled, and all are sweating furiously in the afternoon heat.

The court is so small that the chain-link fence around it also serves as the out-of-bounds marker. A team called Our Gang is playing another named Hollywood in a swift contest that resembles the whirl of mice darting about in a cage. Every so often a player is rammed into the fence, and the refs reluctantly whistle a foul. But mostly the players just play. No blood, no harm.

"I thought maybe Booger might show up," says Danielle Gardner, a tall, lean woman in denim shorts and a T-shirt, leaning against the steel mesh. She is the director of a feature documentary about street ball called *Soul in the Hole*, which opened last week in New York City and Los Angeles. The movie, shot over four years, follows a Brooklyn team called Kenny's Kings as it prepares for and competes in the summer tournament at a playground called the Hole in Bedford-Stuyvesant. Booger Smith, all five feet eight and three-quarter inches and 148 pounds of him, is Gardner's leading man, her Denzel Washington.

He is also her Tupac Shakur. For Booger, whose real name is Edward Smith but who has been nothing but Booger since a cousin called him that years ago for unknown reasons, is on the cusp of joining the pantheon of playground failures, the demigods who had it all and trashed it. Booger is 21. He's been shot twice; he has no college degree; he has hardly ever laid eyes on his father, and he's had a falling out with his mother; he has a 3-year-old daughter; he is on his own. "He's a great guy," says Gardner. "A sweetheart. Everybody likes Booger. I think he's scared now, nervous. He just needs a break."

Also watching the action is Ray Haskins, the basketball coach at Long Island University in Brooklyn. Most of the guys on his team play summer ball, which is O.K. with him. "In the summer you experiment," he says, watching a player dunk so hard that the court fence quivers wildly along three of its four sides. "You play against other great players and see if you can make the things you see out there part of your game. If a new wrinkle works, you use it. A basketball player's game is always under reconstruction."

Last season LIU went 21–9 and made its first appearance in the NCAA tournament in thirteen years, due largely to the arrival of a Brooklyn kid who transferred in after spending two years at Rutgers. His name is Charles Jones. He's a slender and versatile six-foot-three guard who is what basketball people refer to as a scorer. Not a shooter. Not a gunner. Not a bomber. Not a slasher. A scorer. Last season he led all Division I players in scoring, with 30.1 points per game.

Jones is a good friend of Booger's, having played with him for years on Kenny's Kings and other clubs. It is a haunting aspect of *Soul in the Hole* that in candid pregame huddles, opposing teams talk about stopping Booger but are largely unconcerned about Jones and his mates. And those mates include Jason Hoover, a former All-Conference player from Manhattan College; Javone Moore, the alltime assists leader at Canisius; and Seldon Jefferson, the 1996–97 team MVP at West Virginia.

Jones has come to West 4th Street on the subway, the entrance to which is only feet from the court. People are lining the outside of the court now: casual fans, hoops junkies, vagrants, mothers with children, children without mothers, commuters, tourists.

Jones and Haskins shake hands; then the player moves off to chat with Gardner, who has captured on film a big chunk of Jones's basketball obsession. Haskins and referee Roland Rooks, the father of Los Angeles Lakers backup center Sean Rooks, are talking about the best street players they've seen. "I gotta go with Kurt Sumpter," says Rooks. "Back in the early '80s. Six-two. Strong. Don't know if he ever played anywhere [in college]."

"Booger Smith is the most exciting thing I've ever seen," counters Haskins. "You ought to see him. I'd watch him play anywhere. It's all there. He's got a great attitude. Just ain't got no pencil."

Indeed, academic troubles combined with a blasé attitude about his future led to Booger's downfall at Arizona Western, a junior college in Yuma, where he played for slightly more than a semester in the 1993–94 season. "He hadn't even graduated from high school when he came to Yuma," recalls former Arizona Western coach Dave Babcock, now a scout for the New Jersey Nets. The story Babcock heard is that Booger got kicked off the basketball team in his junior year for shooting dice, and quit school in his senior year. "He only played after Christmas for me, but even then he made third team all-conference," he says. "Averaged 21 points and 12 assists a game. I've been a coach for fifteen years, and he can do things I've never seen before. Breaks down a defense better than any player I've ever coached. But the big thing for him is the call of the streets. I couldn't get him to commit to going to class, and my conscience wouldn't let me bring him back."

So after one year he cut Booger loose. "I wanted him either to get a job," says Babcock, "or go to special reading classes at Medgar Evers [College in Brooklyn] with a guy I know there, a great teacher. Do either one. Booger did neither."

A year and a half later, in August 1996, Babcock weakened. "Booger convinced me to give him one more chance," he says. "So he came out, and he was in terrible shape. He'd been shot in the thigh that summer. I'd heard it was a random drive-by, but I didn't feel good about it. So I sent him home again." And that was it.

In *Soul in the Hole*, a 17-year-old Booger has the first lines of the movie: "If I don't make it to the NBA, I'm gonna be a drug dealer. Somehow I've gotta get me a Lexus. Whatever it takes." Gardner caught the yearning with her camera, and now she is trying to make sure Booger doesn't take the wrong path to satisfy it. She talks with him almost daily, encouraging him to make something of his basketball gifts, to break from the stasis of the 'hood. He seems to appreciate the words, because he calls her more than she calls him. But his life is stalled, and he is staring at the bottom, wavering.

"Booger talked to a psychic the other day," Gardner says. "He said she told him, 'This is your window of opportunity.' Of course it is. Another college. Play in Europe. He's got to do something."

The Ghetto Boyz are in black, and Biv 10 is in white. The two teams are playing at 155th Street and Eighth Avenue in Harlem, at historic Holcombe Rucker Park, in what is now called the Entertainers' Basketball Classic. This is a tough part of the city — walk through the police line first, please, get patted down — but it's where pros and street players used to mix it up in the earliest days of the asphalt competition, where you might have seen Kareem Abdul-Jabbar or Julius Erving trading elbows with some guy named the Eraser or Mr. Clean.

This new league is still much like the old Rucker tournament of the 1960s and '70s, except that this one was started by a rapper deejay named Greg Marius in 1980 at a park on 120th Street and Madison Avenue. The rappers, whose music is the electric vapor that floats like a thunderhead over the city game, at first played in the games, but soon they were stacking their teams with ringers rather than singers. "I saw what the guys were doing," says Marius as he hands cordless microphones to Tango and Cash, the deejays for tonight's game, "so I loaded my own team, Disco 4, with guys like Pearl Washington [of Syracuse] and [UNLV's] Richie Adams and [Arkansas's] Kenny Hutchinson, serious players. So you know we won the tournament."

As the hoops talent grew, so did the crowds. Marius brought his thriving league to 155th Street a few years back, and now pros such as Kevin Garnett, Joe Smith and Allen Iverson occasionally stop by to play with the boys of summer. There was a rumor that Booger might show up to play with the Ghetto Boyz tonight, but no luck. It is still so hot at dusk, over 100°, that anyone could be excused for not playing ball. But heat doesn't stop the city game. And the players are out — Ron-Ron, Da Main Event, Superman, Lefty, Half-Man, the Terminator — running fast and strong.

Everybody has a "game" in summer ball, a signature style that defines him the way a haircut or a tattoo or a favorite T-shirt does. The Terminator is a muscular, high-flying forward. But he has an oddly retro style. He lays the ball in on breaks. He does not shoot from outside. He does not dribble between his legs. He does not hotdog. "The Terminator will not dunk!" roars one of the deejays after the forward banks in another layup. "He will not shoot a jumper! And he'll score 50!" To take such a stance, to not do what is possible, is a form of brilliance. And it excites the crowd.

Half-Man jams the ball home. "Half-Man, half amazing!" screams Tango into his mike.

A player races down the lane, right through the defense, to throw in a double-clutcher. "It's the red-carpet treatment!" wails Cash.

The coach of the Ghetto Boyz, a small young man in new Filas, nice shorts, an expensive gold watch and a T-shirt that shows a human-faced mouse smoking a huge joint, seems unfazed by any of the action. He has a studious Rick Pitino–like crouch that he alternates with a concerned Pat Rileyesque arms-crossed stance. Like most of the summer coaches, this man is not a coach by trade. He goes by the name Mousy — nobody has heard him called anything else. The back of his shirt reads LIFE IS FULL OF IMPORTANT CHOICES, and those choices, listed above drawings of marijuana leaves, are: PURPLE INDICA, VIRGIN ISLAND BUDS, JAMAICAN SINSEMILLA, COLOMBIAN GOLD.

Not so calm is the coach of Biv 10, an intense man named Richard Wheeler. He starts using profanity as his team falls behind. That's a basic no-no in a realm where too many verbal disputes end up being settled by Mr. Glock and Mr. Remington. Marius tells Wheeler to cool down.

"F— you!" says the coach.

"Man, you got to quit using the word f—," says Marius. "It's the rules."

"I can't fire my team up?" Wheeler bellows. "There's lots of coaches who curse more than me!"

"No, there aren't."

"Bobby Knight?"

"How much does he make?" Marius snorts.

"I don't care. That's who I am. F— you!"

It's hard to say where the discourse is headed, but suddenly it is halted in midstream. A peal of thunder and a great flashing strobe of light have split open the sweltering night sky, and rain abruptly pours down in sheets. In less than a minute the court and stands are empty. In five minutes there is hardly a person in the park, except for a half-dozen or so vigilant New York City cops.

Meanwhile, at Hunter College on East 68th Street, Charles Jones is unaffected by the storm. He is playing in that rarest of summer events, an indoor tournament.

On his team, United Brooklyn, is street-legend-made-good Lloyd Daniels. Daniels had all the dark lore going a few years back — the heady rep, the bad attitude, the wounds from gunshots that nearly iced him — but he fought back to make it in the real world, eventually playing three seasons in the NBA. That showed the downside of being a playground deity who succeeds in the public arena: he wasn't a very good pro. So how good could he really have been in the playgrounds? His reputation, like those of all asphalt stars, had been enhanced by eager observers who, as chroniclers of his raw dominance, grabbed a bit of their own immortality.

If you never leave the streets, logic says, who knows how good you could have been? Daniels blew it, in that sense. Far better to be Earl (the Goat) Manigault, one of the earliest fallen princes of the city game. The six-foot-two Goat blew what he had — titanium leg springs, ball-handling magic, creative court genius — on heroin in the '6os. People say the Goat was the best ballplayer ever. But we'll never know. And that, too, is a legacy of the urban game.

United Brooklyn coach Sid Jones is a short, serious man who doesn't think much of street reputations. "Booger?" he says, scowling. "He's exciting. He can do wonderful stuff. But I'm a pro-level coach. I'm trying to get players jobs, trying to get them ready for the next level. Booger is small, and he doesn't play big."

The coach watches the next squad of hopefuls warm up. "They all say they want to get to the next level," he says ruefully. "Until they get too close to it. You know, it's not all about talent."

Now Charles Jones sits in a coffee shop near a basketball court in lower Manhattan, eating a jelly-filled doughnut and drinking iced tea. Jones is not yet 22, but he feels old, he says. "Back in '92 and '93 I'd play four, five games in a day," he says. "A game at 10:30, noon, 4, 6:30, maybe one real late. All over. Lafayette Gardens, Kingston Park, Soul in the Hole, CYO games, Citywide. That's when I was a lot younger. I've been playing so long." He shakes his head. The city game is both a blessing and a task.

"You'd be so tired, so dehydrated," he says. "Wouldn't pee for days, it seemed like. Hell, you didn't have time to think about going to the bathroom. But it's still fun. Life is short, have fun, you know? I'm always trying to make a name for myself. I get so hyper before games, and it's because I don't want to lose. Not any of the games. Nowhere. College ball tends to get very political, but street games are real. The refs even get caught up in the emotion. There are lot of good players in college, but a really good street game? Man. There is nothing like it. The Soul in the Hole, I couldn't wait to play in that. Right in the neighborhood, people saying, 'Yeah, this boy can play.'

"Sometimes street ball is harder than college, like when you're six-three and you have to guard a center, or you only got four players and you have to pick up a guy from the crowd. You don't do that in college. And you can't play zones in street ball because people want to see action."

He sips his tea. A large gold head of Jesus hangs on a chain from his neck. "Coming up you always sort of knew the best players weren't in organized ball," he says. "You'd hear about some supposedly great [college] player, then play against him in an AAU game or something, and you'd say, 'What, this guy?' In any park there are players better than me. Oh, yeah. You want a name? O.K., Tone from Brownsville. Just Tone, don't know any other name. Man, can he play. Hell, my brother Lamont. He's 25, but he is for real. Played in the CBA. Division II All-America at Bridgeport. Boogs? That's my man. Known him since he was nine. He could always play. I wish he was with me in school."

The young man who scored 37 points for LIU against Villanova, 28 against Minnesota, and 46 against St. Francis pauses. "I don't know what's gonna happen with Booger," he says. "Hopefully, somebody will see him and pick him up. You never really can tell."

Back when I spent those summer days of 1973 and '74 in Brooklyn, checking out the basketball scene, I heard all about the great ones who never got picked up. Players like Joe (the Destroyer) Hammond, who supposedly was making so much money in the park games that the NBA cash didn't interest him. People like superscorer Pee Wee Kirkland, the Harlem hotshot who went off to the penitentiary on a drug charge. People like the late, high-rising Herman (the Helicopter) Knowings, a six-foot-four-inch ball of muscle who, lore has it, could hang in the air like a cloud of smoke. I saw the Helicopter once at City College in Harlem, sitting impassively in the stands watching a summer game. He was 30 and no longer played, but he had a kind of quiet, athletic grace to him. Was it true what they said about him, I asked. Could he really pick quarters off the top of the backboard? Did he really dunk over Willis Reed and Nate Bowman at the Rucker, at the same time? Was it true, as one coach had told me, that Herman could put his chin on the rim? And what about the three-second stories?

"Yeah, a couple times guys faked me in the lane, and before I'd come down the ref would call three seconds on them," he said after a time, quietly and without expression. "But I don't know, it's all talk, talk. It's nothing."

Of course, there were those city long shots who made it big, like five-foot-eight Charlie Criss, who played for eight seasons in the NBA from 1977 to '85, and Connie Hawkins, who was a four-time All-Star with the Phoenix Suns in the early '70s. But it is the failures who stick in our minds, linger there restlessly like the great tragic heroes of literature. The Goat lingers most of all.

Now 53 and on a waiting list for a heart transplant to replace the one he pretty much destroyed with his needle and smack, the Goat works with young ballplayers at Goat Park, his own little patch of city blacktop at 99th Street and Amsterdam Avenue in Manhattan. Manigault moves slowly these days, though occasionally he'll show a quick step or two to get a kid's attention. But there was a time when he could dunk two balls at once; dunk one ball, catch it and dunk it again; take off from behind the free-throw line and dunk any way you wanted. "They listen to me," he says of the troubled kids who come by to play in his Walk Away from Drugs tournaments. "I tell 'em everything. My whole life. Hold nothing back." The wasted chances, the lack of discipline, the bullheaded defiance, the absent father, the fear of success. All of it, he says. Just lays it out.

"Booger, Booger," says the Goat, almost to himself. "I think I've heard of Booger. He played in my tournament, I think. I heard he got shot. You know, there is something distracting him from making it. Who knows what it is. A girl? The streets? There's always something. But you have to stay away from the things that prevent you from succeeding. You have to give yourself a chance. You can always fall back on hard times."

Up at the Entertainers' game at night in the throbbing heat, the deejays Tango and Cash are giving folks a hard time. They rip and they rap. They bip and they bap. But not everyone is amused.

The coach of the Crusaders, a tall, stylish, shaved-headed man in black alligator-skin shoes, black linen pants, a cream-colored linen shirt and copious gold jewelry, does not need any part of the deejays' cracks. He stands by his bench, head tilted, and says in the scariest of tones, "Do you know who you're f—ing with?" Apparently the deejays do, because they say nary a word in response.

Charles Jones is playing for Sugar Hill, and as his team warms up, I look around at the crowd. Next to me is a muscular young man in a red Michael Jordan jersey, red baseball cap, and a left biceps tattoo with the twin barrels of a shotgun pointed my way under the inscription 2 TA THE HEAD. Not far from him is a skinny middle-aged man wearing sunglasses. He is Joe Hammond, the Destroyer himself. People say the Destroyer did stuff back in the '70s that picked up right where the Goat left off.

I ask Hammond how the current Rucker games stack up against the ones he used to play in. "There's no comparison," he says. "All the pros used to play here. Wilt, Tiny, Julius, Kareem. It changed when pros quit playing on concrete."

And what about the stories of him turning down the NBA's cash because he made more playing in the street? "The Lakers offered me $50,000 when I was 19 to come there and play," he replies. "Jack Kent Cooke. But I made enough in New York."

"Who paid you?" I ask.

"Guys."

"Drug dealers?"

"Drug dealers?" he says quizzically, from behind his shades. "Well, they had money."

I look around as the game begins. There is Richie Parker, the penitent onetime high school sex offender who plays for LIU with Charles Jones. Parker takes a 15-foot jumper. The ball rotates with that sweet sideways spin he puts on it, and it goes straight in.

There is a funny-looking six-foot-six-inch player with remarkable dribbling ability. The crowd calls him Alamo, which changes to Ally-Mo! as he does his show, laughing and talking trash the whole while. "The Black Widow!" screams Tango. "Alfred Moses!" I find out later that the young man's name is Tyrone Evans. Nobody has any clue why he's called Alamo or whatever.

For a moment I find myself transported back to the city game of more than two decades ago. It is the same. What has changed? Better shoes, baggier shorts, smaller hairdos, more tattoos, beepers, cell phones, designer water, nose rings.

But nothing's really changed. Not a thing. The city game has a rhythm that is immutable, like surf on a rocky coast.

Yesterday on West 4th I ran into my old friend Rodney Parker, the freelance ticket agent and street scout from Brooklyn who had been my guide and companion in my first foray into the playgrounds long ago. He was still doing the same stuff, he told me. And the street talent? The barrel had more fish than ever, he said.

"Two years ago I got fifteen kids into schools all over Texas," he said. "Junior colleges. I knew some people. Almost all the kids were from the Bronx, all great talents. And all but one of them is gone. Typical odds. The failure rate is high. And the one kid who did make it just got thrown out of school for breaking into a car.

"I deal with misfits. One of my guys got out of jail at Rikers Island. The kids without any problems, they don't need me. Everybody knows who they are. And you know what? This year I got orders for ten more kids. Move 'em in, move 'em out. What do the schools care? There's more talent than twenty years ago. It's everywhere. It's like a pair of shoes — don't like 'em? Get rid of 'em."

The bubbling humanitarian who used to play street ball with a Brooklyn kid named Lenny Wilkens gave me his salesman's eye. "I got a kid who's 15, he's gonna be the next Jordan," he said. "His name is Smoosh. There's gonna be a sneaker named after him. Six-one, with arms that make him six-four. Best skills I've ever seen. Ever. Want to meet him?"

"What's his real name?" I asked.

"I don't know. Smoosh, that's all. Want to meet him?"

Maybe another day. Instead, we went to Foster Park in Flatbush, just a number 5 train ride under the East River and out to Nostrand Avenue in Brooklyn. This was once Rodney's park. His apartment on the sixth floor of the nearby Vanderveer Homes looked out on the teeming courts below. This was where he watched Brooklyn stars such as Vinnie Johnson and Mike Dunleavy and Albert King develop. This was where he introduced me to the peacock of them all, Fly Williams, back when the Fly was the leading freshman scorer in the nation at Austin Peay in little ole Clarksville, Tennessee, and his possibilities seemed limitless and his problems surmountable.

Fly blew it all, of course. After a stunning series of bad educational and career moves, followed by brief employment with the St. Louis Spirits of the ABA, Fly got shot, went to prison, and fell from sight. I often wondered if he was alive or dead. He had been a wild and crazy guy, at times a genuinely funny guy, but he brought so much of himself to the game that sometimes it hurt to watch him act out his passion play in front of the world. In one college game he wore his trunks backward. In prep school he once dribbled off the court in the middle of a game to get a drink of water. I had seen him dunk over Moses Malone, score 40 points in a half of a park game, shoot cherry pits out of the side of his mouth where a couple of teeth were missing. He was first-team All-Failure, that much was certain.

But lo and behold, look who was sashaying across the heat-rippling courts of Foster Park at midday but someone who looked precisely like a scaled-down adolescent edition of the Fly. And why not, for this was 16-year old James (Fly) Williams III.

"I was doing laundry," said the slight youth, a blue Michigan jersey hanging loosely from his small shoulders, a jeweled stud in his ear, the word FLY freshly inscribed in tattoo ink on his right forearm, the word YVONNE on his left. "Somebody said there were guys here asking about Fly Williams," he said.

We were, I told him. Who is Yvonne?

"My mom," he said. "Fly is my dad. I got the tattoo last month, and my mom went with me because I don't turn 17 until August. Getting old, man."

I had to shake my head because for an instant I thought I had sailed back through the years and was talking to this boy's father. I remembered when the older Fly had told me he felt like an old-timer. This boy looked the same, talked the same. Did he play ball the same?

The youngster shook his head. "I'm a biker," he said. "A street rider. I do freestyle tricks. I do the grasshopper, jump over benches, walls. I got a Mongoose Hooligan. I work in a bike shop, and I want to grow up and be a mechanic. I don't do nothin', just ride bikes, chill, mess with girls."

How is his father?

"He's O.K. He does some reffing."

Fly Williams as a ref? I couldn't imagine it.

"I feel fine having him as my dad, a man who played ball," said the youth. "It would have been better if he'd played longer, but then maybe I wouldn't be here, either."

The youngster squinted into the sun. "You know, basketball doesn't look like that much fun," he said. "Now I see why my dad doesn't talk about it anymore. I used to steal cars, but basketball helped me get out of that. All I did when I was playing was throw fancy passes — people said I was a showboat, like my father. But then I got turned off on basketball, all the traveling, going to parks, playing games, arguing with people. I got tired of it. So now no basketball, no fights. Just bikes."

Tillary Park, Brooklyn, 6 P.M. The small blacktop court with yellow lines slopes toward Tillary Street, beyond which is LIU and downtown Brooklyn. Just down the block is Westinghouse High, the school from which Booger Smith never earned a diploma.

Trees give welcome shade to part of the court; the blazing sun is still baking the city. Tonight in the first game of the Pro Hoops Summer Basketball Tournament the gray-shirted Around The Way team will be playing orange-shirted Fort Greene. Rumor has it that Booger may show up to play for Fort Greene. But then, maybe he won't. No one is sure.

His old coach, Dave Babcock, is trying to get Booger a workout in front of some scouts who might be able to hook him up with a team overseas or maybe a CBA team. "He's not at the NBA level now," says Babcock. "It's about the mental side. Does he really want success? Is he committed?"

Here is Booger now, walking unobtrusively into the park, his orange T-shirt radiant against his dark skin. He is small and wide-eyed, with a wispy mustache and his hair done in a boxy cut that starts far back on his forehead. He has no bulging muscles, no extra-long limbs, no physical qualities that would make anyone take a second look. He shakes hands with his teammates but says little. He is just another anonymous young man among millions.

I introduce myself to Booger and tell him I've been waiting to meet him and see him play. I tell him I haven't been able to reach him on the phone, that nobody answers the numbers I call, the numbers I was told were his or belonged to people who knew where to find him. He nods politely.

I recall what Arizona Western athletic director Ray Butcher had said about the point guard: "He is just a little booger, I liked the hell out of him," he said. "But he's his own worst enemy."

"So what are your plans?" I ask.

He shrugs.

"The NBA?"

"No, I want to go overseas," he says. "Somewhere."

"What about college, say, an NAIA school?"

"College? Yeah, if I could."

"So for now," I offer, "you're just kind of hanging?"

"I'm kind of hanging," he agrees. "Staying in shape."

A spectator walks up and nods to Booger, holds out his cupped palm with a freshly rolled joint in it. "I know you want some," says the man. Booger shakes his head and walks away.

The game starts, and the action is lively. Neither team has a true center — the tallest men on the court are maybe six-feet-six — so the emphasis is on ball handling and penetrating. As always, outside shots are risky, what with the wind, the tilt of the court, and the uneven light.

Booger starts slowly, but at the quarter he already has six points and five assists. He controls the ball as if it were secretly hooked to his hand and couldn't possibly get away. He has a gift that is rare indeed for the flashy player: he throws the simple, expedient passes as easily and readily as the fancy ones.

On the sidelines people are buzzing, waiting for Booger to detonate. In the second half he does. He dribbles through traps like water through a net; he throws a no-look bounce pass that leads to a mighty dunk. He throws two perfect alley-oop passes in a row, to players who seemed to be hidden in the pack.

At 16 Booger left his mother and moved in with Kenny Jones, the coach of Kenny's Kings, for three years. Jones is, or was, sort of like a father to Booger, and of the young man Jones says, "Do I worry about him? All the time. But not on the court. Being on the court is like a sedative for him. He's very calm."

Indeed, Booger is calm now, and he grows calmer as more and more of Around The Way's efforts go into trying to stop him. Charles Jones's brother Lamont is playing for Around The Way, and he can't stop Booger. Nobody can. A week ago in a game at the Hole a defender severely sprained his ankle as he reached for the ball after Booger did a crossover, behind-the-back move. The untouched man fell to the pavement yelping in pain.

The remarkable thing about many of Booger's moves is that he cannot replicate them off the court. They are unplanned, unprac-

ticeable responses to stimuli. A hoops magazine asked Booger to do
a couple of things for its cameras last year, and he failed miserably.
"Once I asked him after a game, 'Where did you get that move?'"
recalls Kenny Jones. "And he said, 'They made me do it.'"

Now Booger does something unbelievable. He wraps the ball
around the head of his defender with his right hand, catches it in
his left, and lays it in. This does not seem possible without the
cooperation of the opponent. But these guys want to bury Booger.
They are not accomplices.

Then Booger does something else. He does it so quickly that
afterward spectators cannot be sure they actually saw what they
thought they saw. Booger bounces the ball between the legs of his
foe and then, as he spins around the man, catches the ball blindly
behind his back and continues dribbling to the basket. Or something like that. In the blink of an eye.

After the game one of Booger's teammates, six-foot-five-inch,
25-year-old Anthony Heyward, Jr., better known as the Biz, talks
about his efforts to help Booger. The Biz played the past two years
in a pro league in Uruguay, and the year before that he played in
Finland. The Biz is a polite, well-spoken, no-nonsense man, and he
says he hopes to get Booger a chance to go to South America with
him. "This summer I'm trying to be around him as much as possible," the Biz says. "I'm not exactly worried about him. But I'm
trying to keep him away from the wrong people."

Heyward is drenched in sweat, the champagne of the city ballplayer. He thinks for a moment. "It's not that he's a bad kid," the
Biz says. "It's just that sometimes things don't work out."

I shake Heyward's hand and turn to find Booger. I look everywhere.

But Booger is gone.

DAVID JAMES DUNCAN

Bird-Watching as a Blood Sport: On the Redemptive Pain of Loving in the Natural World

FROM HARPER'S MAGAZINE

The light of the body is the eye: if therefore thine eye be single, thy whole body shall be full of light./But if thine eye be evil, thy whole body shall be full of darkness.
— Matthew 6:22–23

ON CERTAIN NIGHTS when I was a boy, I used to lie in bed in the dark, unable to sleep, because of eyes — staring, glowing eyes, arrayed in a sphere all around me. The eyes seemed to be alive, though they were not visibly attached to bodies or to faces. They were not, so to speak, attached to emotions either: they conveyed no menace, no affection, no curiosity, no consternation. They simply watched me with a vigilance as steady and beautiful as the shining of stars at night.

Because their beauty was so evident, the eyes would not have troubled me were it not for this: I could not escape them. They had the ability to go on staring whether my own eyes were open or shut; they could, in other words, move with me from the real into the imaginary world. I was in awe of this power. My mother and father, the moon and the sun, the entire world would vanish when I closed my eyes. But the eyes in the sphere would not. And I didn't even know whose eyes they were! I wanted very much to find out.

I told my big brother about the sphere and asked if he'd ever seen such a thing. His reply was confident but not too consoling: he laughed and told me I'd flipped my lid. I tried my mother. She, too, laughed. "What an imagination!" she said. I let her know, with reluctance, that I did not consider the eyes imaginary. "If they're not imaginary," she said, laughing no longer, "you should ask Jesus to make them go away."

I did ask Jesus. But the eyes went right on staring. And although I spoke of them no more, I was glad that this was Christ's response to my prayer. The sphere of eyes had never threatened or damaged me. It was intense. It was beautiful. Why should I want it to go away? That no one but I seemed to see such things — this was a worry. But the sphere's sudden appearance in bedtime darkness felt like a wonder out of some old myth or fairy tale, and I wanted my life to feel like that. So, much as I wanted to know more about the eyes — who they belonged to, what they wanted of me — I quit worrying and let them blaze away. I really had no choice. And in ancient tales the young heroes are patient. I tried to be the same.

In late winter, when I was ten, I made perhaps my first conscious connection between the mysteries of the inner life and those of the outer world. It happened on a long hike through a doomed suburban forest, when I spotted the largest nest I'd ever seen in the top of a towering, seemingly unclimbable cottonwood tree. Partly to dumbfound the older boys I was with, partly out of incomprehensible yearning, I began shinnying up the limbless lower trunk. Ninety or so feet later, I was clinging to tiny branches just under the massive nest and two magnificent great horned owls were circling the treetop within twenty feet of me. Circling and staring — till somewhere inside I felt it: the sense of a sphere. Vigilant, unreadable eyes, watching. Me at the center . . .

The nest was so wide that there was no way to climb, or even to see, up into it, so I reached into it with a bare hand. I learned later that had it contained owlets I would have been attacked, and possibly killed, when the adults knocked me out of my precarious perch. But though their orbit of the tree became tighter and they began to let out quiet cries, the owls did not attack: as luck would have it, my groping hand found not owlets but two large, warm eggs. Again out of mixed motives — bravado, yearning, a pagan fantasy to possess my own magnificent bird — I stuck one egg in my coat pocket, then shinnied back down the tree.

The boys below greeted me with everything a conquering hero could hope for: praise for my climbing, awe of my defiance of the adult owls, envy of my prize. "You crazy asshole!" one of them kept saying, in a way that made clear his desire to be thought the same. But seeing the mother owl return to the nest, knowing the egg beneath her was now destined to be raised alone, the word "crazy" struck me as too kind. I was just a garden-variety asshole. I'd done something stupid, knew it, and knew I lacked the strength and courage to climb the tree again and undo what I'd done.

I tried to make amends in a more arcane way: leaving my friends and their embarrassing praise, I trudged home through the woods, keeping a warm hand around the egg the entire way, then fetched a shoebox, a soft towel, and a lamp with a flexible neck, wrapped the egg in the towel, bent the lamp over it, and began trying to convince myself that I had created a viable nest.

To my amazement, the egg was convinced: that night it began to hatch. And the next morning my mother, knowing real education when she saw it, let me stay home from school to watch. It was a surprisingly arduous process. From first crack to full emergence took twenty hours: eggs, to judge by this one, are no easier to escape than wombs. The owlet was four inches long, naked and exhausted, its pink flesh blurred by an outlandish aura of slush-colored fuzz. Its eyes were enormous but covered with bluish skin: no staring, no sense of the mysterious sphere this time. In fact, I'd never seen a pair of eyes look less likely to open or to see — for I was their adoptive mother.

The owlet rested briefly after breaking free, then commenced a ceaseless, open-beaked, wobbly begging. Panicked by the conviction in its body language, I telephoned the zoo, reached its bird keeper, received a scolding for my nest robbing and a prediction of doom, but still proffered the tweezered egg and hamburger and eye-droppered milk that the keeper recommended. And again, to my amazement, the owlet responded. It enjoyed my cooking, it suffered my touch, it responded to my mothering precisely long enough to make me love it. Only then did it proceed to die. Even at birth, horned owls are tough: it took a full day to stop eating, two days to stop begging, another half day to stop writhing and die.

What did not die — what lives in me even now — are the circling, vigilant eyes of the parent owls. The eyes that I betrayed. *Vigilant, glowing eyes, arrayed in a sphere all around me* . . . Even to mention such a thing puts me — both as a storyteller and as a character in my own story — in way over my head. Yet if deeper truths do indeed dwell in depths, there would seem to be no way to reach them without some risk of drowning.

There I'd lie, then, once in an unpredictable while, year after boyhood year, surrounded by eyes. Eyes that always appeared after the room was dark, the house quiet, and I lay still, yet far from sleep. They did not appear by opening; they simply eased into visibility the way stars do at dusk. They never blinked, never retreated, never glanced to either side. They watched me, period. By no other eyes have I ever felt so purely perceived.

In appearance they were distinctly nonhuman. They reminded me a little of angels, a little of owls, and a little of wild animals whose eyes are suddenly lit by the headlights of passing cars. They varied in size — or else stared at me from varying distances. They varied in color too. I recall shades of green, yellow, orange, all of which seemed wrong for angels. It also seemed angelically wrong, but beautifully so, that these colors glowed.

Another over-my-head mystery: the eyes in the sphere would array themselves not just in front of me but above, below, and behind me. What I mean to imply is a physical impossibility. The sphere of eyes was visible in all directions. In its thousandfold presence I became a point of pure perception suspended inside an encompassing globe. For a long time I drew no conclusions from this; I merely basked in it. As I grew older, though, I realized that I must see the sphere not through physical eyes, or even through my mind's eye, but through an eye that I hadn't been aware of possessing — an eye that could see in all directions at once.

Nothing else on earth had enabled me to see in this way. Nothing else had ever watched me in this way. So no matter how many times the sphere came, I felt awestruck by its arrival. Awestruck and compelled, no matter how late the hour, to stare back. But to be surrounded and stared at creates an air of huge expectation. In the eyes' presence, something enormously good or bad always seemed about to happen. And suspense is exhausting. So it was always I who lost consciousness and left the eyes staring at no one. Until, one winter not long before adolescence, I realized that for weeks now, or perhaps months, the vigilant sphere had ceased to visit.

I've seen nothing like the sphere of eyes since boyhood. But I've described my recurring vision (or pathosis) for a reason: I have continued now and then to encounter actual bird eyes — like those of the circling great horned owls — that have suddenly struck me as living refugees of that mysterious childhood sphere. I've even begun, thanks to these ongoing encounters, to suspect that the sphere, though unseen, might in some way still surround me . . .

In 1968, just days after receiving my first driver's license, I am driving through a small town in a nighttime line of commuter traffic when I see, in the headlight beams of the car ahead of me, a small brown ball rolling in the street. The car does not slow as it drives over the ball. Seeing no kids at the curb, I, too, choose not to slow. Then the ball rolls out from under the car in front, appears in my own headlights, and I see that it is not a ball but a balled-up screech owl.

It is uninjured but blown off its feet. And having failed to slow, I now have no choice but to straddle it. It stares straight into my headlights, eyes glowing as I take aim — and I feel myself fall, once again, into a watched center, feel something very good or bad about to happen. Then it does. Just as I pass over, the owl catches its balance, gathers itself for a leap into flight, and I feel — in the soles of my feet, in my legs, and all the way up my spine — the fatal thud of its head against the bottom of my car. I see, in the rearview mirror, the epileptic thrashing and the cloud of feathers, see the next car, too, run it over, and the next and the next. I do not go back. I already knew that I can revere a creature, mother a creature, want nothing but to love a creature, yet still kill it. I also know that what can't be killed — what will remain inside — is that moment's glowing contact with its eyes.

Highway 101, Tillamook County, Oregon. Again alone in a car, on the bridge over Beaver Creek, I turn toward the railing and see a solitary snipe (*Gallinago gallinago*). My field guide calls the snipe "a secretive bird of . . . marshes, and sodden fields." But this one is standing, calm and incongruous as a would-be bus passenger, right on the bridge's concrete sidewalk. I immediately brake — having learned the necessity of this from the brown ball years before. But as I pass by the snipe doesn't fly, doesn't even flinch. Knowing that something isn't right, I pull over, walk back to the bridge, and creep up on the bird, hoping it won't flush out in front of a passing car. It watches me. I move in close, cup it in my hands. No struggle. The snipe just stares. I stand it in my palm. Free to fly, the bird stays, a child's dream — the wild creature you can pet — come true. I stare at it. It stares at me. Cars come and go. The bird radiates warmth. My hand returns it. The sphere closes around us. It is the peace of the sphere itself, I believe, that keeps me from seeing for so long that the entire top of the bird's skull is gone.

I carry the snipe under the bridge, sit cross-legged by the creek where no one can see me, and stand it again in my palm. I then begin trying to concoct a rite that will remove the treachery from a mercy killing. I start with simple admiration: the camouflage plum-age, satire-shaped tail feathers, earth-probe bill, black pearl eyes. I then try memory: fishing alone on the wide-open estuaries, I have come upon many a *Gallinago gallinago,* and the memorable encoun-ters have all been the same. Silent and unseen, from very high in the sky, a lone snipe drops into a dive, builds up great speed, and, as it nears the ground, veers. This veering is their magic: it turns the tail feathers into drumsticks and the sky into a taut skin that explodes in an impossibly loud sound known as "winnowing." A nineteenth-century ornithologist likened the snipe's winnowing sound to "the cantering of a horse . . . over a hard hollow road." An accurate description, as far as it goes. But the terror of these horses, when you're alone on a misty estuary, is that you've no hint of their existence till they're suddenly riding down on you out of empty grayness.

I congratulate my snipe, as part of our death rite, on its ability to terrify. I sing to it, stroke it, beg its forgiveness. It stands in my palm, pulse bubbling in the hopeless wound, watches me serenely, lets me say or do as I please. All in all, though, I feel our preparatory rite is a near perfect failure, for in admiring and stroking and singing to such a bird, love begins. It is love, therefore, that I must crush with a rock, and love that I entomb, still warm, in a little stone cairn. It is love whose two black pearls join my growing sphere. So it is love that still watches me. Never blinking. Never closing.

There is a passage in Plato that won't leave me in peace. "The natural property of a wing is to raise that which is heavy and carry it aloft to the region where the gods dwell," Socrates notes in the

Phaedrus. Later, he says that "all are eager to reach the heights . . .
[but as most souls] travel they trample and tread upon one another,
this one striving to outstrip that. Thus confusion ensues, and conflict and grievous sweat. Whereupon . . . many are lamed, and many
have their wings all broken, and for all their toiling they are balked,
every one, of the full vision of being, and departing therefrom, they
feed upon the food of semblance."

In this speech, Socrates takes for granted two things I've always
felt but have never heard a salaried American teacher mention.
One is the idea that all of us in a sense "eat" with our eyes but that
what we eat, thanks to our collective trampling and treading, are
illusions: "the food of semblance." The other is the powerful link
between spiritual life and bird life. The natural property of a wing is
indeed to carry that which is heavy aloft, literally and spiritually.
And the American relationship with the wing is characterized by
the shotgun, the drained wetland, and the oblivious speeding car.

A second Platonic passage that haunts me, this one from the
Timaeus, is an account of the origin of vision. When the gods put
together the human body, Plato writes, they placed "in the vessel of
the head . . . a face in which they inserted organs to minister in all
things to the providence of the soul . . . And of the organs they first
contrived the eyes to give light . . ." Not to receive light: to give it. As
the *Timaeus* has it, the gods made "the pure fire which is within us
. . . to flow through the eyes in a stream smooth and dense . . ."
When the outer light of day meets this inner light that proceeds
from us and the two lights "coalesce" upon an external object, the
result is "that perception which we call sight."

This passage resonates beautifully with Christ's "The light of the
body is the eye." And with Walt Whitman's "From the eyesight
proceeds another eyesight . . ." And Rumi's "Close both eyes/to see
with the other eye." And Lao Tzu's "He who having used the outer-
light can return to the inner-light/Is thereby preserved from all
harm." Yet we discussed no such theories of vision in any church,
school, or science camp I ever attended. The older I get, the more
serious this omission feels.

I was raised, like most pop-science-and-Kodak-educated Americans, to believe that the eye works like a camera: an external light
falls on an external object, glances off that object, enters the pupil
(aperture), alights upon the retina (film), is delivered by the

nerves (mailed) to the brain (darkroom), processed instantly (just the way we Americans like it), then stored in the memory (photo album) as an image (snapshot). This metaphor works well enough as a mechanistic description of the eyeball. What we Kodak customers tend to forget is that the eye is only the instrument of sight, not the sense of it.

If we focus not on how the eyeball works but on how we experience our sense of sight in action, the camera becomes a hopelessly inept model. We all live, at all times, in the center of an extremely complex, perfectly visible sphere. There is at all times a visible ceiling or sky above us, a visible floor or ground below, and an almost infinite number of visible objects occupying a 360-degree surround. What we see of this up, down, and surround is, almost literally, nothing. Human vision is as remarkable for what it screens out, or simply fails to see, as for what it actually perceives. Our sight zooms in constantly on details, blinding us to the surround; it pans, constantly, over the surround's surface, giving us "the view" but no detail; it is sidetracked, constantly, by desire, fatigue, daydreams, moods, fantasies, during which we see outward objects yet perceive them not at all. This is hardly the performance of a Kodak product. If our eyes were intended to be cameras, we all deserve our money back.

Human vision in action reminds me of many things more than cameras. A fiberscope, for one. The various forms of fiberscope (arthroscope, proctoscope, etc.) consist of a bundle of transparent fibers through which images can be transmitted, enabling surgeons to probe the human body, focus on minuscule bits of tissue, enlarge and project these bits on a monitor, and operate on this "technologically enhanced" tissue with previously impossible accuracy. Vision, as I experience my own, is a similarly abstract, selective, and often surgical procedure — a procedure I perform involuntarily on the body of my world, with sometimes joyous, and sometimes deadly, results.

Another analogy between vision and fiber-optic surgery: any fiberoptic surgical device does not merely transmit images of tissue; it also illuminates tissue. The interior of our bodies cannot be lit from outside: what a surgeon perceives through an arthroscope is therefore dependent not on external lights but on a tiny light inside the device itself. In a similar way, our perceptions of the word depend not only on exterior lights that bounce "camera-style" off of objects and into our eyes but on an internal light or energy that proceeds "arthroscope-style" from within, outward, illuminating the few objects we choose to perceive.

If this sounds too wild or metaphysical to describe plain day-to-day seeing, it's a metaphysics that we all practice constantly, in perfectly mundane ways. While writing the preceding paragraph, for instance, I swiveled my eyes from the page to grab a blue ceramic coffee cup from a shelf directly behind me. En route to and from this cup my eyes moved across dozens of plainly lit objects. Yet I perceived none of them. By retracing, slowly, my eyes' route to the cup, I see that they swept across a brass banker's lamp, a Japanese painting of Ebisu playing a red fish on a cane pole, a photo of Meher Baba feeding a monkey, an old L. C. Smith & Bros. type-writer, a bunny-ears cactus, an almost life-size figurative sculpture, two jars full of pens and pencils, fifty or so books, and a large window. Yet I saw none of this. Something in me sought an object it knew to be blue, behind me, and full of hot caffeine — sought it so decisively that I turned 180 degrees, "filming" all the way, yet made an essentially blind turn.

This "seeing blindness" is the great contradiction of human eyesight. Why, with our eyes open, don't we simply see every well-lit object? "[C]onfusion ensues, and conflict and grievous sweat." For we are "balked . . . of the full vision of being" and do indeed "feed upon the food of semblance." Vision is a form of reception. But to an even greater extent it is a form of selection and projection. And what concerns me, what scares me at times, is the extent to which my selections and projections are at my command.

How to see more? How to see more clearly? Light is a form of energy. Humans possess energy and to some extent control its ebbs and flows. Can we then aspire to control our inner light? Can we direct the eyes' arthroscopic procedures? How sure are we, lacking such direction, of the surgeon's integrity, or even of his identity? We know so little of inner light sources, speak so little of them, sound so flaky when we do, yet our seeing illuminates so little of our world! I want to know how to aim my inner light, how to clean its lenses, how to recharge its battery. I want access to the control panel, to the joystick, or at least to the bloody on/off switch! I want hours, innocuous hours, in which to fool with my light till I know just how and just when to aim it, and how far, high, and deep it can shine. Because without such control — without a reliable, directable inner light source — I frighten myself. For I have sometimes looked at a living object, even a beloved object, and have seen illusions, shadows, nothing at all. And still I have performed the surgery . . .

I am haunted by a grebe. A grebe encountered and arthroscopically operated upon by my own two eyes, in the mid-1980s, at the height of the Reagan-Watt-Crowell-Bush-Luhan-Hodell-Hatfield-Packwood rape and pillage of my homeland, the Oregon Cascades and Coast Ranges; height of the destruction of the world I had grown up in and loved and given my writing life to; height of an eight-year spate of Pacific Northwest deforestation that outpaced the rate in Brazil; height of the war on rivers, birds, wildlife, small towns, biological diversity, tolerance, mercy, and beauty; height of my personal rage; the depth of my despair; height of my need for light.

Far from aware of this need, I took a long walk, on the first clear afternoon following a tremendous November storm, on a deserted Pacific beach — a beach beautifully wed, in the entire 360-degree surround, to my mood. The storm surf and swell were enormous. The air was a constant, crushing roar. Spindrift was everywhere. So were sand dollars, washed up by the storm as if even the ocean, in that self-absorbed era, were liquidating its inventory in the name of quick currency. The hills to the east were logged bald. The sun, as it sank, grew enormous and red. The stumps and my skin fumed the same angry orange. My shadow grew a hundred feet long, fell clear to the high-tide line, which to my half-crazed King Learian satisfaction was a graveyard: storm-killed murres, oil-killed puffins, carcasses of gulls tangled in washed-up shreds of net, the carcass of a sea lion shot, most likely, by a fisherman who blamed it for the salmon no longer returning from a drift-netted, trawler-raked ocean to rivers mud-choked by logging.

As a lifelong Oregon coast fisherman, I had a few beautiful secrets. I could, right up until that autumn, still sneak into one stream in a virgin cedar- and hemlock-lined canyon, find big, wild steelhead and salmon in a place that felt primordial, and have them all to myself. That year, however, the elk from the vast surrounding clearcuts — hundreds of cuts, hence hundreds of elk — had been squeezed from their once vast range into that last intact canyon. And having nowhere else to go they crossed and recrossed the stream every day, right in the gravel tail-outs where the salmon and steelhead spawn, till they obliterated the reads, pulverized eggs and alevin, turned my secret stream's banks into an elk-made quagmire reminiscent of the worst riparian cattle damage I'd ever seen — a quagmire that sloughed into the little river with every rain, suffocating the salmon fry that had escaped the countless hooves.

When native elk, to remain alive, are forced to wipe out native salmon, it is time, in my book, to get sad. I quit fishing, exercised my rights as a citizen, and wrote "my" Republican senators the usual letters of distress. They answered with more loads of three- and four- and five-hundred-year-old logs shipped away to Japan as if they were nosegays the senators had grown in their own D.C. flower boxes. Meanwhile, robbed of food and habitat by the same vast clearcuts, the black bears came down out of my home forest, moved into a marsh near town, and lived by raiding garbage cans and dog-food bowls at night. Since this posed a danger to humans, the Fish and Wildlife people came in and shot them all, six in a week. And the owl that used to sing to me mornings, attracted by the lights after I'd written all night — the owl that scared me worse than winnowing snipes, actually, because it happened to be a northern spotted, which has an insane guffaw of a morning cry — was now a silence, a nonexistent pawn, a hated cartoon on some poor dumb logger's cap. And in its stead, as if even the Pentagon grieved its passing, we'd built a forest-funded graphite bomber whose stealth in flight was as perfect as an owl's.

So down the storm-smashed beach I strolled that bleak November, kicking at dead birds and drowned logging dreck, wondering what reason I still had to be grateful to live on the "scenic" Oregon coast, wondering what possible definition of "democracy" I represented through my freedom to write, without persecution or incarceration, such words as

Dear Senator Packwood,

I know you've got huge personal problems, but please! Our home here is dying, the only home we have, and we're bound by a political system in which none of the forces killing us can be stopped except through you. So please don't get mad, don't think this is political or personal, please know I'm only begging for our lives when I say that our

last few trees are still falling and our mills have closed and our people
are sad and broke and lied to. And our schools are in ruins, our totem
owl dead, and our elk jammed in a last few canyons, pulverizing our last
spawning beds with hooves they've no other place to set down, so that
the salmon we cherish, salmon our whole Chain of Being needs to
remain unbroken, salmon that have forever climbed these rivers, nailing
their shining bodies to lonely beds of gravel that tiny silver offspring may
live, they no longer come. And our bears, old honeypaws, the joy their
tracks alone gave our children, they, too, gone, and skinned, their bodies, so human! And our kids, our voteless kids, their large clear eyes now
squinting at stumps and at slash burns and at sunlight that shouldn't be
there, squinting at Game Boys and TVs and anti-queer ads, squinting at
anything rather than turning open-eyed to windows and seeing places so
ancient and so recently loved, huge groves and holy salmon, clouds of
birds and dream-sized animals, a whole green world so utterly gone that
already they begin to believe that they only dreamed, they never really
knew, any such blessings . . .

What I knew, there on the beach, was that I'd be writing no such
letter. My politics had become raw pleas for mercy. Prayers, really.
And I pray to God, thank you, not to men like Bob Packwood.

I turned, tired, back to the dunes, to my car, and to the road
through the clearcuts to a cold house I'd once wept with joy to call
home. But just shy of the first dune — eyes red as fury, red as the
fast-sinking sun — sat a solitary, male western grebe.

And I was back in the mysterious sphere.

The grebe was sitting in a curl of kelp weed at the storm's high-
water mark. His eyes, in the evening sunlight, were fire. In the
center of each blaze, a black point: punctuation; hot lava spinning
round a period. A stillness, deep contact, was instantaneous. A
life-and-death contract should have been, too. But — sick of humans, sick of my own impotence, sick with the knowledge of how
much had been destroyed — I gazed out at the grebe through my
sickness. That its body was beautiful I saw as tragedy. That it seemed
uninjured I saw as irony. From studying wildlife-care books and
visiting wildlife-care centers, from firsthand experience with scaups
and gulls and murres, I knew that seldom do humans make a
difference once a seabird washes ashore. God knew what brought
this bird to this beach — hidden damage from a net, spilled oil,
hidden disease, weakness from lack of food in a dying sea. But it
wouldn't be here at all, I thought, if it weren't too late already.

Yet, in perfect contradiction to this pessimism, I felt fear. The molten eyes, the bird's very health and size, intimidated me. Its beak was a dagger. When I'd move close, its neck would draw the dagger back, ready to stab. To capture the grebe I'd have to take off my coat and smother it. The beach was cold; the walk back would be long. Once I got it in my car it might fight its way free. Once I got it home, then what?

Light is a form of energy that flows in waves. When a healthy wave strikes an object, we see that object in what we call its "true colors." When a lesser wave strikes the same object, we see even the truest colors as shades of gray. The sun striking that November beach was brilliant. The grebe's eyes were two brilliances. The world was doing its part. It was a wave, a light that failed to come from me, that allowed me to leave that beautiful bird where it lay.

A premonition, or maybe a desire to return to the scene of the crime, brought me to the same beach three days later. I found the grebe in the same curl of kelp, very recently dead, its body, wings, and plumage still perfect, its burning eyes plucked out by gulls. This was bad enough, but months later, when I dredged up my sad tale for a bird-loving friend, he hit the ceiling. When a grebe, he told me, any grebe, is washed up on a beach like that, all it needs is to be set back in the water. Grebes require a runway of flat water to take off flying, but they don't need to fly in order to live: even in storm surf they can swim like seals and hunt like little sharks. The grebe I'd found was a fisherman, like me. Just as I can't walk on water, he couldn't walk on land. "He was a hitchhiker," my friend told me. "Needed a lift of a hundred yards or so. And you refused to pick him up."

Years passed, storms came and went, I walked mile upon penitent mile on those same beaches. I never saw another grebe. I only added two molten eyes to my sphere.

Yet once those crimson eyes became part of me, something changed. Perception, that grebe taught me, is a blood sport. Life itself sometimes hangs by a thread made of nothing but the spirit in which we see. And with life itself at stake, I grew suspicious of my eyes' many easy, dark conclusions. Even the most warranted pessimism began to feel unwarranted. I began to see that hope, however feeble its apparent foundation, bespeaks allegiance to every unlikely beauty that remains intact on earth. And with this inward change, outward things began to change, too.

Hurrying home in my pickup, late (as usual) from a fishing trip,
I rounded a blind curve on a coastal byway, noticed a scatter of
loose gravel on the asphalt in front of me, and felt an impulse.
There was a steep, logged-off slope above this curve. A solitary elk
could have kicked such gravel onto the road while crossing. I'm a
hell-bent driver when I'm late; I go barreling through mud and
gravel, even dodge fallen trees without thinking twice. But this
time, though I saw nothing, I had that sudden sense of something
good or bad impending, slammed on the brakes, and as my truck
slowed from fifty to thirty to ten I was amazed, then elated, to see
the gravel turn into birds.

Pine siskins — a whole flock, parked right on the two-lane asphalt. I crept my bumper up next to them. They didn't fly. Maybe
thirty siskins, refusing to budge from the road. Reminded me of
late-sixties college students. I got out of my truck, walked up, and
joined them. I liked the late sixties. Such easy excitement! Now I,
too, could be killed by the next vehicle to come barreling round
the curve!

All but one siskin flew as I sat down next to them. The flock then
circled back overhead, chirping vehemently, begging the flightless
bird to join them. The siskin in the road, a little male, had been
nicked by a previous car, had a small wound above his eye, was in
shock. Were it not for my strange impulse, I would have massacred
an entire flock of avian altruists as they huddled in sympathy
around a helpless comrade. Something inside me, I realized, was
wildly more aware of things than I am — two imperceptible points
of molten red, perhaps. I took the wounded siskin home, kept him
in my bird box overnight, drove him the following morning back to
the curve where I'd found him, and released him in perfect health.
I was a happy man.

That was just the beginning. I remain haunted by the grebe, but
it's been a wondrous haunting, for with the accompanying refusal
to despair, a new energy began to flow. Not dependably; it's something to pray for, not something to be smug about. But I began,
especially when driving, to feel a simple alertness and an occasional
intuition: thousands of road miles, thousands of glimpsed roadside
movements, and thousands of half-glimpsed roadside eyes began to
work in concert to help me avoid killing, and occasionally even to
save, a few animals and birds. I am not laying claim to supernatural

skills. I still sometimes kill by accident, and the intuitions that save lives are almost all purchased, like so many mercies, with an earlier being's innocent blood.

Exactly a year after I abandoned the grebe, I was driving home down Oregon Coast Highway 101 in a torrential November rain. It was a Sunday night. A steady line of weekend storm watchers was returning to Portland in the pitch dark. The road looked like a narrow black river topped by two endless rows of insanely speeding boats. Because of the terrible visibility, I was watching the road lit not just by my own headlights but by those of the pickup in front of me. It was in the pickup's lights that I happened to glimpse a brown ball rolling along the streaming road.

I hit my brakes instantly, certain of what it was. I was also certain, because it was rolling when I glimpsed it, that it had been run over at least once already, and that the pickup would run it over again. There was time, before the truck did so, for a one-syllable prayer: I shouted, "Please!" — terrifying my two passengers. But as I braked and pulled hard toward the highway's right shoulder, the ball rolled out, unscathed, in the pickup's tailwind and tailwater, then righted itself on the road as I shot past. It was an adult pygmy owl.

I knew by its ability to regain its feet that the owl was not hopelessly injured. But it was too disoriented to escape the road. And in my rearview mirror, approaching at fifty or so miles an hour, I saw its doom in the form of at least ten cars. Though I'd braked as fast as I could, momentum had carried me perhaps two hundred feet past the owl. I pulled on the parking brake before my truck stopped rolling, jumped out without a word to my stunned companions, and took off running.

The approaching line of headlights was maybe two hundred yards away. I couldn't see the tiny owl in the dark and distance. Ten cars doing fifty, me on foot doing maybe sixteen, a living bird somewhere in between. I didn't do the math. I just ran. And how right it felt, no matter what! How good it felt to tear eyes-first into another November gale, straight down the lane in which a helpless bird huddled, straight into the headlights of ten city-bound cars — for in this running I'd found a penance that might let me again meet, without shame, the crimson gaze of a grebe.

I've played enough ball to have a good sense of trajectories and distances. I knew, the instant I spotted the fist-size silhouette in the

lead car's high beams, that my hands would never reach it in time. I
also knew that the lead car's driver wouldn't see me or the tiny owl
till he or she was upon us, and so wouldn't slow for either of us. I
still couldn't stop running. It still felt wonderful. To be an American, a lifelong motorist, and a bird lover is to carry a piano's worth
of guilt on your back. I was outrunning my piano.

The owl had been staring, stupefied, at the approaching cars.
When it heard my pounding feet, it swiveled its gaze at me. Instant
sphere. Great good or ill impending. I heard cars in the opposite
lane coming up behind me and realized that if the cars in my lane
did see me, they might be frightened into swerving into a head-on
crash. I was risking lives besides my own. I had succumbed to a kind
of madness. Yet as I sprinted toward the cars I had an unaccount-
ably calm vision of a conceivable, beautiful outcome.

The lead car saw me and hit its horn just as I reached the owl. I
swung my right foot in the gentlest possible kick, chipping the bird
like a soccer ball toward the road's shoulder. I followed the bird
instantly, not quite needing to dive as the lead car shot past, outraged horn blaring. All ten cars shot past. I ignored them, searching the rain gusts and night air. And at the edge of the many
headlight beams I suddenly saw my tiny owl in uninjured, earnest
flight, circling straight back toward the traffic-filled highway.

I don't know what my body did in that moment, whether my
heart stopped or my eyes sent out energy, whether my lips and
lungs actually uttered the "Please!" When your whole being yearns
for one simple thing, it may not be necessary to add the words. All I
know is that a gust of sideways rain blasted my owl, its wings twisted
in response, and it rose inches over the crisscrossing headlights and
car roofs, crossed both lanes, left the highway, and vanished, without once looking back, into the forest and the night.

The eyes, it has been said, are the "windows of the soul." Since
the soul is not a literal object but a spiritual one, eyes cannot be the
soul's literal windows. But they are openings into and out of living
human beings. When our eyes are open, they become not one of
our many walls but one of our very few doors. The mouth is another such door. Through it we inhale air that is not ownable, air
that we share with every being on earth. And out of our mouths we
send words — our personal reshaping of that same communal air.

Seeing, I have come to feel, is the very same kind of process.

Through our eyes we inhale light and images we cannot own — light and images shared with every being on earth. And out of our eyes we exhale a light or a darkness that is the spirit in which we perceive. This visual exhalation, this personal energizing and aiming of perception, is the eyes' speech. It is a reshaping of light as surely as words are a reshaping of air. I therefore feel responsible for my vision. My eye-speech changes the world. Seeing is a blood sport.

I'm still in way over my head. I believe that this is my Maker's intention. I'm in so far over my head that I believe I'll need wings to get out. But even over my head I sense that if all souls are one and the eyes are its windows, then those siskin, owl, snipe, and grebe eyes must all, in a realm outside of time, be my very own. So in killing or saving those eyes, in abandoning or loving them, I kill, save, abandon, or love what is outside of time — that is, what is eternal — in myself. This is Buddhist platitude, Christian and Islamic platitude, Native American platitude too, and platitudes don't make very good literature. But they make excellent aids to memory. And in a world in which one's living eyes and body must fly into split-second meetings with the eyes and bodies of others on wet night roads, storm-smashed beaches, in treetops or on blind curves, one needs all the aids to memory one can get.

The God of the Bible commences creation with an exhalation of light from spirit. Shiva is said to be capable of destroying creation by simply opening an eye. Through a life spent looking, or refusing to look, at an endless stream of other creatures, I've learned that by merely opening my eyes, I, too, take part in the creation and destruction of the world. By abandoning a grebe that entered my sphere of vision, I closed two beautiful molten windows through which I might have gazed upon a real salvation. By kicking a twice-run-over owl skyward, I opened two wondrous dark windows upon the same. One of the terrors of being human, and one of the joys, is that for all our limitations and confusions we have been given power. The life that terrifies me and the life that I adore are one life.

J. R. MOEHRINGER

Resurrecting the Champ

FROM THE LOS ANGELES TIMES MAGAZINE

1.

I'm sitting in a hotel room in Columbus, Ohio, waiting for a call from a man who doesn't trust me, hoping he'll have answers about a man I don't trust, which may clear the name of a man no one gives a damn about. To distract myself from this uneasy vigil — and from the phone that never rings, and from the icy rain that never stops pelting the window — I light a cigar and open a forty-year-old newspaper. • "Greatest puncher they ever seen," the paper says in praise of Bob Satterfield, a ferocious fighter of the 1940s and 1950s. "The man of hope — and the man who crushed hope like a cookie in his fist." Once again, I'm reminded of Satterfield's sorry luck, which dogged him throughout his life, as I'm dogging him now. • I've searched high and low for Satterfield. I've searched the sour-smelling homeless shelters of Santa Ana. I've searched the ancient and venerable boxing gyms of Chicago. I've searched the eerily clear memory of one New York City fighter who touched Satterfield's push-button chin in 1946 and never forgot the panic on Satterfield's face as he fell. I've searched cemeteries, morgues, churches, museums, slums, jails, courts, libraries, police blotters, scrapbooks, phone books and record books. Now I'm searching this dreary, sleet-bound Midwestern city, where all the streets look like melting Edward Hopper paintings and the sky like a storm-whipped sea. • Maybe it's fatigue, maybe it's caffeine, maybe it's the fog rolling in behind the rain, but I feel as though Satterfield has become my own 180-pound Moby Dick. Like Ahab's obsession, he casts a harsh light on his pursuer. Stalking him from town to town and decade to decade, I've learned almost everything there is to know about him, along with valuable lessons about boxing, courage and the eternal tension between fathers and sons. But I've learned more than I bargained for about myself, and for that I owe him a debt. I can't repay the debt unless the phone rings.

2.

We met because a coworker got the urge to clean. It was early January, 1996. The cop reporter who sits near me at the Orange County edition of the *Times* was straightening her desk when she came across an old tip, something about a once-famous boxer sleeping on park benches in Santa Ana. Passing the tip along, she deflected my thank-you with an off-the-cuff caveat, "He might be dead."

The tipster had no trouble recalling the boxer when I phoned. "Yeah, Bob Satterfield," he said. "A contender from the 1950s. I used to watch him when I watched the fights on TV." Forty years later, though, Satterfield wasn't contending anymore, except with cops. When last seen, the old boxer was wandering the streets, swilling whiskey and calling himself Champ. "Just a guy that lived too long," the tipster said, though he feared this compassion might be outdated. There was a better-than-ever chance, he figured, that Satterfield was dead.

If Satterfield was alive, finding him would require a slow tour of Santa Ana's seediest precincts. I began with one of the city's largest men's shelters. Several promising candidates lingered inside the shelter and out, but none matched my sketchy notion of an elderly black man with a boxer's sturdy body. From there I drove to 1st Street, a wide boulevard of taco stands and bus stops that serves as a promenade for homeless men. Again, nothing. Next I cruised the alleys and side streets of nearby McFadden Avenue, where gutters still glistened with tinsel from discarded Christmas trees. On a particularly lively corner I parked the car and walked, stopping passersby and asking where I might find the fighter from the 1950s, the one who called himself Champ, the one who gave the cops all they could handle. No one knew, no one cared, and I was ready to knock off when I heard someone cry out, "Hiya, Champ!"

Wheeling around, I saw an elderly black man pushing a grocery cart full of junk down the middle of the street. Rancid clothes, vacant stare, sooty face, he looked like every other homeless man in America. Then I noticed his hands, the largest hands I'd ever seen, each one so heavy and unwieldy that he held it at his side like a bowling ball. Hands such as these were not just unusual, they were natural phenomena. Looking closer, however, I saw that they complemented the meaty plumpness of his shoulders and the brick-wall thickness of his chest, exceptional attributes in a man who couldn't be getting three squares a day. To maintain such a build on table scraps and handouts, he must have been immense back when.

More than his physique, what distinguished him was a faint suggestion of style. Despite the cast-off clothes, despite the caked-on dirt, there was a vague sense that he clung to some vestigial pride in his appearance. Under his grimy ski parka he wore an almost professorial hound's-tooth vest. Atop his crown of graying hair was a rakish brown hat with a pigeon feather tucked jauntily in its brim.

His skin was a rich cigar color and smooth for an ex-boxer's, except for one bright scar between his eyebrows that resembled a character in the Chinese alphabet. Beneath a craggy five-o'clock shadow, his face was pleasant: dark eyes and high cheekbones sat astride a strong, well-formed nose, and each feature followed the lead of his firm, squared-off chin. He was someone's heartthrob once. His teeth, however, were long gone, save for some stubborn spikes along the mandible.

I smiled and strolled toward him.

"Hey, Champ," I said.

"Heyyy, Champ," he said, looking up and smiling as though we were old friends. I half expected him to hug me.

"You're Bob Satterfield, aren't you?" I said.

"Battlin' Bob Satterfield!" he said, delighted at being recognized. "I'm the Champ, I fought 'em all, Ezzard Charles, Floyd Patterson—"

I told him I was a reporter from the *Los Angeles Times,* that I wanted to write a story about his life.

"How old are you?" I asked.

"I count my age as 66," he said. "But *The Ring Record Book,* they say 72."

"Did you ever fight for the title?"

"They just didn't give me the break to fight for the title," he said woefully. "If they'd given me the break, I believe I'd be the champ."

"Why didn't they give you the break?"

"You got to be in the right clique," he said, "to get the right fight at the right time."

His voice was weak and raspy, no more than a child's whisper, his words filled with the blurred vowels and squishy consonants of someone rendered senseless any number of times by liquor and fists. He stuttered slightly, humming his "m," gargling his "l," tripping over his longer sentences. By contrast, his eyes and memories were clear. When I asked about his biggest fights, he rattled them off one by one, naming every opponent, every date, every arena. He groaned at the memory of all those beatings, but it was a proud noise, to let me know he'd held his own with giants. He'd even broken the nose of Rocky Marciano, the only undefeated heavyweight champion in history. "He was strooong, I want to tell you," Champ said, chuckling immodestly.

It happened during a sparring session, Champ said, demonstrating how he moved in close, slipping an uppercut under Marciano's left. Marciano shivered, staggered back, and Champ pressed his advantage with another uppercut. Then another. And another. Blood flowed.

"I busted his nose!" Champ shouted, staring at the sidewalk where Marciano lay, forever vanquished. "They rushed in and called off the fight and took Rock away!"

Now he was off to get some free chow at a nearby community center. "Would you care for some?" he asked, and I couldn't decide which was more touching, his largess or his mannerly diction.

3.

"I was born Tommy Harrison," he said, twirling a chicken leg in his toothless mouth. "That's what you call my legal name. But I fought as Bob Satterfield." His handlers, he explained, didn't want him confused with another fighter, Tommy "Hurricane" Jackson, so they gave him an alias. I asked how they chose Bob Satterfield and he shrugged.

As a boy in and around Chicago, he built his shoulders by lifting ice blocks, a job that paid pennies at first but huge dividends years later in the ring. At 15, he ran away from home, fleeing a father who routinely whipped him. For months he rode the rails as a hobo, then joined the army. Too young to enlist, he pretended to be his older brother, George, paying a prostitute to pose as his mother at the induction center.

He learned to box in the Army as a way of eating better and avoiding strenuous duty. Faced with older and tougher opponents, he developed a slithery, punch-and-move style, which must have impressed Marciano, who was collecting talented young fighters to help him prepare for a title shot against Jersey Joe Walcott. Upon his discharge, Champ became chief sparring partner to the man who would soon become the Zeus of modern boxing. Flicking his big fists in the air, each one glimmering with chicken grease, Champ again recreated the sequence of punches that led to Marciano's broken nose, and we laughed about the blood, all that blood.

When he left Marciano's camp and struck out on his own, Champ won a few fights, and suddenly the world treated him like a spoiled prince. Women succumbed, celebrities vied to sit at his side. The mountaintop was within view. "I never really dreamed of being champ," he said, "but as I would go through life, I would think, if I ever get a chance at the title, I'm going to win that fight!"

Instead, he lost. It was February, 1953. Ezzard Charles, the formidable ex-champion, was trying to mount a comeback. Champ was trying to become the nation's top-ranked contender. They met in Detroit before a fair-sized crowd, and Champ proved himself game in the early going. But after eight rounds, his eye swollen shut and his mouth spurting blood, he crumbled under Charles's superior boxing skills. The fateful punch was a slow-motion memory four decades later. Its force was so great that Champ bit clean through his mouthpiece. At the bell, he managed to reach his corner. But when the ninth started, he couldn't stand.

Nothing would ever be the same. A procession of bums and semi-bums made him look silly. Floyd Patterson dismantled him in one round. One day he was invincible, the next he was retired.

As with so many fighters, he'd saved nothing. He got $34,000 for the Charles fight, a handsome sum for the 1950s, but he frittered it on good times and "tutti-frutti" Cadillacs. With no money and few prospects, he drifted to California, where he met a woman, raised a family and hoped for the best. The worst came instead. He broke his ankle on a construction job and didn't rest long enough for it to heal. The injury kept him from working steadily. Then, the punch he never saw coming. His son was killed.

"My son," Champ said, his voice darkening. "He was my heart."

"Little Champ" fell in with the wrong people. An angry teenager, he got on somebody's bad side, and one night he walked into an ambush. "My heart felt sad and broke," Champ said. "But I figured this happened because he was so hotheaded."

Racked with pain, Champ left the boy's mother, who still lived in the house they once shared, not far from where we sat. "Sometimes I go see her," he said. "It's kind of hard, but somehow I make it."

Park benches were his beds, though sometimes he slept at the shelter and sometimes in the backseat of a periwinkle and navy blue Cadillac he bought with his last bit of money. He missed the good life but not the riches, the fame or the women. He missed knowing that he was the boss, his body the servant. "The hard work," he whispered. "Sparring with the bags, skipping rope. Every night after a workout we'd go for a big steak and a half a can of beer. Aaah."

Finishing his lunch, Champ wrapped the leftovers in a napkin and carefully stowed them in a secret compartment of his grocery cart. We shook hands, mine like an infant's in his. When we unclasped, he looked at the five-dollar bill I'd slipped him.

"Heyyy," he said soulfully. "Thanks, amigo. All right, thank you."

My car was down the block. When I reached it, I turned to look over my shoulder. Champ was still waving his massive right hand, still groping for words. "Thank you, Champ!" he called. "All right? Thank you!"

4·

Like Melville's ocean, or Twain's Mississippi, boxing calls to a young man. Its victims are not only those who forfeit their wits and dive into the ring. The sport seduces writers, too, dragging them down with its powerful undertow of testosterone. Many die a hideous literary death, drowning in their own hyperbole. Only a few — Ernest Hemingway, Jimmy Canon, A. J. Liebling — cross to safety. Awash in all that blood, they become more buoyant.

For most Americans, however, boxing makes no sense. The sport that once defined the nation now seems hopelessly archaic, like jousting or pistols at six paces. The uninitiated, the cultivated, the educated don't accept that boxing has existed since pre-Hellenic Greece, and possibly since the time of the pharaohs, because it concedes one musky truth about masculinity: hitting a man is sometimes the most satisfying response to *being* a man. Disturbing, maybe, but there it is.

Just the sight of two fighters belting each other around the ring triggers a soothing response, a womblike reassurance that everything is less complicated than we've been led to believe. From brutality, clarity. As with the first taste of cold beer on a warm day, the first kiss of love in the dark, the first meaningful victory over an evenly matched foe, the brain's simplest part is appeased. Colors become brighter, shapes grow deeper, the world slides into smoother focus. And focus was what I craved the day I went searching for Champ. Focus was what made a copy reporter's moth-eaten tip look to me like the Hope diamond. Focus was what I feared I'd lost on the job.

As a newspaper writer, you spend much of your time walking up dirty steps to talk to dirty people about dirty things. Then, once in a great while, you meet an antidote to all that dirt. Champ wasn't the cleanest of men — he may have been the dirtiest man I ever met — but he was pure of heart. He wasn't the first homeless heavyweight either, not by a long shot. Another boxer lands on Skid Row every day, bug-eyed and scrambled. But none has a résumé to compare with Champ's, or a memory. He offered a return to the unalloyed joy of daily journalism, not to mention the winning ticket in the Literary Lottery. He was that rarest of rare birds, a people-watcher's version of the condor: *Pugilisticum luciditas.* He was noble. He was innocent. He was all mine.

I phoned boxing experts throughout the nation. To my astonishment, they not only remembered Champ, they worshiped him. "Hardest hitter who ever lived." "Dynamite puncher." "One of the greatest punchers of all time." Boxing people love to exaggerate, but there was a persuasive sameness to their praise. Bob Satterfield was a beast who slouched toward every opponent with murder in his eye. He could have, should have, would have been champion, except for one tiny problem. He couldn't take a punch.

"He was a bomber," said boxing historian Burt Sugar. "But he had a chin. If he didn't take you out with the first punch, he was out with the second."

Every fighter, being human, has one glaring weakness. For some, it's a faint heart. For others, a lack of discipline. Satterfield's shortcoming was more comic, therefore more melodramatic. Nobody dished it out better, but few were less able to take it. He knocked out seven of his first twelve opponents in the first round, a terrifying boxing blitzkrieg. But over the course of his twelve-year professional career he suffered many first-round knockouts himself. The skinny on Satterfield spliced together a common male fantasy with the most common male fear: loaded with raw talent, he was doomed to fail because of one factory-installed flaw.

Rob Mainwaring, a researcher at boxing's publication of record, *The Ring* magazine, faxed me a fat Satterfield file, rife with vivid accounts of his fragility and prowess. Three times, Satterfield destroyed all comers and put himself in line for a title shot. But each time, before the big fight could be set, Satterfield fell at the feet of some nobody. In May, 1954, for instance, Satterfield tangled with an outsized Cuban fighter named Julio Mederos, banging him with five fast blows in the second round. When Mederos came to, he told a translator: "Nobody ever hit me that hard before. I didn't know any man could hit that hard." Satterfield appeared unstoppable. Six months later, however, he was stopped by an also-ran named Marty Marshall, who found Satterfield's flukish chin before some fans could find their seats.

Viewed as a literary artifact, the Satterfield file was a lovely sampler of overwrought prose. "The Chicago sleep-inducer," one fight writer called him. "Embalming fluid in either hand," said another. Then, in the next breath, came the qualifiers: "Boxing's Humpty-Dumpty." "A chin of Waterford." "Chill-or-be-chilled." It was a prankish God who connected that dainty jaw and that sledgehammer arm to one man's body, and it was the same almighty jokester who put those Hemingway wannabes in charge of chronicling his rise and fall.

Mainwaring faxed me several photos of Satterfield and one of a wife named Iona, whom he divorced in 1952. The library at the *Times*, meanwhile, unearthed still more Satterfield clippings, including a brief 1994 profile by Orange County Register columnist Bill Johnson. ("Bob Satterfield, one of the top six heavyweight fighters in the world from 1950 to 1956, today is homeless, living in old, abandoned houses in Santa Ana.") From Chicago newspapers, the library culled glowing mentions of Satterfield, including one describing his nightmarish blood bath with middleweight Jake LaMotta, the fighter portrayed by Robert De Niro in Martin Scorsese's 1980 *Raging Bull.* Midway through the film, Satterfield's name fills the screen — then, as the name dissolves, LaMotta–De Niro smashes him in the face.

5.

"Mr. LaMotta," I said. "I'm writing a story about an old opponent of yours, Bob Satterfield."

"Hold on," he said. "I'm eating a meatball."

I'd phoned the former champion in Manhattan, where he was busy launching his new spaghetti sauce company, LaMotta's Tomatta. His voice was De Niro's from the film — nasal, pugnacious, phlegm-filled, a cross between Don Corleone and Donald Duck. At last he swallowed and said, "Bob Satterfield was one of the hardest punchers who ever lived."

Reluctantly, I told LaMotta the bad news. Satterfield was sleeping on park benches in Santa Ana.

"You sure it's him?" he said. "I heard he was dead."

"No," I assured him, "I just talked to him yesterday."

"Awww," he said, "that's a shame. He put three bumps on my head before I knocked him out. Besides Bob Satterfield, the only ones who ever hurt me were my ex-wives."

LaMotta began to reminisce about his old nemesis, a man so dangerous that no one dared spar with him. "He hit me his best punch," he said wistfully. "He hit me with plenty of lefts. But I was coming into him. He hit me with a right hand to the top of the head. I thought I'd fall down. Then he did it again. He did it three times, and when nothing happened he sort of gave up. I knocked him on his face. Flat on his face."

LaMotta asked me to say hello to Satterfield, and I promised that I would. "There but for the grace of God go I," he said. "God dealt me a different hand."

I visited Champ that day to deliver LaMotta's best wishes. I visited

him many times in the days ahead, always with some specific purpose in mind. Flesh out the details of his life. Ask a few more
questions. See how he was faring. Each time the drill was the same.
I'd give him five dollars and he'd give me a big tumble, making
such a fuss over me that I'd turn red.

"A boxer, like a writer, must stand alone," Liebling wrote, inad-
vertently explaining the kinship between Champ and me. To my
mind, anyone who flattened Rocky Marciano and put three bumps
on Jake LaMotta's melon ranked between astronaut and Lakota
warrior on the delicately calibrated scale of bad asses, and thus
deserved at least a Sunday profile. To Champ's mind, anyone willing to listen to forty-year-old boxing stories could only be a bored
writer or a benevolent Martian. Still, there was something more
basic about our connection. As a man, I couldn't get enough of his
hyper-virile aura. As a homeless man, he couldn't get enough of my
patient silence. Between his prattling and my scribbling, we became
something like fast friends.

Our mutual admiration caused me to sputter with indignation
when my editors asked what hard evidence I had that Champ was
Satterfield. What more hard evidence do you need, I asked, besides
Champ's being the man in these old newspaper photos — allowing
for forty years of high living and several hundred quarts of cheap
whiskey? Better yet, how about Champ's being able to name every
opponent, and the dates on which he fought them — allowing for
an old man's occasional memory lapses?

If the evidence of our senses won't suffice, I continued, let's use
common sense: Champ is telling the truth because he has no reason
to lie. For being Bob Satterfield, he gets no money, no glory, no
extra chicken legs at senior centers and soup kitchens. Pretending
to be a fighter forgotten by all but a few boxing experts? Pretending
in such convincing fashion? He'd have to be crazy. Or brilliant. And
I could say with some confidence that he was neither. Even so, the
editors said, get something harder.

6.

Champ's old house in Santa Ana sat along a bleak cul-de-sac, its
yard bursting with cowlick-shaped weeds, its walls shedding great

slices of paint. It looked like a guard shack at the border crossing of some desolate and impoverished nation.

An unhappy young woman scowled when I asked to see Champ's ex-girlfriend. "Wait here," she said.

Minutes later, she returned with a message: go away. Champ's things have been burned, and no one has any interest in talking to you.

Next I tried the Orange County courthouse, hoping arrest records would authenticate Champ. Sure enough, plenty of data existed in the courthouse ledger. Finding various minor offenses under Thomas Harrison, alias Bob Satterfield, I rejoiced. Here was proof, stamped with the official seal of California, that Champ was Satterfield. A scoundrel, yes, but a truthful one.

Then I saw something bad. Two felony arrests, one in 1969, one in 1975. Champ had been candid about his misdemeanors, but he had never mentioned these more serious offenses. "Oh, God," I said, scanning the arrest warrant: "Thomas Harrison, also known as Bob Satterfield . . . lewd and lascivious act upon and with the body . . . child under the age of 14 years." Champ molesting his girlfriend's 10-year-old daughter. Champ punching the little girl's aunt in the mouth.

"Did you know [Champ] to be a professional prizefighter?" a prosecutor asked the aunt during a hearing.

"Yes," she said.

"Did you know that he was once a contender for the heavyweight boxing championship of the world?"

Before she could answer, Champ's lawyer raised an objection, which the judge sustained.

Champ pleaded guilty to assaulting the aunt — for which he received probation — and the molestation charge was dropped.

Then, six years later, it happened again. Same girlfriend, different daughter.

"Thomas Harrison, also known as Tommy Satterfield, also known as Bobby Satterfield . . . lewd and lascivious act."

Again, Champ avowed his innocence, but a jury found him guilty. In May 1976, Champ wrote the judge from jail, begging for a second chance. He signed the letter, "Yours truly, Thomas Harrison. Also Known as Bob Satterfield, Ex-Boxer, 5th in the World."

This is how it happens, I thought. This is how a newspaper writer learns to hate the world. I could feel the cynicism setting inside me like concrete. My reprieve from the dirtiness of everyday journalism had turned into a reaffirmation of everything I loathed and feared. My noble warrior, my male idol, my friend, was a walking, talking horror show, a homeless Humbert Humbert.

7.

He greeted me with his typical good cheer, doffing his hat.

"Hey, Champ, whaddya say!?" he cried. "Long time no see, amigo."

"Hey, Champ," I said, glum. "Let's sit down here and have a talk."

I led him over to some bleachers in a nearby baseball field. We passed the afternoon talking about all the major characters of his life — Marciano, Charles, Little Champ. Abruptly, I mentioned the ex-girlfriend.

"Now that I'm on the outside looking in," he mumbled, "I see she wasn't 100 percent in my corner."

"Because she accused you of doing those awful things to her baby?"

He lifted his head, startled. He was spent, punch drunk, permanently hung over, but he knew what I was saying. "They just took her word for it," he said of the jury. "The only regret I have in life is that case she made against me with the baby." Only a monster would hurt a child, Champ said. He begged his ex-girlfriend to recant those false accusations, which he blamed on her paranoia and jealousy. And she did recant, he said, but not to the judge.

More than this he didn't want to say. He wanted to talk about Chicago, sweet home, and all the other way-off places where he knew folks. How he yearned for friendly faces, especially his sister, Lily, with whom he'd left his scrapbook and other papers for safe-keeping. He told me her address in Columbus, Ohio, and her phone number. He wanted to see her before he died. See anyone. "Get me some money and head on down the road," he said, eyes lowered, half to himself.

A cold winter night was minutes off, and Champ needed to find a bed, fast. This posed a problem, since taking leave of Champ was never fast. It was hard for him to overcome the inertia that crept into his bones while he sat, harder still to break away from anyone willing to listen. Watching him get his grocery cart going was like seeing an ocean liner off at the dock. The first movement was imperceptible. "See you later, Champ," I said, hurrying him along, shaking that catcher's mitt of a hand. Then I accidentally looked into his eyes, and I couldn't help myself. I believed him.

Maybe it was faith born of guilt. Maybe it was my way of atoning. After all, I was the latest in a long line of people — managers, promoters, opponents — who wanted something from Champ. I wanted his aura, I wanted his story, I wanted his friendship. As partial restitution, the least I could give him was the benefit of the doubt.

Also, he was right. Only a monster would commit the crimes described in those court files, and I didn't see any monster before me. Just a toothless boxer with a glass chin and a pigeon feather in his hat. Shaking his hand, I heard myself say, "Go get warm, Champ," and I watched myself slip him another five-dollar bill.

8.

LaMotta would not let up. He refused to let me write. Each time I tried, he swatted me around my subconscious. "Besides Bob Satterfield," he'd said, "the only ones who ever hurt me were my ex-wives." Men seldom speak of other men with such deference, such reverence, particularly men like LaMotta. One of the brashest fighters ever, he discussed Satterfield with all the bluster of a curtsy. "You sure it's him?" he'd asked, distressed. "I heard he was dead."

You sure it's him? The courts were sure, the cops were sure, the editors were pretty sure. But I was getting ready to tell several million people that Bob Satterfield was a homeless wreck and a convicted child molester. Was I sure?

I phoned more boxing experts and historians, promoters and managers, libraries and clubs, referees and retired fighters, and that's when I found Ernie Terrell, former heavyweight champion. I reached him in Chicago at the South Side offices of his janitorial business.

"You remember Bob Satterfield?" I asked.

"One of the hardest punchers who ever lived," he said.

I've been hanging out with Satterfield, I said, and I need someone who can vouch for his identity. A long silence followed. A tingly silence, a harrowing silence, the kind of silence that precedes the bloodcurdling scream in a horror film. "Bob Satterfield is dead," Terrell said.

"No, he's not," I said, laughing. "I just talked to him."

"You talked to Bob Satterfield."

"Yes. He sleeps in a park not ten minutes from here."

"Bob Satterfield?" he said. "Bob Satterfield the fighter? Bob Satterfield'd dead."

Now it was my turn to be silent. When I felt the saliva returning to my mouth, I asked Terrell what made him so sure.

"Did you go to his funeral?" I asked.

He admitted that he had not.

"Do you have a copy of his obituary?"

Again, no.

"Then how do you know he's dead?" I asked.

Suddenly, he seemed less sure.

"Hold on," he said. "We're going to get to the bottom of this."

He opened a third phone line and began conference-calling veteran corner men and trainers on the South Side. The voices that joined us on the line were disjointed and indistinct, as though recorded on scratchy vinyl records. Rather than a conference call, we were conducting a seance, summoning the spirits of boxing's past. He dialed a gym where the phone rang and rang. When someone finally answered, Terrell asked to speak with D.D. The phone went dead for what seemed a week. In the background, I heard speed bags being thrummed and ropes being skipped, a sound like cicadas on a summer day. At last, a scruffy and querulous voice came on the line, more blues man than corner man.

"Who's this?"

"It's Ernie."

"Ernie?"

"Ernie."

"Ernie?"

"Ernie!"

"Yeah, Ernie, yeah."

"I got a guy here on the other line from the *Los Angeles Times*, in California, says he's writing a story about Bob Satterfield. You remember Bob Satterfield."

"Suuure."

"Says he just talked to Satterfield and Satterfield's sleeping in a park out there in Santa Ana."

"Bob Satterfield's dead."

"No," I said.

I told them about Champ's encyclopedic knowledge of his career. I told them about Champ's well-documented reputation among cops, judges, and reporters. I told them about Champ's face matching old Satterfield photos.

"Then I will come out there and shoot that dude," D.D. said. "Because Bob Satterfield is *dead.*"

Ten minutes later I was in Santa Ana, where I found Champ sweeping someone's sidewalk for the price of a whiskey bottle. It was a hot spring day, and he looked spent from the hard work.

"Look," I said, "a lot of people say you're dead."

"I'm the one," he said, bouncing on his feet, shadowboxing playfully with me. "Battlin' Bob Satterfield. I fought 'em all. Ezzard Charles, Rocky Marciano—"

"Don't you have any identification?" I said, exasperated. "A birth certificate? A union card? A Social Security card?"

He patted his pockets, nothing. We'd been through this.

"In that case," I said, "I'm going to have to give you a test."

Far from offended, he couldn't wait. Leaning into me, he cocked his head to one side and closed his eyes, to aid concentration.

"Who was Jack Kearns?" I asked, knowing that "Doc" Kearns, who managed Jack Dempsey in the 1920s, briefly managed Satterfield's early career.

"Jack Kearns," Champ said. "He was the first manager I ever had."

"All right," I said. "Who's this?"

I held before his nose a 45-year-old wire photo of Iona Satterfield. Champ touched her face gingerly and said, "That's Iona. That's the only woman I ever loved."

9.

Asked to explain myself, I usually start with my father, who disappeared when I was seven months old, walked away from his only son the way some people leave a party that's grown dull. At precisely the moment I learned to crawl, he ran. An unfair head start, I always felt.

As a boy, I could repress all stirrings of curiosity about him, because I knew what he sounded like, and this seemed sufficient. A well-known radio man in New York City, he often came floating out of my grandmother's olive-drab General Electric clock-radio, cracking jokes and doing bits, until an adult passing through the room would lunge for the dial. It was thought that The Voice upset me. No one realized that The Voice nourished me. My father was invisible, therefore mythic. He was whatever I wanted him to be, and his rumbling baritone inspired mental pictures of every male archetype, from Jesus to Joe Namath to Baloo the bear in *The Jungle Book*.

Over time, I grew impatient with the mystery surrounding him, the not knowing, particularly when he changed his name and vanished altogether. (Seeing fatherhood and child support as a maximum-security prison, he took a fugitive's pains to cover his tracks once he escaped.) As his absence came to feel more like a constant presence, I spent long hours puzzling about the potential intersections between his identity and mine. My predecessor in the generational parade, my accursed precursor, was a voice. It unnerved me. It unmanned me. One day, shortly before my seventeenth birthday, I made what felt like a conscious decision to find him. At least, that's what I thought until I met Champ, who forced me to see that no such conscious decision ever took place, that I'd been trying to find my father all my life, that every man is trying to find his father.

True, a love of boxing and a budding disenchantment with daily journalism sparked my original interest in Champ. Then a genuine fondness made me befriend him. But what made me study him like an insect under a microscope was my inescapable fascination with anyone who disappears, dissolves his identity, walks away from fame and family. When pushed to deconstruct my relationship with Champ, I saw that we were trading more than fivers and fellowship. Champ was using me as a surrogate for his dead son, and I was using him as a stand-in for my own deep-voiced demon, whom I met after a brief, furious search.

We sat in an airport coffee shop and talked like strangers. Strangers who had the same nose and chin. I remember random things. I remember that he was the first man I ever made nervous. I remember that he wore a black leather coat, ordered eggs Benedict and flirted relentlessly with a waitress, asking like some fussy lord if the chef made his own Hollandaise sauce. I remember that he was portly and jovial, with wild eyebrows that forked straight out from his head. I remember laughing at his stories, laughing against my will because he could be painfully funny. I remember breathing in his peppery scent, a uniquely male cocktail of rubbing alcohol, hair spray and Marlboro 100s. I remember the hug when we parted, the first time I ever hugged another man.

But what we said to each other over the hours we sat together, I don't know. The meeting was so emotionally high-watt that it shorted my memory circuits. My only other impression of that night is one of all-pervasive awe. My father, my mythic father, had boozed away his future and parlayed his considerable talents into a pile of unpaid bills. I saw none of that. If losing him was a hardship, losing my mythic idea of him would have been torture. So I chose to see him as a fallen god, an illusion he fostered with a few white lies. I loved him in the desperate way you love someone when you need to.

Now, months after meeting Champ, I asked myself if I wasn't viewing this poor homeless man through the same hopeful myopia. If so, why? The answer dawned one day while I was reading *Moby-Dick*, the bible of obsession, which provides a special sort of reading pleasure when you substitute the word "father" for "whale": "It is a thing most sorrowful, nay shocking, to expose the fall of valor in the soul. . . . That immaculate manliness we feel within ourselves . . . bleeds with keenest anguish at the undraped spectacle of a valor-ruined man."

When the valor-ruined man is your father, the anguish quadruples and the manliness hemorrhages. Sometimes the anguish reaches such a crescendo that you simply disobey your eyes. Anything to stanch the bleeding.

Because he recalled the specter of my father and his equally enigmatic cop-out, Champ might have revived that early talent I showed for self-deception. He also either benefited or suffered from the trinity of habits that constitutes my father's legacy. An obsession with questions of identity. A tendency to overestimate men. And an inability to leave the past alone.

10.

Not every homeless man can look nonchalant speaking into a cellular phone, but Champ acclimated himself to the technology, even if he did aim the phone at that part of the heavens where he imagined Ohio to be. He told his sister he was fine, getting by, and urged her to cooperate. "Please," he said, handing me the phone, "let this man look at my scrapbook."

Establishing Champ's credibility was one thing. Establishing mine with his sister was another. Lily couldn't imagine what I wanted from her poor brother, and I couldn't blame her. I tried to explain that Champ merited a newspaper story because he'd contended for the title.

"You remember your brother fighting," I said, "as Bob Satterfield?"

"Yes," she said casually.

"And you have a scrapbook with clippings and photos?"

"I've had that scrapbook for years."

I asked her to mail me the book, but she refused. She wasn't about to ship a family heirloom to someone she'd never met. Again, I couldn't blame her.

It was then that I heard from a former boxing writer. He'd been watching TV recently when he hit on something called the Classic Sports Network, which was airing a prehistoric episode of Rocky Marciano's TV show, wherein Marciano analyzed a 1951 bout at Madison Square Garden between Rex Layne and Bob Satterfield.

When the tape arrived the next morning, I cradled it like a newborn to the nearest VCR. There was Marciano, pudgy and past his prime, a real-life version of Fred Flintstone. Beside him sat his guest, comic Jimmy Durante. After several excruciating minutes of idle chitchat, Marciano turned to Durante and said, "I want to show you the Bob Satterfield–Rex Layne fight."

Durante's eyes widened.

"Satterfield?" he said.

"You remember him?" Marciano asked.

"So help me," Durante said, "he's my favorite. A great, great fighter. I thought he'd be a champion."

"He had the punch, Jim," Marciano said, shaking his head.

The screen went dark. A ring appeared. In the foreground stood a man in a hooded robe, his back to the camera. On either side of him stood corner men in cardigan sweaters, "SATTERFIELD" emblazoned across their backs. Doffing his robe, the fighter started forward, his torso atremble with muscles. Slowly he turned toward the camera, and I saw that he was not Champ. The resemblance was strong, as the resemblance between Champ and old photos of Satterfield had been strong. But they were different men.

My stomach tightened as the "real" Satterfield threw a walloping right. Layne dropped to one knee and shook his head, not knowing what hit him. I knew exactly how he felt.

Champ a fake. Somehow I felt less betrayed when I thought he was a child molester. It made me sick. It made no sense. He knew too much about Satterfield. He knew the record. He knew Doc Kearns. He recognized Iona. Plus, he was built like a fighter — that body, those hands. Yes, I thought, he's built like a fighter.

I phoned *The Ring* and asked Mainwaring to check his records for a heavyweight named Tommy Harrison. Minutes later, he faxed me the file. There, at long last, was Champ. This time, no allowance needed to be made for the passage of years and the corrosive effects of whiskey. That body, those hands.

Besides his name, it seemed, Champ was frequently telling the truth. Not only did he break Marciano's nose, the injury postponed a storied rematch with Walcott. Like Satterfield, he *had* been a highly touted contender, a guy within striking distance of the championship. Like Satterfield, he *had* fought Ezzard Charles. In fact, Harrison and Satterfield had fought many of the same men.

Opponents weren't the only thing they had in common. Both were Army veterans. Both were right-handers. Both were built like light-heavyweights. Both were anxious to break into the heavyweight division. Both were clobbered when they tried. Both retired in the mid-1950s. Both were born in November; their birthdays were one day apart.

"He's fast," Marciano said of Harrison in one clipping. "Has a great ring future. In a year or so, if I'm still champ, I expect trouble from him."

The file proved that Champ was a fraud, or delusional, or something in between. But it couldn't explain his motives, nor account for his corroborative sister. In fact, it raised more questions than it answered, including the most pressing question of all: if Champ wasn't Satterfield, who was?

Ernie Terrell said Satterfield was dead. But I couldn't find an obituary — not even in Chicago. How did a fighter of Satterfield's stature not rate a death notice in his native city?

Phone directories in scores of area codes listed hundreds of Satterfields, too many to dial. A search of databases throughout the Midwest found one Illinois death certificate in the name of Robert Satterfield, a truck driver buried in Restvale Cemetery, Worth, Illinois. Under next of kin, a son on the South Side of Chicago.

"Robert Satterfield Junior?" I asked when the son answered the phone.

"Yes?"

"I'm writing a story about Bob Satterfield, the heavyweight of the 1950s and I was wondering if you might be any—"

"That's my father," he said proudly.

11.

The neighborhood was dodgy, some houses well kept and others falling down. Few addresses were visible and some street signs were gone, so I drove in circles, getting lost twice, doubling back, and that's when I saw him. Bob Satterfield. In the flesh.

After staring at old newspaper photos and studying the tape of his fight with Rex Layne, I'd committed Satterfield's face to memory — never realizing he might have bequeathed that face to his son. Seeing Satterfield Jr. outside his house, the resemblance fooled me like a mirage, and I did what anyone in my shoes would have done: I backed straight into his neighbor's truck.

The first time I ever laid eyes on Bob Satterfield, therefore, he flinched, as though bracing for a punch.

After making sure I'd left no visible dent, we shook hands and went inside his brick house, the nicest on the block. The living room was neat and intensely bright, morning sunlight practically shattering the glass windows. He introduced me to his wife, Elaine, who took my hand somewhat timidly. Together, they waved me toward the couch, then sat far away, grimacing.

They were visibly afraid of me, but they did everything possible to make me feel welcome. She was all smiles and bottled-up energy; he was old-school polite, verging on courtly. He'd just finished a double shift at O'Hare, where he loaded cargo for a living, and he actually apologized for his exhaustion. I looked into his basset-hound eyes and cringed, knowing I'd soon add to his burdens.

I started by acknowledging their apprehension. As far as they knew, I'd come all the way from California to ask questions about a fighter few people remembered. It seemed suspicious.

"But the first time I heard the name Bob Satterfield," I said, "was when I met this man."

I dealt them several photos of Champ, like gruesome playing cards, then court papers and clippings describing Champ as Satterfield. Another profile had recently appeared in a college newspaper, and I laid this atop the pile. Lastly, I outlined Champ's criminal past. They looked at each other gravely.

"I hate this man," Elaine blurted.

Satterfield Jr. lit a cigarette and gazed at Champ. He murmured something about a resemblance, then walked to a sideboard, from which he pulled a crumbling scrapbook. Returning to his chair, he balanced the book on one knee and began assembling photos, clippings, documents, anything to help me recognize that Champ's impersonation was no victimless crime.

While I scrutinized the scrapbook, Satterfield Jr. talked about his father's life. He told me about his father's close friends, Miles Davis and Muhammad Ali, who met his first wife through Satterfield. He told me about his father's triumphs in the ring and the difficult decision to retire. (After suffering a detached retina in 1958, Satterfield fled to Paris and studied painting.) He told me about his father's ancestry, back, back, back, and I understood the desperation seeping into his voice, a desperation that made him stammer badly. He'd opened his door to a total stranger who repaid the hospitality by declaring that countless other strangers believed his beloved father was a "valor-ruined man." I'd walked up clean steps to talk to clean people and made them feel dirty.

Lastly, Satterfield Jr. produced his father's birth certificate, plus a 1977 obituary from a now-defunct Chicago newspaper. To these precious items he added a photo of his parents strolling arm in arm, kissing. When I told Satterfield Jr. about Champ pointing to Iona and calling her "the only woman I ever loved," I thought he might eat the coffee table.

"That somebody would intrude on his memory like this," Elaine said. "My father-in-law was a man. He was a man's man, nothing like the men of today. He was a prideful man. He continued to work up until his operation for cancer. If a person knows he's dying, and he still gets up to go to work, that says a lot about him as a man, and if he knew some homeless man sleeping on a park bench was impersonating him—"

She stopped herself and went to the window, struggling to keep her composure. Satterfield Jr. now began phoning family.

"I'm sitting here with a reporter from the *Los Angeles Times*," he shouted into the phone, "and he says there's a man in California who's telling everybody he's Bob Satterfield the fighter. He's homeless and he has a very bad record, and he's been molesting children and he's using Pop's name. Yeah. Uh huh. Now, now, don't cry . . ."

12.

An old boxing hand once said, "You never learn anything until you're tired," and by that criterion I'm capable of learning plenty right now. After the overnight flight, after the cab ride through the rainy dawn to this downtown Columbus hotel, I'm tired enough to understand why Champ's sister doesn't trust me, and why she's turned me over to Champ's nephew, Gregory Harrison, who trusts me even less. I left word for him two hours ago saying I'd arrived, but he seems like a guy who'd rather give me a stiff beating than a straight answer, so the chance of seeing Champ's scrapbook seems remote.

Above all, I'm tired enough to understand that Champ isn't Satterfield, never was Satterfield, never will be, no matter how hard I try. But I'm also tired enough to understand why he pretended to be Satterfield. He became Satterfield because he didn't like being Tommy Harrison.

It was Satterfield Jr. who made me appreciate how ripe his father was for imitation. Fast, stylish, pretty, Satterfield was Champ's superior in every way. He was the ballyhooed one, the better one. Yes, he had the famously weak chin. But he led with it, time after time, meaning he had one hellacious heart. Champ must have studied Satterfield from afar, longingly, as I did. He must have gone to school on Satterfield, devouring facts about his life, as I did. He must have viewed Satterfield as a model, an ideal, as I also did. One day, Champ must have spied Satterfield across a musty gym, perhaps with Doc Kearns, or a smoky nightclub, where Iona was the prettiest girl in the joint, and said, "Ah, to be him." From there, it was a short, dizzy trip to "I *am* him."

As a man, you need someone to instruct you in the masculine verities. Your father is your first choice, but when he drops out, you search for someone else. If you're careless, the search creeps into your psyche and everyone becomes a candidate, from homeless men to dead boxers. If you're careless and unlucky, the search devours you. That doppelganger eats you up.

"One of the primary things boxing is about is lying," Joyce Carol Oates writes in *On Boxing*. "It's about systematically cultivating a double personality: the self in society, the self in the ring."

What Champ did, I think, was sprout a third self, a combination of the two, which may be what Champ has been trying to tell me all along.

After Chicago, I wanted to scold him about the people his lies were hurting. But when I found him wearing a ten-gallon cowboy hat and a polo shirt with toothbrushes stuffed in the breast pocket, my anger drained away.

"Champ," I said, "when you pretended to be Bob Satterfield, weren't you afraid the other Bob Satterfield would find out?"

Without hesitating, he put a hand to his chin and said, "I always figured the other Bob Satterfield knew about me. As long as everyone got paid, I didn't think the other Bob Satterfield would mind."

"What?"

"This is just you and me talking," he said. "But my manager, George Parnassus, he told me like this here: 'If you go to fight in Sioux City, Iowa, and you say you is Bob Satterfield, then you get a big crowd, see? But if you say you is Tommy Harrison, and like that, you only get a medium-size crowd.'"

Champ's manager had been dead twenty years. But his son, Msgr. George Parnassus, was pastor of St. Victor's Roman Catholic Church in West Hollywood. I phoned Parnassus and told him about Champ, then asked if his father might have staged bogus fights in the 1950s. Before TV came along, I ventured, most fighters were faceless names in the dark, so it might have been easy, and it might have been highly profitable, to promote lookalike fighters in out-of-the-way places. Say, Sioux City.

"Why do you say Sioux City?" he demanded.

"Because Champ said Sioux City."

"My father moved to Sioux City in the 1950s and staged fights there for a number of years."

Which is why I'm in Columbus this morning. I owed it to Champ to take one last stab at the truth. I owed it to myself. More than anyone, I owed it to Satterfield, whose absence I've come to feel like a constant presence.

"I've had a lot of disappointments," Satterfield told a reporter in 1958, sitting in a hospital with his detached retina. "I don't remember all the disappointments I've had." Maybe, forty years later, he's still disappointed. Maybe he knows someone swiped the only shiny prize he ever had — his good name — and he can't rest until he gets it back. All this time, I've been casting Satterfield as Moby Dick, myself as Ahab. Now I'm wondering if Satterfield is the real Ahab, and Champ the whale. Which makes me the harpoon.

The phone rings.

"I'm downstairs."

13.

Champ's nephew is sitting in the middle of the lobby, unaware or pretending to be unaware that people are staring. It's not that he looks out of place, with his floor-length black leather overcoat and gold-rimmed sunglasses. It's that he looks famous. He also looks like a younger, fitter, toothier version of Champ.

He shakes my hand tentatively and we duck into the hotel restaurant. The place is closed, but a waiter says we're welcome to have coffee. We sit by a rain-streaked window. I thank him for meeting me, but he whips off his sunglasses and stares.

"I'm not here for you," he says. "I'm here for my Uncle Tommy. And before I tell you anything you need to know, I need to know from you why you would get on a plane and fly all night, come all the way from California, to Columbus, Ohio, to write a story about *my uncle?*"

I try explaining my complicated relationship with his uncle, but the subject makes me more mumbly than Champ. Interrupting, he says softly: "Uncle Tommy was the father I should have had."

He tells me about the only time he met his uncle, a meeting so charged that it defined his life, and I wonder if he notices the strange look on my face.

"My uncle Tommy was like the Last Action Hero," he says. "I wanted to be just like him."

"You were a boxer," I say.

"I was a sparring partner of Buster Douglas," he says, sitting straighter.

His nickname was Capital City Lip, but everyone nowadays calls him Lip. With the waiters watching, he throws his right, jabs his left, bobs away from an invisible opponent, taking me through several hard-won fights, and I'm reminded of the many times his uncle broke Marciano's nose for my enjoyment.

"When you hit a guy," he says dreamily, "when you hit him in the body, you demean his manner, you know? You sap his strength, you impose your will on him. I was in the tippy-top physical shape of my life! No one could beat me! I was *good!*"

"What happened?"

He purses his lips. His story is Champ's story, Satterfield's story, every fighter's story. One day, there was someone he just couldn't beat.

"Now I race drag bikes," he says.

"Drag bikes? Why?"

"Because someday I want to be world champion of something."

His father got him interested, he says, mentioning the man in a curious way. "My father walks down the street, people part ways," he says. "Big George, that's what everyone in Columbus calls my father. He was a boxer, too, although he didn't go as far as Uncle Tommy."

Feeling an opening, I try to tell Lip about my father. He seems confused at first, then instantly empathetic. He understands the link between boxing and growing up fatherless. Maybe only a boxer can fathom that kind of fear.

"Have you ever heard the name Bob Satterfield?" I ask.

"Yes, I have heard that name."

As a boy, Lip often heard that Uncle Tommy fought as Bob Satterfield, but he never knew why.

He promises to bring me Champ's scrapbook tomorrow, then take me to meet his father. I walk him outside to his Jeep, which is double-parked in a tow zone, hazard lights flashing, just as he left it three hours ago.

14.

White shirt, white pants, white shoes, Lip comes for me the next morning looking like an angel of the streets. As we zoom away from the hotel, I scan the backseat, floor, dashboard. No scrapbook. The angel shakes his head.

"Aunt Lily just doesn't trust you," he says. "I was over there all morning, but she won't let that book out of her house."

I groan.

"I looked through the book myself, though," he says, lighting a cigarette, "and I don't think it has what you want. This Bob Satterfield, the book has lots of newspaper articles about his career, and there's a picture of him with my uncle — "

I wince.

" — and an article saying Satterfield and my uncle Tommy were scheduled to fight."

Disconsolate, I stare at the bullet hole in the windshield.

We drive to Lip's father's house, where a candy-apple red Cadillac the size of a fire engine sits outside, license plate "BIG GEO." Lip takes a deep breath, then knocks. Whole minutes crawl by before the door flies open and Champ's brother appears. He looks nothing like Champ, mainly because of old burn scars across his face. But wrapped in a baby blue bathrobe and glowering hard, he does look like an old boxer. He turns and disappears inside the house. Meekly, we follow.

Off to the left is a small room crammed with trophies and boxing memorabilia. To the right seems to be the living room, though it's impossible to tell because all the lights are off. Big George keeps moving until he reaches a high-backed chair. Despite the oceanic darkness of the place, he remains clearly visible, as if lit from within by his own anger. I can see why he's such a force in Lip's life. He scares the wits out of me.

Rubbing his palms together, Lip tells his father I'm writing a story about Uncle Tommy.

"Hmph," Big George scoffs. "Tommy. He's a stranger to me. He's my brother and I love him, but he's a stranger."

"Have you ever heard the name Bob Satterfield?" I ask.

"Bob Satterfield," Big George says, "was one of the hardest punchers of all time—"

He coughs, a horrifying cough, then adds:

"—but he couldn't take a punch."

"Do you remember Tommy ever fighting as Bob Satterfield?" I ask.

"Tommy never fought as nobody else."

He stands and goes to a sideboard, where he rifles through a stack of papers and bills. "Here," he says, yanking loose a yellowed newspaper account of the night in 1953 when Champ's life began its downward spiral.

"Tommy wasn't ready for Ezzard Charles," Big George says with sudden tenderness while Lip and I read over his shoulder. "They rushed him."

The three of us stand together, silently, as though saying a prayer for Champ. Then, without warning, Lip breaks the mood, mentioning a beef he's having with Big George. They start to argue, and I see that Lip brought me here for more than an interview. He's hoping I can play referee. As with Champ, I was too busy using him to notice that he was using me.

Father and son argue for five minutes, each landing heavy verbal blows. Then Big George makes it plain that these will be the final words spoken on the subject.

"The Bible say this," he bellows. "Honor your parents! Honor your mother and father! Regardless what they say, what they do, all mothers and dads love their children! All of them!"

"He's lying to you," Lip says when we get in the car.

I look at him, startled.

"About what?"

"He knows all about Satterfield."

We drive to a beloved old gym that former champion Buster Douglas helped rebuild after knocking down Mike Tyson. Inside, we find Douglas' father, Bill, training a young featherweight. When Lip tells Douglas that I'm writing about his uncle, "a former heavy-weight con-TEN-der," Douglas nods his head several times, and I feel Lip's self-worth balloon with each nod.

We watch the featherweight work the heavy bag, a black, water-filled sack that hangs from the ceiling. Each time he snaps a hard right, the bag swings like a man in a noose. His name is Andre Cray, and he's 25. Rawboned and scowling, with a flat head and rubbery limbs, he looks like an angry Gumby. When his workout ends, we ask him why he chose boxing as a trade.

"To me it's like an art," he says quietly, unwinding the padded white tape from his fists.

But this isn't the real reason, he admits. Growing up without money, without a father, boxing was the only straight path to manhood. Many of his friends chose the crooked path, a choice they didn't always live to regret. Those who prospered in the crack trade often gave Cray money and begged him not to follow their lead. Some even bought him gloves and shoes, to make sure the streets didn't claim another boxer.

He remembers those early patrons, uses their fate as inspiration. His future is bright, he figures, if he can just protect his chin and not lose heart. In 19 fights, he's scored 17 wins. When he loses, he says, the anguish is more than he can stand.

"You have family?" Lip asks.

"Yeah," Cray says. "I have a son. He'll be 1 on Tuesday."

"What's his name?"

"Andre Cray *Junior.*"

"I imagine he inspires you a lot."

"Yeah," Cray says, looking down at his oversize hands.

Lip nods, solemn. Douglas nods. I nod.

15.

Like a favorite movie, the one-reel *Satterfield Versus Layne* says something different every time I watch, each punch a line of multi-layered dialogue. After several hundred viewings, the core theme emerges. It's about pressing forward, I think. Ignoring your pain. Standing.

"Satterfield is out of this world," Marciano says in his narrative voice-over. "He's one of the hardest hitters I've ever seen."

Satterfield lives up to his reputation in the very first minute, greeting Layne with a vicious second-clefter on the point of the chin. Kneeling, Layne takes the count, then staggers upright and hugs Satterfield until the bell.

Satterfield, in white trunks, with a pencil-thin mustache and muscles upon muscles, is a joy to look at. Decades before Nautilus, his biceps look like triple-scoop ice cream cones. By contrast, Layne looks like a soda jerk who's wandered mistakenly into the ring. Over the first three rounds he does little more than push his black trunks and flabby belly back and forth while offering his square head as a stationary target.

Still, Layne seems the luckier man. In the sixth, Satterfield puts every one of his 180 pounds behind a right hook. He brings the fist from behind his back like a bouquet of flowers, but Layne weaves, avoiding the punch by half an inch. "Just missed!" Marciano shouts. "That would have done it!"

Had that punch landed, everything would be different. Layne would be stretched out on the canvas, Satterfield would be looking forward to the title shot he craves. Instead, the eighth begins, and Satterfield's wondering what more he can do. It's LaMotta all over again. No matter what you do, the other guy keeps coming — obdurate, snarling, fresh.

Far ahead on points, Satterfield can still win a decision, as long as he protects himself, covers up, plays it safe. He does just the opposite, charging forward, chin high, the only way he knows. In the kind of punch-for-punch exchange that went out with fedoras, Satterfield and Layne stand one inch apart, winging at each other from all directions, Satterfield trying frantically to turn out Layne's dim bulb — until Layne lands a right hook on the magic chin.

"I don't think [he] can get up," Marciano says as Satterfield lies on his back, blinking at the house lights. "But look at this guy try."

Boxing's Humpty-Dumpty. The book on Satterfield proves true. Or does it? Always, this is the moment I hit the pause button and talk to Satterfield while he tries to tap some hidden wellspring of strength. Somehow, he taps it every time, a display of pure grit that never fails to make my heart beat faster.

"He's hurt bad," Marciano says, as Satterfield stands and signals the referee that he's ready for another dose. Dutifully, Layne steps forward and sends a crashing left into Satterfield's head. Then a right. And another right. Finally, the referee rushes forward and removes Satterfield's mouthpiece. Corner men leap into the ring. Photographers with flashes the size of satellite dishes shoot the covers of tomorrow's sports pages. Amid all the commotion, Layne takes a mincing step forward and does something shocking.

It's hard to believe, in an age of end-zone dances and home-run trots, that boxers in a bygone era often hugged after their meanest fights. (Some actually kissed.) But Layne gives that postfight tenderness a new twist. As Satterfield sags against the ropes, dead-eyed, Layne reaches out to touch him ever so lightly on the cheek.

It's a haunting gesture, so intimate and unexpected that it begs imitation. Like Layne — like Champ — I want to reach out to Satterfield, to show my admiration. I want to tell him how glad I am to make his acquaintance, how grateful I am for the free instruction. More than all that, I suppose, I just want to thank him for the fight.

One day, after watching his greatest defeat, I visit his impostor.

"Heyyy," Champ says, beaming, waving hello. "What do you know about that? Hey, your picture ran through my mind many times, and then I'd say, well, my friend, he give me up."

He's wearing a white karate uniform, mismatched sneakers and a shirt from the Orange County Jail. Clouds of flies swarm around his head and grocery cart this warm November afternoon, Champ's sixty-seventh birthday. Tomorrow would have been Satterfield's seventy-third.

There are many things about Champ that I don't know, things I'll probably never know. He either got money to be Satterfield, then forgot to drop the con, or wished he were Satterfield, then let the wish consume him. Not knowing doesn't bother me as I feared it would. Not getting his scrapbook doesn't torment me as I thought it might. Every man is a mystery, because manhood itself is so mysterious; that's what Champ taught me. Maturity means knowing when to solve another man's mystery, and when to respect it.

"Been traveling," I tell him. "And guess where I went?"

He cocks his head.

"Columbus. And guess who I saw? Your nephew, Gregory."

"That's my brother's son!"

"Yep. And guess who else I met. Big George."

He pulls a sour face, like his brother's, and we both laugh.

We talk about George, Lily and Lip, and Champ grows heavy with nostalgia. He recalls his childhood, particularly his stern father, who hit him so hard one day that he flayed the muscle along Champ's left bicep. Champ rolls up his sleeve to show me the mark, but I look away.

To cheer him up, to cheer us both up, I ask Champ to tell me once more about busting Marciano's nose.

"Marciano and I were putting on an exhibition that day," he says, crouching. "We were going good. But he had that long overhand right, and every time I seen it coming, I'd duck it. And I'd come up, and I'd keep hitting him on the tip of his nose."

He touches my nose with a gentle uppercut, flies trailing in the wake of his fist.

"On the tip, on the tip, I kept hitting," he says. "Finally, his nose started bleeding, and they stopped the fight."

Smiling now, more focused than I've ever seen him, Champ says he needs my advice. He's been reviewing his life lately, wondering what next. Times are hard, he says, and maybe he should head on down the road, polish up the Cadillac and return to Columbus, though he fears the cold and what it does to an old boxer's bones.

"What do you think?" he says.

"I think you should go be with people who love you and care about you," I say.

"Yeah, that's true, that's true."

We watch the cars whizzing by, jets roaring overhead, strangers walking past.

"Well, Champ," I say, slipping him five dollars. "I've got to get going."

"Yeah, yeah," he says, stopping me. "Now, listen."

He rests one of his heavy hands on my shoulder, a gesture that makes me swallow hard and blink for some reason. I look into his eyes, and from his uncommonly serious expression, I know he's getting ready to say something important.

"I know you a long time," he says warmly, flashing that toothless smile, groping for the words. "Tell me your name again."

LINDA ROBERTSON

On Planet Venus

FROM TROPIC

ON A TYPICAL AFTERNOON at the Williams house, practicing French comes before practicing tennis.

Venus Williams and her sister Serena can see their three private practice courts from the bedroom window, the green windscreens emblazoned like billboards with their last name in big white letters.

But the courts at the family's 10-acre compound in the pine woods of northwest Palm Beach County will remain empty today. Venus, 16, and Serena, 15, have homework to do.

There may be nothing unusual about teenagers studying textbooks, except that Venus is no average teenager. She has been a celebrated prodigy since she was a kindergartner and is among the hottest prospects in professional tennis, a girl who could become the Tiger Woods of her sport.

Most young pros spend grueling days honing their backhands, not their French accents. Missing practice might mean missing out on ranking points, paychecks and endorsement deals.

Venus is nonchalant about skipping practice, and tournaments. The traveling circus of the women's tennis tour has encamped at a Hilton Head, South Carolina, resort this week without her. While her would-be opponents perform before cheering crowds, she hears cows mooing on the neighbors' property. Pastoral, peaceful, *normal.* Just the way her father likes it.

Serena rolls onto her stomach on the bed, trying to evade a puppy who wants to gnaw on her book. She reads a story called *La Vase Extraordinaire.*

"Today, Jeanine is walking with her friend Monique," Serena says in French. "They pass a store with something interesting in it."

Venus stops tapping on her computer keys to interrupt Serena. "It's not the best literature," she says.

The sisters break into giggles.

This smiling portrait is a refreshing one in the gallery of glum-faced girls who, pulled by their parents, left childhood behind in the chase for championships.

The Williams girls' upbringing has been extraordinary nonetheless. Before either was born, their father, who had never hit a tennis ball, crafted a plan to make his children the best players in the world. His inspiration: one day, while watching a tournament on TV, he saw the winner collect a $30,000 check. Then and there he decided to create a sports legend.

To a remarkable extent, Richard Williams has succeeded, in spite of an unorthodox approach. He put his daughters on the slow track. Venus has played only a smattering of pro tournaments since Richard touted her as "Cinderella of the ghetto" and she signed a seven-figure promotional contract with Reebok at 14. She is still labeled a phenom even though she has not won a tournament since she quit the junior circuit at age 11 and is ranked number 87 in the world. The real phenomenon is that the unabating buzz of anticipation about Venus is greater than her accomplishments on the court.

Richard says he wants to preserve an atmosphere of normalcy, but what other world-class players are rewarded with fifty dollars when they lose matches so they don't become obsessed with winning, or practice with partners who also mow the family's lawn?

Richard imposes a different type of discipline, too — in place of the regimented dedication most players know, a rigid adherence to family harmony. Or else.

"Strict discipline has to start when the child is born until age 12, when the skull closes, so that it's ingrained in her," he says, not pausing to explain. "The first time my kids disobeyed I whipped the hell out of them. The next time, I asked them to move out."

Courting Disaster

Richard Williams says he wants his daughters to bloom slowly and naturally in a sport known for its hothouse flowers. The list of girls who traded their adolescence for trophies haunts women's tennis. Jennifer Capriati smiled sweetly for the cameras at 13 and stared sullenly from a police mug shot at 18, after she was arrested for marijuana possession at a Coral Gables motel. Tracy Austin had the aching back of a 60-year-old by the time she was 17. Andrea Jaeger burned out before she hit 20.

Those are just the famous ones, the ones who made it to the top 10. Countless others succumbed to the grind of the pro tour or fell off the ladder while climbing the fiercely competitive junior ranks.

Too often when a girl tumbled her father was doing the pushing. The number 15–ranked pro Mary Pierce hasn't seen her father, Jim, in four years. She fled from him, alleging years of verbal and physical abuse. Steffi Graf's father, Peter Graf, is fresh out of jail and awaiting the rest of his sentence for evading taxes on $28 million of Steffi's earnings. Stefano Capriati marketed his daughter so aggressively that the women's tour allowed her to turn pro at 13. Jennifer wound up in rehab and is attempting a comeback at 21.

"It's always a thing between fathers and daughters," says Seena Hamilton, the doyenne of junior tennis who has run the top national junior tournament, Miami's Easter Bowl, for thirty years. "Fathers love their little girls and little girls are easier to control than little boys. All these men had tremendous ambition they realized through their daughters, who just wanted to please their dads."

Sometimes, that love curdles. Jim Pierce, unemployed and worried about chest pains, writes letters and leaves messages for Mary that are never returned.

"I'm so sorry I ever heard of tennis because it cost me my family," he says. "I spent years grooming her. Now she's got $4 million in the bank and I don't even have enough to fill up my tank at the gas station."

The World According to Richard

Richard Williams saw the wreckage and decided to take a detour. After watching Venus go undefeated in junior tournaments from age 9 to 11 — a rare feat in the competitive southern California district — he staged a disappearing act. He says Venus was getting too good too fast and junior tennis disgusted him. He saw too many stage mothers and fathers with stars in their eyes and calculators in their pockets, too many bratty kids throwing their rackets and getting slapped and yelled at by their parents.

"It's the parents' ego. The money in tennis can make a good parent a crook. They do four things: buy a Mercedes or a Rolls-Royce, join the polo club, build a swimming pool, and tell you what a great job they've done," he says. "As long as I have enough to go to McDonald's I'm happy."

Yet Richard has a 1996 Mercedes *and* a 1986 Rolls-Royce registered in his name and parked in the yard with eight other cars. He lives on a half-million dollar estate. He says the money comes primarily from his own businesses, but there are many such apparent incongruities between his actions and words.

After declaring that "any father who lets his daughter turn pro at 14 should be shot," he entered 14-year-old Venus in her first pro tournament just before the Women's Tennis Association raised the age of eligibility. Although he says "I'm holding the reins tight until she's 18," he insists Venus made the decision to go pro herself.

He preached the importance of education and a normal life for his kids while pulling them out of school and enrolling them in a tennis academy in Florida. He criticized controlling parents while supervising everything from Venus's forehand to her interviews to her trademark beaded-cornrow hairstyle. He lambasted parents for "prostituting their daughters" by turning them into marketing commodities, then negotiated the contract with Reebok, rumored to be worth $2 million.

To Richard, there are no contradictions. "People can call me crazy and stupid, but I'm gambling now so that in the long run my kids can say they had fun growing up and I did it the right way."

Richard says other fathers in his position might have cut dozens of deals. "If I get a hundred calls, I respond to one. I've kept it to a low level."

While looking out for his daughters' welfare, he has made shrewd marketing moves.

"He built up the Venus mystique after Capriati's rise," Hamilton says. "People say he's exploited his children but I say he's exploited tennis. He's outsmarted them. He played off the negativisms that plagued Capriati."

Richard is a tall, slightly stooped man who smokes brown More cigarillos and is given to maundering monologues about such topics as black people, white people, Chinese people, rich people, poor people, the banking industry, the family unit, education and his business acumen.

When he goes off on one of his sermons, Venus stops smiling, lowers her eyes and fiddles with her beads.

She's more comfortable praising her father's decision to keep her and Serena out of tournaments. In 1991, he packed up the family, moved from Los Angeles to Florida, and let the mystery grow.

"We set a precedent," Venus says. "We were brave and smart enough to find a different way. People ask, 'What is that family doing?' We keep them wondering. Maybe I'll run the Kentucky Derby next."

"You ought to be a politician, girl," Richard says.

"Thank you, Daddy."

Career Counseling

Venus is set to play in her first Grand Slam, the French Open, a week from tomorrow. She has a qualifying requirement her opponents won't face. Her father told her: if she wants to play, she must first learn French. Which is why Venus is hitting the books instead of tennis balls on this day.

At home, grades are more important than groundstrokes. Richard, 55, wants his children — five daughters — to have careers. And not in broadcasting or coaching.

"Look at John McEnroe or Tracy Austin or Chris Evert on the TV. Wouldn't that make them sick? Their whole life is tennis," Richard says. "To be a commentator, now that's a fool. I don't want my kids to be one-dimensional."

Venus is six-foot-one and carries herself not like a self-conscious girl but one who has treated a lifetime of stares as compliments. She doesn't speak like a squeaky, stammering adolescent. Only the braces give her away.

Serena is polite and witty, too, but her manner mirrors her solid physique. Let Venus banter. Serena will be blunt. Everyone in the family affectionately calls her "the mean one" and "the one with the temper."

After tennis, Venus intends to be an architect, Serena a veterinarian. The oldest daughter, Yetunde, 24, has been in medical school since age 16 studying to become a cardiologist, although Richard, saying he wants to protect her privacy, won't specify which school. Both Isha, 23, and Lyndrea, 18, are Howard University students in Washington, D.C. Isha plans to become a lawyer, Lyndrea a plastic surgeon.

"I chose every field my kids went into by the time they were 8," Richard says. "By 12, they made plans to go into that business. By the time they're 20, that business should be up and running. We try to get Venus to make a commitment to retire from tennis by 24 so she will be able to catch up on her college studies."

Richard says he would rather see Venus living in a dormitory than living as a hotel suite nomad, traveling from one tournament to another, signing autographs, ordering room service, shilling for corporate sponsors — that just isn't normal.

Of course, it isn't normal for a 16-year-old to read *How to Form and Operate a Limited Liability Company.* But that's the book lying on the bed next to *Animal Farm* and a math textbook. Learning about investments is also part of the girls' education. According to Richard and Venus, she bought her first house at age 7.

"I taught her about foreclosures, leases and lease options, and how to buy a house with no down payment," Richard says. The little girl became an instant landlord, he says, using rent to pay off the mortgage.

But buying houses, apparently, is just a sideline. Venus spends most of her time studying, playing guitar, riding her water bike in the pond on the property and driving around in her Toyota 4-Runner with Serena. And they love to go surfing at Jupiter beach, inspired by their favorite videotape, *Endless Summer.* Aside from practicing a fraction of the thirty-hours-a-week regimen of most elite players, the girls enjoy the usual teenage pursuits.

Except for TV, "which leads to reclining and snacking and staying up late," Venus says.

Except for dating, which Venus, who is a month shy of 17, says doesn't interest her. "When you're ready to date, you're ready to move out of the house," says Richard, who has raised his daughters as Jehovah's Witnesses.

"We don't celebrate holidays or believe in political parties and

we know this world is passing, that it's getting worse every day,"
Venus says.

Venus and Serena don't socialize with friends, either. "I don't
really have any friends from school," Venus says. "Serena and I
pretty much hang out together." After a period of home-schooling
by Richard, their mother, Oracene, and an older sister, Venus and
Serena are going to a private Christian school, which they won't
name, with a curriculum of "finance, taxes, investments and an-
thropology," he says.

"We have a good relationship because we don't fight," Serena
says. Then, doing her best Sigmund Freud impersonation, she
adds in a mock-German accent: "Favoritism is not shown. That
leads to envy, which leads to conspiracy, which is called neurotic
behavior. Then I would have to trip her when she walks down the
stairs."

As the girls' heads shake in another eruption of giggles, their
beaded cornrows click like Morse code.

Lawn Tennis

On a steamy afternoon, while Venus and Serena practice with male
hitting partners, Richard takes a break from his coaching duties.

"Gotta cool off," he says, removing a woman's straw hat from his
head and driving his Lincoln rapidly 150 yards across the yard from
the courts to the pond, where he rides one of the water bikes
around in circles for fifteen minutes.

After he drives back to the courts, he directs two young men who
have been mowing the lawn and watering the plants to hit with
Venus and Serena.

"Yes, Mr. Williams," one man says.

"And get some more balls," Richard says.

"Yes, Mr. Williams," the other man says.

Williams wanders around the clay court cleaning the lines with a
rolling brush, taking bites from a Big Mac and cracking jokes.

Venus plays a few games, laughing whenever her shots go long.

"You look beautiful, Venus Williams," Richard says.

"Thank you, Daddy," Venus says.

Observers of Venus's game say she lacks coaching, the kind of tedious, thousands-of-balls-a-day critiquing to improve her foot-work, shot selection and volleying. More importantly, she lacks match-play experience.

Says longtime commentator Bud Collins: "Venus starts with a handicap. In a highly organized sport like tennis, it's always been done *our* way and Richard is doing it *his* way. A lot of people think he's a charlatan, perhaps out of jealousy. It's like saying we'll build a car without an engine. This noble experiment certainly ought to fail, but if it doesn't, it would be a tremendous lesson for everybody and I'd say hallelujah."

Tom Gullickson, U.S. Davis Cup coach: "It's one thing to be a good ball striker and another to learn how to compete on those days when you're not striking the ball well. Until somebody plays and wins, it's all speculation, and a good sales job.

Martina Hingis, the 16-year-old from Switzerland, took the traditional path. She turned pro just two weeks before Venus, also at age 14, and two and a half years later, she is number 1 in the world, while Venus is number 87.

The feeling on the tour is that time is running out for Venus to prove she's a serious contender. Richard seems to have acknowledged as much by planning to enter her in twelve tournaments this year, including the French, Wimbledon and the U.S. Open — all firsts for her.

"The aura of potential greatness is something she has on her side," said Bob Williams, president of Burns Sports Celebrity Service, which has marketed Michael Jordan among others. "Tiger Woods is paving the way for minority athletes, and Lord knows, tennis is hungry for a new star. But I don't think she can linger much longer. Sooner or later, winning is what counts."

The Discipline of Tennis

To critics who suggest that Venus needs a professional coach, Richard responds that no professional coach could outcoach him or outplay him. To demonstrate, he picks up a racket and hits against the two men.

"Tennis is such an easy game. Look at this forehand. Have you seen a better forehand?" he says, hitting an average-looking shot. He's joking. Maybe.

"Now I'll show you some trick shots," he says, hitting the ball between his legs or from behind his back. "This is what you call black tennis.

"I taught Venus how to serve. I tell her not to serve above 108 mph so she doesn't ruin her shoulder. Watch this serve, with no warm-up," he says, then slaps it into the net.

Richard concludes his demonstration with convincing impressions of the serving motions of John McEnroe, Boris Becker, and Pete Sampras.

"People say Venus needs a coach," he says. "Who can coach her better than me? I don't want somebody telling her what to do like she's a zombie. What if she said she'd rather go surfing than go to Wimbledon? I'd let her."

Later, at the house, Venus and Serena get ready to take the dog to the vet. First, Richard asks for "one more ice cube" in his glass of water, and the girls get it for him. Then, in a reverential ritual that is repeated whenever they enter or leave his presence, they lean over to kiss their father goodbye.

"Thank you, Daddy," Venus says.

"I love you, Daddy," Serena says.

The girls are extremely pleasant to everyone. Richard brought them up to be "nice young ladies." Inside the house, he has posted notices: "You are a professional tennis player. You are the most polite and gracious person in the world."

Richard taught his daughters to respect people, even if people were disrespectful to them. He recalls when one daughter responded in kind to a racial slur.

"I beat the living daylights out of her," he says.

When Yetunde, the eldest, failed to do the dishes properly one too many times, Richard packed her clothes in a suitcase and left it on the sidewalk.

"She had to stay outside all night, and, guess what? It rained," he says. "Poor Yetunde was crying. I let her come back after she'd agreed to a year's worth of punishment: washing the dishes, mowing the lawn and doing work for the underprivileged."

When Venus forgot to clean up after her pet rabbit for the third time, Richard made sure she would not forget again.

"I beat her all around the house and yard," he says. And when she was younger and did not do well in a class, "I went to the school and took the belt to her in front of her friends," he says.

Richard says if more parents followed his example, the country's rates of teenage pregnancy, drug use and AIDS would drop.

"You hear these spoiled brats telling their mom to shut up. Hit junior in the head and smoke him in the ass and junior won't talk back anymore," he says. "He'll respect you and be scared of you."

Venus says that she doesn't resent the discipline or wish for more independence.

"It goes better if you just listen. You can't rebel against them," she said. "But to tell the truth if I want something I go to my dad. I'll tell him a store is having a sale on jewelry and he'll say, 'How much do you need?'"

Taking Care of Business

Richard grew up in Shreveport, Louisiana, the son of a single mother who cleaned schools, picked cotton, and taught him the value of hard work. He claims — with a straight face — that he had his first job at age 2, delivering phone books: "Man, they were heavy!"

He worked at a grocery store, a car wash, and a cookie factory.

"Taking those cookies off the belt and packing those cookies without having time to breathe convinced me never to be without an education," Richard says.

In high school, he was a star athlete. Although he says the New York Knicks offered him a tryout, he wasn't interested in a career in sports. He moved to Los Angeles and talked his way into jobs at a bank and a department store before starting the White Glove Cleaning Company, then went into the business of buying and selling homes with no money down — a technique he learned from a man he met on a golf course. He also owned a security business, which he sold. Today, he says he owns an auto parts business, a small lending institution, and a security firm, but won't reveal their names or specify their locations. He also says he "goes to the worst ghettos I can find" to counsel low-income kids and is trying to raise $300,000 to fund his nonprofit program. He'll only accept contributions from blacks. Venus donates some of her prize money and hold clinics for the kids, he says.

Although Williams puts considerable time into marketing and

coaching his daughters, he says their earnings are not the primary source of income for the family.

"People never ask Monica Seles's dad or Martina Hingis's mother if they're living off their daughters. They only ask black people. Every penny I earn, I really earn it. I make more than Venus."

In fact, Richard says he is so busy with his various enterprises he won't accompany Venus to the French Open.

"I don't have time to sit at a tennis tournament turning my head back and forth when I could be making money or working with the kids in my program," he says.

Jim and Mary

The French Open is where Jim Pierce's world began to collapse. In 1993 he was ejected from the stadium for screaming curses from the stands. He was thereafter banned from women's tournaments.

Pierce's daughter Mary got a restraining order against him. She said she could no longer endure being hit and berated. He hasn't seen her in the four years since.

When Pierce talks about Mary, his arms go numb. His chest constricts. He needs a drink of water.

"Feel my hands," he says. "Don't they feel clammy to you? I get this twitching in my neck like there's a fish on a hook underneath my skin."

He used to be his daughter's coach. Now he makes and sells jewelry out of a modest apartment in Delray Beach, where he keeps plastic grocery store bags full of mementos from Mary's career.

What Mary called abuse, Pierce called motivation. He says she left him so she, her mother and her brother could keep all of Mary's money. He wants to reconcile but can't get through to his daughter to remind her of all the good times.

As proof, he pulls out old notes from Mary, fingered to the consistency of tissue paper.

"You are the greatest dad in the world."

"I came up to kiss you good night but you were already asleep. I just wanted to tell you how much I love you."

And this one, torn into two pieces, both saved: "Daddy, thank you for being the greatest coach in the world."

Pierce, 61, thumbs through snapshots, including one of himself as a young, blond, handsome man, next to which he has taped a photo of young, blond, attractive Mary.

"When they tell a girl to separate herself from her father it's like she's taking a knife to her own throat," he says. "She's cutting herself off from the person who carried her in his arms, who called her daddy's little girl. Mary, you're my twin. When you hurt me, you hurt yourself."

Pierce rubs his tightening jaw, then clenches his fists as he examines his outstretched arms. The daughter he adored has gotten so out of shape "you can see the meat hanging over her bra strap. All she had to do was walk into the sunshine and hit a yellow ball back and forth. I'm stringing the rackets, carrying the bags, making the arrangements, doing the coaching. If the family makes the money, the family shares the money. The mother wanted control of it. They stole from me. They have millions and I can't get a penny. I'd just like enough money to go to the doctor. Here, feel these hands."

Pierce admires the way Richard Williams has beat the system in tennis while keeping his family intact and his daughters loyal. The two men are friends. In one of the rambling greetings Richard frequently records on his answering machine, he expressed sympathy for Pierce.

"The reason Mr. Jim Pierce's heart almost stopped was because he's worrying like a dog about Mary who doesn't give a s— about him. Jim, they're treating you like a black man, but old Richard Williams is right with you."

A Cinderella Story

Venus Ebonistarr Williams might be any other top 100 tennis player trying to make a name for herself if not for the place where she grew up. The heroes of modern-day fairy tales usually have humble beginnings. Venus spent her first eleven years in South-Central Los Angeles, in the inner-city neighborhood of Compton, which her father calls "the worst ghetto in the world, a place infested with drugs."

Then came the day he noticed that the winner of a televised tournament got a check for $30,000, "which was more than I made in a year. Venus wasn't born yet, but I decided she would be a tennis player."

Richard bought some videos and books and taught himself to play. When Venus was $4\frac{1}{2}$ years old, he loaded up a laundry basket with balls and took her to the park in East Compton — not the ideal place to practice, considering that the nets sagged and the courts were littered with broken glass. But it was perfect for myth-making.

The thumping of police helicopters drowned out the thwacking of tennis balls. The gang members and drug dealers who fre-quented the park did not want to share their turf and once shot at Richard and the girls, Richard says.

But eventually, Richard won over the gang members, who be-came like big brothers to Venus and Serena.

Rick Macci, the girls' former coach who runs an academy in Fort Lauderdale, recalled the first time he went to Los Angeles to hit with them.

"Richard talked me into coming by saying, 'The only thing I can guarantee you is you won't get shot,'" Macci says. "He picks me up in a Volkswagen bus that's wobbling, with two weeks of McDonald's wrappers on the floor and a spring in the seat that harpooned me. There were thirty guys playing basketball, twelve people passed out on the grass and a lot of shady characters. But they parted like the Red Sea as we walked to the court, acknowledging Venus, Serena and Richard as if they were celebrities."

Richard has videotapes from those days. They show a little girl who was tall and powerful for her age. They show a father who put out a newsletter on his girls, coaching his daughter how to hit and how to smile and answer mock interview questions.

"She was a hot property; I got more calls about her than I ever did about Pete Sampras or Michael Chang," said Jim Hillman, di-rector of junior tennis for the Southern California Tennis Associa-tion. "She appeared on a lot of TV shows, and her father was always very protective when the camera crews came out. He had some plans even back then. They had an attorney walking around with them. He knew how to promote those girls. Some public relations firm ought to hire him."

Venus was so dominant, her only loss came when Richard per-suaded her to forfeit a match she was winning so her cowering opponent wouldn't be chastised by her parents. With Serena winning steadily in her own age division, Richard decided his girls didn't need junior tennis. He moved the family to Macci's academy in Florida, where, for the first time, an experienced coach set about polishing their raw talent with intense instruction five hours a day.

Macci saw the same competitive fire in the Williams girls he had seen in Capriati, his pupil for ten years before she abruptly left for another academy, a huge endorsement deal and a top-10 ranking.

Macci reluctantly went along with Richard's tournament ban for Venus.

"The way he held her back was a little extreme," Macci says. "To go three and a half years just practicing — talk about boring. She wanted to play so much."

In the fall of 1994, Richard and Macci chose an Oakland, California, tournament for her pro debut.

"People thought Elvis was coming," Macci says.

Richard surprised Macci by taking the girls to Disneyland for two days, then Venus won her first-round match, over number 59 Shaun Stafford. She led number 2 Arantxa Sanchez-Vicario 6–2, 3–1 before losing. More fuel for the hype machine. Nike, Reebok, IMG, ProServ, Advantage International, and Don King came calling.

"Richard interviewed everyone, picked their brains, had them do presentations," said Patrick McGee, an Advantage International agent. "For someone who had no knowledge of the business, he did a masterful job."

Venus signed with Reebok, but she did not sign with a management company or an agent.

"Richard decided he could do it just as well himself," McGee says.

Macci, who had been coaching the girls on scholarships, wanted a contract, too. He couldn't help feeling he was being used.

"You help someone financially, physically and emotionally, you do the dirty work setting the foundation of a player's game and it's only fair you are compensated," Macci says.

But Macci and Richard couldn't agree on terms, and they parted ways in 1995. Earlier this month Richard gave him some money for his years of working with the girls and discussed having Macci coach them on occasion.

Nick Bollettieri, who coached Andre Agassi, Monica Seles and many more big names, has put himself in Venus's orbit after months of wooing Richard.

"I'm taking Venus to the French Open, dear," he says, quick to add that Richard will have ultimate control. "I'm going to look, listen and stay in the background. Richard is different, but I'm different, too, dear. Characters go with characters."

On the rare occasions she has played, Venus has not been a flop. In 1996, she lost to Graf, 6–4, 6–4. In March, she beat number 9 Iva Majoli and led number 8 Lindsay Davenport before losing. At Amelia Island in April, she lost 6–4, 6–0 in the second round to number 30 Chanda Rubin, who is also black, but gets a fraction of the attention directed at Venus.

"Off the ground, Venus is like Seles. At the net, she'll be like Navratilova. She makes a lot of errors but she's not afraid," Macci says. "She will be top 10 by the end of the year if she plays enough. Of course, whenever she loses, people will say it's because she didn't compete enough. That will haunt her forever."

Star Wars

In March, after two years of maybes, Venus entered the big tournament in her own back yard, and ecstatic organizers of the Lipton Championships in Key Biscayne couldn't resist plotting a draw with maximum drama. In the first round, Venus would warm up with number 526 Ginger Helgeson Nielson. In the second, Venus, tennis's revolutionary, would face Capriati, tennis's cautionary tale. And in the third, Hingis, the 16-year-old hare who sprinted to the top, vs. Venus, the 16-year-old tortoise who hoped to catch Hingis in the long run.

Venus beat Nielson in three sets. Then Capriati, up 5–1 against Venus, self-destructed, losing a tiebreaker and going down in three sets.

The result, and the contrasting press conference demeanors of Capriati and Venus, seemed a clear validation of Richard's grand plan. Capriati slumped in her chair, spoke in a monotone of "you knows" and "yeahs" and "whatevers" and perpetuated her image as a disaffected, droopy-eyed youth. Venus was utterly charming. Reporters from around the world filed stories filled with comments like this one:

"I finished nine out of fourteen geometry assignments and nine out of thirteen chemistry assignments and I took a French test and English quiz. I'm allergic to bad grades. I once got a 60 on a test. After a match I've never cried, but after that test I cried."

Oracene Williams watched her daughter sign autographs on the court and answer questions from the press. She is a religious woman. She worries that the humility she and Richard sowed in her daughter will be washed away in a flood of adoration.

"Venus matured a lot in the last six months, but I don't think she's mature enough," Oracene says. "This is scary to me — the fast life, the craziness, the risk that she'll idolize herself and not become aware of who she is and who she isn't. The destruction of herself — that's my greatest fear. They build you up, and when you start doing bad, they take you down. If it was up to me she'd be a missionary somewhere helping people."

The next day, Venus's third on the center stage of stadium court, she and Hingis met in a match promoters hyped as Chapter One in a rivalry that could someday evoke Evert–Navratilova, forgetting, apparently, the other 108 players then ranked higher than Venus.

At first Venus was a sight to behold, whipping her groundstrokes deep into the court, overpowering the five-foot-six Hingis with 106 mph serves and attacking Hingis's 75 mph serves. Venus's braids swung with each shot, her red, white and blue beads clacking like castanets. On impact, she let out a grunt, making it seem like she was hitting the ball even harder. Venus went ahead 3–0. Was the enigma going to ruin Hingis's coronation?

Hardly. Hingis kept her poise, and, once she figured out the pace of Venus's laserlike groundstrokes, began moving the ball around, varying the rhythm, tying up Venus's size 11 feet.

Hingis won the first set 6–4. She won the second in twenty minutes, 6–2. While Hingis displayed a symphony of shots, Venus drummed the same beat. Finesse and experience proved superior to power.

In the press conference, Venus also met her match. Hingis's creativity on court equals her charisma off it. She opened by flicking "a nice present" toward reporters — one of Venus's beads she had picked up on the court. Although the media pushed the rivalry angle, Hingis dismissed it.

Told of Venus' prediction that she and Serena would "be fighting to be the two best players in the world" Hingis replied: "Oh, that's nice. I don't have so much self-confidence at winning one match."

Venus, in no mood to chat after the loss, turned testy. When asked if she sensed the importance of her first match with Hingis, she said: "Could you tell me what's important about it? I don't know why you're asking me that if you didn't answer the question yourself."

Richard, who later claimed he was glad his daughter lost, cut off the questions, hustling her out to the car and back to the house in the woods, where they could put the four harried days at Lipton behind them and get back to normal.

The rest of 1997 is sure to be even more of a test of Richard's master plan. Three Grand Slams are yet to come, unless Venus decides to skip them and go surfing instead. In Paris, London and New York, there will be more fans, reporters, photographers, agents and coaches grasping at Venus than there were in Key Biscayne. No stopping the unveiling now.

Richard has longed for and dreaded this juncture in his daughter's life. Soon, her true standing in the sport will be revealed. He's in no rush to find out. Whatever happens, Venus's happiness is all that matters. Besides, he has another card up his sleeve. Don't forget Serena. She's only 15.

"Serena will be better than Venus," he says. "She's more aggressive. She has a better all-around game."

Serena's keeping a low profile for now. Father knows best.

Says Seena Hamilton, who counts prodigies the way most people count sheep: "I don't know if he can pull off the same miracle twice."

ROBERT COLE

Cale Registering on a Hook

FROM THE COLLEGE OF NEW JERSEY REVIEW

WE USUALLY STARTED our basketball schedule around December 7, but because of the long football season, our first game my senior year was not until December 17, the week after the senior class play was held on the gym stage. I was the father in the play, my usual role. I got good roles in all six of the plays I was in — scores of lines to memorize, directors always in suspense as to whether I would — but I was always either a heavy or a straight man. Blustery father in the junior class play, blustery father in the senior play, blustery high school principal in a one-act Our Miss Brooks comedy, interlocutor for two minstrels (wrote my own song cues), MC for the Christmas pageant. I got ready for two plays between football and basketball seasons as a senior.

Months after the junior class play (*People Are Funny*, from the Art Linkletter radio show, as so many of our school plays were from radio shows), I wrote at the end of the playbook, "I had more fun in this play than in any play or any activity I've ever been in. I only wish that I'll never forget all the happy times we had in this play." But the satisfaction passed quickly with the production because plays weren't much appreciated by the rest of the school except as ways to be excused from class for the morning-after performance. Sports had far more weight. Our senior play was *And Came the Spring*, by Marrijane and Joseph Hayes, the most serious play I was in, a family comedy about adolescents growing up, directed by our senior English teacher, Mrs. Preston Crosby, the most sophisticated influence — and therefore one of the most tolerant people — at Shady Spring High. Jack Wills got to kiss Ann Gose in the senior play, which held everyone's attention, audience and backstage, there rarely being more than one stage kiss a year, and then he made his exit out a stage window, the way we egged him on to do, instead of out the stage door.

"Look, he's going out the window," a voice carried across the gym floor from the bleachers fifty feet away. One of the rigid limitations imposed on the use of the new gym by Mr. Saunders and Coach Rogers was that no chairs could be set on the floor. Mustn't scratch that gleaming maple finish. This destroyed rapport between actors and audience. The most you could even see of the audience was the reflections of stage lights off their eyeglasses, like distant fireflies. You also weren't allowed to chew tobacco in the new gym, the way Lelan Richmond had done in the old gym. Coach was furious when two players from Clear Fork insisted on it. They spit on the sidelines during a game.

Coach hoped he finally would have another winner this season, after the two straight 2–19 teams. He had started five sophomores as a unit last year, looking toward 1954–55, but then one of them quit, and it became increasingly clear that only two of the other four would play well consistently. Then another regular from last year, Big Monk, decided not to play, and suddenly Rogers was shuffling players around, trying to find a way to win. Nine of the twelve boys on the squad started at least twice. I loved it. As an odd senior, it gave me a chance to play. But it seemed like we were running late all season, and never could catch up to what we might have been. We would play several great halves, and we built up to a few good games, but then we'd come apart.

The pace of things had quickened for me personally. The year before I had gone home to bed to rest before every game, but this year I would go at least once a week on game days to have my newly acquired flattop reshaped. I'd seen the haircut in comics and sports magazines, and our football hero, Pansy James, wore one. But when I asked Mr. Smith, my barber in Beaver, to cut it, he created something that looked like a haystack, soft and shapeless on the edges, not crisp and square and level the way it should have been. And I wasn't about to ask old Ben Pendleton, the other Beaver barber, to try to cut one. Stoical, prune-faced old Ben. How could he respect a new style like a flattop? Nothing moved him, we thought. "He wouldn't change his expression if you ran a red-hot poker up his ass," Dossie McGraw used to say. Ben was a nice guy, he just couldn't cut it. Then someone said there was a guy in Beckley named Surbaugh, in the basement of the Beckley Hotel, could cut a good one for $1.25, and all the Beckley boys went there, so we started going up, Jack Wills, Jack Wallace and me. Flattops were still a novelty out in the county. Dossie had said that a guy from Marsh Fork yelled when I went into a game, "Hey look at that guy! He's goin' bald from the ears up!"

Wade Surbaugh, the barber, had a neat flattop himself, but we learned it was actually his assistant, Manuel, a wavy-haired Spanish guy, who was the master barber, so we'd wait for him, but listen to Surbaugh's patter. I was proud to have my senior picture taken in a Manuel flattop, my first suit (gray gabardine), and my yellow and black bow tie. "Oh, a university haircut!" my young Aunt Sereta said, delighted, when I gave her a print.

Surbaugh had sort of a Sad Sack look, and he gave Jack Wills and me a metaphor for life: "I went in the closet at home the other day, looking for something, and I got lost back in there in all those coats and things, couldn't see, like to never got out. The way things are goin', I wished I'd stayed in there." When things went wrong Jack and I would say, "Wish I'd stayed in that closet." We'd remind Surbaugh of it every time we came in. Coach Rogers started his four juniors the first two games, which we lost, and I didn't play much. I was, however, entrusted to take some Varsity Club dues money (I was the president) and go to Beckley and buy Coach two sports shirts for a special Christmas assembly. I knew he liked to wear bright patterns and liked to button his shirts at the neck under his sports jackets, so I went up to Silver Brand and picked out two I thought fit that style, one a shiny silver, the other a shiny black, both with subdued little raised diamond patterns. I tried to remember to watch for him to wear the shirts after Christmas holidays, but I must have missed it when he did.

Basketball practice was great during the Christmas break — no school, no homework, play ball all morning, swing by the house for a monster ham and cheese and peanut butter sandwich and some caramel cake and lots of milk, then thumb up town and buy some incomparable hot dogs and hamburgers and orange pop at the New Deal Lunch, then mess around, go see some movie like *Attila the Hun* at the Beckley or *Hajji Baba* at the Lyric.

It was especially great this year because Lelan Richmond worked out against us several times, getting ready for the Alumni game New Year's Eve. I was excited anytime I was on the court with Lee, because I'd never seen anyone play basketball like him. He had a few days off from Morris Harvey College and brought along his teammate, Don Stover, who had been Class B All-State at Pax. One of my great moments came in a scrimmage that week when Lelan was guarding me in the pivot. I got the ball to the right of the lane, with my back to the basket, faked to my left as if I were pivoting to try a predictable right-handed lay-up, but then pivoted quickly back the other way and down the lane for a left-handed lay-up. I was wide open. The move completely fooled Lelan, who was playing me "half-a-man to the right." As I started back down the court, I heard Stover ask Lelan clinically, "How'd he pick you, Lee?" "I didn't know he could shoot left-handed," Lee answered in a very low voice.

I got my first start in the alumni game, and was made captain. That gave me the honor of going out to the center circle before the game to meet with the opposing captain and the referees, who were Coach Wetzel and Jim McNeish, a former coach at Shady. I divided my attention between them and the cheer, "He's a peach, he's a dream, he's the captain of our team — Bob, Bob Cole!" Most of the time I didn't hear the cheers, but I knew them from cheering the varsity as a jayvee, and I was waiting to hear the one for the captain. I also liked "Boom-a-lacka! Boom-a-lacka! Bow wow wow! Chick-a-lacka! Chick-a-lacka! Chow chow chow! Boom-a-lacka! Chick-a-lacka! — who are we? Shady Tigers! Victory!"

As he had threatened to do last year, Coach Rogers reformed the alumni game by limiting players to recent graduates, and so we were playing a real Shady All-Star team — Lelan Richmond, Bob Pettry (just back from starring in army basketball in Japan), Tom Quinn (a coach), Jack Lilly (a local amateur hotshot, a grumpy guy I didn't like and whose shots I was eager to block), Pilgrim Meadows, and a couple of guys from last year. The refs called twice as many fouls on the alumni as on us, and kept the game close. Fouls were important in most of our games, because we played run-and-shoot fast-break ball and rough and ragged defense, and usually at least two or three of us would foul out each game.

Despite the presence of Lelan Richmond, I did not play inspired basketball. Coach stayed with me, however, and I started all three games the next week when classes resumed. Monday we made the long 40-mile ride to Concord College (Corncob, we called it) in Athens, to play powerful Concord Training, and Coach put me on big Stanley Gunter, a gangly forward who was averaging about 25 points a game. Coach usually would assign me to cover the opposition's high scorer, if he was a center or forward, and I loved the challenge. Against Gunter, I did it right. Playing right in his face and crowding his jump shot, I held him to six in the first half, and got nine myself, three on one play where I faked him, went up, made the shot and drew the foul and made the foul shot, too.

"Great fake, Bobbus!" my close friend Jack Wills told me at halftime. "They all go for the fake, don't they, no matter how good they are." It was nice in the college dressing room, warm and dry and clean and freshly painted, not like most places we played, and it was good to hear Coach read the halftime totals from the scorebook and be only four behind a team like Athens. But I fouled out in the third quarter and Gunter ran wild. The *Post-Herald* was really nice to me the next morning:

> **ATHENS, Jan. 3** — Athens High racked up its fifth victory in a row here tonight as it reopened its basketball schedule after the holidays to take Shady Spring High of Beaver into camp, 65 to 46.
>
> It wasn't until the third period that the local Trojans were able to open up a commanding lead over the visitor and it was Bob Cole's fouling out that seemed to provide the spark to the Athens quintet. Cole's defensive work was a standout for the visiting Tigers.
>
> But with his going, Stanley Gunter began to warm up toward the twine and he tipped a total of 34 for his evening's performance, more than half of which came after Cale left the game.

Forget the typo, I'd never seen a local player get so much credit in the paper for playing defense, and I felt really good Tuesday morning as I was leaving the library and ran into Coach Rogers. I shut the door behind me, and Coach said confidentially, "Well, I know one boy who'll do all right tonight if he plays like he did last night against Gunter."

"Thanks, Coach," I said, and he grinned and went on by me. I felt even better than I had. It carried into that night's game, and I drove on Oak Hill's center and fouled him out in the first quarter, and made eight of ten free throws. Every time I'd look up to gauge the goal for a foul shot, I'd glance through our new glass back-boards — bankin' boards, we called them — and see the band up there in the loft, and Miss King, the director, looking at me, and I'd flip up my one-hand push shot and it would go in. "Gee, that boy sure can shoot fouls," Oak Hill's substitute center said before he fouled out, too. Unfortunately they called close to fifty fouls in the game, and I was gone in the third quarter, very upset at the fouls called on some of my shot-blocks and very upset at having to leave a game in which I had twelve points at the half. We lost 65–64. I would've expected a better result because the referee was Bob Porterfield, the Washington Senator pitcher from over near Prince-ton. But he killed us the way he did the Red Sox.

We had now lost twenty straight games over the last two years, but we broke the streak that Friday down at Clear Fork, with a big rally in the second half, in the only game I ever started against my cousin, Donny Mullins. We came back home against Marsh Fork, and I was assigned to guard the best shot in the league, Larry Cassell, and got to be game captain, too. I was taller than Cassell, so I forced him out of the pivot, and thought I'd give him the outside shot. He took his time and hit it. "Get on him!" Coach glared from the sideline, and then he pulled me, and Cassell hit even more against my substitutes.

I watched a close, tense game. We tied it near the end of the third quarter and then they were called for walking in the forecourt and someone hustled the ball in to Jack Wallace and he turned and sank an incredible two-hand set shot from three-fourths the length of the court as the quarter ended. But the refs wouldn't allow it, claiming we had to put the ball in play from the sideline, not from under the basket the way we had.

Cassell finally beat us with a couple of free throws, 77–76, and Coach Rogers had had enough. He brought up from the freshman team the most promising prospect in the history of the school, a graceful six-foot-three center named Kenny Ward, and he decided to start a funny little sophomore guard, Roger Cochran, who would tell us before games, "Rough up the hairs on your legs, boys, so you look mean." (Dossie McGraw observed that you could tell the bas-ketball boys who had played football: their calves were suntanned. The suntans did set us apart. When MacRae Lilly had joined the football team last August from Army reserve camp, he stood out like an albino in the dressing room. He was white-skinned because, he said, the Army required soldiers to be fully clothed on all maneuvers, so no time would be lost to sunburn treatment.)

I was benched to make room for Ward and Cochran. And in a winter severe even by Raleigh County standards, our season was further disturbed by two postponements in two weeks, because of the latest of a series of heavy snows. Despite the snow, we drove down the treacherous Helen Mountain road to Mark Twain to play on that tiny old court with the running track circling above, and a crowd of a hundred, and I came in during the second quarter and shot a perfect game — eight for eight from the field — and we ran over Mark Twain with the most points a team had ever scored for Coach Rogers, 86–71. "All I saw all night long was Cole grinnin' and goin' up for the rebound and puttin' it back in," one of their players told Coach. But when we came out to the car, we thought we were going to be stuck in Stotesbury for the night.

Snow was tumbling down and Coach needed a push to get moving, and after we gave it, he yelled back, giggling, "Can't stop for you, boys, or I'll never get'er started again," and he kept creeping on up the hill, with three or four of us running after, yelling, "You bastards," and the smart guys who had stayed in the car laughing like sons of bitches. We must have run a mile up Helen Mountain, nothing but the wonder of blizzard, dark, and headlights, throwing snowballs, having a hell of a time, no one on the road but us or we probably would've got our killing done.

Coach said it reminded him of the time they rode all the way home from a college game with the windows down in a snowstorm because someone dared someone to, or someone was lettin' stinkin' farts, he couldn't remember which.

I thought I was rolling now, but I'll be damned if that following Monday, when I came up from the dressing room ahead of everyone else to get loose early, really feeling good, I didn't run into one of those accidents that should never happen. I was shooting and following my shots, and went up for a rebound and came down on something soft. Ow! My ankle turned and I went to the floor. It was some little bastard from the 12:15 phys. ed. class, not even supposed to be on the floor. I was dismayed and Coach was furious, and chewed his ass good. I wasn't worth much for the next three games.

Then we went to Marsh Fork, and I was determined that if I got in, I would try to get even with Larry Cassell for burning me so bad in the earlier game. I did hold him down in the second half, and I got fifteen points myself, including a jumper from the corner like Fred Schaus. We lost again, but I did enjoy it when their coach came up to me while I was finishing off a basket of fruit their home ec. girls gave us after the game, and said, "Good game, big fella." Just like Uncle John and Coach Van Meter.

The fruit was part of a program around the southern part of the state that year to improve sportsmanship and cut down on the violence at games, and it seemed to work well. I wish I'd had something to cut down the violence against me in practice, because the very next day I got hit in the right thigh and started downhill again. It was very tender two nights later, but Coach rewarded me for Marsh Fork with a start against Trap Hill, and put me on their skinny center, Wiley Trent, one of the few boys I faced who still wore country-long, slicked-back black hair. He shot a kind of country-style lay-up, too, kicking his right foot forward as he drove, and he drove it right into my tender thigh. I thought I'd been burnt, hot pain shooting up and down the hip, and when I tried to keep up with a fast break we ran off his rebound, all I could do was drag my leg behind. "Oh, Bob, you looked so hurt!" one of the cheerleaders said later. Coach Wetzel constructed a covering for the sore spot, a football thigh pad taped to my leg on top of rolls of sponge, but I didn't play much for the rest of February, about a quarter of the season. I was glad we had another game postponed by snow.

I finally got to start with three games left, and embarrassed myself. We were playing Pineville, which usually had a lineup of three or four Goodes (rhymes with moods) and a couple of other guys. This year Butch was the best Goode, and he was a great one, a towheaded high-driver who released the ball far above us, and who had scored thirty points the first time they clobbered us. But for this game Pineville had added another threat, and Coach hoped I could neutralize him.

His name was Joe Tilley and he was a giant, six foot six, bigger than any other high school player I had played against or even seen at Beckley games. When I first saw him, during warmups that night, I could think only of George Mikan, because Tilley was so tall — and so broad. I wanted the job of guarding him, but somehow I got disoriented and couldn't follow the defensive plan, which was for me to play in front of him, keep the ball away from him, the way Coach had done against the great George King years ago.

I kept getting behind Tilley, not because of his moves, but because of my timidity. I didn't think I was afraid of him, because he didn't look or act mean. I kept trying to talk to him, to kid him, but he didn't think anything I said was funny, and just ignored me. He got only one goal off me in the first half, but he got five in the third quarter when they won it, and I thought I had missed a great chance. I felt like a fool and I scored only two points. "Well, Wills," Coach Wetzel said later to Jack, "I see you put in the paper where Cole went 8-for-8 down at Mark Twain. Are you going to say he was 0-for-11 at Pineville?" Jack didn't.

The nature of our team was shown by the way we came back from a 25-point loss at Pineville and upset Stoco the next night. We were up and down all year, and although Coach's promotion of Kenny Ward from the freshman to the varsity gave the team a player of great natural ability, it was hard to predict what Kenny would do from game to game, and he wasn't ready to carry the team. And so while we were much better in the second half of the season, going from 2–11 to 5–4, we still were irregular.

The irregularity made us all tend to remember our good individual games, and built a lot of enmity toward whomever Coach Rogers chose to start a given game. The worst instance of this dissension came during a practice session late in the season when some of us, notably myself and Lewis (Lucy) Redden, a senior guard who hadn't started much since early season, were outraged at being replaced in a scrimmage by the juniors and Sammy Grose, a sharpshooting sophomore with whom I used to chase flies in the summer.

Two winters before, Lucy and I had been forced out, not good enough even to practice with the varsity, playing the afternoons away at Dossie McGraw's slate-dump goal. Now here we were, being pushed out again. Be god damn! Sitting on the stage, we began to ride the juniors pretty hard, and Coach stopped practice and asked, "What is all this?" Surprisingly, given the traditional military lines of discipline that prevailed in sports, several of us were allowed to speak our piece, the sense of which was that we didn't think there was all that much difference among our abilities and we hoped we all would get a fair chance to play.

Maybe it cleared the air, because we went into the sectional tournament with a lineup that Rogers hadn't used before — two juniors, two sophomores, and a freshman — the best we had, and we ran over Hinton 82–65 in the best game we played all season, a wild game in which 62 fouls were called. But it wouldn't have happened without two of us seniors. Kenny Ward couldn't function, and I came in eager to play late in the first quarter, and by halftime had scored seven points and got seven rebounds, and helped foul out Hinton's six-five pivotman. And when we mopped up in the fourth quarter, Lucy Redden was there with seven points. That's what we could do as a team, even with our best player having an off-night. Now we got to play our archrival, Sophia, in the semifinals.

I was building toward a state of abandon. This could be my last game for Shady, maybe my last game forever in official competition before a big crowd. It was the tournament, too, a special magic for me, and I had so much to make up for, all the dreams from my paper sports days, all the groping and awkward years, all the flat-out failures from inexperience, fear, and lack of skill, all the inexplicable letdowns after great starts, all the time lost to football and dumb injuries and bad calls and coaches' experiments — all overbalancing the promise of the few times when I had played the game right.

And I'll be god damned, here I was again, on the bench, watching us start off to lose another game to Sophia. Way behind already in the first quarter. Ward was faltering again and I thought Coach would be calling for me, and I made up my mind that I was going to shoot every time I got my hands on the ball. Coach said in my ear, "I want you to go in there and do what you did last night — bring us back." "Yes, sir," I said, watching the floor. He called time and gathered us around, restraining his anger, trying to rally us. "They're leaving that middle open and I want somebody to get it in to the pivot. Cochran, do you and Cole think you can do it?"

We went back out on the floor, and Jack Wallace threw it in to Cochran under the other basket. I watched from the low pivot as they started upcourt, and then I broke up to the foul line, too soon, but Cockhound, a little guy, reared back and fired it to me half the length of the court, between the hands and arms spread like branches in Sophia's zone defense. I got it, took a big stride out the foul line to the right, pivoted, leaped, and hooked, oblivious to the consequences, thinking only, hook it, slam against the glass, bank down into the net, swish! Oh god damn!

The Shady corner screamed, we had our first field goal of the game, "Cole registering on a hook," as the *Post-Herald* said the next morning. What a shot, a twenty-foot hook shot! I didn't try to figure it out. I was going to do it now. Gimme that ball, George Mikan said. Put some hair around that hole and I'll put it in. I started through my repertoire. Another pass in from Cockhound, go right, jump, pivot, jump-turn-shoot shot. Two! Horse in the backyard! Got the ball again, felt crowded on my left, head-faked that way, reached back with my right foot, took a long stride down the lane — went the other way, faked you, you son of a bitch — left-handed rolling lay-up.

"I didn't know he could shoot left-handed," Lee had said. It was all blurs of blues and movements, scuff sounds, grunts, shoves, bright lights, a din of yelling, all right in front of the Shady section, only the basket was clear, and everything was going in, Richwood all over again. Sophia took Eanes off me, tried McKinney, then called time and I came back out matched against Big Hugo. I was going to work this sumbitch. Down the lane to my right, up with the lay-up, he was too slow this time, goal's good and shot one, Shady.

Downstairs at the half, Coach read the book. "Cole's got fifteen" — as much as I'd ever got in a varsity game — "let's just keep gettin' it to him." Only two other guys had a goal and we were down nineteen. We came back up now and Sophia put their best player, Eddie Atkins, on me, the son of a bitch. It was bad enough that he had beaten me out with this girl earlier in the season, but now he had to bring back all these bad memories. Primo Molinari had set me up with the girl, but then she got interested in Eddie, and he rode home with her from their Ansted football game.

Shit, Coach always made us stay with the team bus on road trips, but over at Sophia they didn't even practice half the time, and still beat us, and rode home with their girls. Damn Atkins should've been illegal, the way he could jump, and he always got close to thirty points. Six-two, wiry muscles, long-legged as a possum, country face, long, flappy hair, so damn cocky, somehow he transferred from Mark Twain to Sophia and they won everything, football and basketball.

I couldn't touch him. This was my last chance, third quarter, other end of the floor from the Shady section, seemed like a desert, but the ball came in to me on the right of the lane (how did I get over here?), here's Atkins, but shit, they all go for the fake, don't they, so I give him the head and shoulders, and glance over my shoulder to see how he took it, and damn! there's his sneaker up at my eye level — he's way up there — sumbitch can jump, but wait a second, he'll be down, now I go up, space all to myself, ten feet out, just me and the soft lights and I can almost touch the basket, little easy jump shot — ohh! God damn! How did the rim stop it? Jack Wallace took over the scoring and I got only one goal that quarter and was on the bench at the end.

I hung around in the dressing room, but it was over, I had to shower alone, everyone else had gone up to watch Beckley beat Stoco, and I started crying. Coach Wetzel looked in, understood, and said gently, "It's all right, big horse, remember the good games." I went upstairs near halftime of the second game and there was Dad, wearing his gray hat and blue quilted jacket. He squeezed my arm hard and affectionately, told me I played a good game, and gave me a five-dollar bill. He never had done that before, and the thought began to grow in me that he had missed the game or at least my big half, but I was afraid to ask him. It was hard for him to get home from the mines in time to eat and get to our games, and I knew he would if he could, and I didn't want to know if he hadn't. He had to go, so I went and sat down with Burnice Bucklin, in the Shady seats, which had thinned out some. "Damn, what were you doing out there?" he asked me, grinning great big. "People couldn't believe some of those shots you were taking. They'd start to say 'He's not going to shoot that shot, is he — veeeaaaa!'" He made me feel better.

I got with Jack Wills and we were surprised to run into Larry Cassell from Marsh Fork, standing off in a corner of the stage, wearing a blue and white Edwight Grade School cap and his black and orange varsity jacket. Marsh Fork had been upset in the Class B tournament the night before. "What you wearin' that cap for — startin' all over again?" I asked, trying to be friendly to someone I greatly admired. He was a nice guy. "May as well," he said shyly, with his open, good-old-boy grin, "ain't done nothin' yet." I thought, boy, I wish I'd done a fraction of the nothin' you did. But I didn't say the obvious.

Next night Jack Wallace and I watched together as Beckley mauled Sophia, 78–44, in the championship game, an exhibition

of jump-shooting that "had the capacity crowd of 1,500 or so ooh-
ing and ah-ing," as Bob Wills wrote in the *Raleigh Register* the next
morning. When the Beckley boys released their jump shots, they
would bounce on their toes two or three times and hold their
shooting pose as if they were trying to influence the ball into the
basket. I never would try that because I was afraid I'd look silly if I
missed. My American Legion baseball buddy Sam Caudill gave
me some satisfaction by practically stifling Eddie Atkins, and I was
absolutely elated by what happened afterward when they announced the all-tournament team: ". . . Bob Cole, Shady Spring,"
Mr. Saunders' voice boomed over the PA, and the crowd cheered,
and I got to walk out on the floor with Jack Wallace, who naturally
made it, too, as he did almost every all-tournament team he ever
could have, and there I stood in a semicircle with three Beckley
boys and Eddie Atkins and two guys from Stoco and Jack Wallace,
and most of them probably going to play in college and here I
made it even though I was a substitute. I'd have my name in one of
those little honor lists the *Register* always set off with heavy rules and
inserted like a box in the middle of the tournament stories, the
little boxes I'd been marvelling over since I was twelve.

All-tournament. Section 19-A all-tournament. Bob Cole, Shady
Spring. Boom-a-lacka!

Mr. Saunders was impressed, too, and called a special assembly
Monday morning to honor Jack and me and the cheerleaders, and
the school, which was named Best Cheering Section, maybe with
some advantage since it was our home court. I had worn my sharp
gray pegged flannels and my bright orange-red checked corduroy
shirt, and I felt dressed for the occasion and on top of the mountain. For the next several days Jack Wallace and I kept it alive by
ragging each other in geometry class, each saying the other was
picked for the team only because of a queer relationship with the
Post-Herald sports editor. "Dance with me, Georgie," we'd mock
each other after the Etta James song.

Like Larry Cassell coming to Shady, I drove over to Fayetteville
the next Saturday for the regional finals, and was part of an SRO
crowd that saw Beckley beat undefeated Gauley Bridge.

Dad and Ron woke me up gently the next morning to show me in
the paper that I'd made honorable mention on the All-Coalfield
Conference team. I said, "Thanks," and lay in bed and read the

long story that said, "The composite All-Coalfield player, an average of the first eight players, would be almost six feet, two inches tall, almost 18 years old, a senior in school, and would weigh 172 pounds," my numbers almost exactly, and I liked being listed with all those other boys I thought were so good. And we were taller than the All-State team had been a couple of years ago. Altogether a very nice feeling, being honored as one of the best players in the five-county region. But then the bastards didn't pick an All–County League squad. I might have been third team on that.

RICK TELANDER

Over the Hill, My Ass!

FROM ESQUIRE

I'VE LOST A STEP, I can't leap like I used to, and the rim looks a little hazy from the three-point line. But I can take you to the hole on one leg. And I may have to.

I am sitting here, hurting bad, and I feel lost. Moments ago, I rose from bed to check on a child wailing down the hall, and though I know the sound of such night terrors well — my own preadolescent wee-hour howls resonate yet in my 46-year-old skull — I thought for a moment this was something different. I knew deep down it was only Zack, my 5-year-old, facing up to his dark dreams once again, but my foggy brain had posited something else: this is precisely the sound of you, middle-aged man, fading away.

I took a step and my right knee nearly buckled. I leaned on the bed, hunched like an old gardener. My back didn't want to straighten out. I took another step and my left knee nearly continued its bend, as though it were some kind of catapult that needed full compression before it would launch its cargo, my body, back on its course. Both my ankles ached, and my right hip socket seemed full of sand. My left shoulder, which had borne the brunt of my bed-leaning, felt somehow out of whack, as though if I weren't careful and put slightly more torqued pressure on it, it would pop out of its socket. Which would be bad news, because tomorrow I have a pickup basketball game.

So in the droning grayness of 4:00 A.M., while my son fights off the ogres of his imagination, I've got a few monstrous fears of my own: just how well will my rapidly decomposing body hold up tomorrow while I again play a game ostensibly invented for men half my age?

This may sound self-obsessed, if not downright ludicrous, to those sane, rational souls who gracefully step aside for the spryer, younger generation. Not me. Forget it, you smirking, hip-hop, ear-ring-encrusted bucks. You may be lithe and quick, but I'm smart and mean. I have to be. Here are the medical facts: I don't have any diseases that I know of. And I'm not overweight — though my waist now has the gentle bloom of a former athlete's starter gut.

Nor do I have chronic arthritis or any operation-needing, mal-functioning joints. In fact, the only surgical procedures I have un-dergone have been relatively uneventful cuts to remove my tonsils and my appendix. The former happened forty-one years ago, the latter four years ago, and, as far as I know, neither did anything to me except make me miserable for a week or so. I have never broken a bone that I know of. X-rays now indicate that I chipped parts of both my right and left ankles at some time, years ago, but I couldn't tell you when, and I've never worn a cast or a splint, except on my left ring finger during my college-football days, when I dislocated it while making a goddamned she-boy tackle on a third-string run-ning back in a controlled scrimmage.

Stitches, there've been a few.

Sprains? Lots. Mostly ankle sprains from coming down on oppo-nents' feet in basketball (probably the cause of the chips). There was a torn right-shoulder muscle — again back in college football — which the team doctor took care of with a mighty injection of cortisone, a true miracle drug, my friends, even if it has deleterious side effects if used too often. For, as I say, what doesn't?

One time, about a decade ago, a very large man who didn't know his head from his asshole ran me into the padded stanchion sup-porting the basket, and I couldn't raise my left arm above my nipple for nearly two months. And the socket still clicks occasion-ally Of course, I have had a number of slight shoulder separations simply from tackling, being tackled, falling down, whatever, from childhood to adulthood, and they haven't helped the cause, either. I have patellar tendinitis in each knee, strictly from overuse, and I use ice bags and take ibuprofen on account of it. I have a "degen-erative disk" (doctor's words) in my lower back that makes standing for long periods and sleeping in odd positions fairly painful. I had that condition diagnosed when I was twenty-two. It also is allegedly the result of "overuse," though how one overuses one's spine by that tender age is beyond my knowledge, and certainly I did little more by twenty-two than any other athletic male with a slightly wild streak would have done.

I have a chronically stiff neck (on the right side), which was made chronic when I used too much weight and tipped too far to the left while engaged with a Nautilus neck machine eight years ago, performing what may be the dumbest muscle-strengthening exercise on this planet unless you intend to use your neck for something other than a stand upon which to rest your cranium. Which I do not.

I think I have a budding hernia. No big deal. If I try to throw a rock hard or a softball without warming up for several minutes, I feel a ligamentous twinge in my elbow that says, I could snap if that's what you want. The equally unfriendly twinge I feel in my right shoulder when I try to hum a ball says, How does rotator-cuff surgery sound?

But who cares? I am a nobody. Nobody out there cares about my body except me. Not even my wife on some days. I came into the kitchen recently, hobbling as I always do after a game, and as I sat at the table, stinking with sweat, groaning involuntarily, with an immense bag of ice on this knee, then the other, I asked my wife if she didn't think me somehow a noble and empathetic creature for this steadfastness I held in the face of the raging gale of physical deterioration known as the dimming of the light.

"You're a wimp," she said. "You're dripping on the floor." And she left the room.

I do not have to hurt like this, but I choose to. So it's a good pain, in a sense. I thank God I can still compete at all but I do not like seeing the candle flicker this way. Here's the problem: I didn't play basketball yesterday. Nor the day before that. I played three days ago. When I was 25, I could play from sunup to sundown and feel nothing. And now seventy-two hours go by and I am still spavined and weak.

Is this how God taps you on the shoulder, before he slaps you silly? As I cantilever myself out of bed at daybreak in my now-tranquil house, an abode that like so many of my possessions seems as though it cannot be mine, that it must belong to my parents, for I am still a child, the thought occurs to me: am I scared to death of dying? Or am I simply frightened of the day that I will ache so much that rather than go out to play, I will slide back into the warmth of the bed and remember past glories?

I saw my old football pal Pat Harrington standing by our hot tub one morning in Santa Monica when a group of us were gathering to head out for a little outdoor hoops. I knew he wouldn't join us. He is 48 years old, six-five, 235 pounds, and a former high school All-American in both football and basketball. He was a promising tight end at Northwestern until he ruined his knees early on, and now just flying out from Chicago in a coach seat proved to be almost more than he could handle, painwise.

I asked him something I'd never thought to ask him before: did he miss playing games?

"Every day," he said quickly and with a thin smile, as though he'd been waiting for the question for years. "Every single day. Some of us miss it too much to stop."

Like me and my friends, who missed games so badly that at ages when we should have been doing color commentary for our sons and daughters in the family den, a bunch of us 35- to 49-year-olds actually played in the Northwestern alumni-varsity spring football exhibition last year. None of the old-timers were hurt seriously in that fray, though one friend of mine, who's 44, cracked a couple of ribs and messed up his knee. That sting was put into perspective, however, when he had triple-bypass heart surgery a short while later. Twenty years of two packs a day is even worse, it seems, than a 20-year-old fullback comin' at you. Myself, I took only one serious blow in the game, when I ran with a fake punt and got labeled by a linebacker named Geoff Shein, whom I would have run over in my prime. I'm telling you.

Why do I do it? Why do I let myself in for such abuse, being pole-axed by the disrespectful young Shein? I remember sitting at a bar in 1983 with Packers quarterback Lynn Dickey, then a 33-year-old vet, who had suffered in his career a dislocated left hipbone and shattered hip socket, a broken and shattered left fibula, an 18-inch steel rod pounded down through one leg, severe shoulder and knee tendinitis, and so many surgical repairs on various body parts that he couldn't remember them all. He was preparing to play that week, despite being in great pain from a post-spinal-puncture headache, incurred after he received a spinal injection for pain in his back.

I asked him why he was doing it.

Dickey shrugged and said in his slow Kansas drawl, "What's one more torpedo in a sinking ship?"

Some of my cohorts have flat-out given up on the physical stuff. As I talk to them, I realize that we have all assumed different postures and gaits for wending our way down the long hall. Most of us don't really care about looking that good anymore; is there, after all, anything more absurd than a man on his death bed with big lats, a facelift, and hair plugs? But while there are those who don't give a damn about appearance, there are yet those of us who want to hold on to a measure of youthfulness.

I want to retain a modicum of an athlete's grace and ease because I need it to be able to play the games I want to play. The way I want to play them. Which is not an old-man, shuffle-up-the-court, walk-to-first-base, no-fast-serves way. God, do I love games. I need to play.

I used to hide the fact, even hide my athletic skills — as if such things detracted from the work of the mind. Now I don't care. Now, in fact, I realize that the body exalts the mind, oils it. The problem is, I've come to this realization at a time when it's my body that needs the oil.

I remember a cartoon in *The New Yorker* in which a slovenly old man says to his haggard wife as he reads at the kitchen table and she scrapes dirty dishes into the sink, "Elsie, it says here that if you exercise, your body secretes a juice that makes you feel good."

Screw the juice. I'm not talking about fitness or endorphins; I'm talking about going out and being a guy, playing softball, broomball, soccer, hoisting a weight or two, sprinting after a Frisbee, skiing like a madman down a moderate-to-easy slope, doing cannonballs off the high board, grabbing your kid and maybe throwing the little guy up in the air like a pillow and catching him without ripping a deltoid or bursting a bursa or, God forbid, blowing out part of your weakening abdominal wall.

Of course, there are dangers. A friend of mine, Steve Salzman, a marketing consultant in suburban Chicago, blew his knee out playing hoops thirteen years ago, when he was 32, and he still dreams about what he was until that moment. "I jumped up to tip in a ball off the glass, and when I came down, my left leg was straight when it hit the floor, and I tore the anterior cruciate ligaments in half," he says. "I went to Dr. Clarence Fossier, the Bears' team doctor at the time, and he said, 'It doesn't look good.' I said, 'Will I be able to play ball?' and he said — and I remember this so clearly — 'Not as well as you could before 2:00 P.M. on August 26, 1983.'"

Which is the way it goes. I read about free radicals and the right amount of this vitamin and that supplement for maximum benefit, and blah, blah, blah — it all leaves me thinking of those grim-faced mopes at health clubs everywhere, grinding away at machines very much in the way Ponce de Leon's men must have hacked away at the vines and thorns shielding the always-receding Fountain of Youth. I even chuckle at wealthy zealots like the octogenarian "godfather of physical fitness," Jack LaLanne, who said, "Warming up is the biggest bunch of horseshit. Does a lion warm up when he's hungry? No!"

Everybody's got a shtick these days, something to help you stay young, but we deserve some integrity as we move on down the pike, not just the beckoning fingers of a bunch of quacks. It's difficult to tell whether the pains that nag at an active man's body come from the attrition of aging or just the compounding effect of physical insult. Sweet Jesus, we become like eggshells, drained of our yolks, mere facades.

In a media softball game at Wrigley Field back in the mid-eighties, I hit what I thought was a double but was actually a single, and as I sprinted for second base in preparation for my humiliation, I tore my right quadriceps muscle, went down, and semi-crawled toward the bag. The second baseman crouched and cheerily waited for my arrival. Tagged out, I stood up and tried to walk to the dugout. I sat down when I had crossed the third-base line, and then I started to faint. I would have puked if I hadn't been so nauseous.

The Cubs' trainer saw me, looked at my face, and told me to come into the clubhouse when I could make it. Eventually, I dragged myself in there, and he had me lie on a training table while he packed the entire top of my upper right leg in ice. He wrapped the big plastic bag with an elastic bandage, told me to stay where I was, and went about his business.

I turned my head from side to side and realized I was lying between Cubs pitchers Rick Sutcliffe and Steve Trout, who were treating their own injuries on their own slabs. I said, "Hi," and that was it. I still felt ready to faint. I lay back and closed my eyes and heard the muted sounds and vibrations of the real game starting outside. Somebody else might have waxed poetic and said this was an amazing, semi-real major league experience, but for me it was just gloom. I realized that I was taking my injury more seriously than Sutcliffe and Trout, the two professional athletes between whom I was sandwiched, were taking theirs. For them, injury was a threat to their profession. For me, it put my very life at risk.

This brings to mind a corollary to Murphy's Law: What can go wrong with the mortal coil will. I am ever so thankful for each development in sports medicine and sports therapy. Like lots of veteran guys, I take anti-inflammatories — Nuprin, Advil, or some old, hoarded prescription stuff I got from a mountain-climbing doctor friend — before I play. Science helps you adapt. Last night, my wife was making margaritas, at my request, and I caught her using my basketball ice, and I asked what in the hell she thought she was doing.

"What a baby," she said, shoving a frothy blended drink my way. "Just take this and shut up."

I am afraid of growing old. I am afraid of dying. Do they let you take your jump shots in heaven? Though I thought he was a buffoon back in the sixties, I now have a deepening respect for that psychedelic jock Timothy Leary, who died last year at 75 of prostate cancer. He was "thrilled" about this final trip and said, "How you die is the most important thing you ever do. It's the exit, the final scene of the glorious epic of your life."

Kind of like that last pickup game, the one you can never bring yourself to say is the last one. As NBA player Marques Johnson said to a reporter way back in 1980, "When I'm playing ball, it's like I'm not even part of the earth — like I belong to another universe."

So what do you do? You whoop into the storm, grinning, or at least with teeth clenched in a grinlike arrangement — looking, as my friend Steve Salzman puts it, like a possum shifting peach seeds — dribbling the ball, ready to gear down but ready to fight the whole thing right to the bitter end. Will you play in one of those silly fifty-and-over leagues? Are you kidding? Never! Well, maybe. Probably. Oh, Christ, absolutely.

So here I am in the shank of the afternoon, when most men who act their age are hunkered down in front of consoles or perched on barstools. I'm sprawled on the carpet in front of my closet, girding for battle. You know the drill. You put on your jock (my, how you have come to love and respect that dependable, liberating, three-strapped slingshot, with all it portends!), your gym shorts, the T-shirt from Farragut High School (1995 Chicago City Champions, which you got on a visit to that inner-city school to check up on then-student Kevin Garnett), your patellar brace, your ankle pre-wrap (done in imitation of the style used by Dick Hoover, your college trainer a quarter century ago), three pairs of socks (Calvin Murphy wore six), then the shoes — Nikes, Reeboks, whatever they are — the sweats, then down the stairs, out the door, and into the car for the drive to the forum, the meeting hall, the vortex.

The excitement builds. The anticipation. And the question: God, what have you got for me today? And your battle cry: because I'm coming to play.

This could be my last game, but here we go, screw it. I'm about to play basketball with a bunch of similarly arrested guys I know and love. By some quirk of good fortune, since I am a sports writer by trade, I live next to the Chicago Bears' practice facility in suburban Lake Forest. My property line abuts the west end zone of the practice field at Halas Hall, and I can see, among other things, president Mike McCaskey's office desk, when his curtains are open, the leaves are off our trees, and I am taking a piss in our first-floor bathroom.

So the Bears' front-office basketball fanatics, assistant PR man Doug Green prime among them, often call me when a pickup game is afoot at the gym a block away. Green called earlier, and as I swiftly walk toward the gym, I wonder who will be there today, who will have survived, who will have succumbed, how much longer I myself will last.

Assistant trainer Tim Bream went down with a partially torn anterior cruciate ligament a month ago. He won't be there. And offensive coordinator Ron Turner (now head coach at Illinois), an "older gentleman" about my age whose brother Norv coaches the Washington Redskins, hurt a disk in his back two weeks ago and is still recovering. Perhaps forever. On the phone, I told the slender, 29-year-old Green — whom I once elbowed smartly (by accident)

in the eye socket, opening a tidy, three-inch slit on the arrogant
youngster's face — that, gee whiz, my buddy Ron might be toast
for life.

"Don't think that hasn't been noticed or mentioned," said Green
smugly.

As I walk past Halas Hall itself, I see Brian McCaskey, Mike's
brother and one of our regular players. He was out for a while with
a badly sprained ankle, made a brief comeback last week, and now
has a strange, lopsided look to his face. "Broken nose," he says.
"Green's elbow." Scratch another player. I see defensive coordinator Bob Slowik. "My calves," he says. Scratch one more.

We shoot for teams and soon have a four-on-four game, challeng-
ers sitting on the sideline. My team, with marketing director Ken
Valdiserri, scout Mike McCartney, and an intern named Scott, beats
a team with quarterbacks Erik Kramer and Steve Stenstrom and
wide-out Michael Timpson on it. Timpson, remarkably, is clueless.
He's a first-team receiver but a very bad basketball player. He is
good-natured, however, and merely smiles when an older gentleman, me, positions successfully for a rebound or scores on a fifteen-
foot jumper. It strikes me that I could take him and, in one week of
intensive basketball instruction, turn him into a factor on the court.
But I'm not going to. I am certain there are moments when I look
hideously misplaced in an athletic endeavor such as this. But there
is compensation in life. And this is it. Cunning and grizzle can still,
at times, whip pure stud-meat, untapped, untrained talent.

In the next game, I guard my 42-year-old, back-from-the-dead
pal, Ron Turner. I tell him how pleased I am to see that he's still
with us. He says thanks, then adds needlessly, "I'm too old for this."
His game is half what it was just two months ago. He has gone from
being an active small forward to a stationary point guard who
doesn't bend for errant balls and whose once-lethal fadeaway is
easy to disrupt.

"You know the real pity here?" I say during a break, feeling
compassionate in my vigor. "None of these young pricks will remember we once had games."

As my victorious team prepares for round three, I find myself
thinking about a younger guy I know who was playing at a YMCA
and blocked an old man's shot so hard that the man died. Well, not

exactly from the block and not instantly. "I don't think I killed him," said the youngster. But the geezer did keel over for good just seconds after the facial, and he no doubt took that youth-laden insult with him as one of the sadnesses he pondered while sailing down the long, dark tunnel toward the white light.

Or you know what?

Maybe he didn't. Maybe the rejection was one of the old guy's major delights. I'm thinking just now it might have been something he didn't exactly appreciate but he nevertheless was ever so thankful for. Because it happened in a game. Because he was out there.

ELWOOD REID

My Body, My Weapon, My Shame

FROM GQ

I DID BAD THINGS FOR FOOTBALL. Because I could. Because I was 19 years old, weighed 270 pounds, had 5 percent body fat and had muscle to burn. Forget touchdowns, I played football for the chance to hit another man as hard as I could — to fuck him up, move through him like wind through a door. Anybody who tells you different is a liar.

There is the fear that any hit may be your last. That some bigger, stronger, better player will come along — take you down to the turf and end your career with the snap of bone or the pop of an anterior cruciate ligament.

The moment of impact goes like this: you slam helmet-first into another person's back until you can hear the air whoosh out of his lungs. Or better yet — you ram a forearm so hard into his throat that the crunch of cartilage and the fear in his eyes give you pause. Time stops. No pain, only a sucking sound as the physics of the impact sort themselves out — who hit whom first, angle, shoulder, mass, helmet, speed, forearm. Silence follows the cruel twist of limbs as the pain rushes in the way oxygen blows through the streets of a firebombed city, leaving flame in its wake. The pain is good. Both of you know it, and for a few precious seconds the world has order. Hitter and hittee. Motherfucker and motherfucked.

* * *

I came by football through my father. I played because if you were big, it was what you did in Cleveland. To do anything else was to be soft or queer. As long as I could hit and tackle, nobody made fun of my size. I played football, and that was all you needed to know about me. Then there were the men — the coaches who demanded a single-minded intensity from me each time I strapped on the pads. Even then I knew these were men who kept basements full of plaques and trophies from their glory days, collected beer steins and fell into deep depressions when the Cleveland Browns lost or their wives bore them daughters instead of sons. Their solution to everything was to hit harder. The word was forever on their lips. They scrawled it on chalkboards and spat it in my face: *Hit. Hit. Hit.* They knew how to infect eager minds with the desire to someday play in the pros. And when one of these potbellied men screamed at me to kick ass, act like a man or gut it out, I did, because I wanted to believe that a sport or even life could be boiled down to a few simple maxims. I was big, and I could hit; therefore I had purpose.

In high school, my scrawny body filled out as I moved from junior varsity to varsity and then to captain of a mediocre football team. College scouts came to time me in the forty-yard dash, watch me lift weights and eye me coming out of the shower as if I were a horse they might someday bid for at auction. I can't say I didn't enjoy the attention, but I began to realize that as a potential college-football recruit, I was expected to behave like one. I had to shake hands and look scouts in the eye and thank them for coming to see me. I had to talk sports, tell them who my favorite players were, what team I liked in the Super Bowl. I had to be smart but not too smart. Grades mattered only because colleges like "no risk" players, guys who can be recruited without the worry that they'll flunk out. I couldn't tell them that I didn't care who won the Super Bowl, that what really mattered to me was books. That when I finished *One Flew Over the Cuckoo's Nest* or *Heart of Darkness,* my heart beat faster than it ever had on the football field. I knew that I had to keep this part of me hidden and let the scouts and coaches see the bright-eyed athlete they wanted to see.

Pursuing a football scholarship became a full-time job. Everything I did was for my body. I ate well, went running at night, swallowed handfuls of vitamins, swilled gallons of protein shakes and fell asleep rubbing sore muscles. Everything fell away as I focused on using this body I'd nurtured and cared for, asking it to come back day after day, stronger, better. And it did. Even after the most torturous practices, my body responded by snapping back, fresh and ready to go. If there were limits, I had yet to find them.

On the field, I plugged my heart in, throwing my body at tail-backs with reckless abandon. I went both ways and loved every minute of it — reveling in the sheer exhaustion that came every fourth quarter, when it was all I could do to hunker down into a three-point stance and fire out. To be better than the man lined up across from you was to summon your body to do what it didn't want to do — what it would normally resist doing off the gridiron. Great ballplayers are full of hate and a kind of love for what they are capable of inflicting on another man. And in between whistles, I hated.

When the first recruiting letter arrived, I had this feeling that I was standing on the cusp of what I imagined to be greatness. I saw television, cheerleaders and, I suppose even then, the endgame — the NFL.

"This is a great opportunity," my father said, holding the letter in his hands as if it were alive.

I nodded, knowing that the ante had been raised. I was no longer playing because I liked to hit but for the chance to get out of Cleveland and escape the factory-gray fate that awaited me.

I escaped by signing a letter of intent to play ball for one of those Big Ten colleges, where football is king, the coach is feared and anybody wearing a letterman's jacket is instantly revered. I felt important, my head swirling with the possibilities that seemed to shimmer before me. I had worked hard; my friends had gone out drinking or had sat around watching television, but I'd been running and lifting. Now I felt as if I had been rewarded and every-thing would be O.K.

That was ten years ago, and what I did both on and off the field for football is preserved forever in the aches, pains and injuries that haunt my body, lurking no matter how many aspirins I chew or how early I go to bed.

When I report to freshman summer camp, there are thirty or so other new recruits sitting around a huge indoor practice facility. Some of them are bigger and stronger than me, guys with no necks and triceps that hang off their arms like stapled-on hams. The speedsters and skill guys, mostly thick-legged black dudes with gold chains and shaved heads, pool over into their own corner, staring down at their feet as if the secret of their speed lay somewhere underground. The oddball white guys — quarterbacks, tight ends, and a few gangly-looking receivers — find one another and talk like bankers, in slow, measured tones.

I make my way over to the group of big guys who stand, shifting foot to foot, in a loose semicircle, until the coaches walk in and everybody snaps to attention. I am relieved to find that they look like all the other coaches who have ever yelled at me or offered arm-swinging praise. They are the very same gray/white-haired men, swaddled head to toe in loud polyester, I've been trying to impress my whole life.

Nobody says a word. Instead, the coaches stand there looking at us the way a mechanic eyes his socket wrenches, as tools to be picked up, used and thrown aside. There is only this simple equation: as a ballplayer, I am expected to do as I'm told, lay my body on the line or else get out of the way for somebody who will. Everybody in the room knows and understands this and, when asked, will put himself in harm's way with the dim, deluded hope that he will come out the other end a star.

The speech begins, and it's like every other coach's speech, only this time the coach spouting the platitudes owns our bodies and our minds for the next four years, five if we redshirt. He lays down the rules — the same rules I've heard all my life about what I can and can't do — about how we're here to win and anything less is simply unacceptable.

Then his theory of football: "Domination through hard work, men," he says, his short body quivering with anger. "More hard work until we come together as a team of men focused on one thing: *winning*. Am I understood?"

"Yes, sir," we answer.

"Good then," he says. "I'll accept nothing less than smash-mouth, cream-them-in-the–ear hole football. That is why you are here, and I will not tolerate softness or excuses. You are here because we think each of you will someday become a ballplayer. You are not yet ballplayers, but if you do what we ask, you will become ballplayers, and for that you are lucky."

All thirty of us grunt, "Yes, sir."

Then this no-neck guy, his face swollen with fear and desire, leans into me and says, "I wish we could skip the bullshit, strap on the pads and sort out who's who."

My first inclination is to laugh, to tell him to relax. Instead, I lid my eyes and clench my jaw and tell him that yes, that would be good, that I too like to hit.

Coach finishes his rah-rah speech, and the air is heavy with anticipation as the realization washes over everyone in the room that all of the lifting and running has come down to this — the chance to prove ourselves by putting our bodies on the line with guys who are every bit as strong and as fast.

Then we're marched off to the training room, where a team of doctors pokes and prods us as if we were cattle heading to market. By the time we're through, everybody has a nickname: Fuckhead, Slope, Rope, Sith, Crawdaddy, Pin Dick, Yo Joe, Hernia, Bible Boy, Vic, Napalm, Six-Four, Too Tall, Dead Fuck, Flat-Ass Phil, the Creeper, Revlon. Somebody tags me with Sweet Lou Reid because before every practice I listen to "Coney Island Baby."

On our first day of padded practice, the line coach, a man with steel blue and gray hair, cold eyes, and a hatchet nose, marches us over to a row of low metal cages. "Get into a three-point," Coach says as he lines us across from one another on opposite sides of the cages.

I hunker down, straddling one of the boards, and look out at the man in front of me.

"Hit!" Coach screams.

And with a blast of his whistle, my college football career begins. We hit and fall to the ground, fighting and spitting until he whistles us back to attention. We line up and do it over and over. After ten minutes, I am bleeding from three different places, my arms are numb, and my right thumb hangs from my hand at an angle I know is wrong. But to stop and go to the sideline is to pussy out. So I play through the pain, and after a few more hits I don't care what happens to my thumb.

The rest of practice takes place in five-second bursts, until our pads, wet with blood and sweat, hang on us like second skins. Everything is done harder and faster. Fights break out without warning. Two long-armed D-backs start swinging at each other, and the coaches let it go until the taller one splits his hand on a facemask. Blood flies from his smashed paw as he spins around like some shoulder-padded Tasmanian devil. One of the coaches finally grabs him by the facemask and drags him to the sideline, leaving his opponent alone and bewildered, with nothing to do except join the huddle. Guys suffer knee injuries, pop hamstrings, tear Achilles tendons, while others just go down with silent, allover injuries that are the same as quitting — telling the team you can no longer take it. During the first week, nine walk-ons clear out their lockers and quit.

We learn to live with injuries and spend what little free time we have complaining and scheming about our positions on the depth chart. Hernia has a bruise he can move up and down his forearm. Bible Boy's knee is fucked, and my shoulder slides in and out of place so much that I no longer notice it. All of us have scabbed-over noses and turf burns on our shins that crack and fill our shoes with warm blood the minute practice starts.

After practice and a shower, I stand in front of the mirror and stare at the road map of bruises, cuts, and mysterious pink swellings. I touch each bruise, scrape, and swelling until I feel something, and I know that my body is still there, capable of doing what I ask of it.

When the upperclassmen report to camp, we become their tackling dummies. Even the coaches forget about us and concentrate on the home opener four weeks off. I'm moved from defense to offense because my feet are too slow and my "opportunities," Coach says, are better on the other side of the ball. He tells me that offense is the thinking man's side of the ball, that it is about forward motion and scoring.

I adjust, and within a week I become an offensive lineman. Every day is the same grind — the same flesh-filled five yards on either side of the ball, where we grunt, shove, kick, and gouge at one another. In the trenches, success is measured in feet and inches, not long touchdown runs or head-over-ass catches that bring crowds to their feet.

After three weeks, I begin to root for injuries. Not only do I want the man in front of me on the depth chart to go down but I begin to look for ways to hasten his downfall. I am not the only one. More than once I see guys twisting knees in pileups, lowering helmets into exposed spines, gouging throats and faces with the hope that a few well-placed injuries will move them up the depth chart. The coaches seem to encourage this ballplayer-eat-ballplayer mentality, pitting starter against backup and watching as the two players wrestle and pump padded fists at each other long after the play has been blown dead.

But it is off the field that the real training happens, where I learn about how the team is not really a team. Offensive players hate defensive players. Linemen hate ball handlers because they get all the glory and half the aches and pains. It goes without saying that everybody hates the kickers because of their soft bodies and clean uniforms and the way they run warm-up laps out in front, making the rest of us look bad.

There is also a silent division between blacks and whites. Any white guy who hangs with the brothers and listens to their music is called a "whigger." Black guys who hang with the white guys are called "Oreo-cookie motherfuckers" or sellouts. In the locker room, when there are only white faces around, some guy will call a black guy who fumbles the ball or hits too hard in warm-ups a stupid nigger, and I know that I am supposed to nod in agreement or high-five the racist bastard. And when I don't, there is another line drawn.

But somehow it all comes together, and there are times when black and white, offense and defense, and even the kickers seem to be part of the same team, especially when practice is over and we're all glad to be walking off the field, happy to have seen our bodies through another day, united by our aches, pains, and fatigue.

I learn that among the linemen there are those who belong and those who don't. To belong means to go about the game of football grim-faced, cocksure of your ability to take any hit and keep moving. The guys who zone out on God, refuse the pack or are refused by it end up falling by the wayside, unnoticed by the coaching staff and their fellow players.

Then there are the guys who have already made it — broken out of the pack to start or platoon with another player in a starting position. Among the linemen, they are called "the fellas." Coaches love the fellas because they have proven themselves. But what really distinguishes a fella is not his success on the field but rather his

ability to wallow in the easy gratification afforded any athlete at any
university that is nuts for football. Everything is permitted — drinking, scoring chicks, fighting off the field — because he has survived
the mayhem and the mindless drudgery of practices. I hear the
stories over lunch or in the locker room after a workout: how to
score with a woman nicknamed "the Dishwasher." How to persuade
one of the brains or geeks to cheat for you. How to cop free meals
at restaurants or free drinks at a bar. How to wrangle free T-shirts
from the equipment manager. How to pass the drug test. And, most
important, how to act like you don't give a shit, because you've got
it coming to you.

We win our Big Ten opener, and for a few minutes in the locker
room the air seems to vibrate with goodwill and camaraderie. Even
I who have stood on the sideline getting rained on feel like a player
as I listen to reporters question today's heroes. After the coaches
leave, word that there will be a party at a fella's house percolates
through the sweaty room.

When I enter the party, the room seems to be in some sort of
drunken-action overload. Near the keg there is a makeshift wrestling pit, circled by grubby couches full of squealing teased-haired
women who look at me briefly, decide that I am not a starter and
look away. I am handed a beer and told to drink. My beertender is a
huge, smiling defensive tackle named the Wall, who watches as I
raise the cup to my lips and sip.

"What's a matter with you?" he says, pointing at the beer. "We've
got beer and a roomful of chicks who want to fuck us 'cause we won
the game. What more do you want?"

"I'm just a frosh," I tell him.

"Skip the *Leave It to Beaver* bullshit and drink," Wall says.

I nod, drain the cup and follow him to the kitchen, past heavily
made-up groupies who stare at me now that I am with Wall. There
are others, big guys mostly, and we keep pace with Wall, who tosses
back beer as if it's water. After every round, somebody slops an arm
around me or smacks me on the shoulder, and for a moment I feel
the tug of the fella fraternity.

What happens next is what happens in varying degrees at every
subsequent party. Fights erupt over women, favorite teams, etc.
There is a girl in an upstairs bedroom handing out blow jobs or an

underclassman who is too drunk and vomits before he is stripped naked and thrown out a window or tossed down the stairs.

I down half a bottle of Everclear grain alcohol when it is handed to me and let a sad-eyed chubby girl in tight jeans sit on my lap. As the liquor hits my brain, I realize that there are no victims here, even as I watch this girl get talked into going upstairs with three guys. Later I see her in the front yard, leaning against a lamppost crying, as several players throw empty beer cans at her and call her a whore. Everybody, including the skinny-shouldered engineering student and the jock-sniffing schlub with stars in his eyes whom we occasionally torture and torment, knows the deal and comes back for more. We have something they want, and they'll take anything we have — even the laughter and the cruel pranks — just to be near us, to wear one of our sweatshirts or to talk to us about the game. And it all seems so normal. When our starting defensive tackle rams a frat boy's head into a steel grate, not once but several times, there are no repercussions because he is a star and the team needs him. There are rules on the field and in the locker room when we are around the coaches, but off the field, anything goes.

And I do bad things because I want to belong. I hide the part of me that enjoys classes and reading in my room after practice. I know better, yet I find myself doing the same stupid shit I see others do, and nobody tells me that it's wrong. Nobody blinks when I walk into a party, pick up the first girl I see and pin her to the ceiling until her laughter turns to screams and then finally to tears. I put lit cigarettes out on the back of my hand to prove to the fellas that I don't give a fuck — that I am above pain, above caring what happens to my body, because I am young and I am a ballplayer and my body seems to have no limits.

At another party, I split a frat boy's nose for no particular reason other than that I am drunk and it feels like the right thing to do. He goes down, holding his nose, and I hop up on a thick oak banister, close my eyes and walk, not caring if I fall or if someone pushes me. When I do fall down two flights of stairs, I pop right back up, though my knee doesn't seem to be working, and there are several fraternity brothers closing in on me. Instead of running, I go outside and proceed to kick in the basement windows until I hear police sirens and escape into the snowy back yards. The next day, I am sober and ready to practice, and only at that point do I feel remorse. But then there is the first hit, and my body hurts, my joints crack, and I am absolved.

One night at a party during my sophomore year, I am asked by a fella if I want to help him videotape some girl giving head to a couple of guys in an upstairs room. I nod drunkenly and follow him through the forest of oversize flesh and dull-eyed groupies to the stairs, where he turns around and winks at me. For a moment, I'm not sure if he's joking or not. The music is loud — too loud. There are women playing quarters at a table to my right and guys staring at *Hustler* magazine on a couch in the corner, while several sophomores write their names with a permanent Magic Marker on the body of a passed-out frosh and discuss shaving his balls.

"You ready?" my guide asks. I can tell he's waiting for me to say no so he can call me a pussy or a Boy Scout. I look around at the monster bodies of ballplayers acting like children grabbing at toys, and I realize that I've finally become what the coaches and my fellow players have always expected me to become — a fella, a person living in a world of no consequence. I am not a star or even a starter; still, everything I do is acceptable, allowed and in the end . . . empty.

I look at the hulking player as he awaits my response. Part of me wants to go upstairs and rescue the girl, take her away. But I know she'd only be back next week, drunker and more willing, and I would be there, too, and maybe then, a few beers to the better, I'd say yes when asked if I wanted to help with the videotaping, because I could, because it is expected of me and because it is what a fella does.

I turn to go, but before I can get to the door, Fuckhead jumps on my back and screams, "Isn't this great?" I shake him off and toss him to the floor, tell him no and walk outside, feeling cold and hollow. But most of all, I feel simple and stupid, because I can't see a way out. If I quit, I lose my scholarship and go back home to Cleveland having failed. If I choose not to partake in the fun, there will be a line drawn and I will be exiled into the lonely world of those who practice but who will never play or belong. That is my problem, that I want to belong at any cost. I still have the dream that someday I will become a starter, and the pro scouts will come to

time me in the forty-yard dash and I will have a chance to go to the
next level.

It starts with a tingling in my arm, one of a thousand jolts of pain
that have run through my body that I no longer seem to notice.
Only this time it doesn't go away.

I hear one of the coaches screaming, "Get up, Reid. Get the fuck
up and get your ass back to the huddle."

Without thinking, I roll to my feet and try to shake it off. When I
rejoin the huddle, the coach glares at me and another play is called,
and I line up, hit and do it again, the pain lingering in my spine.
Then one morning I awake unable to raise my arms above my head.
After swallowing a handful of Tylenol Threes and a few anti-inflammatories, I go to practice and hit. My arms dangle from my shoulders, bloodless and weak, forcing me to deliver the blows with my
head and helmet. The coaches scream when I am slow to rise after
the whistle. And when the pills wear off, the numbness is replaced
by a hot poker of pain and a dull, crunching sound in my neck.
After I miss a block, Coach sends me to the sideline and motions for
the trainers to have a look. I explain and point to my neck as they
walk me to the training room. It is the longest walk of my life, and
no one even turns a helmet in my direction. In the training room, I
am told to lie still while the trainers pull my pads off and wrap ice
bags around my neck.

I sit the sideline for a full week. No one except the trainers and
the team doctor says a word to me, and it's all right, because for
once I am outside looking in at the football machine as it whirs and
clicks along without me. But by the end of the week, I want more
than anything else to peel the ice bags off my neck and shoulders,
strap on pads and prove that I'm still one of them. I think that this
time it will be different, that I can hit and go about the game I've
played and nursed my body for without acting like one of the fellas
off the field.

So when the team doctor works his way up my arm with a safety
pin, poking my flesh and asking, "Do you feel this?" I say, "Yes."

"And this?"

Yes, yes, and yes. Although I have no idea where or if he is poking
me. He plays along with the charade. There are no X-rays, only ice
and pills that make my head feel like it's stuffed with cotton. After

the pain has subsided, I am put on a cycle of cervical steroids and must report to the training room twice a day to have my blood pressure monitored.

In a week, I am back on the field, and everything falls into place. My legs move and my body goes where it's directed, but the pain won't go away. I imagine a rotten spot in my spine, a cancer I want to cut out. My body learns to hit all over again, making small adjustments in some vain hope that the injury will go away and with it the nerve pain that seems to lurk after every collision.

Instead the pain gets worse, and most nights I'm back in the training room with the other gimps, begging for ice and more pills that I hope will somehow allow me to hit again. Nobody questions the toughness of the guys who are hauled off the field with their knees turned inside out or the players who are knocked cold and can't so much as wiggle a toe. But I look healthy. There is no blood, no bone poking through skin, no body cast, no evidence that I am injured. I can walk and talk and smile, and in the eyes of the team the real problem is that I can't stand the pain.

I go another month, practicing when my neck will allow, sitting the sideline when it won't. Finally, I'm referred to a neurologist. This time there are tests: X-rays, CAT scans, an MRI, and an EMG. When a nurse pumps two needles into each of my arms, telling me my mouth will taste like I have a spoon in it and that I'll feel nauseous, I smile, happy to have the pain and the sickness so controlled.

As I stare into the fluorescent lights with the taste of metal in my mouth, I know that something in my body has given out, that I somehow deserve this for not wanting to be a fella.

When the tests are over, I am not allowed to see the results. "We'll have them sent to the team doctor," the technician tells me.

"Am I O.K.?" I ask, wanting this guy in a white smock with his needles and nurses to tell me that I'm all right — that I'll have my body back. But I know that I'd only throw it away again, out on the field, to prove that I am one of them.

Instead, there are other tests, more pills, and a neck brace. I start going to the parties, watching the fellas go about their fun, envious of what their play and performance has earned them. To prove to the fellas and myself that I still matter, I get drunk, head-butt walls, and stick needles into my numb hands, despite rational thoughts that tell me what I am doing is stupid. I am careful to inflict this abuse only on myself, to show them that the injury they can't see is real and I can stand even more pain than they can imagine. So I let someone push a stapler into my biceps over and over until my shirt turns red, and for a few precious minutes the fellas pay attention to me — one even shakes his head and calls me a "sick dog motherfucker." And I'm proud. The pain leaves, and my body feels like it used to — large, powerful, and capable of great things.

Then there is the morning, the staples still scabbed into my arms, the cigarette burns on the backs of my hands. But worst of all, there is the silent crunching in my neck and the dead feeling in my fingers. I stand in front of the mirror, staring at the smooth outline of my neck muscles, the slope of my shoulders. I know one thing: I no longer want to play football the way the best of them do — dying between whistles as if you are born to it and there is no other option. Still, when I'm called into the head coach's office and told that I can no longer play, I walk out of the room despising my neck, my body, and the fact that it will no longer have the opportunity to hit another man.

Some guys go through life feeding the athlete inside with weekend-warrior games of touch football, season tickets, tailgate parties, and war stories about what it was like to play. Athletes don't, as they say, die twice; instead, part of them remains 19 years old forever, with the body ready and willing to prove itself all over again. I had to kill that 19-year-old, the one who enjoyed being able to prove himself to the world with sheer brute force: hitting, taking, and not thinking.

After college I headed for Alaska to get away from football. I became a frame carpenter and spent my days pounding nails and lifting twenty-foot sections of wall until my back and neck shivered with pain and my arms went numb. Every time I went home sore, bruised and full of splinters, it felt good — punishment for failing at football and at being a fella. Work helped to kill the jock in me. Falling off buildings and being crushed by two-by-fours dropped by stoned Hi-Lo operators finished what football had started. There were days and even weeks when I couldn't pull myself out of bed. And I liked it, because for once I could see the end — somewhere, sometime I would no longer be able to use my body, and what would be left would be the guy who loved reading and talking about books.

Later I would work as a bouncer, a bartender, a grunt laborer, a truck dispatcher, and a handyman. When I needed money, I rented out my body to schizophrenia-drug-testing programs at a VA hospital. The drugs left me with waking aural and visual hallucinations for days. I thought I was Miles Davis and that I could hear ants crawling in the grass. There were other tests with needles and electric current and more drugs. I didn't care. I got paid for all of it and never once questioned why I wanted to do this to myself. But somewhere along the line, the jock in me died.

Now I'm a guy who used to play. I rise out of bed each morning to a symphony of cracks and crunches. I have pain from football injuries I don't remember. My shoulders still slop around in their sockets if I don't sleep in exactly the same position every night. Sometimes my neck and back lock up without warning, and I fall, and I'm reminded that I did bad things for football and it did bad things to me. It left me with this clear-cut of a body, a burned-out village that I sacked for a sport.

TAD FRIEND

"Uno...Dos...Tres... Urrrrnggghhh!"

FROM OUTSIDE

IN A DUSTY PELOTA COURT in the old Basque village of Arcangues, Migueltxo Saralegi squares his shoulders and throws his hands to the sky. Wearing blue shorts with white thigh pads, a leather waistcoat, and two black tummy belts, he cuts a heraldic figure. Saralegi's reach is actually to expand his lungs, but his aspect makes one imagine he's summoning ancient gods.

Now the stone lifter bends over a lead-filled block of granite. Grasping handholds on its far side, he bucks the awkward object onto his padded thighs, his face crimsoning as his lungs explode in a whoosh. The stone weighs 250 kilograms — 550 pounds. Saralegi slides his hands to the stone's base and then jumps back while levering it end over end to his chest. For the third combination in this dance of balanced force — Saralegi should be the hero of every mover who ever schlepped a grand piano — he drives his torso back again and boosts the stone to his left shoulder. He cradles it there, then removes his hands and pirouettes before shrugging the stone onto a foam hassock.

Two hundred tourists give Saralegi a polite golf clap. Rich Germans and Brits sprung from four gleaming buses, they are kitted out in red "Basque" berets and cloth belts, and everyone carries a glass of rum punch. After witnessing dances, a pelota match, and woodcutting, they are in a folkways frame of mind — curious to see more Basque exotica, but emotionally disengaged. Saralegi has a parallel view: he drove two hours into France from Pamplona solely for the money. He gets about four hundred dollars; the tourists get a show. No harm done.

Yet the 29-year-old actually holds the world's stone-lifting record of 326 kilos, or 717 pounds, and in three days he'll attempt a new mark of 327 before an entirely different audience: knowledgeable Basques primed by a daylong "festival of hunting and fishing." To the Basques, these *herri kilorak* — "rural sports," derived from clearing the land and from farming — epitomize their manly culture. Such contests include log-chopping, scything, handling oxen and donkeys in stone-dragging races, running with 200-pound sacks on one's shoulder, tossing hay bales over an elevated rope, and most impressively, the *harrijasotzaile,* or stone lifting. Stone lifting is "no longer a folkloric exhibition, or for circus strongmen," the local *Diario de Navarra* proudly editorializes. "It requires much more strenuous training than a weight lifter['s]." In November and December, when Saralegi bulks up for the following summer's record attempts, he lifts 88,000 pounds *per day.*

To put it in terms that every American can understand, Saralegi's record of 326 kilos is equivalent to hoisting seven supermodels. Indeed, Saralegi calls the record stone La Gorda — the Fat One — as if it were a fleshy but fickle mistress. In cold weather he wraps her in a blanket, and if she refuses to come to his shoulder he mutters, "She didn't want love today." If she balks repeatedly he calls her *culebra!* (snake) and *puta!* (whore).

Now Saralegi rolls out a granite ball that weighs only 220 pounds, and the announcer invites the audience to give it a try. Three men come and strain at the sphere, then slink off to general giggling. No tourist has ever lifted it above the instep of an Italian loafer. Saralegi, who's maintained a fixed expression throughout these indignities, whisks the ball to his shoulder in one pull and whips it around his neck six times. The applause is much more appreciative; their representatives' humbling has given the audience a connection to the feat.

Afterward, as the tourists are herded off to a ghastly "Basque" feast, I try the granite ball myself. By straining till my eyeballs fill with blood I nudge it perhaps six microns. "How much does he think I could lift?" I ask Edurne Percaz, the voluble brunette who works at a Pamplona gym with Saralegi and who is serving as

my translator. (Saralegi, who suffers interviews warily and whose
Spanish has an elementary-school flavor, is happiest conversing in
Euskara, the k-, x-, and z-riddled tongue spoken by one-fourth of
the 2.5 million Basques.) His surprisingly gentle hand envelops my
biceps; next to his 290-pound Clydesdale frame I feel like Ichabod
Crane. "Fifty kilos," he says in Spanish, "but tell him seventy to
make him happy.

"I'm sorry," he adds pityingly, "but we are just stronger. It's the
race." The Basques believe they are Europe's oldest people, having
inhabited the land straddling the Pyrenees since at least 4000 B.C.
They have the world's highest percentage of Rh-negative blood and
claim to be bigger and stronger and braver than any arriviste Ary-
ans, Franks, and Normans, claim to be the world's toughest soldiers
— claim, in fact, to have landed in America before Columbus. "We
do our tasks," Saralegi says. "We have a history with the stones. An
Italian man with the same muscles can't pick up our stones — because he has no reason to."

And with that Saralegi picks up his stones, slides them onto
a handcart, and dollies them up wooden planks into the back of
his beat-up Peugeot van. Then the world's greatest stone lifter takes
a push broom and sweeps up the woodcutter's sawdust, working
steadily with workmanlike strokes until everything is tidy, until the
job is done.

The streets of this Pamplona neighborhood are full of Basques who
are sweaty and cheerful and rather drunk on *kalimotxo,* their digni-
fying name for red wine mixed with Coca-Cola. I am equally sweaty
and cheerful, and just possibly more drunk. A spontaneous festival
has broken out here in Milagrosa: Teenagers thread in and out on
stilts; dancers click fingers and shake leg bells as they sing "Azuri
Beltza"; children parade in pointed hats crowned with feathers,
wearing twin cowbells attached to the backs of their wool doublets.
When they hop in unison the streets ring. A man inside a mechani-
cal bull's body that shoots out sparks chases the children about in a
cloud of smoke and happy screams.

At midnight we pause for dinner at the Sorgintze bar. We've
already hit the Sorgintze four times, acquiring new friends with
each pass. I am surrounded by grinning Saralegi supporters gob-
bling up trenchers of greasy cod and toothsome asparagus. Mean-

while Saralegi, preparing for the record attempt in two days, has already been asleep for three hours at his mother's house in nearby Leitza. In his home village Saralegi can ramble with the dogs and feed the cows and never answer the phone. He can dream tidy dreams. If he raises the stone, he will reward himself only with a gigantic ham sandwich.

"Migueltxo is a champion, a monster," says Josu, shaking his head at such self-denial. "But all Basques can lift 100 kilos — how much can you lift?"

"One hundred kilos at least," I say, made rash by *kalimotxo.*

"I can lift 150 kilos," says Zube. I am astonished: Zube works at the Volkswagen factory, but he is as soft and mild as a tub of sweet butter. "But just now I have a bad back," he admits, having caught my eye.

"Men are always boasting about these sports because they have nothing to do, really," Percaz whispers to me before addressing the table: "Women are the kings of the Basque household, and men are the kings of nothing." All the men groan and roll their eyes.

About 2 A.M. the kings of nothing lead us down the street to an outdoor concert for Basque independence. The black eagle of freedom flutters on yellow pennants, and the square is thronged with *jarrai,* the radical young separatists who last year rampaged through the city of Bilbao, burning banks and buses. The women have brightly hennaed hair, the men a punk look: shaved heads with rattails, piratical earrings, and Che and *Amnistía!* T-shirts.

Some 500 of the older colleagues of the *jarrai,* the Marxist-Leninist Euskadi Ta Askatasuna, are in prison. A terrorist group whose name means "Basque Homeland and Liberty," the ETA has killed more than 800 people since it was founded in 1959 to battle Franco, who seemed intent upon genocidal revenge for the Basques' having opposed him in the Spanish Civil War. First Franco's German allies bombed defenseless Guernica in 1937; later Franco exiled 200,000 Basques, put 100,000 in prison, and outlawed the Basque language.

But when I ask about the ETA, everyone frowns. Their extremism is out of favor now that their pressure has led to limited self-determination: today the Basques have their own schools, television, and police force. Zube gestures to the crowd, as if to say that tonight everyone just wants to drink and throb around. "That is the stereotype Americans have," says Percaz, "that we all shoot people. And your other stupidity is about running the bulls at San Fermin."

Pamplona's eight-day Fiesta de San Fermin, beginning every July 6, was first made traveler's legend by Ernest Hemingway in *The Sun Also Rises*. Hemingway described an unlucky runner being gored to death, and nearly every year nowadays, as the men flee the rampaging bulls in the daily race through the streets, a drunk American stumbles, forgets to hurl his rolled-up newspaper aside — bulls charge at movement — and gets himself ripped a new one.

Handing me another scarlet drink, Percaz explains that for the Basques, this chase down slick flagstones is a way to triumph over death, to feel life coursing through your veins. "You have to grow up watching it to truly understand. That man trains all year long to run the bulls," she says, pointing to a slight, potbellied gentleman, whose training protocol seems to be chugging *patxaran* liqueur until it dribbles down his chin.

"I could run the bulls as well as that guy," I say. "And next year I will." This is the *kalimotxo* working its ruination, yet my brainstorm seems fiendishly plausible. I will run every morning of the fiesta, hoping to survive till the somewhat easier *encierro,* the *encierro de la villavesa:* all the bulls are dead, so the proud warriors lope in front of a bus.

"*You* can't run the bulls," Percaz says, tossing her hair. "Not really."

"Anyone can *run,*" I say.

"You don't understand anything," she says. "Nothing. And tell me this while we are speaking of Americans who have no good ideas in their head: why don't you have topless bathing?"

I mumble something about our Puritan forebears. "Here I can kiss my friends on the lips in public," she interrupts.

"But not with the tongue," I counter.

"Yes," she says. "Sure, why not? You are 150 years behind us sexually."

"Maybe in public," I say, hazily trying to mount a defense of American debauchery. "But in private we are tremendous bedroom athletes."

"No," Percaz says decidedly. "No, I have been to America."

The next afternoon we drive to Lumbier for a village sports festival. Beside the road an occasional red-tile-roofed village shoots up from the swaths of green wheat and then is gone. They are somehow dustier and more insular than other Spanish villages, and more helter-skelter than French Basque villages. Poplars line the river course and hills crowd in, unsettling the eye like a bunched-up quilt on an unmade bed.

In Lumbier we are nearly bowled over by a parade of 15-foot-high papier-mâché "giants," including Ferdinand and Isabella. We follow a huge, sad Don Quixote through the stone valleys to the square. (Quixote was far too inept to be a Basque, but he makes a splendid costume.) Every Basque town has an annual festival, seizing any reason to party: honoring the Virgin Mary, celebrating fishwives, or simply seeing who can pull the head off of a greased goose. Lumbier's festival, for instance, is to celebrate expatriates from the Navarra province, none of whom seem to be here.

Yet in the square the presentation of rural sports has attracted perhaps five hundred people. First is the *sokatira,* the tug of war, which the Basques claim to have invented. Then comes the *aizkolaris,* in which two men race to chop through a succession of wide beech logs, teetering atop them with their axes flashing in the hot sun.

Then a special exhibition: Nartxi Saralegi, Migueltxo's 37-year-old brother, places his 6-year-old son, Ruben, atop a small log and hands him a George-Washington-and-the-cherry-tree-size ax. Nartxi points to a spot on the log, and the boy makes the first cut. Nartxi touches another spot, lower down. And so it continues for hundreds of tiny blows, including one that narrowly misses Ruben's toes as he slips off the log. When the beech finally splits, the applause is warm and generous.

Finally the announcer introduces Iñaki Perurena, a butcher from the Saralegis' home village of Leitza and a legendary stone lifter: he raised the single-lift record from 250 kilos all the way to 318 and still holds records for lifting 267 kilos with one hand and for revolving the 100-kilo stone around his neck 36 times in a minute. Perurena is 40 now, his gingery hair and beard thinning. He is a little chubby, perhaps, and his brow shines with sweat. But he takes the microphone eagerly: "Friends, thanks for gathering to see our countrymen's work made sport. I am happy to see so many of you here, because it means we will never lose the traditions. And it is our traditions, special to us alone, that make us who we are." He stretches his hands to the sky, pauses dramatically, and then runs to the 200-kilo stone with the quick steps of a lover.

As he lifts it four times to gathering applause, I talk with Nartxi Saralegi, who holds his son tenderly but looks a trifle grim. The Basques love Perurena's gusto and still consider him the sport's eminence, though Migueltxo topped his single-lift record four years ago and has raised it six times since. "Perurena is a showman," Nartxi says, "grabbing the microphone though there is already an announcer. I only wish they were the same age, just once, so everyone would see that Migueltxo is *better*. Still," he acknowledges, "Migueltxo would never be able to make that speech." Migueltxo is like Ferdinand the Bull, possessing none of the I'm-the-man braggadocio required to cross over from athlete to cultural (and advertising) phenomenon. "I try and try to get him to talk, to gesture to the crowd," Nartxi says, "but I cannot even get him to tell *me* about his feelings."

Ten years ago Nartxi, a Navarra champion in woodcutting but never world-class, saw his youngest brother's career languishing in Leitza. Migueltxo's only training was lifting the stone, as it had been since age 11, when he spied a 65-kilo stone around the house and found it "a temptation." At 18 he was stuck on the 280-kilo stone. So Nartxi installed Migueltxo in his house in Pamplona, had his wife cook him special fat- and sugar-free lunches and dinners, and built him a training area in his garage, where he would lift stones regularly with Nartxi when he wasn't lifting weights with his trainer. Nartxi became almost a father to Migueltxo, even more so since their father died last year.

"I control everything," Nartxi says simply. "I am sharper, more open-minded, and I have more concentration — many times I have made Migueltxo lift when he is not feeling like it." Nartxi's frustration is evident: to make ends meet, both men must work at the Gymnasio Jolaskide, Migueltxo as a fitness trainer, Nartxi as a receptionist. Nartxi believes he could go much farther in the sport, for he has the mind and passion of a great lifter — but it is Migueltxo who has the body.

That body has been reinforced like a missile silo. I later ask Saralegi's trainer, a slim, bullet-headed man named Jose Luis Tovias, what I would need to do to become a stone lifter. He laughed for a while. "Go to Lourdes," he said at last, ashing a cigarette. "Seriously? Well, first get your weight up to 130 kilos," he suggested, plumping me up 50 kilos, "but by eating only proteins. No hamburgers, no lamb. No alcohol. Then the basic exercise is the squat, because the most important muscles are the quadriceps and the back. Migueltxo does 500 kilos" — 1,100 pounds — "five times in a row." Saralegi also bench-presses 450 pounds and curls 200 pounds. Eight years ago he totaled his car but emerged unscathed. The doctor told him, "Your body was ready for a big shock."

"Migueltxo doesn't have the quick strength in the wrists and the knees to be an Olympic weight lifter," Tovias said. "He has a slower force. But it's mentally more difficult. He has time to think between the three movements, time to feel his body falling apart." Saralegi knows he has only a few more years to make records and hopes to reach at least 330 kilos before his knees give way.

Here in Lumbier comes the hope of the future: Perurena's 13-year-old son, Inaxio, will lift a 90-kilo stone four times. His father hovers nervously as Inaxio makes the sign of the cross and tips the stone back on shaky, coltish legs. Perurena can't resist helping a little on the final lift, so the referee requests a relift. Inaxio staggers under the weight but ultimately raises it, to sustained cheering. Then Perurena lifts 250 kilos four times, huffing and clutching his lower back in between reps so that the audience bends and jerks with him in silent unison, willing the stone up. After the last hoist he spreads his arms in happy exhaustion. "I want to be like my father," Inaxio tells me, his face reverent.

Perurena then comes over to talk, crowding me cheerfully with his elbows and stalking the conversation like a boxer, his blue singlet soaked with sweat: "We are not force men only — we have feelings," he says. "The stone gives me everything. The view of my life always has the stone in the middle of it." He folds Inaxio in a sideways hug. "When he was three I let him start touching the stones — and it's important that he's listening to this interview. It's not just the lifting; it's the life. Lifting and teaching Inaxio to lift are different pages of the same book."

And Saralegi, I ask? "We are very different," he says. "My son should learn from Migueltxo how to train, which I never did so much. But Migueltxo's focus is to hold the record stone — that is his only goal, his only interest in this task of ours. For me, I will do this the rest of my life. Even when I have no hair, when I am as bald as the stone, I will be lifting with pride in my job. And the people will come see me to encourage, and to relish the effort."

Migueltxo Saralegi eyes La Gorda nervously, as if his mistress had picked a fight. Two days ago he added a kilo to it and spray-painted the new number in red: "327 K." He also lifted it in practice. But now he stands on a small platform in the Salburua fields outside Victoria at 5:30 on a hot, still Sunday afternoon with several thousand people watching. It is a strange, jerry-built venue, removed from the rest of the festival happenings. Basque television broadcasts all of Saralegi's record attempts, so the stage bustles with cameras and technicians and is further checkered by five sponsors' banners, including Volkswagen and Kaiku Milk. For the record attempt he'll be paid about $12,000 — enough to buy a new van.

Saralegi rosins the stone's edges as if he were dusting it with diamonds. Incongruous *trikitixa,* Basque accordion ditties, play on the loudspeakers. "We have to be very quiet for the moment of the great deed," the emcee bellows, "quiet like we are in church." Saralegi grimaces — all that silent expectation only increases the pressure. His best friend, a plumber named Ibon, towels Saralegi's red, sweating face.

Nartxi fixes his brother with his fierce green eyes. "You are going to do it," he commands. Migueltxo scuffs at the floor with his special red and white shoes, and Nartxi, who misses nothing, insists, "The floor is not as bad as we thought — you are 100 percent!" In fact the stage is much too bouncy, and its planks are dangerously far apart. After Nartxi checked out the footing yesterday he told Ibon privately, "Migueltxo won't do it."

"It is too hot, and the floor is very bad," the TV announcer intones, and Nartxi whips around, glaring. But Migueltxo's concentration is such that he hears none of this. He turns to stare out the back of the stage into an empty green field, taking huge breaths that echo through the microphone. Two black eagles rise above the field, circling on the convection currents. He mimes the lift to himself, picturing where the stone will touch his body. Beside him Nartxi shadows the movements in tandem, leaning in as if to merge his strength with his brother's.

Then Saralegi turns and begins. He hoicks the weight to his

thighs, his eyelids closing over with the effort. The huge stone seems to be squeezing him. After a steadying pause, he jumps back and pulls it to his chest. This is the lift's crucial maneuver — akin to balancing a plate on a stick with your nose and jumping back to steady it, only the plate is top-heavy and weighs 719 pounds. But Saralegi's heel catches in a crack and his body shivers sideways. Nartxi, miming alongside, has his notional stone shoulder-high, but Migueltxo's stone hovers just out of control in midair. Ibon and Nartxi leap forward, but Migueltxo has already thumped the stone onto the tuffet.

The applause is generous and encouraging, and he gives a scrunchy-faced wave. But he stares angrily at the stone, measuring its edges with his hands. As Ibon wipes his face again, he murmurs, "The floor is a whore." Only once has he nabbed a record on the second try — the first effort saps 20 percent of his energy — but Nartxi doggedly psyches him up: "Breathe, breathe!" Migueltxo braces and heaves, but the stone makes it only halfway off his thighs. He waves again but looks crestfallen.

Nartxi tries to spin the failure. "In a way it's good," he says afterward, "because the people need to see that this is not easy to do, that he requires good conditions." Meanwhile, a Viscayan stone lifter named Zelia is metronomically hoisting a 150-kilo stone, aiming at his own record of 52 lifts in 10 minutes. Zelia has asthma, and by the time he has broken the record with 56 lifts he is utterly out of air and topples sideways into his handlers' arms. The crowd loves it, the drama as much as the record.

But Migueltxo, who hasn't much use for Zelia, remarks that "that record is easier, because the man can always lift the stone. In my record, sometimes the winner is the man, sometimes the stone." Rendered smaller and more loquacious by defeat, he now sits readily for an interview with *Diario de Navarra*. "The first problem is that the stone was very heavy," he explains — a funny line, were his intent not so methodical.

Almost drowning out Migueltxo's plain talk are the hugely amplified announcements of Tom Knapp, an American trapshooter in the neighboring field. Knapp throws two clay targets into the air, shoots one, ejects the cartridge, shoots it, and then shoots the other target. His buttery voice rides over the cheering, announcing "A *muy rápidas* Berelli! And so easy-loading!" It becomes clear that the exhibition is purely an ad for the Berelli rifle. Knapp mentions Berelli thirty times in a minute — "It's like having two Berellis in one — a semiautomatic Berelli and a pump Berelli!" — as he blows balloons and vegetables to smithereens.

Nartxi listens to all this odious persuasion — "I have a new product from Berelli for the ladies of the house only!" — with surprising care, sifting, within his manager's role, for promotional tips. "If Migueltxo were an American it would be the best," he says at last. "He would understand . . ." He gestures delphically, a glyph of love and frustration. "He would understand that part of the job is to sell himself." But Migueltxo pays it no mind at all, only rolling his eyes and waving good-bye as he's ushered off for his urine test.

DAVID FINKEL

Golf's Saving Grace

FROM THE WASHINGTON POST MAGAZINE

THE BALL: SO WHITE. The grass: so emerald. The creek: so turquoise. The trees: so stately. The entire scene: so beautiful. So
genteel. So manicured. So velvety. So perfect.

This is the Masters golf tournament, in mid-April, on a Friday
afternoon. The ball belongs to Tiger Woods, who is standing on the
13th green, about to begin his ascension. He hasn't yet won the
tournament; that won't happen for another two days. He hasn't yet
become mythical; hasn't yet had Oprah say to him that "you are my
hero and America's hero because of the hope that you've inspired
in everybody"; hasn't yet inspired thousands, or is it millions, to be
so hopeful that they rush out and take up golf. He has, to this point,
dropped out of college, won some tournaments, agreed to $60
million in endorsement deals, turned 21, gained some measure of
fame. The fame, however, is nothing compared with what is about
to happen to him, and that begins now as he attempts his next shot.

It is a putt. The ball is 20 feet from the hole. He is in second
place, one shot behind a player from England named Colin Mont-
gomerie, who is well known among golfing fans in Europe, and
well known among golfing fans in the United States, and little
known beyond that. He is another golfer, in other words, white like
most, circling middle age like most, relatively anonymous, seemingly interchangeable. Unlike Tiger. No one on the PGA Tour is
like Tiger. The hole is a par 5, which means an average player will
likely need at least five tries to get the ball 485 yards from tee to
hole. Tiger's first shot was a monstrous drive, so long that his second shot required a mere 8-iron, which put him on the green. Now

he is about to hit shot number three. As he considers it, thousands of people are considering him. They are lining the green and the fairway, and what distinguishes them most is how motionless they remain as he draws the putter back and brings it forward against the ball. Only when the ball begins to roll do they dare move, and only when it closes in on the hole do they begin to make noise, and only when it drops into the cup do they begin to roar. "Let the record show that on Friday, April 11, at 5:31 P.M. Eastern Daylight Time, Tiger Woods takes his first lead ever at the Masters," the TV announcer says to mark the moment, and all of this — the cheering, the announcer's reverence, the image of Tiger smiling, the sense of importance — goes out to TV sets around the world, including, in Washington, that of Luther Johnson, who doesn't bother to glance up from what he is doing.

He is too immersed in a photo album. He is on his couch, in his living room, in a part of the city that may not be the worst, but is far from the best. "See how small he was? See him in that diaper?" he is saying. He is talking about his son Luke. He is looking at pictures taken in 1981, when Luke was 2 years old and first learning to hold a golf club. "There he is, trying to swing that putter," he says. "It was bigger than he was."

He keeps looking at the photos. It's now 5:35. Luke was supposed to be home more than an hour ago. He's 17 now and a senior at Anacostia High School. "See the swing he had then?" his father says, looking at a picture of Luke when he was 10. "It was a pretty swing." He looks at another picture: Luke holding a trophy, his first. He looks at a picture of Luke when he was 5 and swinging a club that his father had cut down in size, almost in half, to fit him. He looks at another picture: Luke as a toddler, in the living room, putting balls across the beige carpet toward a cup in a far corner. "See, he was a little teeny-weeny dude," says Luther, who closes the photo album and stands up to put it back.

The carpet is still beige. The cup is still in the corner. Back when the first pictures were taken it was just the two of them in the house, and that's the way it is still: a father, a son. Now it's nearing 6 P.M., and the son still isn't home, and the father is saying, "You hope that they learn, that if they see something they'll go a different way," explaining why, in a city such as this, in times such as these, he isn't worried that the son is nearly an hour and a half late.

He looks at the TV. There's Tiger. He's widened his lead to three strokes. History is being made in Augusta. In two days, he will walk the final hole in the safe cradle of white state troopers. Meanwhile, here, in an hour, Luke is supposed to be at a tutor's, so he can work on his math skills, so he can improve his SAT scores, so he can go to a college with a golf team, preferably in a place so warm he can play all year long, so he might one day be good enough to become a professional.

Like Tiger. Who also began playing when he was in diapers.

Except that Tiger grew up in the suburbs, and Luke is growing up in the inner city, where golf couldn't be more foreign. Golf is white. This place isn't. Golf is rich. This place isn't that, either. It is working class, to lower class, to poor. It is row houses and projects. It is graffiti. It is gangs. It is barred windows and doors. It is anything but genteel, manicured, and velvety.

Tiger is supposed to be changing that. Tiger, it is believed, is going to bring golf, at long last, into places such as this.

In one household, though, where a father waits patiently for his son, it is already here. It runs deep. It defines their relationship. It is their bond. It has brought sadness as well as hope. It exists in ways that make Tiger Woods seem not only mythical, but real.

There have been four watershed moments in golf, says John Morris, vice president of communications for the PGA Tour.

The first was in 1913 when the U.S. Open was won by Francis Ouimet, an amateur. "That put golf on the front pages of newspapers not only across the United States but all over the world," he says. "So that was huge." The second: "Bobby Jones winning the Grand Slam in 1930," which was so big that there was a ticker tape parade in his honor. "Then in the late '50s, just as a lot of people were getting televisions, Arnold Palmer came out hitching his pants and attacking greens. He was a perfect television guy, absolutely charismatic . . . And then the fourth one is what we see now with Tiger Woods."

Those are the four. No Nicklaus. No Watson. No Snead. No Nelson. No Hogan. No Sarazen. No Vardon. Great, all, even legendary. But not transforming.

"It seems strange to put a 21-year-old in that category," Morris acknowledges, "but it's the only way to measure his impact."

Which means, then, that golf's fourth big moment is at hand.

In the coming week, the U.S. Open will be played at Congressional Country Club in Bethesda. Tiger is expected here, as is every other prominent golfer in the world, who, like it or not, finds himself a backdrop to this moment. No matter who wins this week, that's the way it is. The moment is Tiger's, the tournament is his to lose. Like the Masters, it is a huge tournament both in terms of implications and history, a tournament that creates legends. Who can say what would happen if Tiger were to win? People still talk about what happened the last time the tournament was held at Congressional, in 1964, when the winner, Ken Venturi, literally staggered through a famously hot and humid final round with a wet towel draped over his head and a doctor in tow to administer fluids and salt tablets. For winning that year, Venturi received $17,000 out of a total purse of $95,400. This year's purse is $2.6 million, with the winner expected to get in excess of $400,000. So some things about golf have changed. Ken Venturi is now a TV announcer. Now there's Tiger. But some things haven't changed at all.

Look through the 1997 PGA Tour media guide, which includes photographs and short biographies of 150 of the top players on the Tour, and you can't help but notice a certain redundancy. Start with John Adams, the first on the alphabetical list, and what you see is a white man. Now go to the end of the list and there's Fuzzy Zoeller, another white man. Now flip at random to any page in between and chances are you'll see the same: white man, white man, white man. Certainly, within the broad category are subsets of background and outlook, but the overall impression is of privilege and country clubs, and the reality of race on the Tour is that of the 150 players, all are white except for the 123rd player on the list, Vijay Singh, who is of Indian ancestry, and the 149th, who is Tiger.

"I'm a Cablinasian," he said to Oprah. "A Cablinasian," she repeated.

"Ca: Caucasian, bl: black, in: Indian, Asian," he explained of his background mix.

"That's what you call yourself?" she said.

"Yeah," he said.

Combine the percentages how you will; in the inner city it is the African American percentage of Tiger that resonates deepest, distinguishing him as the latest in a short line of touring professionals composed of Charlie Sifford, Ted Rhodes, Lee Elder, Calvin Peete,

Jim Thorpe, and Jim Dent. Maybe there have been a few others, largely forgotten in the margins, such as John Shipley, a man half-black and half-Indian who in 1896 nearly won the second U.S. Open ever played, but at most there have been less than a dozen black professionals among the legions of white ones, which is why John Morris includes Tiger's emergence on his list.

"The impact he's had in broadening the diversity of our audience," he explains — that's Tiger's significance. The true test of impact, though, is less with the person than with the effect: how it filters down from the source, how it's embraced by that audience, and how it reduces distances between places such as Congressional and, twenty or so miles away, Kenilworth Park, where Luther Johnson one day brings Luke.

It is the day after Luke was so late and eventually came home safely, just as his father knew he would. He had stopped to play basketball, that's all. He had seen some friends, one had a ball, they went to a court, they played. That's what it takes for basketball, unlike golf, which involves so much more. Balls by the dozen. Clubs. Shoes. A glove. This. That. And space, lots of space, which is why, so many afternoons, they come to this park along the Anacostia River.

It used to be a landfill. Then came a layer of dirt. Then came an attempt at grass. Then came weeds. Now it's a place to practice. Luke arrived home from school this day in baggy pants and a way-too-big shirt and black boots with the tongues folded forward, and his father told him to put on athletic shoes, and Luke did as he was told, and here they are, by themselves in this vast, empty bit of moonscape.

Luther reaches into the car trunk, grabs an old broom handle with a piece of cloth attached to one end of it, marches off about a hundred yards, and plants it in the ground. That's the flag. Luke, meanwhile, takes out a few clubs and a gym bag filled with old balls, scatters the balls among the weeds and begins to hit them toward the broomstick.

"Attack that ball," his father says, watching the first one go up in the air and fade a little to the right.

Wordlessly, Luke tries again.

"Nope," Luther says, watching the second.

"Nope," he says, watching the third.

"Let your shoulders do it. Keep your club going at that target," he says, watching the fourth.

In fact they are all beautifully hit. The swing is smooth. The balls go high, drop gently, land close. But that's not what the father says.

"Don't dip," he says. "Hit down. Like you're going to kill a worm."

"Keep it compact!"

"Stand up some more!"

"Better. But you're still fighting it a bit."

This is how it goes until Luke hits all the balls, fifty or so, and how it goes after he and his father pluck them from the weeds and Luke starts hitting them again.

"It's simple," Luther says at one point, shaking his head because Luke's big, beautiful shots keep fading. "All you have to do is follow instructions."

"Act as if there's a pond in front of that stick," he says at another point. "You gotta carry that pond."

Luke swings.

Luther winces. "You're in the pond," he says.

"There ain't no pond," Luke says back.

They've been doing this for years. A father, a son. The balls are old, but they're also clean because the father scrubs them in the utility sink while the son is at school. He puts new grips on the son's clubs to accommodate a young man's growing hands. He spends $118 on the son's shoes because a golfer needs good shoes. He says to the son as they hunt for balls in the weeds, "Hey, man, you hit 'em, you should know where they are, I ain't your damn hound dog," but he keeps searching even after the son stops because he wants the son to hit them again, to be better than he is, in every way.

The father is 66 years old. Luke is his fourth child. The other three are long grown, long gone. Somewhere in the area is Luke's mother, whom Luke sees from time to time, but it became obvious early on that Luther would be the one to take on the day-to-day responsibility of Luke, and that's what he has done for the last fifteen years. "I was determined that I was going to take care of this one," is what Luther says about that. "I ran the streets so much, I decided, well, I'll just devote myself to him." So he wasn't an angel, but for his son he has tried to become one. He cooks Luke breakfast. He drives Luke to school. He picks Luke up. He cooks Luke dinner. He is busy trying to get Luke into college: the dining room table is covered with college guides, with applications, with financial aid forms, with catalogs, with scribblings, with lists. And in between everything is golf.

"He's obsessed," says Luke, not meaning anything bad by this, just stating fact.

Luke isn't obsessed. Not yet. He merely loves golf. He shoots in the low 80s at the beginning of summer and the high 70s by the end of summer, and he suspects he could be much better if he played more. As does his father. "If I could take you somewhere where there's nothing but trees and golf courses," he says to Luke one day, not so much dreamily as regretfully. "You can't do it in the city. You just can't do it in the city." Which Luther knows because he couldn't do it in the city, either. He, too, grew up here, not far from where he lives now. He began playing when he was a teenager. First he caddied, then he began going onto the course with the other caddies when they were allowed to play a few holes in the brief minutes between twilight and darkness, then he began playing a lot on the so-so city courses rather than the great suburban courses, then he went into the service and stopped playing entirely, then in his thirties he began playing again. He was good. Often he shot par. Sometimes he broke par. But by then it was too late to do anything more with this than be a golfer who wasn't quite great, who kept playing anyway, who now is a retiree with a modest government pension, with a house that is paid for, with enough of his game left to shoot consistently in the mid-70s, with Luke. They play as much as Luke can afford in time and Luther can afford in money. "At least two thousand dollars a year," is what Luther imagines he spends. In summer, their best time, they might play almost every day of the week, but always in the afternoon when it's cheapest, and rarely on Saturdays when it's more expensive, and never on Sundays when there's church.

Church, in fact, is what caused Luther to miss the last round of the Masters. They began going last year after the unsteadying experience of attending a funeral for one of Luke's classmates, and now they go consistently. By the time Tiger was closing in on the final holes, Luke was home, watching on TV and every so often swinging a 6-iron. The living room ceiling is only eight feet high, but Luke's swing is compact enough and predictable enough that he can bring the club back all the way without scarring the plaster, and the carpet is good enough that it won't fly apart when he brings the club down. Bam! Beautiful swing. Bam! Beautiful. Luther, meanwhile, was still at church at an afternoon function, so Luke slipped a videotape in the VCR, and now, a few days later, they are watching the final hole of the tournament together.

Here comes Tiger to the 18th tee. He is so far ahead at this point, the TV announcers are saying things like, "a virtuoso performance like Augusta has never seen." The only question left is whether he will break the record for the biggest margin of victory ever.

Luther is on the couch. Luke is standing, eating Cheez Doodles. Tiger swings. He is great off the tee, huge off the tee: longer than anyone, straighter than string. But this ball twists immediately and severely to the left.

"Wait a minute. What happened?" says the announcer. "A comprehensive hook."

"That looks like me," Luke says.

"He's cussing," says Luther, watching Tiger, who has whipped around and seems to be saying something to someone in the crowd. "Somebody snapped a camera." Second shot: Tiger is smiling now, even though he is as far left as any player has been off the 18th tee, at least as far as Luther can remember, and he remembers everything about these tournaments, even that a player named Ian Woosnam was almost this far left a few years back. He videotapes the tournaments. He watches them, often at night, analyzing swings, playing and replaying them so he can tell Luke what to do without having to invest money he doesn't have in lessons. Tiger swings, and the ball drops cleanly onto the back of the green.

Third shot: a putt. Too firm. The ball slides past the cup and keeps rolling.

Fourth shot: if Tiger makes this, he breaks the record, and of course he makes it, and the record is his, and the moment is his, and all of golf is his, and now he pumps his fist, and now he walks from the green toward his parents, and now he wraps his arms around his father.

Luke, at this point, has grabbed an iron and is practicing his swing.

And Luther is watching the scene on the TV: Tiger holding on to his father, crying, holding on tighter, holding on and holding on, then after a time going to his mother. "Dad first," he points out.

"I promised myself when Tiger was 2 that I would make two contributions to his golf game: course management and mental toughness, the latter an outgrowth of my upbringing and my years as a Green Beret . . ." Earl Woods, Tiger's father, writes in his book *Training a Tiger.* "So I pulled every nasty, dirty, obnoxious trick on him week after week. I dropped a bag of clubs at impact of his swing. I imitated a crow while he was stroking a putt. When he was about ready to hit a shot, I would toss a ball right in front of his, and it would cross his line of vision. I would make sure I stood in his line of sight and would move just as he was about to execute the shot. I would cough as he was taking the club back. I would say, 'Don't hit it in the water.' Those were the nice things I did. In other words, I played with his mind . . ."

And here Tiger is, nineteen years later, mentally tough, battle ready, golf's Green Beret, about to tee off at a tournament in Florida called the Players Championship. It is another important tournament, though not quite as important as the Masters or U.S. Open. It is a tournament Tiger won't win, not this year anyway, but he is nonetheless the player the fans want most to see. "Oh, God," says a woman in the crowd, watching as he approaches the first tee. It is not adoration in her voice but amazement, caused by the spectacle of Tiger being escorted by ten tournament marshals and an armed sheriff's deputy. It is a phalanx. It is something no other player has. Tiger is in the middle, the deputy follows, and the marshals are split into two lines on each side of him, each side with a stretched-out length of thick rope. They move when he moves. They stop when he stops. In this way he will travel the course.

This is what a father has helped create.

"On the tee, from Orlando, Florida, Tiger Woods," says the tournament volunteer whose job is to announce each player's arrival, followed by:

Cheers.

Quiet.

Stillness.

Smack! Away flies the ball.

"Holy cow."

Farther and farther.

"Jesus Christ."

Flying and flying.

"Tiger!"

"You're the man!"

Off goes the man, off goes his movable barrier, off goes most of the crowd. It is a huge crowd that follows him, including three representatives of Nike, one whose entire job is to be with Tiger at all times, and also a man named Anthony Searcy, a black man, a black man who is 27 years old and married and earns $40,000 a year, a black man who lives on a cul-de-sac in a 1,825-square-foot house with four bedrooms and two baths and a two-car garage, a black man who began playing golf three years ago and now plays twice a week and spends perhaps $3,000 a year on golf course fees and $12.50 a month on gloves and $100 whenever he needs new shoes and who knows how much per year on the balls he likes that go for $27.99 a dozen, a black man who says that when he is paired up with white golfers their reaction is often: "'Here comes another one coming out to try' and they don't shut their mouths until you crush one off the tee," a black man who paid $110 for tickets and $8 for Cokes and $1 for a Snickers bar to spend much of the week watching Tiger Woods. "I don't know," he says, trying to pinpoint why Tiger is so inspiring to African Americans. "He's *pseudo* like you. He's *kind of* like you. He's close enough that I can identify with this guy. He doesn't quite look like me, he doesn't quite talk like me, but he's close. He's close enough."

Off goes Tiger, off goes Anthony, and in another part of the golf course, in the clubhouse, past the security guard, up the stairs and inside the Commissioner's Hospitality Suite, Tim Finchem, the commissioner of the PGA Tour, couldn't seem more pleased. This is what he has been hoping for, the occasion of golf's expansion past the moneyed white male into the great big world beyond. The world of the less moneyed, for instance. And women. "And hopefully, if we can stimulate more interest and access to the game, and generate more minorities playing the game at this level, [we can] push the demographic into the minorities," he says. He is speaking loudly over the sounds of forks scraping plates. It is lunchtime in the Hospitality Suite: a Mexican buffet for one hundred or so close friends of the Tour. "We're working on the business plan now," he continues. "We'll have it done late summer. We're going to go out and start getting funding put together in the fall." Maybe it will take three years, he says, maybe five, but eventually golf will be in all the places it has historically shied from, including the inner city.

The inner city, in fact, is the area that Finchem seems consumed by the most. Around him the sounds of eating and laughing continue, but he is talking about working with cities, working with school systems, working with charitable organizations, working with private corporations, soliciting donations, obtaining titles to abandoned urban patches and building whatever might fit: a 9-hole course, a 3-hole course, a 1-hole course, a driving range. Part of the motivation is business, he says — the more interest there is in golf, the more money there will be for the Tour — but another part, he says, comes from a sense of "social responsibility" because golf is "wonderful," golf is inspiring, golf teaches lessons about life, golf is curative. "Because it's the right thing to do," he says about why golf needs to be in the inner city, and he says this so sincerely, and has said it so often, it has begun to trickle down through the various levels of the very white PGA Tour. Down to Charles Zink, for instance, the Tour's chief financial officer, who says, "The other thing to do is to do nothing, and that's clearly not what we want."

Down to Ruffin Beckwith, executive director of an under-construction project called World Golf Village, which will include a charitable arm to help fund Finchem's plan. "I don't know that we're arrogant enough to see ourselves as rescuing" the inner city, he says. "I mean we're not going to go in and solve the problems. We're not going to stop drugs. We're not going to stop crime. But we do think, over time, we can have a significant impact on a lot of young lives."

Down to Chris Smith, director of special projects for the Tour, who, as he drives one day from the Players Championship to a ceremony at World Golf Village, is listing some of golf's noblest qualities. "Sportsmanship," he is saying. "Integrity. If you can expose kids to something this honorable, you like to think it can help society. That if people could play by these rules, things could be better." He drives and drives until, twenty miles south of Jacksonville on I-95, he turns onto International Golf Parkway, which leads into the village. By next year it will be the site of the official golf hall of fame, a hotel, an IMAX theater, some shops, some time-share sites, some home sites, two golf courses, and other golf-related things that might fit into a project called World Golf Village. But at the moment it is a construction site that has been shut down for the day because 1,000 friends of the Tour were invited to see the place, 700 of whom said yes.

There are bagpipes to greet them. There are trolleys to transport them. There is endless food, and endless drink, and an endless assortment of gifts, including commemorative hourglasses, filled with white sand, "to put in your car and measure the length of your cell phone call," says the woman handing them out, and cigars that, according to the man handing them out, would retail for $12 apiece because they are Cuban seed, aged three years in a Dominican wrapper and "specially made for the occasion."

"We gotta talk business," says one man, puffing away on one of them.

"Yeah," says the man he is talking to, also puffing away.

"We gotta talk numbers," the first man goes on.

"Yeah," the second man repeats.

They puff on, talk on, numbers and business, business and numbers. Meanwhile, not far from them, a woman named Nikki is telling people about a chance to buy, for $85 and up, a commemorative brick that will be inscribed with their name and included in a half-mile-long Walk of Champions. "It's a unique gift opportunity to be a part of history," she says, adding: "There will be six gazebos with computer kiosks that will enable you, using a touch screen, to locate your personalized brick, to make a dinner reservation, or to even make a tee time."

Meanwhile, a man in a blue blazer is saying to another man in a blue blazer, "Saw you motor down here in your 740 SL."

Meanwhile, a helicopter lands. It's Arnold Palmer, in from Orlando. And now comes another helicopter: Jack Nicklaus is here as well. As are Sam Snead, who won 81 tournaments in his day, and Gene Sarazen, who won 37, and Byron Nelson, who won 18 in one year, 11 of them in a row. "He's a man of incomparable grace and humility," Ruffin Beckwith says, introducing Nelson to the crowd, and Nelson, an elegant old man now, looks around and says with grace and humility, "Golfers are the greatest people in the world, and I thank you very much."

There is applause. More food. More drink. More business. More bagpipes, and now, as the walkways become crowded with more and more people, the sound of crackling walkie-talkies: "I need somebody to get Mr. Palmer and Mr. Nicklaus in a golf cart and back over to the helicopters," comes an urgent command. "They've got to get out of here."

A cart appears. The crowd parts. The helicopters lift off. The day goes on. There's a lake. In the middle of the lake is an island. In the middle of the island is a flag. A line forms on the shoreline. Someone has brought clubs. Someone has brought balls. Balls, clubs, food, drink, cigars, a lazy afternoon, a little business and an island green: this is golf, the sport that far away from here, out of sight, in another world, Luther and Luke are going out to play.

They go to Langston Golf Course on Benning Road, just west of the Anacostia River. This is the course where Luther caddied as a teenager and where he learned the necessary skill, at least for that time, of playing at night in the uneven light of car headlamps. It is where Luther has brought Luke so often, starting when he was a little boy, that when Luke appears this day everyone has something to say. They ask about school. "He studying?" asks a man named Biggie. "He says he is," says Luther. They ask about college. "Where I want to send him is Jackson State," says Luther. "It's Walter Payton's brother, that's the coach. I called him. I explained to him that Luke got 780 on the SAT. He said, 'Well he needs an 820 to play.' I said, 'Well, I'm going to send him down, and if possible he can practice with the team his freshman year, and he can play his sophomore year,' and he said, 'No, man, I want him to play his freshman year.'" They ask whether this is the day the son will beat the pants off the father.

"Put that long ball on him," a man tells Luke as he walks by.

"No mercy," Luke says.

They go into the clubhouse, which has a bathroom with a sink that has no plumbing attached to it. "I want something," Luke says, heading for the snack bar.

"Hot dog," says Luther.

"Cheeseburger," says Luke.

"Hot dog's cheaper," says Luther.

They go outside, past the pay phone that is covered with all kinds of scribbled phone numbers and messages that aren't likely to show up in World Golf Village anytime soon. "Drugs — call Lonnie Jr. — on Ely Pl." "Glock 9mm for sale." They walk past the plaque that says the course is on the National Park Service's National Register of Historic Places, and they make their way to the tee. When the course first opened in 1939 as a place for blacks, and only blacks, to play, it seemed on the edge of civilization. No more. Now it is a true inner-city course. RFK Stadium is just to the south, the Metro arches over the southern edge of the 10th hole, and a housing project is just beyond the third green. For a while, kids were coming out of the woods along the third fairway, harassing people, stealing balls. There is a chain-link fence along the back of the green, and every morning the grounds crew spends time gathering up whatever trash is tossed over the fence during the night.

Luther hits first. They are starting today on the 10th tee. He watches his ball sail over Kingman Lake, which is an extension of the river, and come to rest against a construction fence that separates the fairway from the driving range, which is under construction, which was supposed to be finished in early spring, which is nowhere close to being finished, which is why Luther and Luke so often go to Kenilworth Park.

Luke hits second. He draws back his club, and Luther doesn't toss a ball at him, doesn't drop a bag of clubs, doesn't imitate a crow, doesn't stand in his line of sight, doesn't move, doesn't cough, doesn't say, "Don't hit it in the water." He lets his son hit, watches the ball fly over the dirty lake, watches it drop onto the patchy fairway, mumbles something about popping it up, and off the two of them go, past the subway tracks and into an afternoon of golf.

On one hole, Luke puts his hand on his father's shoulder and says to him rather tenderly, "I ain't gonna let you beat me."

On another hole, when Luke is out of earshot, looking for a ball that has gone into the left rough, Luther says, just as tenderly, "After he makes enough mistakes, he'll learn," and then hollers so Luke can hear: "You gotta practice. Practice, practice, practice! Tiger Woods practices before he plays, while he plays, after he's done. The rest of them do, too."

Luke, he calls his son, as well as Lucas, Baby, Babe.

On another hole, when it's clear that Luther will indeed win this day, although not by much, he takes in the setting sun, the long shadows, the other golfers moving around the other fairways, and says, "Look around. There's no other kid out here."

And there isn't. Just Luke. Once, there were others. The city had an active program for young golfers. Luke was in that, and then he joined a golf team that played at a course in Prince George's County, and then he joined the team at Anacostia High School when the coach, a man named Bill Chain, got wind of how good Luke was and persuaded him to enroll there rather than in his neighborhood school. It was something Luke was easily persuaded to do. There was another good golfer on the team, a young man named Donald Brinkley, and Luke was glad to have someone to play with who was his age, and his color, and near his skill level, and whose home wasn't in the suburbs, and who loved golf as he did.

But in the city, things happen, and one day, when Donald Brinkley was 16, he died.

By that time, the city golf program had fizzled out. As had the team that played in Prince George's County because the other players, all older than Luke, not better, just older, graduated from high school and no one was around to replace them. Now it was January 1996, a Sunday, the Sunday the blizzard began, and one of Donald's other friends stopped by his apartment and asked if he wanted to walk down the street to the store. The apartment is deep in Southeast, in a housing project called Benning Terrace. It has long been a troubled area, and Donald had been well on his way to becoming a reflection of that until, when he was 13, he met Bill Chain, who took him under his wing, taught him golf, taught him things about life, took him in many ways into his own family, settled Donald down. Just that bit of attention seemed to have transformed Donald into someone who "ate, slept, talked golf," Bill Chain would say later, but on a snowy day in the dead of winter, when golf is far away, there are only so many things to do. So Donald walked to the store with his friend, and not long after that Donald's mother, Gloria, was outside with her husband when, as she describes it, "I heard four or five shots," and said to her husband, "Did you hear that?" and then Donald's friend came running up, gasping for breath, out of control, saying that Donald had been shot. So many months later, she is still not entirely sure what happened. There was a trial. There was testimony that the man who shot Donald did so after hearing his car alarm going off, that he ran outside, saw his car had been broken into, saw some young men, felt threatened, pulled out a gun and began firing. It also became clear at the trial that Donald had nothing to do with this, that he was just there, that's all, just there, and began running when he saw a man with a gun. "He was telling the dude, 'Don't shoot.' He was telling the dude, 'It wasn't me,'" is how Gloria imagines the moments before her son fell down into the snow. He was shot three times: once in the hand, once in the side, once in the back. "See, they hit him in the hand when he raised them and said, 'It's not me,'" she goes on, certain of this, that first came the hand, then the side as he turned, then the back as he ran, but of course all that she knows for sure is what she saw by the time she got there: "He was in the ambulance, and they were pulling off, and we followed them to D.C. General." And then: "They were taking him into the emergency entrance, and they were pumping his heart, and I knew he wasn't alive." And then: she eventually went home, picked up the phone and called Bill Chain, and soon after that Bill Chain called Luke, and soon after that Luke and Luther began going to church, and soon after that Bill Chain left Anacostia High, and soon after that the golf team fell apart, and now, late in the afternoon, Luke is walking along with his father, the one person who is always ready to play, who is saying, "There's nothing prettier than to be on a golf course with the sun setting and the pretty grass and the fresh air."

It's not that Bill Chain disappeared. He simply moved to another school. He had the opportunity to become a guidance counselor. He figured a guidance counselor could help more kids than a golf coach could, and now he is at Malcolm X Elementary School in Southeast, a school where every afternoon twenty students get together to learn about golf from none other than Bill Chain. He no longer has Donald, he is no longer a coach, he no longer is so certain of things, but he continues to believe that golf can be transforming, that "golf is magical," even in a fenced-in area behind the school where he gathers the children. The grass grows in clumps. No matter. There is broken glass on the asphalt and graffiti on the school. No matter. The clubs he hands out are a mishmash of whatever he has been able to pull together over the years, and there aren't enough for everyone, and there are twenty kids and a mere one of him, but never mind any of that. Why complain? Really. Why? There are far better things to do in an hour.

"What do you think I'm here for?" he says to them.

"Teach us golf," they answer in unison.

"You think I'm out here for any other reason?"

"No."

"'Cause I got better things I could be doing with my time, so I don't want any jiving," he says, and with that he gets down to work.

He shows them the necessary motion for a chip shot. "Rock like a baby," he says. He shows them how to grip the club. "Hold it," he says, "like it's a bird." They grab the clubs. They are not holding birds. They attempt chip shots, don't rock like babies, send balls skidding along the ground, start to fidget while waiting for their next turn, start paying attention to other things like the marching band that is also out here practicing, hoist their clubs like drum major batons, begin dancing around. "Good shot . . . great job . . . perfect . . ." Chain says, meanwhile, hopping from one kid to another, and somewhere in the suburban country clubs there may be one-on-one lessons in technique, but here there is a man who doesn't lose his belief in golf's ability to be a catalyst, not even when he tells one boy who won't listen that he has to go home and the boy dissolves into tears. "See you tomorrow. See you tomorrow. I ain't mad. But you got to listen," he says, and as the boy hurries off, angry, crying, he says to the others, "If you're going to play golf, you got to be serious."

There is so much to learn about life, so much that is golf. Sportsmanship. Integrity. Honesty. Courtesy. Discipline. Seriousness. So they get serious, and the next day they are back, all twenty, holding birds, rocking like babies, and when one boy hits the ball well, he says, "They call me young Tiger," and another boy who has watched golf on television boasts, "I saw Tiger," and when another boy hits the ball squarely, Bill Chain says, "You all hear what that sounded like when that club hit that ball? That's what Tiger's sounds like every time," and is that what this is about? Is it all about Tiger?

"I'm Tiger Woods," say a succession of children on a TV commercial. They are serious children. They are beautiful children, white and black and everything else one would find in the nation of Cablinasia. "I'm Tiger Woods," they keep repeating, and maybe it's marketing, but no matter, never mind, because sometimes from marketing comes inspiration, and sometimes from inspiration comes myth, and Tiger, right now, is mythical. Never mind that he's only 21 and that despite years of crow caws and crashing golf bags he will hook the ball at the sound of a camera shutter. He is perfect. He is everywhere. He's at Malcolm X, inspiring twenty children. He's in the Commissioner's Hospitality Suite, inspiring the commissioner. He's at Nike, inspiring $40 million. He's in Augusta, inspiring white troopers. He's on TV. He's in all the papers. There's a bus. It is filled with schoolchildren. It is lost in the back roads of Florida. He's there, too.

The bus is looking for him. It is the day before the Players Championship and he is somewhere ahead, conducting a children's golf clinic with another golfer, Fred Couples, sweet Fred, weird Fred, who just before the clinic told the press that he didn't expect to do that well this week because of some personal problems. "This is like, you know, I guess the best way to say it, I broke up with my girlfriend," is how he put it. So maybe he's a little blue, maybe he'd rather not be here, but golf is honor, and golfers honor commitments, and here he is, right on time, to talk to a couple hundred kids, the same couple hundred who seem to show up at every clinic like this, the kids who will one day be America's new generation of moneyed white males. Except this year there are thousands of kids, of all types, because of Tiger. Tiger. Tiger. Tiger. He hits a ball, and they scream as it flies away. He asks if anyone has a question for him or Couples, and so many are shouted at him that he says, "Hold on, hold on, we're not going to lose control of this, O.K.? We're going to be respectful, O.K.?" and meanwhile, the lost bus of schoolchildren, which is coming from inner-city Jacksonville, has finally arrived, and the driver has been directed to a parking spot a mile away, and the children have walked through one muddy field after another, and here they are, just in time to see Tiger get in a golf cart and be driven away.

The clinic is over. They've missed it. They watch him vanish, and so deep is their disappointment that PGA Tour officials make hasty arrangements to escort them to the driving range so they can meet another golfer, Larry Mize, who has earned $5 million in his career, who won the 1987 Masters by making an unforgettable 140-foot pitch, but who this day is one of the 149 golfers in the Tour media guide who aren't Tiger Woods. Graciously, he does the best he can. He hits some big drives and explains what he does and autographs golf balls, and the kids are appreciative, but after a while they begin to fidget, and then their attention wanders, and then they turn away from Larry Mize and see that behind them is a beautiful, grass-covered hill. And as one of their teachers, Jill Fritz, will say later, "You have to understand, where we are is pretty trashy-looking. Where we are they see the prostitutes every day, the drug dealers, you know." There isn't much grass, she will say, and there aren't any hills, and so it is understandable that the kids run to the top of this hill and roll down it, and the hill is so soft and wonderful that they run up it and roll down again, and now they are laughing, and now they are laughing so hard they are shrieking, and now one of the PGA Tour officials who brought them here is saying into his walkie-talkie, "What a nightmare," but no matter, really, because every time the kids are at the top of the hill they can look around and see, as Jill Fritz will say, "a whole new world for them," the world of Tiger Woods.

So are they Tiger?

And if they are, what about another boy who is rolling down a hill two days later along the 18th fairway, a boy named Nathan Pabst who managed to get Tiger's autograph a few hours after the clinic, when the other kids were on their way home?

"Tiger was coming off the putting green," says Reasa Pabst, Nathan's mother, recounting this, "and he signed my daughter's poster, he said, 'Ladies first,' and then Nathan was in there getting trampled, and Tiger picked him up and said, 'Everybody back,' and he put him down and signed his autograph and said, 'Everybody go,' and it was cute. He was such a gentleman."

Up comes Nathan from the bottom of the hill.

Unlike Fred Couples, she adds.

"Couples," Nathan says. "Jerk."

"He pushed Nathan out of the way," Reasa says. "He was coming off the putting green, and he pushed Nate and another kid, got in a cart and went away."

"I ran after him and called him a jerk," Nathan says.

"And that wasn't nice to do," says Reasa.

"But he was," says Nathan and off he goes, down the hill, while Reasa says, "My husband thinks he was upset because at the clinic Tiger was getting all the attention." Nathan is 9. He lives in a big house across the street from Vijay Singh. He is in third grade. He just got a puppy. He likes to go to the driving range with his father, and his father likes to play golf at a course that costs $120 a round.

Up he comes from the bottom of the hill.

"It feels like baby skin," he says of the wonderful grass.

Down he goes again.

"Nathan. Everybody's watching. Be a gentleman," Reasa calls after him.

Is Nathan Tiger Woods, too?

Is everybody?

Or is there something else at work here, something larger?

"We dropped him off Friday after school," Luther is saying. He and Luke are at home. The TV is tuned to the news. "It snowed all Saturday and Sunday. It was when the big blizzard came through."

"Mr. Chain called us," says Luke.

"It was that night," says Luther.

"It was early the next morning," corrects Luke, who has the unblemished memory of a 17-year-old. He remembers golf shots he hit when he was 8. He remembers how Donald Brinkley would call nearly every night asking him if he wanted to play. He remembers everything about the call from Bill Chain. "He didn't come right out and say it. He said, 'Luke, how you doing?' He said, 'I have some bad news.'"

So this time, instead of to a golf course, a son and his father went to a funeral and listened to a succession of eulogists. "I loved Donald so much," is how Bill Chain began, and when he could talk no longer he was replaced by a man who'd been the leader of a Boy Scout troop that Donald was briefly in, who said that of twenty-nine boys in the troop, twelve had been beaten or shot, and when he was done the minister said, "Our young people live in a difficult and dangerous world, a world filled with fear and loneliness, a world few parents understand," and in the back, Luther and Luke sat in silence, taking it all in, and since then there's been a routine to their lives: church on Sundays and afternoons with each other in between. "When he got on the golf course, it was quiet, it was peaceful, there wasn't no shooting, there wasn't nothing like that," Luke says of what Donald once told him. "And then he'd go back to where he was."

Which of course was just down the street from where they are now, spending a rainy afternoon inside.

On TV comes something about Fuzzy Zoeller, issuing some kind of apology.

"What happened?" Luke asks.

"He said something uncomplimentary about Tiger Woods," Luther says. "Called him a little boy. Said something about the dinner next year at the Masters, about eating fried chicken and greens."

Now comes a report about baseball player Roberto Alomar shaking hands with the umpire whose face he spat in last year.

Followed by a piece on basketball player Allen Iverson saying that just because some people consider him selfish and contemptuous doesn't mean he shouldn't be the National Basketball Association's rookie of the year.

Followed by another piece on something else, but by that point Luther and Luke aren't paying attention. It's just sports, nothing more, and they have other concerns. Dinner. Homework. College applications. Sleep. School. And now, the next day, since the sun is out, an afternoon at Langston, where Luther has been for much of his life, and Luke has been for much of his.

One more round.

Father against son.

"He could be better. He could get better grades. He could study a little harder," the father says on one hole.

"Well, I don't like playing with him too much. It kind of aggravates me most of the time," the son says on another.

"Get that weight off your right side!" the father hollers.

"But he's all right once in a while," the son says. "He brings me out here. He cares enough to try to help me. He pays for greens fees, pays for shoes, pays for clubs, everything I need. If it wasn't for him, I never would have been on a golf course." On they play. In the distance at one point is the unsettling sight of eight police cars racing along Benning Road in search of a young man, 17 years old, Luke's age, who is wanted for the murder of a police officer a few days before. Their sirens fill the air, but only for a moment, and then it is quiet again, and then golf resumes, and then, with the score tied, Luke and Luther come to the final tee.

Luke hits first. A fade. Into the trees. "You dipped. Hit it! Boom! Whistle through," Luther says. He hits his own ball and watches it soar. "I can work with that."

Second shot:

"You need more club," says Luther.

"You don't even know what club I got!" says Luke.

He swings.

"Oh, man," says Luther. "That's ridiculous."

"Dang," says Luke.

Third shot:

Luther lands on the back edge of the green.

Luke lands just short and to the left.

Fourth shot:

Luke rocks like a baby and chips to within four feet of the cup. "Pretty much how I played it," he says.

Luther putts, comes up two inches short, taps in for a five and walks off the green to see what Luke will do next.

And this is what he does:

He ignores yet another police car screaming by on Benning. He ignores the Metro swooshing by overhead. He lines up his putt, draws back his putter, brings it forward, watches the ball roll past the cup and seems momentarily surprised.

Who is Tiger Woods? Is Tiger Woods Luke Johnson?

He missed. He knows that. He has lost. He knows that, too, as surely as he knows that there have been many worse afternoons. He taps in to make it official and gracefully picks up his ball, and then he walks toward his father, who is waiting for his son.

CHARLES P. PIERCE

The Man. *Amen*

FROM GQ

OK. GOLF JOKE.

Jesus Christ and Saint Peter go out to play golf. Saint Peter steps up to the first tee. He's got the sharp designer vines. Even got a brand-new yellow Amana hat. (Amana sewed up a sponsorship deal long before anyone else, and Nike couldn't even get in the door.) Clubheads that gleam in the heavenly light like stars on sticks. Takes out a golden tee. Puts down a fresh Titleist Balata. Smacks it down the fairway for a clean 265, dead center. Ball sits in the green grass like a distant white diamond. Allows himself a little smirk as he steps out of the tee box. Listens carefully to hear if a cock is crowing.

Anyway, Jesus up next. Old robe. Sawdust up to his elbows (somebody needed a coffee table finished that morning). Got a black rock tied to a cane pole. Got a range ball with a red stripe around its middle and a deep slice up one side. Hits the ball with the rock, and it goes straight up in the air. It is plucked away by a passing pileated woodpecker, which flaps off down the fairway toward the green. Stiff head wind blows up. Woodpecker begins to labor. Just over the front fringe of the green, woodpecker suffers a fatal heart attack. Drops the ball onto the back of a passing box turtle. Ball sticks. Turtle carries the ball toward the hole. At the lip of the cup, turtle sneezes.

Ball drops into the hole.

Saint Peter shakes his head.

"You gonna play golf?" he asks Jesus. "Or you gonna fuck around?"

Is this blasphemous?
Is it?
Truly blasphemous?
Truly?
And what would be the blasphemy?
And what would it be?
The punch line? That Saint Peter is said to be using a curse word
as regards his Lord and Savior?
No, ma'am. Sorry. Please consult Matthew 26:73–74.

> And after a little while, they came that stood by, and they said to Peter,
> "Surely, thou art one of them, for even thy speech doth discover thee."
> Then he began to curse and to swear that he knew not the man.
> And immediately the cock crowed.

Peter was forgiven.
And what would be the blasphemy?
And what would it be?
That our Lord and Savior would play golf?
That He would do anything within His admittedly considerable
powers to win?
No ma'am. Sorry. I believe that Jesus would play to win. I would
not want Jesus in a $1,000 Nassau, not even with four shots a side.
I do not like my chances at that. No, ma'am, I do not. I believe
Jesus would take my money. I believe that He would take it and
give it unto the poor, but I believe He would take it. I believe
that Jesus would focus. I believe that His ball would not find the
rough. I believe that there would be sudden windstorms. I believe
that He would find no water, but that if He did, He would walk
out and knock one stiff from the middle of the pond. I believe
that He would go for the stick on every hole. I believe that the
Redeemer cometh and He playeth to win, or else He'd have
wound up as merely one of the foremost carpenters in Nazareth.
I would not want Jesus in a $1,000 Nassau, not even with four shots
a side.
Is this blasphemous?
Is it?
And what would be the blasphemy?
And what would it be?
That there is divinity guiding the game of golf? That the hands of
God are on a steel shaft, the fingers of God overlapped and strong,

and that the hands of God bring the steel shaft up brightly in the heavenly light — but not past parallel; never past parallel — and then down, hard, to smite the sinful modern world?

Is this blasphemous?

Is it?

In the limo, fresh from a terribly wearisome photo shoot that may only help get him laid about 296 times in the next calendar year, if he so chooses, the Redeemer is pondering one of the many mysteries of professional sports.

"What I can't figure out," Tiger Woods asks Vincent, the limo driver, "is why so many good-looking women hang around baseball and basketball. Is it because, you know, people always say that, like, black guys have big dicks?"

Vincent says nothing right off. Vincent is cool. Vincent played college ball at Memphis State under Dana Kirk, and that is like saying that you rode the range with Jesse James or prowled the White House with Gordon Liddy. Straight outlaw street creds, no chaser. Vincent is sharp. Vincent got into computers back when computers meant Univac, and that is like saying you got into navigation when navigation meant Columbus. Vincent is cool and Vincent is sharp, but Vincent is stumped here for an answer.

He and Tiger have already discussed video games. Tiger likes fighting games. He has no patience for virtual skateboarding. "I get fucking pissed when I've got a station and no games to play on it. It's frustrating," Tiger said. He and Tiger have also discussed the various models of Mercedes automobiles. The day before, Tiger won himself a new Mercedes automobile at a golf tournament outside San Diego. But it was such an ordinary, respectable Mercedes that Tiger gave it to his mother. Tiger likes the more formidable model of Mercedes that Ken Griffey Jr. drives. "That is a great fucking car, man," he enthused. Vincent agreed. But then Tiger came up with this question about why all the good-looking women follow baseball and basketball, and he came up with this theory about black men and their big dicks, and Vincent is not ready for the turn that the conversation has taken.

So I step in. It is said to be the case, I begin, trying to give Vincent a moment to regroup, that women follow baseball and basketball closely because those two sports put them in greater proximity to the players.

"What about golf then?" says Tiger, and now I am stumped for an answer.

Vincent finally tells him, "Well, what Mr. Pierce back there says is right, and what you said, well, there's probably some truth to that too. And the other thing is that there is so much money involved in those two sports that that probably has something to do with it, too." Tiger seems very satisfied with the roundness of this answer. He says nothing for a moment. He looks out the window of the limousine, and he watches the failed condominium developments go passing by.

One day earlier, he had won the Mercedes Championships at the La Costa Resort and Spa. La Costa was the place into which the Mob plowed all that money from the Teamsters pension fund. La Costa is now owned by the Japanese. Jimmy Hoffa must be spinning in the Meadowlands. The Mercedes Championships used to be what the PGA Tour called the Tournament of Champions. All things do change. Still, only golfers who have won a tour event during the previous season are eligible to play in this tournament, which annually kicks off the new tour season. In 1996 Tiger qualified for the Mercedes by winning two of the eight tournaments he entered after joining the tour in September.

At La Costa on Saturday, he birdied the last four holes to move into a tie with Tom Lehman, the 1996 PGA Tour player of the year. On Sunday, however, La Costa was drenched by a winter storm out of the Pacific, and it was determined that Lehman and Woods would play a one-hole playoff for the championship, the $296,000 first prize and the brand-new Mercedes. The officials chose the par-3 seventh hole, which ran off an elevated tee down to a green bounded by water on the left side. Hundreds of people scurried down through the rain, a great army moving behind a screen of trees, a bustling little loop of humanity shivering under bright umbrellas.

Lehman hit first. He caught his shot fat. It landed on the far bank and hopped backward into the pond, scattering a flock of American coots. (These were genuine American coots — also called mud hens — and not the other, more visibly affluent American coots, some of whom were lining the fairway.) Now, there was virtually no way for Woods to lose the tournament. He could reverse pivot and line up the clubhouse veranda, and he'd still be better off than poor Lehman, who had to function amid the ragged and distant hosannas of Tiger's partisans cheering Lehman's misfortune. Instead, Woods took out a 7-iron. As he followed through, a raindrop fell in his eye, partly blinding him.

The ball damned near went in the hole.

The crowd — his crowd, always his crowd now — did not cheer. Not at first. Instead, what the crowd did was . . . sag. There was a brief, precious slice of time in which the disbelief was sharp and palpable, even in the pulping winter rain. Then the cheers came, and they did not stop until he'd reached the green. He tapped in for the championship, the check and the car, which he gave to his mother.

"All right, here's what happened," Tiger would explain later. "If I hit it toward the middle of the green and my natural draw takes over, then I should be right at the hole. If I hit the iron shot I'd been hitting all week, which was kind of a weak-ass-shot to the right, then it should hold against the wind and make it dead straight."

"So I turned it over perfect. I finally hit my natural shot."

And how long did all this calculating take?

"A couple of seconds. Of course, if he'd have hit it close, I probably would've been more aggressive."

The next morning — this morning — a limousine picked him up at his mother's house, and it took him to a photo shoot for the magazine cover that is only going to get him laid 296 times in the next year, if he so chooses. He gave the photographer an hour. One single hour. Sixty minutes, flat, in front of the camera. In the studio, which was wedged into a Long Beach alley behind a copy store and next to Andre's Detailing Shop (if you happen to need an Aztec firebird on your hood in a hurry, Andre's your man), Tiger was dressed in very sharp clothes by four lovely women who attended to his every need and who flirted with him at about warp nine. Tiger responded. Tiger told us all some jokes.

This is one of the jokes that Tiger told:

The Little Rascals are at school. The teacher wants them to use various words in sentences. The first word is *love*. Spanky answers, "I love dogs." The second word is *respect*. Alfalfa answers, "I respect how much Spanky loves dogs." The third word is *dictate*. There is a pause in the room. Finally, Buckwheat puts up his hand.

"Hey, Darla," says Buckwheat. "How my dick ta'te?"

He was rolling now. The women were laughing. They were also still flirting. The clothes were sharp, and the photographer was firing away like the last machine gunner at Passchendaele. And Tiger told jokes. Tiger has not been 21 years old for a month yet, and he tells jokes that most 21-year-olds would tell around the keg in the dormitory late on a Saturday night. He tells jokes that a lot of arrested 45-year-olds will tell at the clubhouse bar as the gin begins to soften Saturday afternoon into Saturday evening.

This is one of the jokes that Tiger told:

He puts the tips of his expensive shoes together, and he rubs them up and down against each other. "What's this?" he asks the women, who do not know the answer.

"It's a black guy taking off his condom," Tiger explains.

He tells jokes that are going to become something else entirely when they appear in this magazine because he is not most 21-year-olds, and because he is not going to be a 45-year-old club pro with a nose spidered red and hands palsied with the gin yips in the morning, and because — through his own efforts, the efforts of his father, his management team and his shoe company, and through some of the most bizarre sporting prose ever concocted — he's become the center of a secular cult, the tenets of which hold that something beyond golf is at work here, something that will help redeem golf from its racist past, something that will help redeem America from its racist past, something that will bring a new era of grace and civility upon the land, and something that will, along the way, produce in Tiger Woods the greatest golfer in the history of the planet. It has been stated — flatly, and by people who ought to know better — that the hand of God is working through Tiger Woods in order to make this world a better place for us all.

Is that blasphemous?

Is it?

There is no place in the gospel of the church of Tiger Woods for jokes like this one:

Why do two lesbians always get where they're going faster than two gay guys?

Because the lesbians are always going sixty-nine.

Is that blasphemous?

Is it?

It is an interesting question, one that was made sharper when Tiger looked at me and said, "Hey, you can't write this."

"Too late," I told him, and I was dead serious, but everybody laughed because everybody knows there's no place in the gospel of Tiger for these sorts of jokes. And Tiger gave the photographer his hour, and we were back in the car with Vincent and heading back toward Tiger's mother's house. "Well, what did you think of the shoot?" Tiger asks, yawning, because being ferried by a limousine and being handled by beautiful women and being photographed for a magazine cover that will get him laid 296 times in the next year, if he so chooses, can be very exhausting work. "The key to it," he says, "is to give them a time and to stick to it. If I say I'm there for an hour, I'm there, on time, for an hour. If they ask for more, I say, 'Hell, fuck no.' And I'm out of there."

Hell, fuck no?

Is that blasphemous?

Is it?

And what would the blasphemy be?

And what would it be?

Can he blaspheme against his own public creation, his own unique role, as determined by his father, his management team and his shoe company? Can he blaspheme against the image coddled and nurtured by the paid evangelists of his own gospel?

Hell, fuck no?

And what would the blasphemy be?

And what would it be?

Can he blaspheme against himself?

God willing, he can.

Two days earlier, while Tiger's father was greeting passersby behind the 9th green at La Costa, Tida Woods was following Tiger around the course. She is a small, bustling woman who occasionally is forced to take a little hop in order to see over the spectators in front of her. On the 15th hole, Tiger left his approach shot short of the green.

"Well," Tida said, "Tiger will chip this one in, and we'll go to the next hole."

Tiger chipped the ball, which bounced twice and rolled straight into the cup.

"That boy," said Tida Woods. "I told you he would do that."

She walked on. I stood stunned under a tree for a very long time and wondered about what I had just seen. I think there are pilgrims at Lourdes who look like I did.

This is what I believe about Tiger Woods. These are the articles of my faith.

I believe that he is the best golfer under the age of 30 that there ever has been. I believe that he is going to be the best golfer of any age that there ever has been. I believe that he is going to win more tournaments than Jack Nicklaus won. I believe that he is going to win more major championships than Jack Nicklaus won, and I believe that both of these records are going to stand for Tiger Woods longer than they have stood for Jack Nicklaus. I believe he is going to be rich and famous, and I believe that he is going to bring great joy to a huge number of people because of his enormous talent on the golf course. This is what I believe about Tiger Woods. These are the articles of my faith.

I believe that he is the most charismatic athlete alive today. I believe that his charisma comes as much from the way he plays the game as it does from the way he looks and from what he is supposed to symbolize. I believe that his golf swing — never past parallel — is the most perfect golf swing yet devised. I believe that he is longer off the tee than any good player ever has been, and I believe he is a better player than anyone else longer off the tee. This is what I believe about Tiger Woods. These are the articles of my faith.

I believe that Tiger Woods is as complete a cutthroat as has ever played golf. I do not want Tiger Woods in a $1,000 Nassau, not even with forty shots a side. I believe he would take my money. I believe I would leave the course wearing a barrel. I believe that the shot that won for him at La Costa was not completely about beating Tom Lehman on that afternoon, because Tiger could have used a lemon zester to do that. I believe that shot was for a couple of weeks or a year from now, when Lehman is trying to hold a one-shot lead over Tiger Woods down the stretch in a major tournament. This is what I believe about Tiger Woods. These are the articles of my faith.

This is what I do not believe about Tiger Woods. These are the theses of my heresy.

I do not believe that Tiger Woods was sent to us for any mission other than that of "being a great golfer and a better person," as his father puts it. After all, this is the mission we all have, except for the golf part. (No just and merciful God would demand as the price of salvation that we all learn to hit a 1-iron.) I do not believe that a higher power is working through Tiger Woods and the International Management Group, even though IMG once represented the incumbent pope. I do not believe that a higher power is working through Tiger Woods and the Nike corporation:

Tiger, Tiger, burning bright
Selling shoes for Philip Knight

This is what I do not believe about Tiger Woods. These are the theses of my heresy. I do not believe the following sentence, which appears in one of several unauthorized hagiographies: "I don't think he is a god, but I do believe that he was sent by one." This sentence presumes, first, that there is a God and, second, that He busies himself in the manufacture of professional golfers for the purpose of redeeming the various sinful regions of the world. I do not believe this about Tiger Woods.

I do not believe what was said about Tiger by his father in the issue of *Sports Illustrated* in which Tiger Woods was named the Sportsman of the Year: "*Can't you see the pattern?* Earl Woods asks. *Can't you see the signs?* 'Tiger will do more than any other man in history to change the course of humanity,' Earl says."

I do not believe that Earl Woods knows God's mind. I do not believe that Earl Woods could find God's mind with a pack of bloodhounds and Thomas Aquinas leading the way. I do not believe that God's mind can be found on a golf course as though it were a flock of genuine American coots. I do not believe — right now, this day — that Tiger Woods will change humanity any more than Chuck Berry did. This is what I do not believe about Tiger Woods. These are the theses of my heresy.

Is that blasphemy?

Is it?

In the beginning was the father.

"I said," Earl Woods insisted, "that Tiger had the ability to be one of the biggest influences in history. I didn't say that he would be. I am not in the business of predicting the next Messiah, nor do I feel that Tiger *is* the next Messiah. That's stupid. That's just stupid."

Earl Woods was a tired man. He had walked the back fairways of La Costa, where he was treated by his son's galleries the way that mobsters used to be greeted by the doormen at this place. But he'd forgotten his folding chair, and he'd forgotten his CD player on which he listens to his jazz music while Tiger plays. He was a month away from bypass surgery, and he was beginning to get cranky about it.

"I'm a terrible patient," he said. "I'm one of those people who say, 'I don't want to be here.' And then I make such an ass of myself that people let me go. They don't have any reason to keep me."

The story of Earl and his son is worn nearly smooth by now. How Earl fought in Indochina as a Green Beret alongside a South Vietnamese named Nguyen Phong, whom everyone called Tiger. How Earl returned from the war with a Thai wife name Kultida, and how they had a child whom Tida named Eldrick — "Fathers are just along for the ride on that one," Earl explained — but upon whom Earl insisted on bestowing his old comrade's nickname. How Earl would take the toddler with him when he went to hit golf balls. How the little boy climbed out of the high chair and swiped at the ball himself, showing superlative form. And how everything came from that — the appearance on television with Mike Douglas when Tiger was only 3, the superlative junior amateur career, the three consecutive U.S. Amateur titles, the explosion onto the PGA Tour at the end of last season.

And it was Earl's apparently limitless capacity for metaphysical hooey and sociological bunkum that produced the gospel that has so entranced the world, the golfing press and large conglomerate industries. Separated into its component parts, Earl's gospel is predestination theory heavily marbled with a kind of Darwinist Christianity and leavened with Eastern mysticism. Simply put, the gospel has it that while Earl Woods was wandering through Indochina, a divine plan was put in motion by which Earl would one day have a son who would win a lot of golf tournaments and make a lot of money because it was his karma to do so, and that, through doing this, the son would change the world itself.

"I think that the *SI* article went a little too deep," Tiger muses. "As writers go, you guys try to dig deep into something that is really nothing." Well, perhaps, but Earl certainly said what he said, and Tiger certainly has profited, because the promulgation of Earl's gospel is as much at the heart of Tiger's appeal as is his ability to go long off the tee.

There is a dodgy sense of transition around Tiger now, a feeling that the great plates on which he has built his career have begun to shift. In December, for example, he and his father fired John Merchant, Tiger's longtime attorney. Moreover, there is a sense among the other people on Tiger's management team that Earl has pushed his own celebrity far beyond the limits of discretion, particularly in his comments to *SI* concerning Tiger's place in the world. At La Costa, after Tiger's round on Saturday, his swing coach, Butch Harmon, dropped by the press room to cadge a beer.

"Earl," he said with a huge sigh, "is getting out of control."

This is not something anyone would have dared to say even a year ago.

It is perhaps understandable. By his play and by the shrewd marketing that has surrounded his career almost from the time he could walk, Tiger Woods is now an authentic phenomenon. Golf tournaments in which he plays sell more than twice the number of tickets they would if he did not. With Michael Jordan heading toward eclipse and with no other successor on the horizon, Tiger Woods is going to be the most popular athlete in the world for a very long time. The old support system worked splendidly as he came up through the amateur ranks. But there are unmistakable signs that it has become seriously overtaxed.

Consider, for example, the persistent rumors that Earl and Tida have all but separated. At La Costa, they were not seen together on the course at all. Tida commuted to her new house, while Earl stayed at the resort. (At the time, IMG insisted that any rumors of a split were not true.) There was no evidence in his room that she had been there at all. There was only Earl, alone in the room, suffused with a kind of blue melancholy, an old man now, and tired besides.

"I'll be satisfied if he's just a great person," Earl says. "I don't give a shit about the golf."

Ah, but he does. He has given up a lot for it. He left another wife and three other children. He has devoted his life, a lot of his energy and a great deal of surpassing bullshit to creating something that may now be moving far out of his control. "I'm not worried now," he says. "Obviously, I will not be here to see the final result. I will see enough to know that I've done a good job."

On the first day at La Costa, Tiger was paired with David Ogrin, a veteran tour pro who'd won the previous year's Texas Open, his first victory after 14 years and 405 tournaments. Ogrin is considered one of the tour's most enlightened citizens despite the fact that he looks like a rodeo bouncer and is the owner of one of America's most genuinely red necks. The two of them reached the 9th tee. Tiger had the honors. He absolutely scalded the ball down the center of the fairway, yards beyond anyone else who would play the hole that day.

"Hey," said David Ogrin in awe and wonder. "Eat me."

It was Butch Harmon's time of day. The son of a Masters champion and the brother of three other PGA pros, Harmon was stalking the practice tee at La Costa in the mist of the early morning. He explained how much of Tiger's power comes from his longer musculature — "almost like a track athlete," he said. "Tiger was born with a beautiful natural flow to his swing. It enables him to come through the ball almost like the crack of a whip. Add to that the fact that he was taught well early, because Earl had a real good concept of the golf swing." And then he said something else — something beyond mechanics, but just as important.

"You know, you can get so wrapped up in this game that you have no fun, and as soon as you know it, your career is over and you never had any," he said. "It's a game you can get so serious on that you can't . . . *play.*"

It is the golf that is the sweetest thing about Tiger's story. It is the golf that is free of cant and manufactured import. To the untutored, Tiger Woods is an appealing golfer because he is young and fresh, and because of the distances he can carry with a golf ball. To the purist, he is appealing because his swing is the purest distillation of Everyman's swing. Unlike John Daly, who approaches a golf ball with a club in much the way Mel Gibson approached English infantrymen with a broadsword, Tiger has a swing that is both controlled and clean. "I never go past parallel," he says. "I think people look at me and say, 'That's the way I want to hit the ball.'"

There was resistance to him on the tour at first, because he had come so far so young. But what overcame that was Tiger's manifest hunger to compete. It is not artificial. It is not feigned. It is real and genuine and very formidable. There is a difference between getting up in the morning to win and getting up to *beat* people. Tiger's gospel says that he has more of the first kind of days than he has of the second. The reality is far less clear. He didn't have to go after the pin on Lehman. But he did. "It's nice to know you're out there with somebody whose sole goal isn't to make third on the money list," says Justin Leonard, a gifted young pro.

"I just love to compete," Tiger says. "I don't care if it's golf or Nintendo or in the classroom. I mean, competing against the other students or competing against myself. I know what I'm capable of.

"You know, the prize money, that's the paycheck. That's the money I earned for myself. All the other stuff, my Nike contract and Titleist and now the All Star Cafe, to me, that's a bank account, but it doesn't really make me as happy as what I earn through blood, sweat and tears on the golf course. That money, I have the sole responsibility for earning that. Just me, alone. All the other stuff can depend on how good your agent is."

It's the gospel that has complicated his life. He can commit minor faux pas that become major ones because they run counter to the prefabricated Tiger of the gospel. Soon after he announced he would leave college to turn pro, Nike featured him in a commercial in which he said, "There are still courses in the United States that I am not allowed to play because of the color of my skin," and the world exploded.

The racial aspect of Tiger's gospel has always been the most complex part of it. At first he emphasized his multiracial background — after all, he is as much Thai as he is American, and Earl is an authentic American ethnic stew. At the same time, Tiger and his management team were pushing him as a racial pioneer along the lines of Jackie Robinson, Muhammad Ali and Arthur Ashe, none of whom considered themselves "multiethnic." The Nike commercial pointed up the dissonance of the two messages. One prominent gasbag of a pundit challenged Nike to find a course that Tiger couldn't play.

It was an interesting case study in the practical application of the gospel. In the first place, if you dressed Tiger up in ordinary golf clothes — an outfit, say, without thirty-three Nike swooshes on it —

I'm willing to bet you *could* find a course in this great land of ours that wouldn't let a black man play. However, the gospel insists that Tiger came to heal and not to wound. There is no place in journalism whiter than sports writing, and there is no sports writing whiter than golf writing, and generally it is the received wisdom that to be great any great black athlete must be a figure of conciliation and not division. Witness, for example, the revolting use of Muhammad Ali in this regard, especially now that he can't speak for himself. The imperatives of the gospel held. The spot was pulled.

There is little question that Tiger has brought black fans into the game, and that he is part of a modern continuum that reaches back to Jack Johnson. Johnson was a hero generally among black people not far removed from *Plessy v. Ferguson.* Later, Joe Louis served much the same function, except that Louis was far less threatening to white people and thus had an easier time of it. (It was with Louis that we first saw white people using a black champion to prove to themselves how broad-minded they'd become.) Jackie Robinson was a hero to those black people who came north in the great migration to work in the factories in places like Brooklyn. Arthur Ashe came along at a time when the civil rights movement had begun to create a substantial black middle class. And now that America has begun to wish for the appearance of the great racial conciliator, along comes Tiger Woods.

"The reason is the timing of it," he says. "Other guys, like Charlie Sifford, they didn't get the publicity, because the era was wrong. They came along when prejudice reigned supreme. I came along at the right time."

I believe that Tiger will break the gospel before the gospel breaks him. It constricts and binds his entire life. It leaves him no room for ambiguity, no refuge in simple humanity. Earl and Tida can't break up, because the gospel has made their family into a model for the "unfortunate" broken homes that produce so many other athletes. Tiger can't fire his lawyer, because the gospel portrays him as a decent and caring young man. Tiger can't be an angry black man — not even for show, not even for money — because the gospel paints him as a gifted black man rewarded by a caring white society. Tiger can't even tell dirty jokes, because the gospel has no place for them, and they will become events if someone reports them, because, in telling them, he does it:

He blasphemes against himself.

I believe in what I saw at La Costa, a preternaturally mature young man coming into the full bloom of a staggering talent and enjoying very much nearly every damn minute of it. I watched the young women swoon behind the ropes, and I believe that Tiger noticed them, too. There was one woman dressed in a frilly lace top and wearing a pair of tiger-striped stretch pants that fit as though they were decals. I believe that Tiger noticed this preposterous woman, and I do not believe that she was Mary Magdalene come back to life.

"See her?" said one jaded tour observer. "Last year she was following Greg Norman, and there were sharks on her pants."

It is not the world of the gospel, but it is a world I can believe. Hello, world.

The 17th hole at La Costa is a 569-yard par 5 that the locals call the Monster. Legend had it that no professional had ever reached it in two. Back up in the tee box, Tiger was getting ready to drive the hole. He had birdied the previous two holes, hurling himself at Tom Lehman, who was still leading the tournament by two strokes. As I walked from tee toward green, I noticed a young couple standing alone, far ahead of the mass of the gallery. They had established a distinct position under a gnarled old jutting tree. The tee box was invisible back behind the crook in the dogleg. A few yards in front of the couple, a browned footpath bisected the fairway.

"This," the man explained, "is where John Daly hit it last year."

The roar came up the fairway in a ragged ripple. And I saw the heads swivel all the way back along the fairway, swivel back and then up, back and then up. And then forward, still up. Forward, still up. I found myself caught up in it, and I saw the ball passing overhead, passing the point where the couple had decided to stand, passing the point where John Daly had once hit a golf shot that no longer mattered.

The ball dropped on the other side of the little brown path. The crowd did not cheer, not instantly. The crowd simply . . . sagged. Then they cheered, and the crowd came tumbling after Tiger along the sides of the fairway. He had hit the ball past everyone's expectations.

Tiger had a birdie in his pocket, unless he jerked it over the flock of genuine American coots and dunked it into the designer pond in front of the green. All he had to do was lay it up, pitch the ball close, and sink his short putt. That was the safe play. That was what he should have done.

Tiger took a wood out of his bag.

The gallery erupted.

It has been a long time since any golf gallery cheered someone for removing a club from his bag. The ovation was not about redemption or about inspiration. It was not about the metaphysical maundering of theological dilettantes. It was about courage and risk and athletic daring. Its ultimate source was irrelevant, but I do not believe this golden moment was foreordained by God while Earl Woods was stumbling around Indochina trying not to get his ass shot off. To believe that would be to diminish God.

And that would be the blasphemy.

And that's what it would be.

He needs so little of what is being put upon him. I believe in the 21-year-old who tells dirty jokes and who plays Nintendo games, and only the fighting games at that. I do not believe in the chosen one, the redeemer of golf and of America and of the rest of the world. I hope he plays golf. I hope he fucks around.

I believe he can blaspheme himself. And I hope to God he does.

These are the theses of my heresy.

"Hey, Darla. How my dick ta'te?"

And I hope the jokes will get better.

It was a savage and wonderful choice that he made, the choice of a man who competes and who knows the difference between those days when you want to win and those days when you want to beat people, and who glories in both kinds of days. The choice he made to hit the wood was a choice he made not only for that day but also for a hundred others, when other golfers will be playing him close, and they will remember what he did, and maybe, just maybe, they will jerk it over the coots and into the pond. If that is the hand of God, it is closed then into a fist.

"Because the lesbians always go sixty-nine."

They will get much better.

He took back the club — never past parallel — and it whistled down, and I could hear Butch Harmon talking softly about the crack of the whip. I heard no sound at contact. The ball rose, gleaming, into the soft blue of the sky. Tiger followed the flight of the ball, stone silent but smiling just a bit. The gallery began to stir as the shot easily cleared the pond and rolled up onto the green no one had ever hit in two before. The smile never made it all the way to his eyes.

This is what I believe in, finally. This is the article of my faith. I believe in that one, risky shot, and I believe in the ball, a distant white diamond in the clear heavens, and the voices that rose toward it, washed in its wake, but rising, rising still, far above the profane earth.

I believe in the prayers of the assembled congregation assembled.

"Youthemanyouthemanyouthemanyoutheman."

"God! You the fucking MAN!"

Amen.

BRUCE McCALL

The Case Against Golf

FROM ESQUIRE

No GAME designed to be played with the aid of personal servants by right-handed men who can't even bring along their dogs can be entirely good for the soul. Wait. Let me take a mulligan here (unique in all sports, that, a sleazy little conspiracy to subvert from within the scoring honor system of this self-consciously honorable pastime) and start over.

Here are the first three lines of the first three books celebrating the game of golf — and not even Barbra Streisand celebrates herself as tirelessly as golf celebrates itself — that I happened to flip open while researching this brief:

Years ago I had a crisis in my golfing life. — Fred Shoemaker

The very summer in which I at last, acting on an old suggestion of my genial publisher, settled to the task of collecting my scattered pieces about golf turned out to be an unhappy one for my game.
— John Updike

This book began the way a round of golf begins — with much excitement, good intentions, and aspirations that were, frankly, grandly delusive. — Lee Eisenberg

Defeat, discouragement, disillusion, thy name be golf. And that's the devout speaking.

Bitter? Sure, I'm bitter. Golf was thrust upon me as a lad of 11, conscripted by my short-fused, club-flinging old man to drag his rattling bag, heavy as a rolled-up carpet, through long, hot thirsty afternoons and into languid sundowns, waiting, waiting, waiting outside the 19th hole. But something heroic there is in belting long

fly balls, not to mention probably sexual as well; somehow I overcame both early trauma and left-handedness and sidled into teaching myself the game — God knows Dad wouldn't — as a righty, in
my early twenties. Or the subduffer's version of the game, flailing at
scabby old CroFlites with rented tin clubs on the scorched hardpan
of bring-your-own-scoring-pencil public courses, alongside my shirt-
less, etiquette-challenged peers.

I believed in Natural Golf. Taking lessons somehow would have
seemed like cheating, even if I'd had the money. You don't hire a
hockey tutor, after all, and there are no croquet pros. Surely it
was within the athletic competence of the normal human male to
achieve some modest level of skill at what, after all, came down
to nothing more than a kind of leisurely medieval form of marks-
manship: you aimed to fit tiny balls into slightly less tiny holes in
the landscape by whacking them with various mallets. What you
needed to know about the game, playing would teach. A couple
of buckets of balls at the driving range to seat in the feel of swinging a club, sure; the odd helpful tip from an equally benighted
playmate — but no game with so simple a goal, I naively rea-
soned, could possibly need profound analysis and expert tutelage
to master.

More weekends over the next three decades than I like to admit
even now were squandered in the grip of this pathetic fallacy. Pathetically, season after season, I persevered. Pathetically, I managed
to bury the fact that I didn't know what I was doing out there and
took the great-circle route to success, rationalizing that better clubs
and tonier venues and the ruboff from more skillful partners would
elevate my game. All they elevated was my sense of futility and then
betrayal. How the gods of golf must have snickered as my stroke
count hung up there in the triple digits year after year. Of course,
like every other desperate, deluded chump, I came to twist the
workings of the laws of probability into proof of underlying mastery: that one perfect fluke stroke one morning long ago, right on
the sweet spot, a shot long and true, amid thousands of muffs
and flubs and shanks and hooks before and after — that was the
real golfing me. If I did it once, I could do it again. This pursuit was
the self-torture of the hamster, pumping away on his treadmill in
his cage, going nowhere. Better yet, think hemorrhoids: the more
maddening the symptoms get, the more madly you agitate the
wound, and the more madly you agitate the wound, the more

maddening the symptoms get. By now, my game had hardened into hapless dufferdom.

It's a spanking September day in 1987 on the 12th tee of a lovely course on Long Island. One, two, three drives in succession produce bouncing grounders straight into the rough. The condescending tact of my partners' silence burns as I rummage for the last ball left in my bag. Snap! Suddenly, I'm bone-weary, no longer able or willing to mask my fuming rage and humiliation in the innocuous banter of the good sport. I'm never going to get better.

Faithful acolyte, trusting servant, I'd given myself to golf as a nun gives herself to God, and what had golf given me in return? The finger.

I would wager that there are more sufferers like me — have-nots hacking through grotesque parodies of the golfing life as limned by the misty-eyed haves, tamping down the bile while setting up for the next foredoomed recovery shot — than the golfing world can dream of. But one of the game's many sinister dimensions is that, cultlike, it enmeshes its doubters and would-be defectors in such guilt and fear that they dare not act. It would be letting down the cause, sneaking out on the towering debt piled up by so freely partaking of its bounty, while with every pitiful gesture mocking and disgracing its noble ideals.

Guys, let me help deprogram you, embolden you, and make you free. Savor the case against golf.

Golf Spelled Backwards Is Flog

As in — Flog yourself! Flogging's too good for me! Flog me some more!

What golf develops best is masochism. It can be no accident that this most self-punitive of games was popularized by the Scots, who found a way to flog their miserable, sinning Calvinist selves further by turning even their raw weather and heather-tufted monoscape into a form of self-flagellation the way they'd already done to music with bagpipes and to food with haggis.

In fact, it's easy to see golf not as a game at all but as some

whey-faced, nineteenth-century Presbyterian minister's fever
dream of exorcism achieved through ritual and self-mortification.
Wash thy ball! Cover up thy vile body! Replace yon divot, to profane
not God's works! Rake ye even the humble sand trap, to please
God's eye! Walk here, walk not there, no infernal carts! Litter not!
The meek shall let the bold play through! Hush thy voice in His
presence! Be still! Repress thine angry feelings! Members only!
Nonmembers — heathens — begone!

Warning: The Surgeon General Has Determined That Playing Golf Is Addictive — and Still He Plays Golf

Mastery of golf requires the perfect simultaneous alignment of so
many human and topographical and meteorological variables as to
overburden the average mind and drive it into the refuge of mysticism in its search for an ordering power: *What if skill is a delusion?
What if golf is a random and chaotic universe ruled by the forces of pure
chance?* Every golfer who ever did everything precisely by the book
only to watch his 7-iron shot plop feebly into a lake has at least
flirted with the idea. Not even the grizzled veteran or the advanced
student of the game can ever entirely overcome the sneaking suspicion that what it really all comes down to is luck. Lucky lie, lucky
roll, lucky bounce. String 'em all together and you're golden.

And thus, like gambling, golf hooks the susceptible and the desperate with the seductive promise of coming up a winner against all
odds via nothing more than the auspices of Dame Fortune. And
thus, like gambling, golf becomes addictive. Just one more round. I
can feel it. Today's the day luck rides in my cart. Today's the day
that higher power makes me destiny's tot, guides me through the
shadow of the valley of incompetence on a giddy roll of clean
fairway drives and miracle putts.

Well, it didn't work today. Maybe tomorrow. I'll just keep playing
until it does. Goddammit, it's only a matter of inches here and a tad
more topspin there. Can't stop now — so tantalizingly close I can
taste it!

And so, lured by his hazy chimera, the addict trudges on. I think
of my poor friend Henry Beard. Henry, lost to his friends and loved
ones, Mensa-busting brainpower indefinitely parked in the locker

room as he enslaves himself, day after day, every day of the year, moving from Southampton to Carmel to Ireland to the Virgin Islands in his mindless, endless pursuit of . . . of what? I doubt that even Henry himself knows. This human golfing machine is the one living links rat who, once off the green, never mention the game. The loony bastard *doesn't even keep score!* Maybe Henry is too far gone. But there is still hope for you. Now that you can see golf plainly, not as just a harmless pastime but for the sinister addiction that it is, you can fight it.

If Golf Were Running Major-League Baseball, Jackie Robinson Would Have Made His Debut at the Age of Seventy-eight

All golfdom hailed Tiger Wood's Masters blitz and instant enthronement. It made everybody just feel heartwarmingly deepdown good, goldarn it. The way a one-hundred-years-or-so-overdue collective sigh of guilty relief ought to.

No cheap shots from this bunker: golf is not racist, no matter what Fuzzy Zoeller might say. (For one thing, guys named Fuzzy are usually capable of saying almost anything.) Let us be understanding: the dated, tight-assed upper-class social conservatism in golf's soul ensures that its glands have always tended to reject diversity. There aren't many blacks or Jews in P.G. Wodehouse, either. But golf embraces the workingman or the bohemian no more warmly. Golf lovingly preserves a sense of its own stuffy Anglo-Saxon elitism.

Gaze upon the timeless architecture of the ideal American country club: the sort of heavy, stone, mock-Tudor pile that could be called early Robber-Baronial, grandiose enough to give Robin Leach a contact high. And inside those places, people are probably still getting *blackballed* by the sergeant at arms for not eating the crust on their white-bread chicken-and-mayo sandwiches.

Who wants to snuggle up to a game — a culture — that exudes at its loftiest and most exalted levels all the gaudy human panache of the 1909 summer picnic of Boston's biggest Wasp law firm?

Of course, *you're* different. Like my non-Wasp friend Lee Eisenberg. In his inspirational spiritual teardown, *Breaking Eighty,* Lee briefly mumbles about founding the Cool Guys Golf Association — nothing polyester, playing without a glove, on rural public courses

— to drive a wedgie, so to say, between golf's Warren G. Harding image and the game he and his friends wish it to be. Fat chance. Like trying to get away with wearing a porkpie hat in the foreign legion, bucking golf's rigid, ancient, and monolithic culture is futile.

Here's a simple way to abolish golf's elitist and exclusionary image and make it a truly all-American sport: ditch that fifties-Republican-martini-drinker's green Brooks Brothers–style sport jacket and make the winner of the Masters slip on something in, say, black leather with plenty of metal studs.

Here, Pull This Condom over Your Feelings

It takes but a single Saturday afternoon watching foursome after foursome limp off the final green at Burning Foot or Winged Tree or any other course in the land to know that most golfers not only never succeed in achieving a consistently proficient level of play but seldom hack their way beyond the dreary lowlands of semicompetence for more than brief, giddy visits. In frustration and bewilderment and heartbreak, the shortfall between the average golfer's hopes for his next round and the tale the scorecard tells eighteen holes later must outdo the failed ambitions of all other pursuits ostensibly taken up for pleasure.

All this is bad enough. But golf's perversely proud status as the least demonstrative of sports, combined with its essential challenge — let's you and your inner self fight — leaves your natural outrage at the inevitable fuckups nowhere to go but back into your own bile ducts. You can't valve off physically, as in tennis or hockey: well, you *can*, but the club-snapping, ball-hurling, cart-kicking berserkoid soon makes himself persona non grata even to his friends. Nobody likes a crybaby. So you have to live inside the ironclad but inhuman myth of golf as a cool, disciplined, deliberative game and of you as a gentleman too self-controlled and mannerly to feel, much less express, any low urge to verbal or physical violence.

But you're not some goddamned stiff-upper-lip Brit twit drilled from boarding school onward to repress his feelings. The bottling up of righteous anger twists the guts, stresses the nerves, balloons the blood pressure. Bing Crosby *died* on a golf course. This is recreation? Who needs this kind of constant, self-administered psychic torture? Why not just go bowling?

If Thoreau Had Been a Golfer, Bet Your Ass He'd Never Have Written Walden

Trust golfers to take the great outdoors and turn it into a Pavlovian dog run. "Great day for golf," you say, stepping up to the first tee. "What a beautiful course," somebody else chimes in. Bullshit. Five minutes later and awe at God's surrounding verdant bounty has telescoped down to glaring at a ball in a stupid sand trap or rooting around in the rough and a view of nature as a series of obstacles arranged for the express purpose of further thwarting your already struggling game. As the idyllic round you had envisioned disintegrates into the duffer's familiar sense of slowly drowning in calm water, you find yourself playing not only against your partners but against God himself. That's not a splendid grove of elms along the right side of the fairway — it's one long corridor of hideous steel columns waiting to be bonked by an errant drive and then bounce the ball right back to you. Those autumn leaves of red and gold are going to be for your ball what the Pacific Ocean was for Amelia Earhart. Uh-oh, a duck-dotted sheet of sky blue water! What a nasty, pointless thing is a water hazard. Natural beauty? From inside your ever-shrinking zone of desperate concentration, you might as well be playing in a concrete drainage ditch for all you notice of hill and dale and bosky dell.

Strategize, calculate, measure, focus, recite the hard-learned mantra of a thousand dos and don'ts as you lurch toward the next crucial stroke. Golf isn't for daydreaming or sightseeing. It's work. Mark Twain was right: golf is a good walk spoiled. Golf is no venue for admiring the scenery. Take the family to a park.

Ah, So That's Why John Updike Loves It

Golf is all about rules that mustn't be broken, techniques that mustn't be ignored, etiquette that mustn't be violated. It's more about what you *can't* do outdoors on a beautiful day than what you can. No wonder Wasps love golf. It must feel like church, like Choate, like their wives.

Golf, Inc.

Golf doesn't feel like fun in the lighthearted, carefree sense that, say, skating and kite flying feel like fun. Thus golf's historically hypnotic appeal to corporate types and the Japanese. To them, it feels better than fun. It feels *familiar,* which obviates any need to exercise the imagination. It is problem-solving made exquisitely, maddeningly complex and as such is not relief from, but a direct continuation by other means of, the tension, drudgery, competitiveness, and rule-boundness of their working lives. No wonder mighty corporations make mascots of the Palmers and Nicklauses and Normans of the world, pay fortunes to play with them, shoehorn them into their ads. They're not only glamorous by the standards of guys who've seen *Les Mis* three times, they're the living incarnations of kindred souls.

It is no accident that my own defection from the golfing ranks so closely coincided with my abandonment of the effort to live a type-A professional life. Moral: Life is for living, bub. Do you sincerely want to devote your precious weekends to aping the inner life of the workaholic corporate striver?

O. J. Simpson Is My Role Model

You could learn to fly a plane or earn your certificate in diesel-engine repair faster and more cheaply than you can buy golf proficiency. This may be the only sport in which even the natural athlete never rises above hacker status without samurai-intense apprenticeship. And the kicker: if you don't keep up the regimen of lessons and tuneups like dialysis treatment and don't keep getting in your thirty-six or fifty-four holes a week, your swing starts getting flecked with dots of rust and verdigris and the extra strokes accrue around your game like flab and you need a golfing vacation in Arizona to recover and there goes the kitchen renovation.

And the thing is that that seems only logical and fair to monomaniacs like you. Golf, like no other game, suckers you into a swinish selfishness about your money and, worse, your family time in the way it tears the Master out of the house for great half-day chunks every Saturday and/or Sunday from April to October (not even to talk about the incremental wastage of lessons and driving-range visits ad nauseam). You prick.

Honestly, Now: Don't You Sometimes Secretly Want to Scream?

Who the hell wants to cramp down his natural responses to fit golf's sourpuss rules of decorum? Anybody seen having a loud good time on the links is a pariah. Open jollity is a fart in church. Besides asking us to embrace its mid-Ohio notions of fashion, golf also expects each man and woman to sport the glum and haunted mien of the Fugitive and to remain resolutely poker-faced even in those rare moments of triumph. The game is played, even at the duffer level, on such a razor-edge of concentrative tension that every stroke must be cradled in a reverent hush. That Barry Bonds addresses the single toughest feat in sports — poling a 90-mile-per-hour fastball into the bleachers — amid forty thousand bellowing sets of lungs is immaterial. Like President-for-the-Foreseeable-Future Laurent Kabila of the Democratic Republic of the Congo, golf makes its own rules, and in golf, a tyrannical silence must ever prevail, the silence not of good manners so much as of ancient druidic superstition, as if to utter human noises in this sacred place would piss off the plaid-clad gods of golfdom and trigger a plague of mashie niblicks clattering down from above. And so: the idiotic spectacle of entire tournament galleries stifling the emission of so much as one soft belch the whole day long while TV announcers whisper their way through the rites before them like mourners at a mob funeral.

Hey, Norman, you Aussie asshole, hook another one! You're gonna whiff it, Tiger! Keep it up, Palmer, atta way to blow a putt! Would the sky fall if golfers took up their own brand of baseball-dugout chatter? Worse — it might enliven the game.

How's About a Quick Round at Sisyphus Hills?

I've saved the bad news for last. What its devotees in their hubris and myopia have never grasped is that golf is *not* a sport like other sports. Can the hymns and paeans; that's not what I mean. I mean it's a freakish, artificial endeavor less akin to tennis or skiing than to juggling eighteen dinner plates on a stick while riding a unicycle.

There is nothing natural about it; that's why golf is so hard. Why no player in any sport is so driven to wallow in swamps of theory and technique and biophysical arcana as deep as those that mire the golfer. Why no golfer ever gets within putting distance of even fleeting mastery without first undergoing the physical and mental drilling of a North Korean midget-sub suicide spy, followed by years of trial and error — mostly error — trying to implant a thousand discrete bytes of wisdom into muscle and synapse. Why golfers are driven forever thereafter to pillage the bookstore shelves and video racks and equipment brochures in the quest for a magic final fix.

They're trying to learn the unlearnable. Golfers think they're playing a normal sport, if one somewhat more frustrating than the average, which should be primarily dependent for success on the usual standbys: power, muscular coordination, mental concentration. Skills that can be learned and then honed. No wonder nine out of ten golfers are doomed to bewilderment and failure. No wonder a 250-pound insurance salesman can whip a poor jock's ass and everybody's surprised. Golfers, poor saps, are blind to the fact that you can't get there from here. That the set of attributes golf rewards — the high-wire acrobat's nanosecond timing, the chess master's hour-in, hour-out laser-beam concentration, Stalin's willpower — are rare, inborn gifts. And that you're about a likely to attain them via diligence and how-to manuals as you are to turn yourself into an idiot savant.

Come to think of it, that's exactly what great golfers are. Idiots savants. So the bad news is actually good news after all. You're hereby released from all further hopeless struggle at learning how to juggle eighteen dinner plates on a stick while riding a unicycle. You're hereby released to find yourself a *real* sport.

CHARLES P. PIERCE

A Big Game

FROM GQ

UPON ARRIVING IN A NEW TOWN, some people visit museums. Other people find the theater, or they go off in search of whatever the local newspaper says is the best restaurant in town. I have one friend who haunts courthouses, collecting exotic criminal proceedings the way some folks collect roadside reptile farms. As for me, I seek out the arena or the ballpark. Even after years of traveling to games, I still listen for distant cheering and look for the glow of lights above the near horizon.

I am a sucker for a Big Game. Which is not necessarily the same as a Championship Game. It is not necessarily the same as an Important Game, as defined by television hucksters. A Big Game is more than that. It is a piece of living history, a theater of the generations with an outcome more compelling than theater of any other kind. Thousands of actors have played Hamlet, but Hamlet always dies. Thousands of players have played in the Harvard–Yale football game, and very few of them have the same story to tell. If all the elements are right, and if history has aligned correctly with the emotion of the moment, I would rather be at a Big Game than almost anywhere else in the world.

In this capacity, I have rooted for small-college basketball teams in Wyoming and for small-college football teams in Mississippi, for minor league baseball teams in North Carolina and for high school hockey teams in Minnesota and for a thousand athletes whose names I have long since forgotten. I have been an Alcorn State Brave and a Mishawaka High School Caveman. (Our women's teams, it should be noted, are gallantly called the Lady Cavemen.) I have been a Reno Silver Sock and an Asheville Tourist. (The centerfield scoreboard read VISITORS and TOURISTS, which I thought was right friendly.) It has been said that we all carry our own America with us. My own personal America comes with six seconds left and the home team — *anybody's* home team — with the ball and trailing by a point or a goal. There is barbecue at the concession stand, and there is beer in a paper cup, and a band is playing across the way. I can be happy there.

In Lawrence, Kansas, where stands the University of Kansas, they long ago set up a memorial to the old man on a bare and windy hill just inside the cemetery gates. But they buried him a few degrees south, in a shady plot, with his family and his fellow Masons, beneath a tall marble tower with a great marble ball set on top of it. His marker is flat, set right there in the ground, the stone so darkened and weathered that it looks like a small vein of iron in the earth. NAISMITH, the stone reads, and beneath it, in smaller letters, JAMES and MAUDE.

Basketball had a single inventor. That we can say this with authority makes the game unique among sports. The Scottish shepherd who first hit a rock with a curved stick, thereby inventing both golf and recreational prevarication, is lost to antiquity. It has never been clear whether the inventor of American football was the first man to run with the ball, the first man to throw a forward pass or the first man to devise a point spread. Baseball has at least four creation stories (at least one of which is an absolute lie), all of which obscure the fact that America's putative pastime is really a British mongrel. Basketball, however, began irrefutably in this country with James Naismith, who is buried in this shady plot in Lawrence, Kansas, where he came to coach at the university and in which function he remains the only men's basketball coach at the University of Kansas with a losing lifetime record.

I mention all of this because it is within basketball that the growth of sports — for good and ill — can be most vividly seen. After all, in certain places, even high school sports have become afflicted with a giantism similar to that which has afflicted the professional games. I can be fairly sure that old Jamie Naismith would not approve of much of it. He was said to be rather stiff-necked in the area of personal deportment. Still, there is evidence that he was not entirely an old fud: we know, for instance, that he played the fiddle, and that "Little Brown Jug" was his party piece.

Across town, on this breezy morning fresh with the onrushing springtime, Kansas is preparing to play Kansas State in basketball for the 237th time. I think that if he could, Naismith — 1–1 lifetime against the Wildcats — would be there on Saturday. I think he would cheer. I think he would shake a pompom. I do not think he would chant "Bullshit!" at a referee — even though nobody ever had better credentials to do so. (Naismith was death on profanity.) But I think he would enjoy a Big Game. I think he'd have — and I'm sure he will one day forgive me for saying so — a hell of a time for himself.

More than anything else, a Big Game needs to have a sense of place. It radiates outward from the arena. It spreads itself beyond the stadium. Children slide down an icy sidewalk toward the warmth of the field-house doors. Halfway up the block, they can smell the popcorn. Time stops at midafternoon. The old men come out in their blazers. The women all wear camellias. The air itself seems to quiver and shake. The first time Florida and Florida State played football last season was a Big Game. It was in Tallahassee, all raucous with accumulated tradition, cheers echoing back through time and the generations. The second time they played football was in the Sugar Bowl. This was not a Big Game. It was merely for the national championship.

Alas, more and more, the Big Game is being overshadowed by the Championship Game, which increasingly is becoming just another television show. For example, there is no more entertaining sporting event in the country than a football game between Mississippi and Louisiana State, particularly if the game is played in Baton Rouge. First of all, the game is played in Louisiana, which, as we all know, is not part of the United States of America in any sense that really matters. Second, the game is played at night, fog swirling through the paludal air and Spanish moss hanging like ghostly fingers from every tree. Third, surrounding the game, there is a sprawling celebration that is pretty much what the Druids would have thrown if they'd had sororities. The game will probably never be a Championship Game, because neither LSU nor Ole Miss has competed for any kind of championship since God was a boy. The people in charge of such things will probably never designate it as an Important Game, either. But it is a Big Game, every year. Big Games are not about trophies and banners. They are not about ratings and rights fees. Instead, memories are at stake, entire lifetimes of them. Bright as midnight torches, they are as warm and genuine as primal fire.

In or near the town of Monona, Iowa, there once was a highway patrolman named Howard Bell. It seems that Bell once nabbed Kansas coach Roy Williams for speeding along Highway 52. Williams was in town recruiting a local high school star named Raef LaFrentz. The following evening, lurking still, Bell ticketed LaFrentz. Three years later, LaFrentz is preparing to play Kansas State, and he has just told the story on a conference call that included representatives of the *Sporting News, Sports Illustrated* and the Associated Press. Howard Bell is now famous, and he doesn't even know it. That is the way things happen today. Radar at the ready, Trooper Bell now cruises the information superhighway.

LaFrentz is preparing to play in a Big Game, though it has ceased to be much of a competitive rivalry. Kansas has won the game nine times in a row going back to 1994, and Kansas State is winding up a thoroughly miserable season. Nevertheless, on the running track that circles the basketball floor in Allen Fieldhouse, students have been camped out for tickets for nearly three days. In one corner, engineering students work out a design assignment using what appear to be Popsicle sticks. Two students have set up a small video arcade near one of the darkened popcorn stands, and a number of others are asleep under blankets. This will be the last home game for six Kansas seniors. The fans are urged to bring flowers and to shower the court with them before the game.

Allen is a genuine field house, one of the very few left. The stands rise steeply away from the court. At either end of the building, the walls come to a peak, with windows set into them. Kansas has been playing in this place since 1955, when it was dedicated to Dr. F. C. "Phog" Allen, Naismith's successor and the man to whom Naismith confided his theory that basketball cannot be coached, that it can only be played. Allen cannot have taken the old man too seriously; Phog coached at Kansas for thirty-nine years.

They have tucked and trimmed and embroidered the place

down through the years. In 1990, as part of the unending renovation, they bought a new scoreboard. This presented them with the problem of what to do with the old one. They planned to sell off the electrical components piecemeal and the metalwork for scrap. Then someone in the athletic department called Kelly Driscoll and told him that if he hustled he could have the old scoreboard for his saloon. Driscoll fired up his truck and took off up Naismith Drive.

On the night before the Kansas State game, the Yacht Club is loud and merry. The fans of one school are indistinguishable from the fans of the other. Up front, near the door, Kelly Driscoll sits at his personal table and watches a Big Game come through the doors of his saloon.

Driscoll is a native Kansan. His hometown is Russell, where his family has been involved for years in Democratic politics and has been something of a burr in the hide of Russell's most famous son, Bob Dole. (Around the Driscoll hearth, Dole is remembered fondly as "the only county attorney we ever had who never won a case.") Recently, when Russell County went Democratic in the state's gubernatorial election, Dole was heard to comment that the Driscolls must have been working overtime. One of Kelly's brothers lives on a farm next door to Russell's other claim to fame: a purported landing area for extraterrestrial spacecraft. What with space aliens coming down from the sky one day and the Washington press corps arriving the next, Russell has had a rough, if redundant, couple of years.

When his friend called him about the scoreboard in 1990, Kelly Driscoll was trying to make a success out of an old singles bar that he'd bought. He ripped the leatherette off the walls and renamed the place the Yacht Club, decking it out in a nautical motif that was approximately as appropriate to Kansas as a rodeo ambience would be to Hawaii. Right from the start, Driscoll's friendship with then coach Larry Brown and with Brown's star player, Danny Manning, made the Yacht Club a sort of unofficial headquarters for the 1988 champions.

The scoreboard dominates the Yacht Club the way a great landscape dominates a Tudor banquet hall. "There was no way we could get the thing through the doors," Driscoll recalls. "So we knocked out one of the back walls and fit the scoreboard right into the hole.

That scoreboard is part of the wall. I don't know what will happen if
we ever sell the place." The scoreboard is permanently set at Kansas
83, Oklahoma 79, the final score of the 1988 championship game.
The score is brighter on a Friday night than anything else in the
place. You can see its glow through the windows from the sidewalk.

It began in 1886 as a cheer for a victorious science club. At odd
points during a game, Kansas fans intone, "Rock. Chalk. Jayhawk.
Kayyy-*yewww!*" The melody of it had whispered at me for years. As I
lounge in my seat in the field house just before the game, it finally
occurs to me that it is a snatch of Gregorian chant, the same haunting strains that I first heard at a Trappist monastery near where I
grew up in Massachusetts. It is a serious, signifying chant, and it
brings back a flood of memories, and not merely of basketball
games but also of something bigger than myself, which is what the
people who wrote the chants had in mind. For a long moment, I am
home again.

The crowd has brought their flowers. Every time a senior is
introduced, the air fills with blossoms. Dressed in tuxedos for the
occasion, the band plays hard and loud, albeit with an unfortunate
tendency toward '70s Toyota-commercial standards. The chant is
much more impressive in its gravitas. Not many people even in
Kansas would argue that this is an Important Game, but it is a Big
Game because it has begun to feel like one. Time stops for a moment. The air in the field house begins to quiver and shake.

Kansas plays a terrible first half, but its team is so patently superior that it takes the game away easily in the second. As the minutes
wind down, the forgotten seniors at the end of the bench are in the
game, and everybody pleads with them to score, and they all do,
and everybody is very happy and pleased. After the game, nearly
everyone stays in his seat, and all six Kansas seniors get to give a
little speech in order to say good-bye.

I do not stay for all these valedictories. The Savior is mentioned
early on, and I have a strict rule regarding the theological specula-
tions of athletes. I discreetly make my way to the door, walking out
into a softening evening.

This was not a Championship Game. It was not even an Important Game. However, it was a Big Game. It was a Big Game because
of the band in its tuxedos, and because of all the flowers cascading

onto the floor, and because of all the little speeches and because of all the people who packed in to watch it at the Yacht Club across town. There is a sense of community here, not only among the people attending the game but also with all the people who attended the previous 236 games Kansas and Kansas State played against each other, all the way back to January 25, 1907, when James Naismith himself masterminded a 54–39 Kansas victory. It is for all of them — all the players and all the coaches, but also for all the people whom the game has ever touched. It is for Raef LaFrentz and for Trooper Howard Bell. It is for the people at the Yacht Club and for the people in Russell — for the Driscolls and the Doles, and maybe for the odd space alien, too. It is for James and Maude, and it is also for me.

Because everyone has stayed for the speeches, the lawn outside the field house is empty and silent. As I walk toward my car, I can still hear the cheering inside the building. Basketball began here. It is a constant and unbroken line from James Naismith — an athletic theologian himself, truth be told — to the seniors giving the speeches in a field house named for one of Naismith's protégés. I believe the old man would have had a time for himself. I believe he would have enjoyed the band in their tuxedos. ("Maude, do you think they know 'Little Brown Jug'?") He would have Rock-Chalked himself hoarse. I think the old man would know a Big Game when he felt it. And maybe, at a loose moment, when Maude wasn't watching, James Naismith would have thrown a few flowers into the air.

The Hustle

FROM SPORTS ILLUSTRATED

IT WAS THE DAMNEDEST IDEA. Here sat Jerry Adelman in his family-owned drugstore across the street from the Los Angeles Sports Arena in the fall of 1960, listening to a ridiculous spiel from Lou Mohs, new general manager of the Los Angeles Lakers, the team that had just arrived from Minneapolis to play in an obscure league called the National Basketball Association. Mohs needed cash to promote his team and was trying to convince Adelman to buy five hundred season tickets and sell them to customers at twenty-five cents over face value. This would give Mohs precious operating capital and Adelman a profit. Perfect, except that Adelman didn't think of himself as a scalper and didn't think of basketball as entertainment.

"Nobody is going to pay to come out and watch your players run up and down the court in their underwear," Adelman told Mohs that day. Mohs persisted, and the 26-year-old Adelman caved in, if only because the cost, four dollars per ticket per game for choice seats, was so modest. "I still didn't think there was a chance we'd make any money from it," Adelman says.

Fade, and cut to 1997. Two days before the Super Bowl, in a hotel room far above New Orleans' bustling Canal Street, Jerry Adelman, now 62 and co-owner, with his brother David, of L.A.-based Murray's Tickets, is busy greeting customers and delivering the more than 2,500 Super Bowl tickets that his national brokering agency had promised. On the street below, Joe Bonino, a muscular, dark-haired 36-year-old in blue jeans and a neat white sport shirt is standing on the trolley tracks that bisect Canal. In one front pocket he has a cellular phone and a pager, in the other enough cash to buy a modest home; hence, he also has an armed, personal security guard standing to his left. Bonino holds a walkie-talkie against his left cheek, alternately speaking into it and straining to hear the squawks that return, while he is approached by a stream of similarly edgy characters, each of whom produces a cache of game tickets and offers them for sale. Bonino, who was once employed by Adelman, now works major events for Golden Tickets, a Dallas-based national ticket broker. His job is to help secure the 2,200 Super Bowl tickets that his clients have already paid for. He would appear to be the most popular man in New Orleans.

It is the fourth Friday in January. Bill Parcells's face fills the newspapers and television screens, and Desmond Howard will soon be Green Bay's hero. But it is the ticket guys who own the Super Bowl. Who own the Masters. Who owned the Final Four last weekend in Indianapolis, when seat-starved Kentucky fans came north and bought their tickets off street corners; late last Thursday morning, the mingling of ticket-rich coaches and hungry ticket guys turned a downtown hotel atrium into a freewheeling marketplace. It is the ticket guys who stand astride the outsized, overpriced, see-and-be-seen world of spectator sports. It is the ticket guys who have changed the way America gets through the turnstiles.

They are part of a boom, in the right place at the right time — at the intersection of sports and society, where games are both a tool for big business and a social status symbol. People want to go to games and see the stars, and ticket guys can usher them through the doors. Brokers have sprung up like software companies or designer coffee shops, and common scalpers have been given new life and a new outlet by the brokers. The ticket business has never been more influential, and the late Lou Mohs has never looked more like a genius.

Ticket guys (their term, not ours) come in three forms, doing the same job in different ways. Most familiar are the hawkers every casual fan has run across outside every arena. Their stock-in-trade is the old-fashioned scalper-to-fan swap. Cash for tickets, and in the door. They work the crowds at their local stadium or arena, selling a ticket for just a little more than they paid. They're the most visible level of a vast weblike business. Beyond them are realms of scalping that are little known or examined. Next come national street hustlers, the gritty middlemen who work all the big events in every major sport, buying from one source (often the local hustler) and selling to another (often a big operator). They're a roving, Runyonesque breed, some of whom put many tens of thousands of miles a year on their cars. Finally come the national brokers, whose seven- and eight-figure businesses primarily serve corporations and the rich, selling tickets by the thousands from posh hotel rooms and by fax and Web site.

They all have three things in common: they must buy low and sell high or perish. They know from memory the arcane and diverse laws that govern their business and that decree it legal in nine states, illegal in nine others and allowed with restrictions in thirty-two. (Georgia is expected to pass a law becoming the tenth free-market state this week.) And all of them would sooner spill free tickets into the wind than talk openly about their incomes. Ticket guys respect police, but, in inverse proportion to the legitimacy of their business, they fear the Internal Revenue Service. High-powered brokers do most of their business through credit cards, leaving a trail that requires paying taxes. But street hustlers and hawkers operate almost exclusively in the untraceable realm of cash-only. They all say they pay taxes, but the veracity of the returns they file on April 15 is highly suspect.

At heart, they are all scalpers. But most of them don't much like the term, and the bigger they are, the more they dislike it. Brokers are the aristocracy of the ticket business — Brooks Brothers to the street hustlers' T.J. Maxx — dealing in a world in which $1,350 is fair market for an upper-end-zone Super Bowl ticket with a face value of $275. But scalping? "We believe there's a big difference between true brokers and some guy who's hawking tickets outside an arena," says Barry Lefkowitz, executive director of the three-year-old National Association of Ticket Brokers. You could start a small riot debating the truth in Lefkowitz's statement. However, it is true that a good broker will never leave you ticketless or sell you something in right field advertised as "behind the dugout." And brokers do have offices and addresses; some even have phones that aren't cellular.

Most of all, a broker is a bridge between some game and some person/corporation/travel agent who wants a ticket but can't find one. Or can't get a good ticket. Bulls–Sonics? Yankees–Indians?

Duke–North Carolina? NBA Finals? World Series? One call to a good broker, and seats can be had. How the broker builds this bridge, and who he builds it for, makes for rollicking business.

Like this: four days before the February 9 NBA All-Star Game in Cleveland, Ram Silverman, a 37-year-old former bartender, and Bonino are splayed across soft chairs on opposite sides of a desk in their downtown hotel room tending two telephones that sit ominously silent. They have promised three hundred tickets to clients for All-Star Weekend, half of them for Saturday night's Slam Dunk contest and the other half for Sunday night's game. Like a short seller on Wall Street, high-powered ticket brokers sell before they buy. They "take orders" for events for which they have no guaranteed tickets, and then they set out to fill those orders before the game, preferably at a cost lower than the client has already paid for the seats, creating a profit margin. It is a precarious and speculative operation. Every major event rolls the broker's nerves through a wood chipper.

All-Star Weekend was supposed to be a small operation for Golden Tickets. Two weeks earlier Golden had filled its Super Bowl orders with lethal efficiency, and the trip to Cleveland was envisioned as a breather of sorts. But shortly after the Super Bowl, Silverman took an order from one of his best clients, a Japanese company, for sixty tickets to each night's activities. Bonino chides him now, as Alice would Ralph, that this late order was a lousy idea. In the coming days street hustlers would say much the same thing, but Silverman was willing to take the risk to keep a rich and loyal customer happy.

"We haven't touched a ticket," says Bonino, in the hotel room. "In fact, we haven't seen a ticket." Silverman smiles wanly. "We aren't really nervous yet," he says. Hours later they would sit down at a Cleveland steak house, giddy with mock celebration. "Two tickets!" Bonino would say. "We picked up two tickets!" Two down, 298 to go. Whatever anxiety the two of them feel is cloaked with an easy familiarity, drawn from almost nine years of similar tightrope-walking without a net.

Silverman, a Chicago native, was tending bar at a T.G.I. Friday's in suburban Dallas in 1987 when he met Debbie Andrews, a ticket broker. "We went to her office a few times, and I was fascinated with the ticket business," says Silverman. "I begged her to give me a job."

She did, but less than nine months later, Andrews was arrested and charged with mail fraud. She pleaded guilty to overcharging clients' credit cards for ticket purchases and was sentenced to nine months in prison.

Silverman quit just ahead of the posse but left with a vision. He went to Steve Parry, a poker-playing friend and well-heeled sales executive, and proposed starting a ticket brokerage of their own. Parry bankrolled the start-up for his wife, Jan, and Silverman, and the two of them set up in a rented house in Plano, Texas, on April 25, 1988. The name Golden Tickets was taken from the precious booty won by five fictitious children in Roald Dahl's *Charlie and the Chocolate Factory.*

They launched themselves in pursuit of the industry's two essentials: loyal clients and a steady flow of tickets from reliable sources (season-ticket holders, team and league management, players and coaches, 800-number ads in *USA Today* and event-appropriate local newspapers, etc.). What they lacked was a "street specialist" who could bail them out of a ticket deficit on the day before the Super Bowl or the Thursday before the Final Four, somebody who could be trusted to take $50,000 to the street and come back with tickets. Enter Bonino, then 27, a lifelong hustler from, by turns, Madison, Wisconsin (where he was born), Los Angeles and Chicago.

Silverman had first met Bonino at the 1988 Final Four in Kansas City. "You could see he was a guy that people respected," Silverman says. This is in reference not only to Bonino's prodigious street connections and subsequent ticket hauls but also to his five-foot-ten, 190-pound build, hardened by hours of weightlifting and boxing. Bonino had started scalping tickets in 1976 as a 16-year-old high school junior in Madison, where he was taken under the wing of Jim (J.R.) Rush, a scruffy hustler — still active — who was two years ahead of Bonino in high school and already a veteran of the streets. Their hot property two decades ago was University of Wisconsin hockey tickets. While a cluster of hopeful scalpers would wait politely outside the arena, trying to buy and sell, Bonino and Rush would take their game to the highway, where cars entered the distant parking lot. To get their hands on tickets, Bonino says, "we'd give them our little boy voices, 'Oh, sir, we really want to go to the game.' And then we'd turn four seven-dollar tickets for fifteen bucks apiece and have enough money for pizza and pinball."

In subsequent years pizza and pinball were replaced by rent and car payments. Bonino's jump from local punk to regional hitter was made during his many visits to Chicago in the early 1980s, when brokers left cold with fistfuls of tickets would give them to Bonino to sell, hoping for any salvation at all from a lost investment. "About an hour later Joe would come back with no tickets and money falling out of his pockets," says one Chicagoan, who now works as Bonino's security guard on the street. Soon thereafter Bonino went national, following concert tours and hot sports tickets, often driving more than five hundred miles a day, unafraid of hostile turf. In January 1986, just before Super Bowl XXI, he stood outside the L.A. Sports Arena holding the ubiquitous SUPER BOWL TICKETS NEEDED sign, trying to buy up everything he could as the host city's allotment of tickets was released for sale to the public. He was confronted by Larry Pederson, a menacing hard-ass who owned a large chunk of the street trade in L.A. from the late '70s through the mid-'80s, at one time controlling more than three hundred Lakers season tickets a game in Magic Johnson's heyday.

Pederson, tall and thick, poked a finger in Bonino's chest and said, "I don't know who you are, but you're in L.A., and that's my town, and I don't want you picking up tickets." Bonino looked up at Pederson. "I'll pick up tickets wherever I want to pick up tickets," he said. Predictably, the two of them brawled viciously, throwing haymakers, as Bonino recalls it, for a solid five minutes before security officers ripped them apart. "I went to the Forum a hundred times after that and never had a problem with Larry," says Bonino. "I think he respected me, to tell you the truth." (Epilogue: Pederson was shot in the head and critically wounded while sitting in his Jeep outside the Forum in February 1989. "He was a rough guy and had to be an enforcer out there," says Adelman.) The fight with Pederson was nothing more than the cost of doing business for any street hustler. Bonino estimates that he's been arrested "at least twenty times" and been in "a million fights."

Bonino's street pedigree was the perfect complement to what turned out to be Silverman's business savvy. In less than nine years of existence, Golden Tickets has grown into a multimillion-dollar operation that routinely turns high-five-figure profits at a single major event. The arc of Golden's success in the '90s has mirrored that of the entire industry. "Ten years ago it was a new industry, and

then there was an explosion," says Mike Schwartz, a national broker
and owner of ABC Tickets, of Wilmington, Delaware.

With the broker boom came large-scale abuses. Truckloads of
Wisconsin football fans traveled to Pasadena in late December
1993 to watch their Badgers play in the Rose Bowl for the first time
in thirty-one years, only to find that travel agents who were either
naive, dumb or unscrupulous couldn't provide nearly 3,800 tickets
they had promised. A month later, at Super Bowl XXVIII in Atlanta,
the street market on tickets inexplicably soared in the final days,
forcing brokers to take huge losses in order to deliver seats. Many of
them bailed out on their orders and skipped town — leaving clients
stranded — only to open up a week later with a new name and a
new 800 number.

In the wake of these events a small group of brokers agreed to
form the NATB. "It was something we had to do, to police ourselves," says Parry, now an ex-salesman and president of Golden
Tickets. There are two hundred brokers in the NATB who encourage prospective ticket buyers and sellers to call the national office
for a report on any member broker before buying or selling. However, there are also at least three hundred brokers who are not
members of the NATB, and countless street hustlers and independent operators who wouldn't consider joining (not to mention
dozens of filthy rich and successful brokers operating illegally in
New York City who are further underground than Jimmy Hoffa and
like it that way).

The best of the brokers operate like futures traders, trying to
nail the value of, say, a Masters badge, three months before the
event. For instance, Golden Tickets sold most of its Super Bowl
tickets at prices ranging from $1,150 to $1,350 (though some of its
prime seats were priced much higher) and tried to fill those orders
by buying seats for $900 or less. Face value on a Super Bowl ticket
was $275 for most seats, but face value, as Silverman says, "is a
meaningless term." Clients are occasionally individuals, but more
and more often they are corporations. Businesses in both the U.S.
(including *Sports Illustrated*) and abroad crave tickets, not just to
romance advertisers and clients but also to reward productive employees.

What better way to thank someone for selling all those desktop
copiers throughout the Midwest than with two tickets to a Bulls

game? In most cases the best way to get those tickets is through a broker. If you happen to need thirty tickets, it's the only way. The arrangement creates an irony whereby some advertising executive sits on the 50-yard line at the Super Bowl holding a ticket that was sold to a lowlife, then hustled to a street punk, then sold to a legit broker. Happens all the time.

For repeat events like Bulls games ($550 for a good seat at a routine regular-season game; $1,250 for a good seat at a big game), Alabama home football games and their ilk, the brokers rely on season-ticket holders. Schools, pro teams and event managers hate this. "The brokers are a major annoyance to us, and our fans don't like them at all," says Bulls principal owner Jerry Reinsdorf, who has revoked the season-ticket privileges of a small number of holders caught selling their tickets. Such pronounced rectitude rings a bit hollow; in truth, teams sometimes sell season tickets to brokers to help boost official attendance. One Midwest broker told *SI* that he owns hundreds of season tickets to games of the pro franchises in his city plus more than fifty each for Notre Dame, Ohio State and Michigan football, all of which help to form the backbone of his business.

Annual events require more resourcefulness, as tickets flow through people who are forbidden to scalp. Silverman simplifies: "We get our tickets from the people who have access to them." Take the Super Bowl. According to the NFL's Super Bowl ticket czar, Jim Steeg, ticket distribution for this year's game broke down this way: 35 percent to the participating teams (controlled by the two owners), 25.3 percent to the league office (including the "people who do business with the league," says Steeg), 29.7 percent to nonparticipating teams (controlled by the owners, although every player in the league is given the right to buy two tickets at face value) and 10 percent to the Saints, the host city's team.

Translation: there are dozens of fertile sources from which brokers can score Super Bowl tickets. The NFL issues a stern warning to teams, which says in part, "Scalping suggests a desire to profit personally . . . on the coattails of the league's popularity. Such conduct will not be tolerated." This solemn rebuke is a joke. Super Bowl tickets are bartered like autographed memorabilia. One broker told *SI* that he picked up 500 of them this year from a single source in Green Bay.

Professional athletes are among the most active of all ticket scalpers. For this year's Super Bowl, Green Bay and New England players were given two free tickets and offered the right to buy about two dozen more. As they are each year, many of these tickets were sold to brokers at a huge profit. (Think about it: if a player buys twenty tickets at face value, it costs him $5,500. He can walk into the parking lot, where dozens of brokers and hustlers wait with sacks of cash, and sell them for at least $18,000, a clear profit of $12,500 in five minutes.) "Even the rich players can't say no to that kind of money," says one broker. In fact, players become attuned to brokers' needs. According to several brokers, one New England player stood on a chair in the locker room in Foxboro in January and shouted to his teammates, "Don't take less than $1,500 for a ticket."

So it's not surprising that brokers and hustlers view any ticket-related news item with healthy suspicion. When it was reported that San Francisco 49ers assistant coach Pete Carroll asked for fifty Super Bowl tickets in his negotiation with the St. Louis Rams for their head coaching job, brokers smirked in unison. Carroll might have fifty friends who want to go to the big game every year, says one broker, but "I see a $50,000 bonus." (Carroll and his agent both deny that Carroll ever made the request.)

Right after player tickets were released for the '96 Super Bowl between Dallas and Pittsburgh, one participating player, through his agent, invited a broker to his house, where fifteen players sold game tickets. The broker arrived with an armed, personal security guard and a briefcase full of cash and left with approximately 270 tickets, worth nearly $300,000 on the open market.

The Super Bowl of college sports, for fans and ticket guys alike, is the Final Four. This year in Indianapolis 34 percent of the 47,000 tickets were sold through the public lottery, for which there were 167,000 applications, including those of a great many ticket brokers who submit multiple applications under various names from various addresses. Each participating school received 3,500 tickets. About 8,000 seats went to the NCAA office and the host city organizers. All of these ticket sources are mined aggressively by brokers, but the best seats of all belong to coaches and are distributed by the National Association of Basketball Coaches. Allocation is determined by a school's NCAA division status and by a coach's seniority. According to NABC executive director Jim Haney, Division I

coaches are usually given the opportunity to buy two good seats —
"lowers between," in the parlance of the scalper. That is, seats in the
lower level between the baskets. And many of the coaches sell these
seats for enormous profits. They can buy tickets for a face value of
$100 and then sell them for $3,000 or more. However, the combination of the cavernous RCA Dome and the scheduling of this
year's event on Easter weekend drove prices down into the $1,000
to $1,500 range, causing much bickering between coaches and
scalpers. The release of the NABC tickets is a scalpers' convention.
One national broker counts thirty coaches among his regular clients. "They all have my pager number, and I never see their faces,"
he says. "It's always a middleman, like a manager [who delivers the
coach's tickets]." The NABC includes a warning against scalping
with the tickets it gives out; its most severe penalty for scalping
Final Four tickets is five years without ticket access through NABC.
But ticket scalping is legal in Indiana, which last week made the
NCAA rule against scalping, and the NABC warning, virtually unen-
forceable.

The practice is so common that St. Joseph's coach Phil Martelli
even joked at a press conference about unloading his subregional
tickets in Salt Lake City, where scalping is legal, because his wife was
going on a spending spree. For lesser lights, a quick scalping profit
is a big deal. Unlike Martelli, some Division I assistant coaches
make as little as $16,000 a year, and they have the chance to make
$3,000 in ten seconds at the Final Four. It's a no-brainer.

The Final Four and the Masters remain the two priciest tickets in
sports. Although the Masters market fluctuates wildly on site, a
four-day badge often sells for more than $2,000. When the Final
Four is held in a venue seating 20,000 or fewer, prices spike. The
'90 Final Four, at 17,765-seat McNichols Arena in Denver, saw what
many brokers recall was the first $1,000 ticket. Six years later a
prime, three-game ticket book for the Final Four at the 19,299-seat
Meadowlands in New Jersey was selling for as much as $10,000.

Yet even when a broker has clients and access to seats, the market
can crush him in a single day. That's what happened at that '94
Super Bowl in Atlanta, when the dearth of street tickets sent prices
spiraling upward. Golden Tickets, for instance, which had taken
client orders at $750, eventually paid more than $1,500 per ticket
to fill many of them. Late on the Friday afternoon before the game,
Bonino ran in from the street and asked Silverman, "How's it look?"

"Not good. We might lose a hundred grand," Silverman said.

Whereupon Bonino ran to the bathroom and vomited prodigiously. "Somebody tells me I'm about to lose more money in a single day than I used to make in a year, I'll throw up every time," Bonino says. Three months later at the Final Four in Charlotte, the brokers turned the tables on the hustlers who had killed them in Atlanta. The market inexplicably bottomed out, and brokers who had taken orders for $1,750 or more were filling them for $750, netting $1,000 on each sale.

This year's NBA All-Star Game in Cleveland provided no such bailout for Silverman and Bonino. Late that Friday afternoon a hotel room bed — which by then should have had a quilt of tickets across it — was adorned by only a dozen tickets. Before Sunday evening's game Bonino would spend countless hours scouring hotel lobbies in search of loose tickets. He would pay an average of $350 for tickets that Golden had already sold for an average of $275, and the company would take a loss. But the orders would be filled, the last for Saturday's Slam Dunk contest with just fifteen minutes to go, and the clients would be happy. "Joe just went nuts for us," Silverman would say, several days later. "When the pressure is on, he just transforms. He comes through; he gets the tickets." Bonino is sheepish about this rare skill of his. "I really don't look to get into fistfights on the street anymore," he says. "But I can get tickets if I have to."

The long, flat run of U.S. 92 that hugs Daytona International Speedway is awash in pedestrians spilling into the late afternoon following the Twin 125 races that are held three days before the February 16 Daytona 500. Most fans wear sunglasses and T-shirts paying homage to their driver of choice. Most carry coolers. Across from the track's main gate, on a grassy area in front of the Ramada Inn (just maybe the most famous hotel in scalping), wooden police barriers and plastic netting form a makeshift pedestrian walkway, and here the call of the street hustler is heard above the excited chatter of the unwashed. Tickets? Anybody got tickets? Anybody need tickets?

Were they not hawking, the scalpers could be part of the crowd, with wardrobes that run from surf dude to golf slacker to auto mechanic. These are the warriors of the ticket business, the national street hustlers, tireless plungers who fly and drive to as many as three hundred events a year, usually arriving without tickets, diving in to buy low off the street and sell high. Although most scramble to come away with $30,000 a year, the best of them can clear up to $120,000, just turning and burning, as they say. "It's the last bastion of capitalism," says Jeff Keylon, a hustler from Knoxville, Tennessee. "You take a guy from Wall Street, he wouldn't last a week hustling tickets." There are no more than fifty or sixty true coast-to-coast hustlers in the country, a Special Forces of scalping. They carry cellular phones and pagers and answer to names Elmore Leonard would love: Eddie the Beard, Richie the Head, Indian Steve, Knockout Pete. They are in South Bend for big games, out along the exit ramp from the Indiana Toll Road early in the morning. They were in Atlanta last summer, trolling Peachtree Street during the entire Olympics. They seldom sleep. Can't turn tickets in bed.

This end of the business knows no qualifications, except that you need enough money to buy your first ticket and enough guts to get out there and sell it for a profit. Street hustlers are young and old, skinny and fat, cheery and grim. Guys like 43-year-old Minnesota Mike, who is already looking forward to the 1998 World Cup in France. "That's a quick $35,000," he says as he works the Daytona crowd. Or like 26-year-old Harley Sroka, who started hustling hockey tickets outside Toronto's Maple Leaf Gardens when he was 13 and now lives in Chicago. He says with much pride that an uncle, Morris (Cooney) Cohen, was "king of the scalpers in Toronto." He taught Sroka everything he knows.

As a group they are desperately compulsive — many are heavy drinkers or drug users, driven to make money by the need to support their habits. Almost all of them are heavy gamblers. Their lives are a gamble. They compete viciously for the same turf, yet against outsiders they are a tight circle of peers, careful with trade secrets or the type of money talk that might attract the IRS.

Leaning against one of the temporary wooden rails in Daytona Beach is a middle-aged man in a white T-shirt and blue jeans with long, thinning white hair swept back into a magnificent fluff at the nape of his neck. Doug the Rug, 54, is a Brooklyn native who has been scalping tickets for four decades. "I started outside Ebbets Field, that's how long I've been doing this," he says. He has just enough New York in his voice to make him seem streetwise, and he speaks just softly enough to get a customer's trust. He points to the speedway entrance across the street and to the dozens of hustlers scurrying about. "Thirty years ago I used to come down here, and the box office was a little wooden box over there, and I had this whole operation to myself," he says. "Too many hustlers now, too many seats."

The Rug stops to work two "straights," scalper slang for regular fans. They offer him two seats for Sunday's 500 (face value for that event ranged from $60 to $160). He pulls a bloated roll of hundreds from his pocket and pays them $1,800 for the pair — which he turns over half an hour later for $2,000. "I'll tell you the best night ever," he says. "Willie Mays Night at Shea Stadium, 1973. They had a box office release of 5,000 tickets right before the game. They were 2-dollar tickets, and the public never saw them. Scalpers bought them all up for 50 cents over face, and we were selling them for twenties. Great night."

If Doug the Rug represents the past of this business, 26-year-old Arizona Nick is the present. He wheels into a strip mall parking lot in a rented black Suzuki Sidekick, his high-end mountain bike folded into the back seat. Nick's fade is bleached punk blond on top, left black on the sides. At the Super Bowl he had a long goatee, but now that is gone. Different site, different look. Word among the hustlers is that Nick is the best in the business right now. His modus operandi is pure survival. On one of his first visits to Chicago, as a teenager, he challenged Bonino and was thrown in jail the next day, courtesy of Bonino's connections.

In the early '90s Nick, who like many street hustlers vehemently refused to be interviewed by *SI*, insisted on working the U.S. Open tennis championship at Flushing Meadow in Queens, New York, despite the fact that New York scalping is notoriously territorial. One of New York's ticket crews beat him up and tossed him off the grounds. The next day he was back. And the day after that. "He didn't give a s—, that's why he's so good," says Phoenix Matt, a lifelong friend of Nick's. The best hustlers, like Nick, use crews to score large numbers of tickets when a box office puts some specific event on sale. They "will get guys on the street and buy them beer or wine to stand in line," says Matt. When tickets hit the street, the guy who can creatively forage best has a huge advantage. It's common for hustlers to try to bribe box office or Ticketmaster sellers. Anything for an edge.

The hustlers' profession is as wearying as selling religion door-to-door, but the economics of it is as simple as fourth-grade math. It was the hustlers who cleaned up at the Atlanta Super Bowl that cost Golden Tickets more than $100,000, extorting enormous prices from brokers at the last minute and making huge profits on their own hustled tickets.

The national hustlers love to see a local favorite roll into an NCAA regional or the Final Four, or to see the likes of Alabama in the Sugar Bowl. "You see Kentucky make a regional in Birmingham, there's a bloodletting," says Keylon. A $75 ticket is suddenly worth $500, and the hustlers know it better than the people who own the tickets.

A budding hustler learns the rules and then climbs. Steve Susce, 36, who now co-owns AAATix, a Birmingham-based ticket brokerage, did some casual scalping of football tickets as an undergraduate at Mississippi State and then attacked the business more seriously in 1987, after the Pittsburgh Pirates released him from a minor league contract. He was living in St. Louis, and he began working college football games at Missouri and Illinois. His learning curve was dramatically steep, involving the common sense economics of scalping — and a bicycle.

"One day I'm working a game at Missouri, and this guy goes blowing past me on a bike holding up two fingers, yelling, 'Need two!'" says Susce. "I thought, Man, that's the way to go. So here's the bike strategy: you're at a stadium for a game, face value is $25. You get different scenarios. Sometimes the ticket is actually worth $75, sometimes it's actually worth $5. So you ride your bike up to the front gate of the stadium early and find out what the game is worth. If it's a $5 ticket, you ride around the stadium as fast as you can, buying every ticket you can put your hands on [at that price]. Then you go out on the highway, and you sell like crazy and make 20 bucks a ticket: 20, 20, 20. The people out by the highway, they don't know it's a $5 ticket yet. Now, if it's a $50 ticket at the stadium, you can't buy a bunch because there aren't any. That's why it's 50 bucks. Demand, but no supply. So you ride your bike out by the highway, take a piece of cardboard and write TICKETS NEEDED, $30. People sell. They think it's a good price, and they don't know it's 50 bucks at the stadium. You buy a stack, ride back to the stadium and sell: 50, 50, 50. Boom, boom, boom."

In March 1987 Susce was scalping his way through the NCAA regionals. He was in Louisville on Thursday, in Cincinnati on Friday, back in Louisville on Saturday, and hawking at a Bon Jovi concert in Lexington on Saturday night. There he was arrested by Lexington police, who confiscated his money and tickets and dragged him to jail, leaving his beloved bike outside Rupp Arena. When he was released without charges on Sunday morning, his tickets and money were returned, but his bike was gone, so Susce drove to Cincinnati to scalp at the regional finals that afternoon. "I get there, and somebody yells to me, 'Hey, I got your bike,'" recalls Susce. "It's this old guy named Walter Anderton, a ticket guy from Memphis, knows everybody and everything. He's dead now, but what a sweet guy. He took me out that night for drinks. He gave me this list of events that I should go to — kind of tutored me."

The list Anderton gave Susce that night is the national hustler's itinerary. They work the circuit: the Super Bowl, the NBA All-Star Game, Daytona, major conference basketball tournaments, the NCAA tournament and the Final Four, the Masters, the Kentucky Derby, the Indianapolis 500, baseball's All-Star Game, and the World Series. And hundreds of smaller events to fill in the empty white squares on a calendar. It is a dizzying schedule, a nonstop train.

Two days before the NBA All-Star Game in Cleveland, in the middle of a bitter-cold Midwestern night, a doughy 32-year-old hustler who goes by the name of Cleveland Chris sat in the lobby of a downtown hotel (the All-Star Game was a home game for Chris) and recounted his past year. "At least 300 events," he said. "Maybe more than that. I'd have to check my calendar." He is wearing khaki shorts, his standard scalping uniform 365 days a year, including the subzero nights when he hawks face-value Cavaliers seats outside Gund Arena for a local broker who needs to unload them. "There's not an event I won't do," he says. "One day a couple of years ago, I'm driving down I-71 to Columbus for an Ohio State football game. I stop, and I'm reading the newspapers, and I see there's this big Canton McKinley versus Massillon high school football game, the one hundredth. I'm thinking, How big must this be? So I go straight there. The stadium only seats about 20,000, and scalpers are getting 50 bucks to get in. I went to work right there."

Sometimes the hustler gets hustled by another hustler. Cleveland

Chris was at the Super Bowl in New Orleans with everybody else. Two days before the game he transacted a piece of business with Dane Read Matthews, a Cleveland broker, that showed the murky waters in which the street ticket business is conducted. Matthews needed two good seats for a client, and on the Friday preceding the game Chris produced what he believed were two such seats — 50-yard line, suite level — and Matthews paid $1,700 each for them. When Matthews checked his seating chart closely, it turned out that the suite was in the corner of the end zone (the Superdome's oddball numbering system made this difficult to discern at first glance), and thus he had to eat a $300 loss on each ticket. After Matthews complained, a livid Chris marched into the New Orleans Marriott lobby in the wee hours of Saturday morning, where he found the hustler who had originally sold him the seats.

"It's late, and everybody's been drinking a little," says Chris. "So next thing you know, I pop him, he pops me, and I wind up in jail until Sunday. I missed Saturday, I missed the game, probably cost me $10,000. I'm sitting in jail, and the cops keep coming into my cell telling me, 'Hey, your beeper's going off every five minutes, what are you, a drug dealer?'" He left town on Tuesday "and went straight to Daytona to work out of my hotel room for the 500."

As Chris talks, his hands crinkle a sports betting sheet supplied by Las Vegas casinos and some bookmakers. "I love gambling," says Chris. "I've made $1,000 today on tickets; tomorrow I'm betting $1,000 on three [college basketball] games." Hustling tickets on the street and gambling on sporting events push the same buttons for hustlers, providing the singular rush of action.

This dual addiction has given rise among scalpers to a new form of hedging on the sports market. A hustler who is anticipating a big ticket score in an upcoming game — provided a certain team advances in a tournament or a playoff — bets against the team whose victory will create the ticket market. If he wins the bet, he's covered for the ticket loss. If he loses the bet, his ticket sales will cover the gambling loss. It's the street hustler's unique variation of a ploy commonly used in more legitimate financial markets.

As long as there are markets where supply and demand fluctuate, street hustlers will be there to cash in. "I could sell drugs for a living because I'm a hustler," says Cleveland Chris. "But why sell drugs and go to prison when I can sell tickets and make money?"

"Give me a crayon and a piece of cardboard," says Susce, "and I'll make a million dollars."

A red Dodge Intrepid idles in the cold beside a slender young man standing on the curb, shivering, outside Indiana University's Assembly Hall. In three hours the Hoosiers will host Ohio State, and this Big Ten basketball game, as always, is a sellout. From the backseat of the car, Brenda Stratman suspiciously eyes 25-year-old Renny Harrison's fanned tickets and asks the price for two good ones. "One hundred each," says Harrison, whose hands are covered by a pair of thin cotton gloves. After a stunned pause, Stratman gathers herself for a counteroffer. "Seventy-five," she says. Harrison shoots back. "Eighty dollars each," he says. "They're really good seats. Don't think about it. Just buy the seats and enjoy yourself."

Stratman slumps back in her seat. She has traveled two and a half hours from Mount Vernon, Indiana, with her husband, Chris, and another couple, Jeff and Mindy Johnson. It was not a trip made lightly: they have driven to Bloomington having agreed that if it's too costly for all four of them to buy tickets, two of them will go elsewhere to watch the game on television. Stratman appeals to Harrison. "Come on," she whines. "You're making so much money." If Stratman buys two tickets for $80 apiece, Harrison will make $100 profit. Face value on the seats is $16 each; he paid $30 apiece to a season-ticket holder who didn't want to attend the game.

This is the ticket scalping your father knew: hometown street-corner scalpers selling tickets for today's game embody the soul of the ticket business. Harrison is the co-owner of an agency (Circle City Tickets), makes good money, and occasionally roams the big events. But he never misses an Indiana home game. On these days and nights he is Every Scalper, of which there are thousands from Oregon to Maine, some selling eight tickets a night, some selling eighty. He is the guy with seats for a game that you want to see. Now.

His business is conducted on "the walk," the local scalpers' universal term for whatever area serves as the common ground for sellers and buyers. Here in Bloomington, as elsewhere, the straights are ever suspicious. "You'll be selling for face [value] at game time," one straight mumbles to Harrison.

"Cheapskate," says Harrison.

As Keylon, the Tennessee hustler who works Volunteers football games on his home turf, says, "You get called a lot of things out here, a lot of cracks about your heritage and all that, but I just tell 'em, 'Hey buddy, I got the tickets and you don't.'" It behooves a straight to be cautious, to carry a seating chart, to work the scalpers and learn the market. At some venues (including New York City's Madison Square Garden) counterfeit tickets are common — good cause to ponder any potential purchase. For their part, outside arenas like the Garden, where scalping is illegal, hustlers must be even more acutely aware of the market and wise to the whims of the police.

On this February afternoon in Bloomington, Harrison arrived at the walk with forty tickets in hand, purchased from various season-ticket holders. His then girlfriend, Stephanie Myers, helped him pick up fourteen more — at face value, a huge score — when the box office had a late release of tickets. Harrison sold all but four of his fifty-four, grossing nearly $1,000, and then bopped down into the well of the arena with three friends to watch the game and cheer for coach Bob Knight's red army from four of the best seats in the building.

Indiana's 93–76 victory made it a good day all around for Harrison. But as he drove home to Indianapolis that night, the paradox of his profession nagged at him. He is a scalper, a good guy and a bad guy at once, providing a service that the public both craves and detests. "The business has a bad reputation for a good reason," Harrison said. "There are a lot of dishonest people in it. I'd like to think I'm separate from those people, but in truth, I'm not."

Rolling in the opposite direction, home to Mount Vernon, is the red Dodge whose passengers eventually bought two tickets at Harrison's drop-dead price of $80 apiece. Jeff Johnson and Chris Stratman sat fourteen rows from the floor, right on the baseline, while their wives went to a nearby restaurant. "I had the time of my life," Johnson said later. "I'll probably go a couple of times a year now. It was more than worth it to pay $80." Here he contained his glee for a beat and considered the transaction that put him in the building. "Of course," he said, "I wish the profit was going to a better cause."

DAVID FERRELL

Far Beyond a Mere Marathon

FROM THE LOS ANGELES TIMES

BADWATER IS A MADMAN'S MARCH, a footrace through the summer heat of the hottest spot in America. It extends 135 miles from a stinking water hole on the floor of Death Valley to a piney oasis 8,300 feet up the side of Mt. Whitney. The course is nothing but asphalt and road gravel. Feet and knees and shins ache like they are being whacked with tire irons. Faces turn into shrink-wrap.

Lisa Smith is 102 miles into it. She has been running, and now walking, for almost 27 hours, through yesterday's 118-degree heat, up 6,000 feet of mountain passes into a 40 mph head wind. The night brought her 40 minutes of sleep, if that — two catnaps.

Her feet are blistered and taped up, and she is wearing shoes with the toes cut out to relieve the pressure. Her right ankle, sprained twice since February, is so swollen she can no longer wear the air cast that was supporting it. She is also cramping with diarrhea.

"It's bad," she says, gasping. "My stomach is killing me."

Grimacing, spitting, bending over at times to fight the nausea, she trudges on, pushing down the undulating highway toward Keeler, a ramshackle mining outpost. Visible ahead is the serrated peak of Whitney, as distant as Oz. If she can hang on, it will take most of the day — and a 4,000-foot ascent over the final 13 miles — to get there.

Every year, two or three dozen elite ultra-marathoners come to Badwater, and every year Badwater beats them down. About a third fail to finish; after 50 miles or 70 miles or 110 miles, the torture exceeds their desire to go on, and they end up rolling away in their cars and minivans, faces covered with wet towels, their bodies stretched out like corpses.

For a thin slice of society — zealots who live to train, who measure themselves by their mental toughness — the ultra-marathon is the consummate test of human character. No other event in sport, except possibly a prizefight, is as punishing, as demanding of the mind and body. No other athlete is more revered than the distance runner. Indefatigable, heroic, celebrated in poetry and myth, the Greek soldier, Pheidippides, ran 26 miles from Marathon to Athens to herald victory over the Persians in 490 B.C., then collapsed and died. It was the first marathon. To fill the unforgiving minute, to persevere, is one of the highest ideals of man — who, after all, was born to hardship, cast from Eden.

The explosion of extreme sports in recent years has produced an unprecedented number of ultra-endurance races. Several thousand men and women travel the country — and abroad — competing in events from 30 miles to more than 300 miles. There are weeklong "adventure races" by foot, bike, and kayak across Patagonia, South Africa, Australia.

In Morocco, there is the Marathon des Sables — "the Marathon of the Sands" — a six-day trek, in stages, across 150 miles of the Sahara. Colorado has the Hardrock 100, snaking 100 miles through the 11,000-foot peaks of the San Juan Mountains. In Alaska it's the Coldfoot, a 100-miler in October with the wind roaring and the temperatures plunging to 40 below.

Death Valley has Badwater: "probably the most physically taxing competitive event in the world," according to the runners' handbook, which warns that you could die out here — though no one yet has. "Heat illness or heat stroke . . . can cause death, kidney failure, and brain damage. It is important that runners and crews be aware of the symptoms . . . vomiting, headache, dizziness, faintness, irritability, lassitude, weakness, and rapid heart rate. . . . Heat stroke may progress from minimal symptoms to complete collapse in a very short period of time."

Twenty-seven runners have entered this year's tenth anniversary race, a field drawn from North America and Europe. Lisa, 36, is the only woman, a fitness trainer from Bernardsville, New Jersey, who has run 60 marathons — her fastest in 2 hours and 48 minutes — and four ultras. Bjarte Furnes, 23, a molecular biology student from Norway, is out to become the youngest ever to finish. Beacham Toler, 69, a retired boilermaker from Amarillo, Texas, is already the oldest; he aims to better a personal best by breaking 50 hours.

The course record, set five years ago, is 26 hours and 18 minutes, but few concern themselves with that or the first place prize money — $500. The main goal is to go the distance, because Badwater, like every extreme race, is less a competition among runners — whose training and talents vary widely — than it is a struggle between each runner and the miles. To conquer the course, you must get through it in less than 60 hours. Those who make it in under 48 — 2 days and 2 nights — are awarded a special memento, a belt buckle, a modest hunk of bronze featuring a bas relief of the desert.

"If I don't make it, I'll be back every year until I do," vows U.S. Marine Corps Major W. C. Maples, 33, a second-time entrant from Camp Pendleton who stands now at the starting line, shortly before dawn. Three years back, during Utah's Wasatch 100, he got off the floor of an aid station despite hypothermia and winced through the last 50 miles with a stress fracture in his right leg.

But Badwater got him a year ago. The Major, as other runners call him, quit after vomiting up a bunch of pink, fleshy tissue that turned out to be part of his stomach lining. It was the only endurance race he failed to complete.

"I have fumed over that," he says. "One way I define a challenge is something that does not have a guaranteed outcome. I know that on my worst day I can strap on a pair of shoes and run 26 miles. But here, no matter what kind of shape you're in, there's no guarantee you're going to finish. I can relate to that. I train for combat. Combat does not have a guaranteed outcome."

The Body Is Under Enormous Assault

The race begins in the dawn glow of a clear, breezy morning, below a craggy cliff of the Amargosa Mountains on the valley's east rim. From a casino-hotel on the Nevada–California border, where the runners spent the night, it has taken more than 40 minutes to reach Badwater, so named for an acrid, amoeba-shaped pool of salt and brimstone just off the road. Its brittle white edges look like crusts of ice, but that is a desert illusion because the temperature at 5:30 A.M. is 92 degrees.

A weather-chipped placard notes that the earth here sinks to the lowest point in the Western Hemisphere: 282 feet below sea level. Minivans and cars fill a narrow parking lot. The support crews tend to number one to four people — wives, coaches, in-laws, friends, gurus, anyone willing to dispense water, food, and exhortations. The vans are packed high with provisions — gallons of water, sandwiches, fruit, candy bars, protein bars, Gatorade, pretzels, crackers, salt tablets, sea salt, socks, shorts, blister pads, tape, towels, ankle braces, sunglasses, sunscreen, five or six pairs of shoes, and a bathroom scale.

Sahara hats are popular — white, Lawrence of Arabia headgear that shades the neck and cheeks. A few runners, like the Norwegian, wear them tailored to hold clumps of crushed ice, a cold skullcap. Dr. Dale Sutton, 57, a San Diego dentist, carries ice atop his head and in hanging pouches near his cheeks as well as in the pockets of his running togs: pinstriped blue pajamas sliced with ventilation holes. He is known as the Pajama Man.

Runners stretch, mingle and pose for pictures — all in eerie quiet, because it is so early, or because they are about to wage combat, or because the open desert sky swallows up most of the sound. At 6 A.M. they assemble on the road. No speeches, no fanfare. They are told to go. They take off to the whoops and claps of the support crews.

In all the miles to follow, these will be the only spectators; no one else will appreciate their toil, except perhaps the whizzing motorists and the occasional bystanders who have stopped for a Coke or radiator coolant in towns hardly larger than a gas station.

At first the road climbs gradually north along the valley floor, away from hills and escarpments named Funeral Peak, Coffin Canyon, and Dante's View. The ruddy desert loam tilts toward ridges to the east and falls to the yellow-white valley bowl to the west. For long stretches there is almost no vegetation, just rocky fields divided by the winding asphalt.

They move at a fast, easy gait. For superbly fit athletes, who train by doing 10 or 20 miles a day, the early stages of a long race often produce the euphoric sensation that they could go forever. Runners like to savor it, aware of their own breathing, the length and balance of their strides.

"I focus on what I'm doing, how I'm feeling," says the man who takes the early lead, Eric Clifton, one of America's great ultra-marathoners. "I'm constantly monitoring myself, keeping my legs relaxed, running smoothly, keeping my arms relaxed. Is my face tensed up? I'm trying to be as efficient as possible."

The 39-year-old movie buff, a theater projectionist from Crownsville, Maryland, has won more than half of the 68 ultra-marathons he has completed; he set an unofficial record last year by running a 100-miler in 13 hours and 16 minutes. Like most who venture into such extreme races, Eric began more modestly, running the 2-mile in high school, later dabbling in 5- and 10-kilometer road races. Once he realized his own exceptional stamina, he advanced to marathons and triathlons, then ultra-marathon cycling races.

With his long, pendular strides and short, pink socks, Eric moves well in front, followed by a pack that includes Lisa and the Major, steady at 9 minutes per mile.

At 7 A.M. the sun emerges above the Amargosas; it is 105 degrees — in the shade. At 7:15, it is 108. At 7:25, it is 110. A hot, dry wind pushes the competitors along. Dragonflies blow around in it. Tinder-dry weeds quiver in the canyon washes. At Furnace Creek, 17 miles out, the runners veer northwest on California 190, passing a borax museum and descending again into the yawning desolation of a dry lake bed where the thermometer reads 114. The asphalt is at least 20 degrees hotter.

Faces and shirts are sweat-soaked. Support vans play leapfrog with the runners, moving ahead a mile or so at a time. Runners stop briefly to drink, many alternating water and electrolyte supplements. How much they drink, eat, weigh, how hot they are, how fast they are going — every detail is logged by crew members, who take on the mien of anxious scientists, recording the vitals of subjects in some grotesque lab experiment.

The body is already under enormous assault; the success of the hours ahead will hinge largely on the fickle alchemy of supplying it proper nutrition. Sweat loss alone in this heat can exceed a gallon an hour. Dehydration is a constant danger. Usually, it is accompanied by the depletion of blood sugar and electrolytes — sodium, potassium, and other ions that are vital to cells and muscles.

Cells die; muscles cramp. In extreme cases, the heart may go into fibrillation, which can be fatal. More often, the body channels extra blood to the heart and brain, robbing it from other places — the skin, kidneys, and bowels. A runner gets the chills. Kidneys clog with protein from damaged muscles, damming up toxins in the blood. The walls of the empty bladder sometimes rub at the pubic bone, causing internal bleeding and producing an intense urge to urinate. Pieces of the bowel or stomach wall may slough off in diarrhea.

Rarely, the body temperature climbs high enough, 104 degrees, to affect the brain; the runner may slip into convulsions or a coma.

Drinking is a safeguard, but huge amounts of water may overwhelm the gastrointestinal tract, causing cramps, bloating, nausea. Even sports drinks may not contain enough electrolytes — or the body may not absorb them well enough — to prevent problems. It is often a matter of luck, experience or genetics that enable one runner to endure while the man behind him folds up like a scarecrow.

Distance Runner's Rite of Passage

Badwater delivers its earliest savagery to those from cooler climes. A Swiss runner with stomach cramps is the first to drop out. Bjarte, the Norwegian, vomits after 18 miles — the beginnings of an agonizing downward spiral that would end with his surrender, 10 hours later, at Mile 53, by which point he had thrown up, in the estimation of one crew member, at least 40 more times.

A 33-year-old Canadian, Paul Braden, once ran a Colorado 100-miler in which his blisters got so bad he had to cut off his shoes with scissors, drain the wounds, and go the last 15 miles with sandals taped to his feet. But that was not as agonizing as the cramps and nausea he now suffers as he nears Devil's Cornfield, a grove of clumpy arrow weed bushes 36 miles out.

With the wind raking across the road, with the temperature reaching 118 degrees, Paul drops a red flag — a legal means of temporarily leaving the course — and accepts a car ride to Stovepipe Wells, a burg at 41 miles consisting of a motel, a saloon and a convenience store. There, officials from Hi-Tec, the athletic-gear company that sponsors the race, help him into the back of a refrigerated bottled-water truck. His legs keep cramping and he is screaming so loud that a few tourists wander over, trying to see what is going on.

A white-haired race official administers a carbonated electrolyte beverage whose effect is immediate: Paul vomits all over the truck bed. The theory is that his balky digestion — gummed up by too much fruit — will now return to normal. Looking queasy, Paul is driven back to his flag. He resumes, suffers more cramps, ends up resting, falling asleep and finally dragging himself back onto the road in the evening, when the worst of the heat is over.

Finishing the race is the rite of passage of the distance runner. The sport culls out the weak and rewards the dogged. The runner learns that pain is temporary, but the gulf between those who drop out and those who finish is vast and enduring. With every step, an investment is made. It is either lost on the roadside or it becomes a jackpot that you reap at the end.

Having completed Badwater three times, Barbara Warren, a San Diego sports psychologist, has found that "the deep satisfaction in life comes from this enormous achievement. You feel like a giant."

Often, athletes spend months training and planning for Badwater, which raises the emotional stake in how it turns out. Paul tried to prepare himself for Death Valley by traveling to Amarillo, Texas, a month beforehand, running 10 to 15 miles a day in 100-degree heat.

The Major began training for Badwater in January, expanding his regimen to include twice-monthly workouts in the desert near Borrego Springs. Every trip he ran 26 to 30 miles, alone, bored, baking in the sun. "By the end of June, I had put in almost 1,600 miles just for this one race," he says. There are other forces: all the Marines at Camp Pendleton who know he is representing the Corps — what will they think if he quits? The lessons he learned from his mother, who has spent 27 years battling a degenerative stomach disorder, and his grandfather, who survived the same malady until he was 87, still mowing his lawn at 86.

If you get through a thing like Badwater, a lot of life's other problems seem far more manageable, the Major says. But the moment you let yourself quit, you step onto a slippery slope. One day you quite at 90 miles and the next you quit at 60. Before long you are getting by with the minimum, rationalizing mediocrity.

"Quitting is a disease," he says. "I can't bear the idea of looking in a mirror and seeing a quitter."

The Major is now bearing down on the 50-mile mark, nine miles beyond Stovepipe. It is well into afternoon. The road climbs; it will reach 6,000 feet at the end of the 18-mile stretch to Towne's Pass in the Panamint Mountains. The wind is coming downhill, and it is directly in the runners' faces — a steady blast that seems to come from some humongous hair dryer. No one runs; they walk tilting into the wind at comical angles, like a bunch of Charlie Chaplins.

The Marine Corps flag snaps wildly from the rear of the Major's support van. His face, faintly freckled, is rigid, his eyes fixed on the road. All of his elaborate philosophy has been bludgeoned down into a tight-lipped, ten-word mantra: "Mind over matter: If you don't mind, it doesn't matter."

Much of the first half of the field is scattered along the 18-mile climb. Eric is still well in front — he's already through the pass — trailed by a runner from Tennessee and then Lisa, in third place, but well back and struggling. Her 10- and 12-minute miles have disintegrated to this: a mile logged at a woeful 25 minutes.

Nauseated, weakened by diarrhea that began the night before the race — a result of nerves, her crew thinks — she is limping too, with an air cast supporting her bad right ankle. It is still hot — 107 at 4:30 P.M. — and she has at least 24 hours to go.

She tries not to think about the punishment ahead. Long-haired and purposeful, a former springboard diver at the University of Wisconsin, she is a staunch believer in mental strength, spiritualism, holistic healing. Like the Major, she is inspired by the courage of others: her younger sister, Julie, a member of her support crew, who overcame life-threatening surgery to repair three small holes in her heart; her cousin Joe, who was Lisa's age when he died last year of AIDS.

"He got a tattoo in New Orleans," she says. "Seven guys all used the same needle. All seven of them are dead."

Music from a movie they enjoyed together, *The Last of the Mohicans,* plays on her headphones.

All the runners are adrift out here, sorting through their thoughts, weighing the reasons to push on. A few miles behind Lisa is the 69-year-old Texan, Beacham, who slumps into a folding chair to gulp water from a plastic bottle.

"This right here is pretty agonizing," he says, but nothing of the ordeal shows on his face, thin as a hawk's. Beacham looks as if everything soft in him has boiled away on the hard roads — and maybe it has. He runs 3,000 miles a year, seven or eight ultra-marathons.

Despite a poor spell at 38 miles, where he had to lie down and take some chicken noodle soup, he is keeping up a formidable pace. The drive seems to come from a fear of growing old, says crew member Jim Davis, who is 58. Ultras are especially important to Beacham because without them, without all the training, he would figure to start withering away.

"I think he wants to get in as many of them as he can," Jim says, "before he gets to where he can't."

Hallucinations Not Uncommon

Evening is falling. The corrugated mountains near Towne's Pass glow warm orange and black, painted by slanting sunlight and shadows. Bruised clouds blow over the ridges. At 7:30, the sun sinks into the clouds rimming 6,585-foot Panamint Butte, gone until morning, and a soft violet haze settles over Death Valley. The plum-colored Amargosas, where the day began, are a ruffled curtain across the other side of the world.

The heat subsides — it is 86 degrees at 8:10, when the first automobile headlights fill the shadows. Eric, the race leader, descends into the Panamint Valley, where indolent followers of Charles Manson are still said to inhabit the brushy foothills near the Barker Ranch.

Eric is now feeling it. Downhills are murder on the thighs; after the intense early pace, his are aching like "somebody was beating them with baseball bats." At Mile 68, near a motel stop called Panamint Springs, he is passed by a 45-year-old investor named David Jones, who has yet to take a rest. Even when he had to vomit, up at the pass, he turned his head, retched and pressed on.

David opens a substantial lead. With the light fading in a landscape of rolling hills and ridges, Eric and Lisa contend for second place. A quick glance up to a stream of purple-orange clouds and Lisa sees a face — her cousin Joe's face, a vision that lasts an instant and is gone. It inspires her, but also saddens her. She cries. She tells her crew about it. Soon, the sky deepens, and even those tangled clouds disappear, leaving her there on the road toiling.

The darkness takes over. She sees a shooting star and is heartened by whatever hope it might portend, but before long she is crying again.

Night is hard. Night is for demons. Night is when rationality shrinks away, slipping down a rabbit hole, and nothing remains but the black asphalt and black sky and the questions that flicker through shorting mental circuits, like: Where is the horizon, what creatures are out here, why does it matter, really, to keep on going?

Hallucinations are not uncommon. Two years ago, when she got through Badwater in less than 42 hours, her first ultra-marathon, Lisa had a conversation with her dead grandmother. She heard babies crying, Indians chanting. "I saw things flying through the air," she remembers. "All the trees on Whitney, I thought they were people climbing."

Others have seen dogs, herds of cows, miniature people pushing tiny sleds, women showering, cactuses magically transformed into rocket launchers, highway skid marks shooting away like harpoons, flying off to infinity. One runner remembers an elaborate bridge under construction, spanning the highway, with an office building next door. Only the next day, when he was driving back over the course and looking for it, did he learn from his crew that all of it was pixie dust.

The runners are illuminated for periods of time by headlights, until the support vans pull ahead, leaving them to catch up again. At the west rim of Panamint Valley is another climb, through a 4,000-foot pass called Father Crowley's. It is cool enough there for long sleeves and sweatpants; the runners change during the stops. Here and there, they nap — half an hour, an hour, rarely longer.

Two more drop out, one because of a long, purple thigh bruise, the result of a pinched nerve and tendinitis. Eric goes lame on the downside of Crowley's; he dawdles through 10 miles in 6 hours and quits at dawn at Mile 94. Having won so many times, he places no stigma on stepping away, regrouping, aiming for another race. That is not the case for the less accomplished. For most who quit, the failure is a trauma almost equal to the pounding of the miles.

A runner who stops ceases to be a runner. It is a death of that identity, marked by an ignominious epitaph: "Did not finish." The phrase is abbreviated on the printouts that list the winners, and the slang verb, "DNF-ing," has an obscene sound, foul with shame. The runner who succumbs often goes to extraordinary lengths for resurrection, training for months and traveling back to the same race, the same course, a year or two later, to try again.

Twenty-four hours have gone by. Fatigue seeps like ice water into bones and joints. Walking is the rule now. Rest stops lengthen. Closing their eyes, they get leg massages. They take time to patch blisters, tape their feet, change shoes. They go up half a size when the swelling is bad. They drink hot soup and get up with the painful slowness of old men.

Gossip travels up and down the course in irregular pulses, moving from race officials to support crews, then to the runners. They crave information about the whereabouts of others, how they are doing. Eric's withdrawal is surprising news. It is rare now that one runner sees another, except on arduous grades or during long stops when someone is passed.

Lisa slips into third place. Beacham drops back into tenth, an hour ahead of the Major. Only twice during the night has Beacham slept, once for 15 minutes, another time for 20. He maintains a steady pace through Crowley's despite a blister on the ball of each foot, wounds that have been growing for almost 60 miles.

"It was pretty painful until I got them lanced," he says, his breath as sharp as piston strokes. "They hurt now, but I can stand it."

Beyond the pass, the road levels out near 4,000 feet, angling northwest along the Saline Valley and the dry Owens Lake bed: contoured terrain that grows nothing but rust-colored scrub. A wall of white mountains fills the far horizon. This is another of Badwater's psychological slams. One of those distant, chiseled peaks is Whitney.

"You can see the finish," says a runner, "but it's 51 miles away."

The sun climbs into the blue vastness of space and they pass one by one down the long, rippled road, a line of asphalt that runs forever.

"The sun's coming up, and pretty soon the sun will go down, and that's what you have to think about," says Dale, the Pajama Man, who at 7 A.M. is distracting himself, playing mental word games, his gangly limbs swinging as if they are loose in their sockets. "You have to disassociate your body from the pain."

At a drink stop, he sips slowly, to avoid spitting it up, and tries to gauge his progress.

"I have, what? Thirty-five miles to go?"
"No," a crew member tells him. "Forty-seven."

"It's Beyond Exhilaration"

In spite of the distance remaining, race officials are able to make a reasonably accurate projection of the finishers. They can see who is going well, the ones who will probably hang on.

David Jones, victorious only once in 57 prior marathons and ultra-marathons, is far ahead in first, already nearing Lone Pine, the tree-lined town at the base of Whitney. He is on his way to clocking 29 hours and 10 minutes, more than five hours ahead of the man in second.

Most of the top 10 runners will earn a buckle. Beacham's blisters will continue to plague him, but he is on his way to finishing in 43 hours and 53 minutes, well under his goal of 50 hours. The Major limps on a swollen right knee and is chafing so badly in the crotch that a streak of blood runs to the knee of his white sweatpants. He crew has dubbed him "Mad Mood Maples"; he is headed for a time of 45:15.

At least 18 others are also on the way to finishing. Seven have quit. That number might reach eight. Lisa is the one in doubt — the only remaining runner in serious trouble who has not yet withdrawn.

At 102 miles, she clings to third, reeling from her bad ankle and diarrhea and sleep loss. To go the next 6 miles to Keeler takes her four hours. Lone Pine is 16 miles beyond Keeler. Morning turns to afternoon. The sun beats down; temperatures soar into the 90s. The highway veers right into Lone Pine, past an airport, motels, diners, then left at a traffic light onto the two-lane road up Whitney.

This final stretch, a 4,000-foot ascent over 13 winding miles, is by far the most daunting. It begins gradually — the road flanked by sagebrush and boulders and tall rock formations that look like brown crispy cereal all glued together. Soon it rises to impossible steepness.

Lisa is still on the lower slopes at 3 P.M., taking ice treatments on her ankles. They are both so badly swollen they barely move. Coming out of the motor home, she is staggering. Turning uphill, her mirrored glasses catching the hot sun, she looks ready to cry. Two crew members walk alongside, ready in case she should collapse.

"Never, Never Quit," says a spray-painted slogan across the back of the motor home, but sometimes such lofty ideals must give way to reason. Her crew huddles in the road, discussing whether to make her stop. Her mother, Dot, squints up the mountain.

"It's scary," she says. "She doesn't want to give up. I think we're trying to make the decision for her. My theory is, live to race another day."

Arguing for surrender is that in two weeks she is scheduled to compete in a 300-mile adventure race, a team event for which she and her friends have paid hefty entrance fees. It is unthinkable to miss it, but the recovery from an ultra-marathon can take weeks. Most runners are fortunate to begin training again in six or seven days; stamina may not return for a month or two.

Lisa, though, doesn't always make the rational decision. Crew member Tony Di Zinno remembers an earlier adventure race, when she suffered a sprained ankle and a hairline fracture of her right leg on the second day out. She strapped on an air cast and kept going, six more days, 250 more miles.

Her hope had been to break the women's record for Badwater — 36 hours and 19 minutes, set during a race that began at night. That goal is now out of reach. With 8 miles to go, Lisa disappears into the motor home. Sister Julie stands outside, helpless, wondering if this is where Lisa will yield.

"She says she's never felt this bad," Julie says. "She can't bend her ankles, they're so swollen. There's no blood in her urine yet, but she thinks she lost her stomach lining."

For almost half an hour, there is only this still-life picture: the motor home under a cloudless sky, the rugged mountainside rising above it. Now and then a breeze stirs, but all the air seems to move at once, muffling sounds, preserving a strange hush. Insects clicking softly in the sagebrush. Inside, Lisa lies on her ravaged stomach. She will explain later that it is unwise at this point to sleep: the body begins to shut down. Instead, she meditates. In her mind she makes a list of all those reasons she should quit, the complaints of 127 horrific miles, every negative thought. When the list is as long as she can make it, she lights a tiny imaginary fire — and she burns it.

The door opens. She is helped down to the pavement, and she turns to confront the mountain.

"I'm going to get to the top."

Upward, then, with the road growing steeper. Her ankles cannot handle the slope, and so she turns around, walking backward, tiny three-inch steps. Up, up, up, staring into the sky, Whitney rising behind her. At 5:45, she is well up the mountain, the road at last curving into the afternoon shadows.

Pine trees begin to appear. Her legs look puffed up, rubbery, but they keep moving. Where the road levels out she turns around, walking forward until it rises again. At six o'clock, she has less than four miles to go. Every step is precarious, but her mood soars — "it's beyond exhilarating" — and she talks in strained breaths about a book, *The Power Within,* by Chuck Norris, and how its lessons helped her through the hard moments.

Less than a mile to go and the road rounds a steep turn. Lisa goes through it backward, her arms out, as if dizzy. Immediately, four Marines — the advance guard from the Major's group — jump out of a van and join her, like jet fighters forming an escort, but they drop away after the final curve, letting Lisa take the last hill alone.

Whitney Portals, where the race ends, is tucked within a nook of chalky granite: a clear pool fed by a plunging waterfall, hillsides thick with tall evergreens. A yellow tape is stretched across the road and Lisa hits it, finishing in 37 hours and 1 minute. It is not the record she wanted, but it is the fastest a woman has gone from a daytime start, when the racers cross the floor of Death Valley in the heat.

Officials, crew members, and five or six bystanders surround her, applauding. She is weeping, relieved, overjoyed, falling into the embrace of her sister, her mom, her friends. She looks up at the sky and says thank you. A huge bouquet of red roses is placed in her arms, spilling over them in a glorious scene of triumph — a portrait somehow perfect, but also fleeting, because Lisa quickly hands the roses away.

"Can't hold them," she whispers. "They're too heavy."

GARY SMITH

A Delicate Balance

FROM SPORTS ILLUSTRATED

CONSIDER YOUR SISTER-IN-LAW. Picture your whole family around the dining room table for the holidays, and start with your sister-in-law as she's spooning the gravy. Think of all her strengths, her good intentions, as well as all the things that make you want to stick your fork into your thigh.

Look, I know you don't know me from Adam — but just indulge me for a minute before the showstopper comes on. Turn to your brother now. You're studying him as he drains his third beer, thinking of all the stupid arguments you've had, all the quirks of his that have made your teeth grind since you were kids.

Now your spouse. Don't worry, she's oblivious; she's yapping to her sister. Consider her moods, her hormones, her chocolate addiction — the whole works. Got it?

Now close your eyes and imagine this. Imagine all of you at that table — brothers, sisters, in-laws — forming a human pyramid. Seven of you, stacked up in three tiers, except you're not on the ground. You're on a wire the width of your ring finger . . . three stories above the ground . . . the person on top standing on a chair . . . and no safety net below. To survive, your family has to synchronize every step and walk from one end of the 34-foot wire to the other. Just one failure to accommodate one of the niggling little pushes or pulls from that sister-in-law, one old jealousy between you and your brother, one bad night with your wife — hell, one cough or sneeze — and it's coffins for all of you.

One more thing. You have to do this not once, but seven days a week, for two years, all over the country. Traveling and eating and sleeping and dressing together, hating one another and loving one another and handing one another your lives again and again and. . . . Look, the Guerreros are almost ready now.

LADEEZ and GENTLEMEN! You are about to witness CIRCUS HISTORY! Fifty years after the Wallenda family ASTONISHED the world with an UNPRECEDENTED seven-man pyramid on the high wire. . . .

This is all you needed, right? You got your kids here, you got your popcorn and soda, and all you want to do is enjoy the circus, and you got some idiot next to you chewing your ear off. I'll shut up in just a second, promise. But there're just a few things I can tell you that'll make what you're about to see, as amazing as it is, even *more* amazing. Like the ringmaster said, the Wallendas were the ones that made The Pyramid famous. They're the family that brought it from Europe back in the late '40s and the pictures made everyone's eyes bug out . . . and then made them cover their eyes fifteen years later when the Wallendas collapsed in Detroit. It was horrible. Karl Wallenda up there dangling by his foot with a cracked pelvis, his ex-wife's niece clawing for dear life to his back, two other in-laws dead on the floor, and his own son paralyzed for life. And have you heard? It's already gotten one of the Guerreros, too. Just a few months ago, not long after the beginning of this two-year tour they're doing with Ringling Brothers. The Pyramid took out their kid brother Walfer, crushed the poor guy's vertebrae and paralyzed him from the waist down. You're probably wondering how the hell the other six survived, but it's not that simple, because—

LADEEZ and GENTLEMEN, the challenge of the seven-man pyramid requires the complete communication, cooperation and concentration of our artists. We ask for COMPLETE SILENCE in the arena!

All right already, I'll whisper. Don't worry, I'm not going to ruin it for you, because I can't. The more you learn about this trick and this family, the more unbelievable it gets. See, it's a family that . . . how can I say this? They all love one another, maybe too much, but hang around them for a few days and you start finding out about the rivalries and spats, conflicts that were never quite resolved. Maybe a little like your family or mine, the difference being, for the Guerreros, that each of those things can play itself out in the most subtle of ways, and kill them.

This might sound strange, but you know how hard it is to keep a family together these days? That's all the Guerreros are trying to do up there. To be *one*, a clan, just like when they were kids in Colombia, even now that they're adults living in America and some of them have kids of their own. Maybe that's unrealistic nowadays, an impossible illusion, and one thing's for sure — it's cost them years of heartache and anger between the ones who held onto that illusion and the ones who gave it up. Until a couple years ago, when they finally came to realize that there was only one way to do it, a way no other family would ever dream of. Because the one thing that can keep them all together is the one thing that can destroy them altogether.

You guessed it. The Pyramid. The Seven.

Ringling Bros. and Barnum & Bailey is proud to present this DEATH-DEFYING maneuver, performed by the sen-SA-tional GUERRERO FAMILY!

See their lips moving up there on the tower platform? They're praying together. *"En el nombre de Dios."* In the name of God. Now they'll start assembling The Pyramid. It's going to take lots of equipment: three crossbars, a metal chair and a balancing pole in each of their hands. And it's complicated. But I'll guarantee you, once they're all up there, you won't be worrying about the details. It'll all be in the pit of your stomach.

There goes Brian French, the only gringo, stepping onto the wire. He's one of the Guerrero in-laws, married to the captain, Jahaida; heavier than you'd picture a wire walker, isn't he? That's because he's not a wire walker. He's an elephant trainer, poor fellow, 23 years old, never walked a wire in his life till the family sucked him into this adventure a couple of years ago. It's easier that way, they kept telling him. No bad habits to break; just do everything exactly the way they tell him to, and he'll be just fine. Only he doesn't believe them, not for a minute, and he's praying like the pope after ten cups of coffee, and he won't be able to see anything, not one glimpse of The Pyramid or of his destiny, because it's all going to happen behind his back. He would much rather, as a matter of fact, lie down and let a pachyderm put its foot on his chest, which he's done hundreds of times in circuses, than do this. The more stressed he gets, the more he eats, and the more Jahaida nags him, reminds him that the high wire is the last place on earth you want to haul an extra thirty pounds.

Now that Brian's far enough out onto the wire, two hooked

braces are being placed over his shoulders from behind. Who's next, slipping his shoulders into the braces that attach him to Brian? The kind of creature the Guerreros fear most on this earth: an outsider. Cappy Acevedo from Colombia, 24 years old, the only nonfamily member in The Seven. Every time he sees the Guerreros playing with their children, his mouth goes dry and all he can think is: what if *I* make the mistake that orphans them? Which is not a far-fetched notion, because, for one thing, he once broke his leg going down a stairway, and he has to support the three hundred pounds of pressure that each man on the base of The Pyramid has to carry. Jahaida keeps trying to transfer the mound of french fries and slice of carrot cake from her husband Brian's plate to Cappy's plate, and to get Cappy into bed by midnight so he won't be off fast-talking the Ringling dance girls in the curve-clutching tights. He's the sweetest guy, but they watch him like a hawk. He's an outsider.

Next, a striking 33-year-old woman from Portugal is stepping from the second level of the platform onto the thin crossbar that's attached to the shoulder braces between Brian and Cappy. That's Aura, a contortionist from a circus family who never dreamed of going near the high wire until she met one of the Guerrero brothers at 18 and married him two weeks later, and suddenly realized she had to learn so much so fast to go up where he went that she ended up in the hospital from a miscarriage that damn near killed her.

For their safety, ladies and gentlemen, there is to be ABSOLUTELY NO flash photography!

Wilson's toeing the wire now, third member of the four-man base, the half brother who ran away at age 12 and never came back to the Guerreros, except to visit . . . until now. The humorous, sensitive one who even today, at 46, can't help wondering sometimes if he's really a Zamudio, his natural father's name, or a Guerrero — if yoking his life to theirs is enough. Who can't help wondering sometimes if the family is criticizing his posture on the wire or second-guessing his steps because it's warranted, or because . . . well, you know how it is with brothers. Because the brother who's about to attach himself to Wilson from behind is the one who used to put Wilson's teeth on edge, the one Wilson always thought was the favored son, his stepfather's first real son. Funny, how he ends up with his fate tied to what he ran away from.

Next: Werner. He's the last man on the base, the short, well-built guy who's shouldering the brace that's connected to Wilson, which has been resting on the lower tier of the platform. He's the 38-year-old brother who was a star on his own in Europe for years, the one you'd think would be in charge, but he's swallowing that bile for now, just thankful after all his years of loneliness to be part of the family again.

He's the handle of a whip: every movement, no matter how small, will ripple through The Pyramid back to him, and he has to absorb that movement, kill that wave, or it'll oscillate back to the others while they're still reeling from the first one. Want to know how he sleeps? He wedges himself against the wall every night so that he won't bolt out of bed with his arms thrashing, certain that he's falling again, the way he did that time in Stockholm, fell so bad he suffered a hematoma eight inches wide and the length of his back. He's the one who took the place of his paralyzed brother.

Now Jenny, the purest daredevil. She's the eldest Guerrero daughter, stepping from the railing on the second level of the platform onto the crossbar that now rests on Aura's shoulders. Jenny has dislocated her hip, sprained her neck in three places, ripped virtually every tendon in one hand, broken her tailbone, dislocated two discs and broken a foot. Way back, before the Guerreros dared try The Seven, Jenny was the family's star, leaping over one of her brothers on a wire thirty feet above the ground, letting him climb onto her shoulders and then carrying him across the air, stuff that no woman had done before. Until that day at the airport fifteen years ago when she betrayed the family — those are her own words — and walked away . . . only here she is coming back to volunteer for the most vulnerable position of all: on the chair at the top of The Seven, almost five stories up.

Now watch carefully. Jahaida, Jenny's 29-year-old sister, is reaching out from the platform and balancing the metal chair on the crossbar just behind Jenny. Jenny's taking a step backwards and slowly lowering herself onto the chair. Below Jenny, Jahaida tucks her shoulders into the brace, assuming the 150 pounds of pressure she has to support, hitching herself to Aura on the second level, and now she's stepping onto the crossbar running between Wilson and Werner.

Jahaida's got one helluva job. She has to keep her poise for every instant of the 34-foot-long journey across the wire, to notice every faint leaning, every infinitesimal loss of harmony, and to correct it, with the subtlest tilt of her body, or with the coolest verbal command, without betraying even a trace of the terror that might be screaming through her heart. It's Jahaida's job to mother them all, psychoanalyze them all, heal them all, hold them all together, even the ones she resented for walking away years ago. She's in the cockpit, the position Karl Wallenda manned four decades ago, only her role is infinitely more complicated than his was because she's a female in a Latin family, not to mention the youngest Guerrero out there, and how in the hell, you might well ask, just as Jenny and Werner and Aura often have, did she ever get to be in charge?

So now they're all in position, but before they start across, before Werner calls out *"Listos?"* (Ready?), let me ask you something: Why is it that people don't consider high wire a sport? Where's the line that separates the two? Strength? Agility? Athleticism? Balance? Teamwork? Damned if I can find it!

At any rate, now you've got the *how,* but you're still wondering . . . *why?* Don't worry. Even the Guerreros still wonder that. Why in the name of God are they doing a damn fool thing like this?

I'll tell you why. And you know what's really amazing? The guy who dreamed this whole thing up, the real reason they're all up there, the one who should be basking in all the glory, can't even be here to see it. He's a thousand miles away feeling proud, but feeling awful, too. He's in Sarasota, Florida, at the side of the one in the wheelchair, the one that the dream cut down. He's their dad, Arturo.

Let me tell you about this guy. He's 67 now, and he can't be more than five feet tall. You think you're looking at a spectacle now, wait till you hear his story — that's a spectacle — and there's no way you're going to make sense of the one without the other. I mean, who'd ever think that an altar boy would run away and join the circus? Who'd ever think that one of the smartest kids in the class, the serious little squirt pulling A's, would up and vanish one day to join the hucksters?

But Arturo was disillusioned, and he was suffocating. His father's parents were rich and educated landholders in Colombia who had disowned his dad for running off with an illiterate Indian woman and having two kids with her. When Arturo was 2 — *poof!* — his dad flew the coop, leaving this poor Indian woman with two little boys and not much more than her wits, her rosary beads and her saints to get her through. She had a stick she wasn't shy about using, and her son Arturo was *going* to wake up while it was still dark to go sell fruits and vegetables in the town market, and he was *going* to run from there to school to get the good grades, and he was *going* to run from school to the rectory to do odds and ends for the priests, and he was *going* to run home and do his homework and go to bed and get up and start all over the next day, and she was *going* to earn enough money prowling the countryside with her truck, buying and selling produce so that her two boys could go to university and reclaim their daddy's place with the elite. . . .

Then the circus came to Cajamarca, the town in the foothills of the Andes where they lived. And here's this 16-year-old kid who's been stashing away pesos for the right moment by slipping them inside a hollow tree in his yard, who can't understand why his mother keeps saying movies are immoral and the circus a perversion, and how the priest can keep saying *amen!*, the same priest who demands Arturo kick back half his pay for the work he does in the rectory.

So the circus came, and Arturo tapped the tree and joined the pagans, and imagine how delicious that must've been. For about five minutes, because right away he knew he'd made a terrible mistake. But he was just as bullheaded as he was smart, and he didn't go back, no matter how guilty he felt, no matter how many days he went hungry when the circus promoters took advantage of him, no matter how many times he got word that his mother still loved him and wanted him back. Not once, for ten years, did he return to Mama, and not once — *ever* — to God. He shot right up the ladder, from candy vendor to carpenter to mechanic to chief of trucks to stilt-walker to clown to the promoter's right-hand man, for godsake, by the time he was 18, because he was a gem amid the peanut shells and sawdust — an honest, humble, diligent, intelligent young man in a circus.

But circus ladders are rope ladders, and they kept swaying and fraying and snapping right in his hands. And each time Arturo was left to wonder: would this have happened, would they have exploited him yet again, if he had a family? You've got to understand, family in a South American country is respect, integrity and wealth . . . and Arturo had cashed all that in — for freedom. Would he ever

admit his doubt to anyone else? Oh, no. Call it pride, call it sin, call
it *cojones,* call it dignity: he'd up the ante. He'd build his own circus,
build his own family. A big family, tight as a fist. A fist that a lonely
little man could raise to the sky.

Weird, isn't it? Ten thousand people, and suddenly it's so quiet
you could hear a family drop. Just like on an airplane when you hit
turbulence — everyone silent except the wailing babies. That's
what it's like until — or *if* — Arturo's family gets across.

Watch their feet. The heel of each gymnastic slipper must come
down on the cable two inches in front of the other toe. They all
take a step together and pause, counting to themselves, *one, two,
three, STEP.* Nothing inside their heads except those three numbers
and God.

You keep watching and tell me what you think; I can never decide
if The Pyramid's a prayer to God, or a thumbing of the nose at Him.
Maybe it would've been better if Arturo had never hoped for The
Seven, dreamed of it, breathed a word of it to his family. Maybe it
would have been better if he'd never glimpsed The Seven that
night in Cali, Colombia, back in 1955 when the Wallendas were
touring South America. But something in that image — one big
family, so trusting, so united, so precise, so majestic, walking across
the void on a thread to the commands of its patriarch, Karl —
touched him, and set off the dream.

That was the year he met Maria Ruth Cortes. Ruth — that's what
she went by — was doing trapeze, just as he was, and she was a
knockout. Get this: her brother would end up having nineteen
children, all in the circus. Her father, at 16, escaped with the aid of
a circus rope over the wall of the seminary he had been forced by
his mother to enter, causing that poor woman to suffer a fatal
heart attack when she learned that he had overthrown God and
family for trapeze. You got it. Perfect marrying material for Arturo
Guerrero.

Sure, they were polar opposites. Ruth was the soft, temperamen-
tal, dependent one, Arturo the aloof, philosophical, hell-or-high-
water dependable one. She would pull south, he would pull north:
don't couples, when they're in love, call that balance? Those three
sons she had from previous lovers — Edmundo, Aston and Wilson
— they were fine with Arturo too, a head start on his fist; instant
respect, automatic clan. They named their first daughter after

Jenny Wallenda, the girl Arturo had seen on the chair on top of the Wallendas' pyramid, and they kept building from there.

The high wire came next. It *had* to. It was the perfect metaphor for Arturo's life: one step from the platform, and you couldn't retreat — it was harder to turn around on the wire and take that single step back than to take thirty more to the other side. And no net. *Ever.*

But he had a problem. He needed a partner up there to do the stunts that dropped the jaws that brought in the money that made sure he never caved in and crawled back to *Madre.* So he would take in a newcomer, feed and shelter him, teach him his tricks, create a humdinger act — and then watch it go up in smoke. The circus would duplicate Arturo's rigging, the partner would steal his tricks, and it'd break Arturo's heart every time. Have you ever met anyone like that? Arturo was always the first to pick up hitchhikers, the first to clothe gypsies and the first to sound the alarm to his family: "Never trust outsiders! Only your family!" So Ruth, who thought he was out of his skull when he first suggested it, and 10-year-old Edmundo, who didn't know any better, ended up as his partners on the high wire. Who else could Arturo trust?

Take another look at Jenny up there on top, Jahaida in the middle, Werner on the bottom. They were on the high wire as *fetuses.* Ruth would suck in her breath, girdle her gut, wrap herself in baggy skirts, go up on the high wire, climb onto Arturo's shoulders, then let little Edmundo wriggle up onto hers . . . *eight months* pregnant . . . *seven* pregnancies. Wait'll you tell your wife that one. Ruth had already lost one baby at seven months when she fell off the trapeze. "Arturo, I have pain!" she cried one night when her contractions started while Edmundo was balancing on a chair on the crossbar between her and Arturo. "Hold on!" cried Arturo.

She held on, was rushed to a tiny clinic, and gave birth to Walfer. That's when the village doctor said, "*No más,* Ruth," and mercifully tied her tubes.

Picture it: Circus Guerrero groaning up the flanks of the Andes in a cream-white '52 Ford truck, its bed jammed with tigers and bears, mountain lions, monkeys and pumas, the cabin jammed with diapers and milk bottles, infants and toddlers and teens. Arturo with a cushion stuffed behind his back so he could reach the steering wheel, and little Walfer riding on his shoulders, clutching his hair around the curves. Arturo watching the Communist guerrillas blink the message up the mountainside as he drove his family through the dark toward another town too remote, too dangerous for any other circus to consider: *Let this one through.* Rolling through town, braying the arrival of Circus Guerrero over the truck's loudspeaker; Ruth unpacking the red tights if they were in a left-wing town, blue for a right-wing one; Edmundo putting bear dung in a jar and selling it to the yokels as tonic for baldness; Wilson sticking flyers in the awestruck children's hands; Aston pounding tent stakes into the earth; Werner and Shirley and Jenny helping the grown-ups set up the seats for another two-show night; little Jahaida and Walfer getting in everyone's way. Arturo wading into the river to bathe the bath-hating bear, the one that nearly tore off his privates with a swipe of its claws. Then all of them — Guerreros, that is — collapsing at night in their home: one room in a local boardinghouse.

When you're living out of a truck, there are no cribs. One baby girl rolled off the bed, struck her head on the floor, and died. After that, to save another one from a similar fate, Ruth wrapped her up like a mummy, but she ended up wriggling under the wrappings and suffocating.

So Arturo's fist kept growing — and losing fingers too. Back in the mid-'60s, 14-year-old Aston and 12-year-old Wilson ran away, ground down by the relentless regimen of cage-mucking and tent-raising, of wire-walking and tumbling under the eyes of a stepfather with a remorseless stick. And they couldn't shake the feeling, whether it was true or not, that Werner was living on Easy Street because he had Arturo's blood. Playtime? Arturo didn't believe in toys. Hell, Arturo didn't even believe in friends. They're bums, he'd say. You give them a hand, they take an arm. Work is your best friend; everything else is just headaches.

For nearly four years the family never saw Aston and Wilson. Guess where they went? To another circus. When they finally came back, it was just to visit. Then there was Edmundo, who had fallen from the wire, broken four ribs and a collarbone. Doubt began creeping into Arturo's mind. Maybe he'd been too hard. Maybe he'd lose all his children to death and defection if he kept taking them up on the high wire, dragging them along on this endless ride. But he felt trapped. He'd invested his life's savings in Circus

Guerrero, and what else could he do? It had been so long since he had picked up a pencil that he had trouble writing.

He agonized and finally, in 1966, decided that 8-year-old Jenny, 7-year-old Werner and 6-year-old Shirley were going to have a school, a home and a warm bed. So one day he showed up at the door of the mother he'd left all those years ago. She hugged them all and cried. Arturo was formal, polite. He offered her the children. The Guerreros split up.

The telegram arrived at Circus Guerrero a few years later. Arturo read it and crawled under the truck, sobbing. Ruth had to claw the message from his fingers to find out. Shirley was dead, killed by a bus.

God, the whole thing would be so incredibly sad, if it wasn't even more amazing. Arturo collected Werner and Jenny, furious with himself for having opened his fist and allowing his family to scatter, angry at the world for tricking him into softening . . . and then smashing him. All his fears had been confirmed. There was no justice, no fairness, no law in the universe except the one he calls the Law of Compensation. No matter what a man does, he pays for it ten times — that's the law. If that's how things worked, if death was waiting everywhere, for the corrupt and the innocent both, then the only important thing was for a family to stick together, go down together . . . but only, goddammit, after *going up* together.

Look. Here's where they stop, dead center on the wire. Here's where they forget everything that's happened and trust one another absolutely. Here's where they pray they have been perfect, because if one of them is leaning when Werner calls, "Stop!" then God help him, because he's going to have to hold that position regardless, while Jenny slowly rises from her seat and carefully lifts her foot up onto the chair . . . and stands to her full height, her full glory, beneath the lights. At that moment, she'll tell you, she feels an aliveness, an awareness in every cell of her body, that she's never felt anywhere else on this earth. And the ones below her will tell you that everything in their lives — their aches, their arguments, their bills — is gone, completely gone. And there's a purity in that stillness, the most terrible of purities, one you and I will never know.

That's the gift Arturo gave them. And if you don't get that, you'll never understand him . . . and maybe you never will, regardless. Because there's no way you or I, never having felt that moment, would ever dream of putting our children through all the hardship and danger that he did.

I'm telling you, I've been around them all — your boxers, your matadors, and your poets too — and there's a purity to this guy Arturo that outstrips all of 'em. He's an atheist who understands the concept of God, and hungers for it. He keeps climbing toward that absolute, no matter how many times reality strikes him down. And he's found it, even if it only lasts for a few minutes, right in the midst of all the hucksters and con artists — no, right above them — and he's passed it to his children. Purity. The magical healing place. Just look how still The Pyramid is . . . all but that little quiver — here, take the binoculars — that quiver in their biceps and their calves.

It was inevitable, I guess, that a guy like Arturo ended up in America. It was only going to be for two or three years, he figured, when he closed up the family circus back in '76. All he wanted was to see the shiny place he had heard so much about, to make some decent money and return. How could he have known?

Just when they had become successful with Ringling, just when promoters all over Europe were panting for them, just when Arturo had turned Jenny and Werner into stars in a three-man act with him, doing all the running and leaps, the rope-jumping and baton-jumping and somersaults that other wire walkers considered lunacy . . . the two of them left. Bang, bang, within nine months of each other in 1982. They were suffocating, they said.

Edmundo . . . Aston . . . Wilson . . . Jenny . . . Shirley . . . Werner. . . . Now the fist was down to just Jahaida and Walfer, the two youngest. Arturo was in the middle of Europe, his act up in smoke, his heart in ruins, his family split — the remaining children convinced that those who had left, even though the family still loved them, were traitors. And itching to prove them wrong, the one place it counted most: on the wire.

Arturo drove the family's silver trailer to an orange grove outside Valencia, Spain, and set up a low wire. Jahaida, 15 years old at the time, was a natural, almost ready. Walfer, 14 — the baby, the soft-hearted one, just like his mom — was another story. For six months, under a relentless sun, a relentless eye, Walfer walked the wire from dawn to dusk, waiting for Arturo's stick to sting his feet when he erred and loathing every second of it. Six months in that orange grove, with no electricity or lights; a half year of black bread and white pea soup. And then months more of drifting through Europe, all but broke, parking in rest stops to sleep, waking up to the knock from police who now considered them gypsies.

Arturo's dream? He couldn't even utter it anymore. No circus would conceive of paying enough money to bring the seven Guerrero children back together unless they did The Seven . . . but how could they do The Seven if each of the seven needed to leave the family and be free?

Then one day, after they'd finally found work in Italy, Walfer fell. He lay there shaking, aching everywhere — his moment of truth. Suddenly it hit him: if he crawled away, if he quit this job he'd never liked and confirmed his father's suspicions about his lack of heart, then . . . it was over. He was the last child, no one to take his place, no one to stand between his parents and a desperate old age. So he got to his feet, and started climbing back up, and the crowd went wild, and he nailed all the crazy jumps Arturo had dreamed up, and that was it: a maniac, one of the world's best wire walkers, was born. A kid who'd end up doing an unprecedented 1,250 jump-rope repetitions on the high wire, who'd become the first man to leap four people on the wire in public and seven in practice — God, I wish he was up there right now so you could see him. A son you could almost . . . maybe . . . rebuild a dream on.

Want to know how Jenny passed her decade and a half in exile? As an Avon Lady, a roofer, a lineman for the telephone company and a souvenir vendor, before finding her own partner — an outsider — and going back up on the wire. Werner? He became a star in his own right all over Europe, with Aura as his partner. But it was never quite satisfying. No matter how many times the poor kid called home and tried to get Arturo to say three words on the phone, tried to share his triumphs and disasters with his family, it was never right.

Finally, even Jahaida left. She snuck out of the back window of the trailer — at 25, for godsake! — to marry Brian . . . only to faint as the justice of the peace read the vows, and scurry back home to Mama and Papa three days later. Then Walfer, after he and Jahaida had finally persuaded Arturo to retire in 1992, when he was 62, went to Europe to be Werner's high-wire partner, just to keep the creditors at bay. Poor guy, 24 years old, cried for so long in the airplane that the flight attendant finally had to ask him what was wrong.

Sure, the kids chipped in and helped their parents buy a house in Sarasota that same year — imagine, all those years with all those kids, and now they buy a five-bedroom house. And sure, they visited their mom and dad. But they were just visits, too often loaded with almost as much second-guessing and feuding as they were with laughter and hugs.

Only Werner, the cockiest one, ever flung the contradiction into his father's face. "How can you say I abandoned the family?" he demanded of Arturo one day. "You left *your* family . . . didn't *you?*"

This is where the Wallendas fell apart. This is where the nephew of Karl's first wife felt his shoulders sagging from all the weight piled on top of him and the 45-pound balancing pole began to drag his hands lower and lower. . . . This is where Brian, Cappy, Wilson and Werner must actually walk uphill, because even the 16,000 pounds of pressure pulling on the cable to keep it taut, from 14 guy wires ratcheted as tightly as the rigging will bear, aren't enough to keep the high wire from sagging at the center under a half ton of human beings and 350 pounds of poles. This is where the Guerreros know why they ended up suffering a year of Florida sun and mosquitoes and two-a-day practice sessions on the wire in Arturo's back yard before they took this two-year double dare. Didn't I tell you that lady behind us trying to hush us earlier would be leaning over my shoulder before I was through?

Look . . . see what's happened? One of them in the base has stepped too fast, or too slow, and they've separated just a hair, but look how it makes the whole thing tremble. This is when they all wonder if they weren't all better off spread across the globe, every man for himself, scrambling to survive, just as they were back in the early '90s.

This is where Werner wonders what drove him and Walfer to the international circus festival in Monte Carlo in January 1994 and what made them get worked up into such a lather, just because seven wire walkers called the White Angels had the audacity to do The Pyramid there, the trick the Guerreros considered their birthright — even if they hadn't done it yet. This is where Werner wonders why he hungered so much for a way back into the family, why he cried, "That's *our* trick! We can't let this happen! We were born to do this!" — and then, when Walfer heard the trumpets too, jumped onto a plane home with him, and convinced the family that they *had* to do The Seven. For Dad! For the family name! For the mortgage payments! For the fist! For the way things always should've been!

Never were so many problems solved by one dramatic stroke. Nobody could remember Mom and Dad looking so happy. Three generations running around the Sarasota house, big steaming bowls of Colombian soup between the midday and evening practices, and then everyone, at the end of the day, jumping into the backyard pool.

You'd think they finally had it made, but let me tell you what happened. Jahaida and Walfer wondered who had elected Werner the boss. Jenny and Werner wondered what made Jahaida and Walfer think they had all the answers, just because they'd stayed at Papa's side longer. A couple of them weren't happy over the money split. None of them could shake the feeling that Arturo, barking suggestions from the ground, was turning them all into children again. And oh, yes, that other problem. They had six — Jenny, Jahaida, Walfer, Wilson, Werner, Aura. They needed seven. Aston, down in Colombia, and Edmundo, off doing trapeze with his three kids, couldn't do it. The Guerreros had no choice but the one they'd all been raised to dread: an outsider.

The Grand Opening came in Amsterdam in December 1994. One of their first practices there, and they came *this close* to kingdom come. A few feet from the end of the wire, a wire walker from Colombia named Jorge — the outsider they'd reluctantly settled on — couldn't bear the strain any longer. He lunged for the platform to save his hide and The Pyramid began to disintegrate. Net? Are you kidding? Not even in practice. Jahaida took three quick steps backward on the crossbar to compensate, and God knows how, but Walfer held on when her last step ended up in his teeth.

But they pressed on. And for two weeks in Amsterdam, and then a few weeks more in Vienna, the standing ovations, the awe, the purity were enough. "This isn't work!" Jahaida would go around saying. "This is fun!" Then The Seven began to flush out every character flaw, pick at every old scar, rub up all the old friction. So what happened? The Pyramid fell apart six weeks after it finally came together, undone by the same old dilemma: What needs too much to be together falls apart. They all quit in Vienna and went home.

Which is where this story would've ended, or never quite begun, if one of the jaws hanging open in Vienna hadn't belonged to the chief talent scout for the Greatest Show on Earth. This guy showed up at Arturo's house late one night and asked a question: would the Guerreros accept one of the richest contracts in Ringling history to do The Seven for two years, beginning in late '96, with Ringling holding an option for two more?

Would they? *Could* they? Of course they couldn't. Of course they did.

I shouldn't tell you what happened next. After all, they're so close to the other end now, and if they can just hold on for a few more steps, we can both go look for a cold beer. It's not the best time to talk about family history following them up to the wire, one of the Guerreros falling, crushing his spine, coming within a whisper of death. But I can't put it off, because everything's linked.

Jahaida and Walfer, fearing their older brother's dominance again, didn't include Werner and his wife in The Seven that would tour America for Ringling. Wilson begged off; he'd had enough. Jorge, the outsider, was axed when he panicked once again. In their places stood a Moroccan named Mustafa, Cappy, and two more Guerrero spouses, virgins to the wire whom the family painstakingly trained for a year: Jahaida's Brian and Walfer's Angelina. This time they asked Dad to be their maestro on the floor, and for both him and their mom to live with them on Ringling's mile-long train.

Then, Werner showed up in Tampa, just as the tour was about to begin last December. He was pining to share the greatest moment in the family's life. Arturo begged the others to take him back into the fist, to let him take the Moroccan's place — that man's poison, Arturo warned them. But they wouldn't listen.

The old man's eyes misted, and Ruth cried, when they saw The Seven walk for Ringling. But then Arturo, feeling badly for Werner, went back to Sarasota with his banished son, leaving the tour a month after it had begun.

The pressure buckled the Moroccan. He smashed his head over and over against a box one night, sobbing that he couldn't take it. Just before it was time to assemble The Pyramid in Asheville, North Carolina, early in February, he did something no Guerrero had ever seen — he leaped from the high wire onto the mat during a performance — forcing the Guerreros to cancel The Seven that night. They had no replacements. They could either keep hinging themselves to a man coming unhinged — or surrender the fat contract and a lifelong dream. Then, about a week later, as they packed up in Greensboro, North Carolina, Jenny, sick of her younger siblings' commands, said she was quitting.

The Seven was swallowing Walfer piece by piece. What would he tell management at curtain time in Richmond two days later? He agonized until nearly 4 A.M., then finally hit the road. An hour and a half later he lost control of his truck and turned it over on I-85. He spent five hours in the emergency room, went nearly forty hours without sleep, and bled internally from the impact of the wreck. Jenny showed up in Richmond after a change of heart, and Walfer, fearing that Ringling was losing all patience, couldn't bear the thought of canceling The Seven once more.

Arturo was the only man with the power to persuade him not to go up, but he was back in Sarasota with the banished Werner. In a fog, without making his customary last check of the rigging, Walfer stepped onto the wire to do the tricks he performed each night just before The Pyramid. He raced toward Cappy — the over-under stunt — and leaped just as Cappy ducked. It's hard to know exactly what happened then. Maybe Walfer missed the jump that badly. Maybe the wire, not quite secured to the tower, sagged when he landed, and then recoiled. He fell, breaking three ribs and puncturing a lung as he struck the cable, his hand grabbing it just long enough to swing him outward, toward the edge of the mats. Half on, half off, he landed, his legs jackknifing over his head, crushing two vertebrae and his spinal cord.

Arturo's face drained of blood when he got the call in Sarasota, and he hopped into a car alongside Werner, with Wilson and Edmundo not far behind. For sixteen hours of extremely risky surgery, the Guerreros, united, waited for the headshake that would signal life or death.

Three weeks later, his family all still at his side, Walfer called them to his bed. Jahaida had made it clear: she was finished with The Pyramid and the wire; she would take care of her brother for the rest of her life. Brian kept it quiet, but he was never going up again either. Walfer cleared his throat, four tubes sticking out of his

chest. "I need to see a light in front of me, Jahaida," he begged.
"You've got to do The Pyramid again."

Jahaida, in tears, finally nodded, and Brian did too. Walfer
turned to Werner. "You and Aura will take my place and Tweedy's,"
he said, using his wife's nickname. He turned to Wilson. "You'll
take the Moroccan's place, won't you?" he asked. Wilson flinched
. . . but couldn't turn him down. For once, he was sure. The family
needed him. *His* family needed him. The Pyramid went on.

I'll be honest. They still argue. But the arguments end sooner
now. Jahaida only has to mention Walfer, and the voices hush. She
tries harder than ever to begin each critique of Werner by saying, "I
know you've been on the wire for many years, but—" and he tries
harder than ever just to shrug and listen. She tries harder than ever
not to take Wilson to task in front of the others, and to treat Aura
as a sister instead of a sister-in-law, and to give Jenny the space
she needs.

It's working right now, and it's fun again, but they admit The
Pyramid's scarier than it's ever been because of how little time the
new members have had to harmonize their steps. For a while there
was a net below them — New York state law — which the Guererros
considered a disgrace, but it's gone again now.

They call home every day, sometimes twice, to talk to Walfer. He
loves to talk but sometimes the pain from his spine grinding against
the two long metal bars the doctors inserted is just too much.
Arturo tells him the doctors are wrong — he'll walk again, walk on
earth and on air both. He tells Walfer he's made of different material than other human beings. Then the others in the room will
look up, and realize Arturo's gone. They'll look outside and see
him in the back yard, walking over the weeds, walking on the wire.

He just didn't want his kids to suffer, like he did. That's why he
couldn't bear to let them go away, even when they grew up. He
can't quite figure out how things ended up this way. "Sometimes I
think that the only thing I ever really planned was running away
when I was 16," Arturo says. "And that everything after that just . . .
just *happened*."

When you ask him if he could've ever imagined it like this,
getting his dream and not being able to see it, getting his family
back together and getting his son in the wheelchair with it too,
Arturo doesn't say anything. He just takes off his glasses and cries.

Look! They're finished! You can breathe again. Listen to the crowd. Now I'm going to tell you the most amazing thing of all. Maybe it's just a joke, but Walfer's said it enough times now that even he's not sure anymore. If he can't get out of his wheelchair one day, if he really can't . . . then he and his wheelchair are going up. Up on the high wire, where a Guerrero belongs.

THOMAS KOROSEC

Goofy Golf

FROM THE DALLAS OBSERVER

IN FAR NORTH DALLAS, just up from the Whataburger and the Just Brakes and the Blue Star miniwarehouses, Jeffery Smith is wandering with his putter among the plastic zebras, dreaming little dreams.

Sure, his sport holds about as much cachet as indoor roller-skating, or bumper pool, or lawn darts. "It's easy to be pretty good," as one miniature golf authority has said. "It's stupid to be very good."

But Smith, a former Deadhead who earlier this year had a pair of crossed putters and an ace of clubs tattooed on his left leg in a display of similar dedication, wants to be more than very good. He dreams of the perfect game. Of getting on TV. Of winning $1,000 a hole in this year's glorious, ultimate round.

People will get hooked on just about anything.

So here he is, banging putt after putt down the synthetic green carpet of Hole 13, Course 2. "This," the 37-year-old exterminating company manager says with easy authority, "is the hardest hole at Coit Road Putt-Putt."

It would be foolish to argue with the man who holds the course records on all three of this Putt-Putt's pint-sized 18-hole tracks — an 11-under-par 25 on Course 2, a 13-under-par 23 on Course 1, and a 14-under-par 22 on Course 3. "I know every inch of it," says Smith, who is among 46 players in the Professional Putters Association, a creation of Putt-Putt Golf and Games, a $100 million-a-year franchising operation covering 246 courses, most in the Southeast and Midwest.

The PPA is about as far down the golf food chain from Tiger Woods as one can go. Still, the competition is brutal. The pro circuit is crowded with Putt-Putt virtuosos from proving grounds like Danville, Virginia; Pineville, North Carolina; Duluth, Georgia; and Kingwood, Texas.

Smith, the defending Texas state champion — he won in 1995 and 1996 — is trying "to move up to the next level" this season and begin winning some of the tour's eleven national events.

Getting that good may be stupid, but there is something in it that is at once addictive and painfully difficult. "I've heard players call it M.F.G.," Smith says. "Miniature fucking golf."

Smith is a man among children as he puts in his four hours of practice on a suburban Saturday morning — one of the three sessions a week he spends working on his game or playing competitively. Around him, birthday parties and kiddie outings meander through the pygmy-proportioned courses, which together with bumper boats, go-carts, batting cages, and a roomful of video games constitute Coit Road Putt-Putt and Games. A temporary sign on the front fence promises: LASER TAG COMING SOON.

Smith's present concern, the malevolent Hole 13, doesn't look all that tough in the hands of a knot of 8-year-olds playing in the group ahead of him. From the rubber tee box, they whack their balls every which way, screaming them down the orange aluminum side rails en route to scores of 3 or 4. One kid, wearing a Goofy T-shirt, finishes out by plopping on his belly, aiming the butt of his putter like a pool stick, and popping his red ball in the cup with a jab.

The way Smith sees things, it's as if there is another Hole 13 out there, existing in a parallel universe — a multifold and sometimes inscrutable place where speed, angles, gravity, even wind and temperature, play their parts. It is a lilliputian world in which all-but-imperceptible marks in the green polypropylene carpet, or dents along the rails, mark imaginary lines along which a perfectly stroked putt will travel and drop in the cup in a single stroke.

In serious Putt-Putt, players want to ace them all — a feat that has been accomplished only twice in competition. A two is par. "When you ace six or more, you have a round going," Smith says.

Hole 13 comes in the shape of a long rectangle at the tee box-end, connecting to a square. The metal cup is located just right of the middle of the square, about twenty feet from the tee.

To trick things up, a foot-tall hump cuts across the rectangle at an angle. Beyond that, the area around the hole tilts slightly from the player's right to left — the consequence of settling cement at the 8-year-old course.

Put it all together, and a ball struck straight at the hole curves left, then right, then left again before it reaches the hole.

"There is something about the carpet now that's messed up my shot," Smith says, referring to the one-bounce-on-the-right-rail strategy that has served him well in the past.

Now, though, his ball is hitting the right rail once before the hump, then skimming along and hitting it again on the far side, sending it wide of the hole. "It's only supposed to bounce once," he says.

When his ball rolls to a stop more than five feet left of the hole, making for a tough second shot, Smith moans. "Not there. When you end up over there, you're hating life."

The reasons behind the changing conditions that have Smith in a momentary funk are all around him. The North Dallas–Richardson-Plano kids that plunk down their five dollars to play a round here are a notoriously free-swinging lot — as evidenced by the dozens of red, yellow, and orange balls in the fake alligator-infested lagoons that run between the holes. "You have to hit it pretty hard to get off the course into there," says Smith, stating the obvious.

The Coit Road course is well known among the Putt-Putt cognoscenti as one of the most difficult in the state because of this constant addition of new dents, gouges, scrapes, and bubble-gum stains.

"Let me tell you, this course changes more than most — it changes day to day," Smith says. "I can literally come out here and play a shot, and tomorrow it will be different. These kids out here are pretty aggressive."

So Smith sets about finding a new way to ace Hole 13, aiming at various dents and marks up and down the right rail. A fiberglass elephant atop the gray Putt-Putt mountain keeps watch over his earnest work.

A trim, athletic man whose curly brown hair is receding somewhat, Smith makes no excuses for his infatuation with what most people perceive to be a game for children, or adolescent dates.

"You say you're a professional putter, and people give you that look of disbelief. They think you're joking," says Smith, who in his day job as general manager of Dallas Pest and Termite Services' Carrollton office oversees seventy-five bug-killing employees.

An easygoing, highly personable sort, Smith does everything he can to explain how the game works at this level, and why someone might ever want to put this kind of time and effort into it.

As a high school senior in suburban Glencoe, Illinois, Smith saw his first Grateful Dead concert at Chicago's Uptown Theater on January 31, 1978. He returned the next night and the next, and in the following few years followed the band to nearly seventy shows.

His Putt-Putt story develops along similar lines.

Smith was on his sofa one Saturday afternoon in 1989 when a Putt-Putt tournament came on cable TV. A skillful golfer with a low, single-digit handicap, he had played a few rounds of miniature golf in Chicago as a kid, but this somehow grabbed him. He wandered over to the recently built Coit Road course that afternoon, and happened to meet Rainey Statum, one of the guys in the televised tournament. Statum, a Houston-area player, told him about a little local event going on at a course in Mesquite the next day. Smith played in five other amateur events that year.

The next year he joined the pros. The PPA invites the 50 or so top players in the country to join, and collects a $500 annual fee. Another 200 proficient players are considered to be regional pros.

So far, Smith says, he's earned about $9,000 in prize money, with his best showing in the Texas state championship — in a state ranking second to North Carolina for its number of courses. About 40 serious players competed in the state event, for which he won $1,500.

During the 1995 championship at his home course on Coit Road, he aced 21 of 36 holes en route to the $1,500 first prize. In 1996, he successfully defended his title against 40 other players in Wichita Falls, acing nine in a row at one point.

A local putter manufacturer, Traxx Golf Company, has begun providing him clubs.

"He's very good, but they're good all over. I wish the ball would fall for him more often when he goes and plays for the big bucks in Orlando and places like that," says his wife, Iris Davila, who married Smith three years ago this October.

They had already been dating for a few years when Smith took up the game, she says. He doesn't ease up a bit when they play together. "He takes it seriously," she says.

It's been said that most women don't understand pro Putt-Putt
— only one of the 46 national pros is a woman — and Davila says
she can see why.

"He spends a lot of time at it," she says, hesitating ever so slightly.
"But it's his thing. It's harmless. I mean, he could be hanging out
in a bar."

Putt-Putt purists will tell you their game differs from other types of
miniature golf because there is no room for luck. There are no
windmill spokes to shoot between, no brontosaurus mouths opening and closing, no live bears swiping at balls.

Putt-Putt courses are made up of 18 of the 188 hole designs the
company has copyrighted. Although Putt-Putt layouts offered windmill holes, skeet-ball target holes, loop-de-loops, and other doodads
in the 1950s and '60s, today the courses are laid out with geometric
precision in an attempt to reward the same skills possessed by
traditional golf pros. The windmills and mock safari animals are
placed off to the side.

Of course, it remains a form of miniature golf, and as such its
roots reach deep into a weird, all-but-forgotten chapter in the history of fads: the year America went loco for miniature golf.

As John Margolies recounts in his book *Miniature Golf* (fittingly
bound in a shaggy chunk of Astroturf), James Barber designed the
first bantam golf course in 1916 on the lawn of his estate in Pine-
hurst, North Carolina. The game gathered little popular appeal
until 1929, when a Tennessee family patented something called
Tom Thumb golf and built their first course at Lookout Mountain,
the eternally cheesy resort. The now-gone Tom Thumbs were little
enclosed courses covered with artificial turf, much like miniature
golf courses today.

Within a year, this novel pastime exploded, taking its place behind dance marathons and hot-dog-eating contests as one of the
zaniest fads of the era, and perhaps the biggest of them all. People
called it "the madness of 1930."

In that single year, more than 25,000 courses sprang up across
the country, including more than 150 on New York City rooftops.
People poured so much leisure time into the game that Hollywood
studios ordered their stars to stay off the mini-links. The game was
so big, they found, it was starting to hurt box-office receipts, which
were down 25 percent that year.

The courses *were* wild. A layout in Los Angeles called Caliente worked around a natural geyser that shot steam one hundred feet in the air. Mary Pickford, the screen actress, opened a course shaded by surreal, Max Ernst–inspired fake palms. Another L.A. course boasted a live bear chained at the edge of the runway who swiped at passing balls. Bobby Jones, the grown-up golf great of the era, gave putting tips on his weekly radio show, while "I've Gone Goofy Over Miniature Golf" became one of the year's most popular songs.

Referring to the onset of the Great Depression that year, humorist Will Rogers said, "There's millions got a putter in their hand, when they ought to have a shovel."

By the end of the year, though, mini-golf crashed harder than disco. It didn't come back until an insurance salesman named Don Clayton arrived two decades later and became the Ray Kroc of putting. In 1954, Clayton laid out a version of the game in his home town of Fayetteville, North Carolina. As the story goes, he called it Putt-Putt, because he wasn't sure how to spell the world "vale" in Shady Vale Golf.

The game boomed with postwar suburbanization, sprouting up next to fast-food franchises and strip shopping centers. Today, Putt-Putt is global. There are eighteen courses in Japan; one in Beirut; and one overlooking Krakatoa on the Bay of Java.

To underline his vision of the game as a thing of skill, Clayton started the PPA tour in 1959. "Our putters are great athletes and great men," said Clayton, who died last year at age 70. "We have made competition out of a thing that was recreational. I believe this is the kind of drive and commitment that made this country great."

There is more than one way to cash in on today's Putt-Putt tour — although Putt-Putt headquarters is far from thrilled about all the informal betting going on around its events.

The biggest money changes hands in "the Calcutta," a country-club betting game in which each player is auctioned to the highest bidder. The bidders who own the win-place-show finishers collect a piece of the betting kitty. At the 1996 Texas state championship, Smith bought himself with a $70 bid. He collected about $600 when he won.

Then there are the "pot games."

Because each course plays differently, players will arrive one or two days before a tournament and learn how the ball will roll. As Smith puts it, "Courses are tougher, better, fairer, faster, slower — they are all different."

During the endless hours of practice before tournaments, seven or eight players will gather and play the field for $2 a hole, per player. If you're at the head of the pack, or the end, you can win or lose as much as $100 a round.

"Guys out there like to turn it up," says David Lynch, a 46-year-old security guard from Mesquite who is one of four North Texans on the national tour. "It can get expensive."

Lynch, who has worked around the Mesquite Putt-Putt on and off for the past ten years, was at that course on a recent Tuesday night, playing in a very tough small-stakes match against Smith and about a dozen others. The money was put up by the players.

Set in a parking lot beside a bland, lunch-box-shaped club-house, the Mesquite course is as cheerless as these little artificial worlds get.

"I bleed orange and green," Lynch says, referring to the ubiquitous Putt-Putt colors. A pear-shaped guy in wraparound sunglasses and a Putt-Putt cap, he says he's been getting more time to practice since his divorce, to which his devotion to the game contributed.

"She said it was a kids' game," Lynch says. "When I worked here, she said it was a kid's job."

Betting aside, the only way to break even or make money as a pro, after expenses, is to move up among the top handful of players nationwide, Lynch says. And only one Dallas-area player has ever done that.

"People stop sniggering when I tell them I earned $75,000 playing Putt-Putt," says Marc Portugal, a 34-year-old marketing operations manager who grew up playing in Waco. Competing at the top levels since he was 16, Portugal has been "on TV" five times and has won the game's national championship twice.

These days, three players make each of the three televised rounds — which pay players $500 or $1,000 per hole in a head-to-head competition carried on ESPN. The nine players are selected in a variety of ways: by winning one of several national tournaments, by being one of the top players throughout the season, or by winning a qualifying tournament.

The national championship, a $20,000 event capping the season, is held in September. It pays $3,000 to the winner.

Jeffery Smith talks about this "next level" as he prowls his dwarfish golf course, showing a visitor how the big boys play. Dressed in a Putt-Putt shirt, with a folded towel and PPA tag dangling from his belt, he looks, well, professional.

He'd play and practice even more, he says, but spring is termite season, and he is busy on his job.

Smith bounces his ball twice off the rubber tee mat before he places it in one of seven indentations, then seeks his aiming mark. "I have to know where I'm aiming. I just don't feel my way around like some of these guys," he says.

Smith becomes so absorbed in his target that when an 8-year-old named Zeke runs up and stand only a foot behind him, breathing hard and talking, he doesn't move a millimeter from his shoulder-square stance.

He is thinking more about such things as wind — which pushes a ball down the carpet more quickly at Hole 3, the one that runs under the concrete mountain and past the waterfall. Temperature, too, enters the calculus. A ball will bounce a bit more off a hot side rail than a cold one.

In a round that takes less than a half hour, Smith aces nine holes with a repertoire of straight shots, elaborate triple-banks, and "touch" putts that pass the hole, bounce off the back rail, and drop in "the back door."

Hole 12 he conquers with a screaming shot that hits a concrete wedge, squirts straight left, bounces off a rail, hits another concrete wedge, and dives into the hole.

Even the sinister Hole 13 yields an ace — one bounce off the right rail. He gets 2's on the rest, for a round of 27.

"The key for me is concentration. I need to improve my mental game," Smith explains after the 18th hole, which he stuffs with his towel so his white PPA ball doesn't get gobbled up like everyone else's.

"I made nine in a row the year I won here," he says. "You get on a roll. You're feeling like you can't miss. You hear basketball players or other athletes getting in a zone. A Putt-Putt putter can too." Facing back toward his Zen garden of a golf course, club in hand, he concludes, "I'm looking for my zone."

JOHN SEABROOK

Tackling the Competition

FROM THE NEW YORKER

THREE YEARS AGO, Paul Tagliabue, the commissioner of the National Football League, decided that the league needed to become more "proactive" about marketing the sport of football, or "the product," as the newer owners call the game. The NFL had severed its long relationship with CBS after the 1993 season, signing on with Fox, and Tagliabue wanted to take a forward-looking approach to marketing which would be more compatible with "the approach to sports television that ESPN and Fox brought to the table, that everyone else is emulating now." As he explained it to me, "It's really an attitude more than something you can quantify. It's more youthful. More iconoclastic." In recent years, the sports landscape in which the NFL competes has been profoundly altered by other forms of media and entertainment. Video games provide some kids with the same sense of action, speed, and power that pro football used to supply; Nintendo, for example, is a major competitor of football that did not exist twenty years ago. On the modern media gridiron, it isn't Johnny Unitas vs. Bart Starr anymore; it's Brett Favre vs. Batman.

Although previous presidents of NFL Properties, the licensing, sponsorship, and marketing arm of the league, had all come from within the league office, Tagliabue thought that the right person to lead a new marketing campaign, like the one the National Basketball Association has employed so successfully in recent years, might be found outside the NFL. He needed someone who could make football attractive to a new generation without disgusting the middle-aged bratwurst-and-beer types who enjoy going to games with their faces painted in the colors of their teams. The situation of the NFL was a little like that of the high school football star who has always had the girls flock to him and suddenly needs to go looking for a date for the first time: it would require the right touch. How do you preserve the unglamorous essence of football, which consists of men colliding with each other, while competing with all the cool new noncontact sports, from snowboarding to street luge?

Neither Tagliabue nor Neil Austrian, an investment banker and former advertising executive whom Tagliabue hired as president of the NFL in 1991, was interested in "becoming a CBS" — that is, allowing the forces of change that had humbled its former network to erode the NFL as well. Recently, polls have shown that football is losing kids to both basketball and soccer. Basketball is now twice as popular as football among 12- to 17-year-olds, according to a 1996 ESPN Chilton Sports poll, and all around the country not as many kids are going out for football as in the past. John Cistone, who coached the varsity team at St. Vincent–St. Mary's High School, in Akron, Ohio, for thirty-nine years, told me, "In the seventies and eighties, we would have seventy-two to eighty-two players on the varsity. Last year, we had forty-four. We've won four state championships, so we have quite a football tradition. But kids don't seem to be interested. The core athletes, they still play football, but the fringe, who were playing football ten or twenty years ago — today they do other things." Terry McBroom, the coach at San Marin High School, in California, said, "Back in the seventies, football was huge. But now we've fallen off. We play in an eight-team league — there've been eight teams for as long as I can remember. But last year Redwood High School and Drake High both suspended their varsity programs. Redwood has twelve or thirteen hundred students, and they couldn't field a football team. 'Course, their soccer is huge."

Football is not "on trend," as the marketers say. Very few girls play the contact version of the game — a serious liability in an era when the growth of women's participation has become "the biggest change in sports in the last decade," according to Dr. Richard Lapchick, the director of Northeastern University's Center for the Study of Sports in Society. And soccer moms don't want their sons playing football. Even though the rate of injuries to young soccer players is actually higher than it is to young football players, football has an unhealthy image: concussions, steroids, widespread use of painkillers, and the fact that pro careers last an average of three and a half years. Not only are the pros unable to play football when they retire; they often can't run, or even walk, without limping.

After a search of the top marketers in various media businesses, the Commissioner settled on Sara Levinson, the co-president of MTV, to take over the job of marketing the pro game. This was an unconventional choice. MTV is the prototypical cable channel, "niche-marketed" to a small, well-researched "demo," while the NFL represents classic network TV: it delivers the only mass audience left in television. Also, MTV sells exactly what my high school football coach tried to drill out of his players. In the mid-seventies, football was defined as everything rock and roll was not: it was discipline rather than hedonism, showing team spirit instead of doing your own thing — a jock/stoner dichotomy memorably expressed in the movie *Dazed and Confused*. What has happened in the intervening decades is that rock's values have triumphed on the media gridiron and football values have withered. The hedonists have ended up kicking the jocks' butts.

The arrival of Levinson, the first woman president at any of the Big Three sports leagues, was something of a cultural shift for the men of the NFL. The league's headquarters, at 280 Park Avenue, is a masculine place. Men occupy the windowed offices on the perimeter; female secretaries work in the bullpens inside, their work surfaces covered with brand-reinforcing giveaway products known in the industry as "glom." Everywhere on the walls are pictures of gritty, heads-up plays by American males. Recently, when one of the executives was dating Sharon Stone, he got high-fives from the guys in the windowed offices whenever he walked down the row. One NFL staffer, a former high school football player, told me, "When Sara got here, some of my buddies called me up and said, 'You're working for a fucking woman?'"

"One thing I noticed was that in meeting guys would sit there, you know, throwing a ball," Levinson told me. "I'd say to myself, 'What the hell is going on?' They would just sit there in a meeting doing this." She made a throwing motion, then went out for her own pass and caught it in an ironically jocklike way.

Levinson is 46, and has red hair, freckles, and a 5-year-old son who is currently into basketball. ("'Michael! Michael!' — that's all I hear," she told me.) She was not a football fan before coming to the NFL. Growing up in Virginia, she had three brothers, but their mother would not allow them to play football. "Jews don't play football," Levinson joked. But one of her biggest projects now is to get women to become avid football fans. According to a fan survey that she commissioned on arriving at the league, 40 percent of the NFL's TV audience is women. When I expressed skepticism about this number, and about whether women could ever be persuaded to feel passionate about such a brutal game, Levinson gave me the impression that the game I knew and loved was not exactly the game she was planning to sell. At a meeting I attended, one of the men working on the Women's Initiative informed his boss, "Our research indicates that women like the tight pants on the players. They like, um, their butts."

"Go figure," Levinson said.

Levinson is iconoclastic — a trait that went over big at MTV but is not so big at the NFL. "At the NFL, authority and tradition are very important," she told me. "At MTV, when we had our tenth-anniversary specials, we would talk about whether we even wanted to call attention to the fact that we were ten years old. Whereas at the NFL we bring out the throwback jerseys and celebrate our seventy-fifth anniversary." Football is the ultimate team sport — it's all about guys in huddles, accepting orders — and, as Levinson quickly learned, the league itself is a team operation. One of the day-to-day tasks at corporate headquarters is to persuade the thirty extremely competitive capitalists who own the pro teams to share almost all of their television and sponsorship revenues equally, in the interest of creating a competitive league and what amounts to a kind of exclusive socialism unlike any other in professional sports. In major league baseball, the owners enjoy much more freedom to make deals with broadcasters and sponsors in their own markets, and there is no true salary cap to prevent rich owners from spending whatever it takes to get star players. (Albert Belle, the Chicago White Sox slugger, makes more money than all the players on the Pittsburgh Pirates combined.)

Today, however, economic and social forces are eroding both the team ethic of football and the team ethic of the league. Some of the new crop of pro players, like the New York Jets receiver Keyshawn

Johnson, the author of a tell-all memoir of his rookie year entitled *Just Give Me the Damn Ball!*, seem to think that they're playing in the NBA. Even more corrosive to team spirit is free agency, under which a player can declare himself on the open market four years after being drafted by a team. Free agency is the devil's bargain that Tagliabue made with the Players Association four years ago to insure labor peace in the league, and it has had a profound effect on both the league and the game. Young players now want to distinguish themselves as individual stars early in their careers, so that they can command higher prices in the open market, and fans risk losing their favorite players to other teams if the players' asking price is too high. (Eighty-nine players have changed teams this year under free agency.) Coaches of losing teams can no longer blame the luck of the draft, or the limited talent pool, for their teams' poor performance — "You don't survive without winning" is how Tagliabue puts it — and that is one reason that there are eleven new head coaches in the league this year. Each owner, in order to be liquid enough to have a 12-million-dollar signing bonus sitting on the table when a superstar free agent visits his office, has had to search for new sources of revenue. This drives up ticket prices, which are rising at nearly three times the rate of working people's wages, and also makes the owners crave revenue-producing stadiums. (Nine new stadiums are set to open in the next five years.) Owners whose cities won't build new stadiums have the option of moving to cities that will, as Art Modell, the owner of the Cleveland Browns, did last year, whereupon the Browns became the Baltimore Ravens.

Sprint, the NFL's official telecommunications sponsor, pays 24 million dollars a year for the privilege, in part because the NFL can guarantee Sprint exclusive rights to games in all local markets, where Sprint is trying to extend its business. Even if an owner believes that he can make more money doing his own sponsorship deal with a local carrier, the NFL's exclusive Sprint deal means his hands are tied. But this may be changing. It was a pivotal moment in the life of the league when Jerry Jones, the renegade owner of the Dallas Cowboys, walked onto the field two years ago during a Cowboys–Giants *Monday Night Football* game, accompanied by Phil Knight, the chairman of Nike, to announce a deal that included "stadium rights" — a hot new revenue source that would allow Nike to display its swoosh in the stadium.

In the meantime, football's ratings remain high. A hundred and ten million people watch the NFL on TV every week; 130 million people watch the Super Bowl. Though the networks that made football the most popular sport in America are in decline, the NFL remains the single largest content provider to network television. Of the top ten most-watched shows ever to appear on television, seven have been Super Bowls, and the ratings of an above-average *Monday Night Football* game, like the Dallas–Green Bay game last year, are higher than those of any NBA playoff game ever. The NFL guys cite these stats for the same reason that a 300-pound lineman runs into you — to knock you over. But even while football remains the most popular spot on TV, its purchase on the national Zeitgeist has slipped. Paul Gardner, in his book *Nice Guys Finish Last: Sport and American Life,* applied Charles Reich's theory of the three stages of American consciousness to sports. Baseball is the sport of Consciousness I, which was nineteenth-century, small-town rural America. Football is the sport of Consciousness II, spanning early-twentieth-century industrialism up through the postwar corporate society. Gardner, who was writing in the early seventies, wondered if basketball — a sport that values skill over force and improvisation over planning, shows the human body in its natural form rather than heavily armored, and, above all, allows its players to express what Reich called "the concept of full personal responsibility" — might become the sport of Consciousness III.

Today, Gardner's analysis looks prescient. The values of brute force no longer resonate as deeply with America as they once did. We are an entertainment and information economy: creativity and entrepreneurship have more currency in our lives than physical labor, and personal initiative means more to us than following orders. The men for whom football was a ticket out of the mines and the mills are now the grandfathers of lawyers or insurance salesmen or McDonald's employees, and the green fields that formed their vistas have been replaced by urban and suburban landscapes. The playing field of the contemporary urban kid's imagination is as likely to be a basketball court or a computer screen or an iron bannister in the park which he slides down on his skateboard as it is to be a football field.

"Basketball is the MTV of sports," Sara Levinson told me in her office one day early in July. "The way TV covers basketball, with the

quick cuts, the music overlaid — it's much more like MTV. So the
NBA skews young. Going to a basketball game — it's like being
inside a video." At MTV, Levinson sold rebelliousness; indeed, she
helped make rebelliousness and anti-authoritarianism a commodity. "Just Do It," the rallying cry of Nike, might not have been
possible without the attitude blazed by MTV. In football, the message has long been "Just Do What the Coach Tells You to Do."
Football players are not encouraged to do much creative thinking,
which may be one reason that kids aren't so interested in playing
the sport. "We have to be careful not to be MTV, because it would
turn off our viewers at the older end of the demo," Levinson went
on. Kids relate to rebelliousness, and the NFL is "not a rebellious
force. We need to get into kids' skins before the rebelliousness
starts to get really loud."

In order to insure that football remains the game that teenagers
play on the lawn at Thanksgiving, the NFL is in its second year of
promoting several new pickup-style football games, all of which are
variants of flag football. David Newman, whom Levinson worked
with at MTV, and who is in charge of special events, told me, "It's all
about getting a football, this unusual-looking object, into a kid's
hands as soon as you can. Six years old, if possible. You want to get a
football in their hands before someone puts a basketball in their
hands, or a hockey stick or a tennis racket or a golf club." Mission-
aries from the NFL go out to youth organizations like the YMCA
and the Police Athletic League in various cities and try to get the
counselors to teach the new games to their kids. "The football in-
frastructure in the urban areas has declined so badly it's almost
disappeared," Scott Lancaster, the director of the NFL's youth football program, said, adding that last year's New York City champion,
Kennedy High School, in the Bronx, had its playing field condemned. It literally collapsed. (The team practiced in a parking lot
and played all of its games away.) Unlike traditional high school
football, however, the NFL's new games are coed, and in designing
them the league has taken from soccer and basketball elements
that research shows kids like, such as continuous play, lots of scoring, and chances for everyone to stay involved in the action. In NFL
Ultimate football you can take only two steps before you have to get
rid of the ball. Flag games are five on five, and no blocking is
allowed, but downfield laterals are, thus creating more opportunities for everyone to score, or at least to touch the ball.

In reaching out to kids, the NFL has to contend with the fact that Nike and Reebok have changed the way that kids see sports. From a modern sports-marketing perspective, football has two basic flaws: you can't see the players' faces and you can't wear their shoes. A Reebok executive estimates that the company spends eight to ten times as much money promoting basketball players as promoting football players, because it sells many more pairs of basketball shoes than pairs of "cleated footwear." Today's sports marketing is about the face, the individual, the personality. The shape of Michael Jordan's head is a brand. When Karl Malone's lips move at the free-throw line, millions wonder what he is saying. And basketball has adapted its own marketing efforts to the techniques of the sneaker-makers. Rick Welts, the president of NBA Properties, told me, "We decided in the early eighties that we were going to focus our marketing on the talent and personality of individual players, that what was different about our sport was that you saw the players so much. We would make an effort to develop them as individuals, figuring people would be drawn to their stories. That strategy wasn't designed for kids, but it turned out that kids in particular responded to the players as individuals." Football players, on the other hand — hulks behind helmets — are faceless performers for the team. Football is about character, not personality. A personality on a football field is like a target the other players aim at. As David Newman conceded, "It's a challenge. Some of our biggest stars, the fans hardly know what they look like."

What, exactly, is Levinson selling, in selling football? People who like to watch the game — my wife, for example — tend to enjoy the ballet part of it: the perfect passes, the circus catches, the great breakaway runs. (She thinks that tackling should be banned from the sport, and that the pros should play flag football.) But my experience of playing organized football is that the essence of the game is hitting, not ballet. Especially if, like me, you weren't fast or agile, the way to excel at football was to hit people as hard as you could on every play. It was fun to run a "counter" (a misdirection play), in which I was the pulling blocker — to ram full speed into the blind side of some dumb lineman who had bought the fake, empty my body into his body, and knock him flat. But to be hit, that made you wonder. Suddenly there is impact, the solid *thwunk* of someone else's body smashing into yours, followed by a silence

except for your own strangled-sounding *"unnngh."* You are flying
through the air, not knowing yet what hit you; your head strikes the
ground first, and a weird, smoky smell comes into your nose. You lie
on the ground moving your head cautiously, because the impact
has obviously torn your brain free from the webbing that connects
it to the inside of your skull. Then you see your opponent standing
over you, laughing at you, or maybe snarling at you — it's hard to
be sure.

This is the least upbeat but perhaps most immutable aspect of
football, and it's something that Levinson will have trouble selling:
football is about hard work, pain, and losing. (Messages that the
game is all about winning — such as "Just win, baby," which is the
Raiders owner Al Davis's hipster re-statement of Vince Lombardi's
famous remark "Winning isn't everything, it's the only thing" —
are actually less than half the story.) Football is the only common
language we have in which to talk about the pitiless, hit-or-be-hit
side of America. The game's origins lie in a hazing ritual that was
practiced at Ivy League colleges in the 1820s, according to Ben-
jamin G. Rader, the author of the 1983 book *American Sports*. Fresh-
men would be summoned to a field to play a rugby-like game
during which the upperclassmen would welcome them to school by
beating the crap out of them. That impulse (often outlawed by
school authorities) found its way into rugby football, which was
popularized in the United States in the 1860s and '70s in part by
the success of the novel *Tom Brown's School Days*. The violence that
had always been implicit in a game that involved men running into
each other had never been fully expressed by the Englishmen who
played it: their class and their decorousness stopped them from
pushing the violence beyond a certain point. The American gentlemen who played the game were not so sporting. There was no rule
that said you couldn't punch your opponents, for example, so in
the American game there was punching.

The men who played this variant of rugby, which was to become
football as we know it, lived in a society that was considerably
meaner than ours. The array of safety nets and government programs that exists today to ameliorate, or at least disguise, the in-
equality of American society had not yet been designed. The poor
immigrant had to contemplate in all its stark, Darwinian unfairness
the wealth of railroad men like Jay Gould. It was a take-or-be-taken

society, and football was a way of making a game out of that, a mean game for a mean world. The bruising union battles around the turn of the century were psychically revisited on the field — there was an undercurrent of brutality that is still very much part of the game. "Hey, baby, this movie is rated R," Bruce Smith, of the Buffalo Bills, said on the sidelines recently, his million-watt smile lighting up his handsome face. "Adult language and violence. Lots of it."

The pro game rose to supremacy among American sports in the 1950s, as the offensive machines increasingly mirrored the corporate ethic of that era: centralization, division of labor, doing what you're told. The greatest innovator in those corporate aspects of the game was Paul Brown, the coach of the Cleveland Browns: he invented the modern "pocket," which the quarterback stands in to throw; brought classroom methods to the game; put coaches in the press box; and was the first coach to call all plays from the sidelines, a technique now standard in the pros. (Today's quarterbacks all have radio receivers in their helmets.)

In the sixties, football overtook baseball as the country's most popular sport. (Baseball got to keep "national pastime" as a consolation prize.) It drew on the turbulence of that decade, both at home and abroad, and may have reached its peak as a national obsession in January of 1972, when Richard Nixon took time out from his "game plan" for ending the war in Vietnam in order to awaken Miami Dolphins coach Don Shula at 1:30 in the morning before Super Bowl VI and call in a play he was sure would work against the Cowboys — a down-and-in pass to Paul Warfield. (Shula ran the play late in the first quarter; it was incomplete.) In a nation seething with pinkos, longhairs, drug takers, and nonconformists, football was a sturdy bulwark, a blocking sled.

Just as offense expressed the Zeitgeist of the fifties and sixties, so defense is true to the spirit of the nineties, because in defense personal initiative is more important than following a present plan. The "sack" — a term invented by Deacon Jones, of the L.A. Rams, to denote the play in which a single defender can cause the downfall of the whole offensive plan by tackling the quarterback behind the line of scrimmage — is the quintessential rock-and-roll play; it's about the triumph of the individual over the system. (Jones described the feeling of a sack as being "like you devastate a city, or you cream a multitude of people. It's just like you put all the offensive players in one bag and I just take a baseball bat and beat on the bag.") The growing importance of the sack in the pro game has created a new kind of athlete, whose body is an impressive combination of the strength and the speed necessary to get through the line to the quarterback quickly. The great defensive ends — like Bruce Smith, of the Bills, and Reggie White, of the Green Bay Packers, who stand six feet five or so and weigh two hundred and eighty pounds but are as quick as little scatbacks over short distances — are to me the most awesome athletes in pro sports.

Left to grow organically, football would naturally express the rock-and-roll impulse that values the individual over the group. Yet even in the age of MTV marketing, football is uneasy with this impulse. The touchdown dance, an eighties innovation, is rock and roll on the largest imaginable stage. (Dr. Harry Edwards, a sociologist at Berkeley and a consultant to the San Francisco 49ers, has described it as "the creation of a vehicle to express that joy for which there is no mainstream language.") But the league discourages these uppity displays of individuality. (In the college game, all touchdown dances are against the rules.) At the same time, in other areas the NFL manages to court the game's potential for show. As defense has got better over the years, the league has made rules limiting what defensive players can do — like the rule that says the defensive backs cannot bump the receivers more than five yards from the line of scrimmage — in order to encourage scoring, because scoring is what people like to watch on television. This is one of the ways in which the value of the spectacle has taken precedence over the nature of the game.

On arriving at the NFL, Levinson set about drawing up a new marketing plan for pro football. Howard Handler, whom she brought with her from MTV, and who had begun his career as a brand manager for Quaker Oats, was the author of this document — called, of course, *Game Plan 1997*. It begins by defining football as "the American essence of human competition," and attempts to put into marketing lingo the worldless passion of the gridiron. It includes, for example, a graphic representation of the NFL's six "Core Equities" and their "Key Symbols":

Action/Power: Hitting, elusive running, circus catches, the NFL Shield.

History/Tradition: Leaves, NFL legends, fathers and sons . . . tailgating.

Thrill/Release: Fans laughing, screaming, frustrated, exultant. Players doing the same.

Teamwork/Competition: Green Bay Packers in the '60s, '69 Jets, the Steel Curtain.

Authenticity: The ball (pigskin), the field, grass, mud . . . sweat, blood.

Unifying Force: The team, friends, families, communities, tailgating.

Also part of the game plan is the "NFL Mission," which focuses on the importance of youth:

Nothing can be more important than how we manage young people (particularly ages 6–11 . . .) into our fan continuum and begin to migrate them toward becoming avid/committed fans.

Critical Action: Generate early interest and enthusiasm. Transform/convert their casual interest into commitment. Amplify to avidity.

How?: Elevate/personalize players; Football education. . . . Increase NFL intersection with pop culture/trends; Continue to give them products that allow them to build and express their loyalty.

Handler's game plan was slipped into a few of the slim folders that Levinson's nine vice-presidents brought to a meeting I attended at 280 Park on a very hot day in July. Three of the V.P.s were people Levinson had worked with at MTV; the rest were longtime NFL guys. No balls were thrown, but there was much discussion of various ways to promote the NFL "brand." Since Levinson's arrival, it has been O.K. to speak openly about the NFL as a brand, and to conceive of the business as a national branding operation, in which the league tries to gain as much leverage as it can by sharing its "brand equity" with "partners." This meeting was a festival of brand names, from Starter to Bud, including Pert Plus, Hershey's, 7-Eleven, Coke, Visa, and Sports Authority. Jim Schwebel, who is in charge of sponsorships, reported that he had "an excellent meeting with Gatorade last week." And Coke's "The Red Zone" campaign, he said, had brought half a million new names to the NFL's database, which the league can now share with its partners, like Sprint.

"That's good," Levinson said.

"I hope the owners are aware of who is bringing all these businesses to the party," Schwebel said. "It's us. Are we going to get the credit? No."

Jim Connelly, the head of licensing, which is NFL Properties' basic and still most profitable business, spoke next. The retail sales of NFL-licensed goods is a three-billion-dollar-a-year industry. Traditionally, the NFL has sold merchandise in downmarket venues like J. C. Penney and K mart — not just clothes but sheets, stadium blankets, wastebaskets, Christmas ornaments, all kinds of "trash and trinkets." ("Stack it high and let it fly" was the unofficial NFL motto.) But lately Connelly has been negotiating partnerships with high-end brands. "Would we talk to Tommy Hilfiger?" Connelly had asked himself out loud when we spoke earlier in his office. "Yes. We're planning on it. You see his nautical attire, or Ralph Lauren's Polo line — everybody is getting into sports to sell their stuff. Maybe we go in the direction of the understated casual look. You can't walk down the street looking like Joe Torre, in pinstripes, and you can't walk down the street in Armani, like Jeff Van Gundy, unless you're rich, but you can wear exactly what Ray Rhodes" — the Philadelphia Eagles coach — "wears on the sidelines."

Connelly concluded his presentation by noting the extent to which the NFL was kicking the NBA's butt in the licensing business. "What's going on with basketball?" he asked.

"They got next," said Handler, sarcastically alluding to the clever turn on the neighborhood-playground line "We got next," which is the NBA's slogan for its new women's league. Earlier, Handler had repeated to me the NBA's marketing slogan, "I love this game," and asked, "What is that? The emphasis should be on 'this,' as in this particular game. Because after *this* game what have you got? The Mailman versus Sir Charles — what the fuck is that? What happens when they're gone?" His point, which I heard frequently at the NFL, was that the NBA has achieved some fast and easy market share from Michael Jordan and a few other great individual players but has neglected to promote the game itself and will suffer when Michael retires.

Sports and entertainment may be growing ever closer together, but there is an important difference between them. Entertainment is an operation driven from the top down, by a few people who try to give the public what they think the public wants. Sports works the other way. A sport is born among the folk, in its relationship with a particular team. Thanks mainly to television, that relationship has turned into a commodity, which marketers try to "grow" into more money by figuring out how the love of a team can be shifted to the love of a product. But, no matter how much entertainment and marketing you can spin out of football, there's a part of the game that remains essentially unmarketable, and nonetheless accounts for football's mesmerizing appeal to its fans. Football players are the faceless heroes whose travails represent your travails; the fact that you can't see their faces actually makes it easier to feel their pain.

This visceral side of the game — the old, premarketing world of football — is on display each year at the Professional Football Hall of Fame, during Enshrinement, a week-long festival at the end of July in Canton, Ohio, attended by half a million people. Naturally, Commissioner Tagliabue appears at this event, and I joined him on a Friday morning as he flew out of the Million Air terminal in Teterboro, New Jersey, on board an NFL-chartered jet. Last year, the Commissioner was loudly booed at Enshrinement weekend, mostly by Cleveland Browns fans who were angry at him for allowing Art Modell to move their team to Baltimore — an outrage that many fans saw as a symbol of what's wrong with the pro game, which is that the business and the spectacle have become more important than the relationship between the teams and their fans. But if the Commissioner was nervous about the reception waiting for him in Ohio this year, he didn't look it. He stretched his long legs in the cabin — tall and trim at 56, he still has his basketball figure from the days, nearly forty years ago, when he was the Georgetown Hoyas' leading rebounder — and reflected on the state of the NFL. "For two decades, up through the nineties, you really had a period of status quo," he said. "And it was great. There wasn't a hell of a lot of change. Now we've got a lot of change." However, he preferred to see change as bringing "creative energy" to the league. He pointed out, for example, the positive side of free agency — that it has allowed the new expansion teams, like Carolina and Jacksonville, to be immediately competitive. "And this has been a big plus as far as bringing new fans to pro football," he said.

Tagliabue was met on the runway of the Akron–Canton airport by Hall of Fame volunteers in new Lincoln Town Cars, which had been lent by local car dealers. He was driven with appropriate pomp to the hall, to speak at an unveiling of new postage stamps depicting famous football coaches, and then to a country club, for a private lunch honoring this year's enshrinees: Mike Webster, Wellington Mara, Don Shula, and Mike Haynes — the Pittsburgh Steelers center, the New York Giants owner, the Miami Dolpins coach, and the Oakland Raiders defensive back, respectively. The invited guests were mostly Hall of Famers from years gone by: Gale Sayers, Paul Warfield, Terry Bradshaw, Deacon Jones, Joe Greene, Ray Nitschke, Joe Namath, Bob Griese. Almost all were wearing the special gold jacket that signifies their place among the 189 players who have been blessed with the NFL's highest honor. Whatever force fields of irony I, a New York smart-aleck in Kitschville, had brought with me were instantly demolished, and I was left standing there with a huge grin on my face as I looked around the room at the heroes of my boyhood.

It was not a particularly healthy-looking group. Many of the players winced, clearly from joint pain, as, one by one, they rose to speak to the new enshrinees and to welcome them to "the greatest fraternity in the world," in the words of Kansas City great Len Dawson. Chuck Bednarik, of the Philadelphia Eagles, the last player to play both offense and defense, was sitting at the table behind me. His knuckles were hugely swollen, and the pinkie on his right hand was broken sideways; it veered away from his coffee cup like some grotesque parody of Emily Post etiquette. Frank Gifford, who, thanks to Bednarik, had been hospitalized with a deep concussion after the Eagles–Giants game in 1960, was seated a few tables away, with Wellington Mara. (The Commissioner wondered whether the guys were ribbing Frank over his recent extramarital escapades, but the presence of the 80-year-old Mara, Gifford's former boss, seemed to keep things above that level.)

The Enshrinement ceremony took place the following morning, outside the hall, which has a huge football-shaped dome as its roof. Although the season doesn't start until August 31st, this was the invocation of it, the ritual arousing of Old Man Football from his sweaty, tormented summer slumber. It had rained earlier, and by the time the ceremony got under way the grass was starting to steam. Paying and credentialed guests were seated on the lawn in front of the hall, while "the people" were gathered on a hill to the right, between a Cyclone fence with barbed wire on top of it and a concrete retaining wall. Most of them were Steelers fans, who had made the two-hour drive from Pittsburgh to witness the beatification of Mike Webster: he had been the center on the great Steelers teams of the seventies, when they dominated pro football. To the left was a raised stretch of Interstate 77 — high enough so that passing semis could see down into the scene. The speeches were punctuated with thundering blasts of solidarity from truck drivers on the job.

The crowd did boo when the Commissioner was announced, but not as loudly as last year. Tagliabue kept his remarks brief, and then each enshrinee was "presented" by someone of his own choosing. Don Shula was presented by his two sons, Dave and Mike, who are both coaches in the league. Wellington Mara was presented by Gifford, who declared that Mara was the father any son would wish to have, the "most honest and decent man I have ever known." In a sign of the times, Mike Haynes was presented by his agent, Howard Slusher, who is now a special assistant to Phil Knight, of Nike.

Finally, Mike Webster was presented by Terry Bradshaw, who had been the Steelers quarterback and the so-called Blond Bomber during their golden age, and who now plays the football buffoon on Fox's NFL broadcasts. Webster, known to fans as Iron Mike, is from Tomahawk, Wisconsin, and was the class of '97 enshrinee who to me best represented the values of old football: with his bulging biceps, he was known for wearing cutoff sleeves in all kinds of weather; he was the rock, the anchor, the guy willing to play in pain, who went for ten years in a row without missing a game until he dislocated his elbow. Though football has evolved into high-tech aerial warfare over the years, the position of center — the one who snaps the ball — hasn't changed since the nineteenth century. It's still a "game" of pushing and shoving and being kicked and punched and bitten.

Bradshaw began by saying of Webster, "I loved him from the very first moment I put my hands under his butt," and he followed with an anecdote about how Iron Mike liked to drink a gallon of buttermilk and take liver pills before games, which meant that by the fourth quarter he was ripping eye-watering farts as Bradshaw squatted over him. (Bradshaw, who can attribute some of his good health to Webster's excellent protection of him, made the Hall eight years ago.) At the end of his speech, Bradshaw produced a football and hollered, "Jes' one mo' time!" Webster took off his gold jacket and squatted, and the Blond Bomber (now mostly bald) got up under his butt for old times' sake.

A few weeks earlier, I had seen a piece on ESPN's *SportsCenter* about Webster's troubles since he retired from football, in 1992. He had lost all his money and his home due to bad investments, and for nearly a year and a half he lived in the back of his car, occasionally sleeping in the Pittsburgh bus station. He has congestive heart disease, and may also be suffering from post-concussion syndrome. He has convulsions and spasms that keep him up at night, as well as a severe varicose-vein condition in his legs, which causes even the smallest cut to "squirt blood everywhere," according to his wife, Pam, who is currently suing him for divorce, and has taken their four children with her to live in Wisconsin. She said she and Mike would sometimes cover his veins with Super Glue, to prevent them from popping in the living room. Toward the end of the ESPN piece, Mike said, "Some things I think horrify me," and, indeed, he looked like a man who had peered into the abyss. He is 45, but he looks 70, easily. Still, he was upbeat: "All I have to do is finish the game. . . . Like John Wayne said, 'I'll finish it, maybe not standing up, but I'll finish.'"

Now, speaking without notes, in a simple, sincere way, Webster asked everyone who cared about football to rise. I jumped out of my chair. Fucking A! I love football! Then he spoke for about twenty minutes, his remarks frequently interrupted by mournful-exultant wails of "Miiike!" floating down the hill from the *Braveheart*-like mass of faces painted black and yellow.

At one point, Webster returned to his semi-mystical theme of the finish. "You only fail if you don't finish the game," he said. "If you finish, you win. You have to measure by what you started out with and by what you overcome. In a lot of ways, we are the same."

The fans up on the hill bellowed savagely. "We love you, Mike! We're with you, Mike!"

"You're going to fail, believe me," he said. "But there's no one keeping score. All we have to do is finish the game and we'll all be winners."

I found myself joining in the din: "Miiike!"

It was a cry of pure American id.

ROBERT ANDREW POWELL

Coming of Age
on the 50-Yard Line

FROM MIAMI NEW TIMES

What politics is to the Cuban community, football is to the black
community.
— RICHARD DUNN, former Miami city commissioner

ON FRIDAY, Gwen Cherry Park rests. An empty Doritos bag tum-
bles across the abandoned main football field, lodging itself in one
of the hollow diamonds of a chainlink fence. With all the kids in
school, no noise bounces off the steel roof of the new gymnasium, a
gift from the National Football League. A low-riding Toyota glides
down NW 71st Street past the Scott housing project, its muted bass
groove cutting the silence, its metallic gold rims glittering in the
light of a sun that burns hot at noon on an early autumn day.

Saturday the park comes alive. Hundreds of neighbors have
turned out to watch the eight Gwen Cherry teams sponsored by
the Greater Miami Boys and Girls Club — all nicknamed the Bulls
— battle for Pop Warner football superiority. Right now the 80-
pound Bulls (Pop Warner teams aren't divided according to age
but by their weight, which ranges from 65 pounds to 140 pounds)
hold a 10–0 lead over Palmetto. Ten-year-old Bulls wide receiver
Sammie Bush, barely taller than a man's hip, snags a lateral and,
finding himself free of any defenders, darts 45 yards for a touchdown. Six coaches dressed in matching blue and yellow shirts, caps,
and sneakers gleefully trade high-fives and slap their clipboards.
Twenty tiny cheerleaders shake pompons.

It's hot out here, it's hot out here
There must be a Bull in the atmosphere!

Beyond the yellow rope that separates the players from their followers, a half-dozen barbecue grills pump out a cloud of charcoal smoke and chicken fat that drifts over the field like a misty blimp. One young spectator parks his rear end on a bicycle seat. His neighbor rests his on a metal folding chair. Standing up in the fifth and highest row of the flimsy bleachers, the gits — local slang for gang members — puff on blunts while they berate the coaches. *Y'all better start throwing the ball!*

The Gwen Cherry Bulls 80-pounders have dispatched their first three opponents this season — South Dade, Richmond, and Tamiami — with relative ease. With a shutout against Palmetto an imminent possibility, Bulls players have already started celebrating. Sammie Bush choreographs Deion Sanders dance steps while linebacker Richard Dunn, son of the former Miami city commissioner, pushes his palms skyward, "raising the roof" on an impending 4–0 record.

"Every Saturday is a festival in this park," beams Charlie Brown, executive athletic director of the Boys and Girls Clubs. "With the inner city, there's basically nothing planned or organized on a weekly basis for people to do. Our football games are a day people can look forward to spending with their neighbors and their families, just enjoying the afternoon."

A fight breaks out on the sideline. Linebacker Steven Green's dad excoriates his son for a mental mistake. The critique is overheard by the boy's stepfather, who is standing not far off, talking on a cellular phone. "That's *my* motherfucking son!" shouts the stepfather, flashing a mouthful of gold teeth. He turns back to his phone: "Excuse me, I got to deal with this guy." Then: "I'll kick your ass right now, boy!"

The men lunge at one another but are quickly restrained by coaches. The natural father slips free and sprints across the field, hurdling the railroad tracks and disappearing into the Scott projects. "Is he getting a gun?" a spectator wonders aloud. Steven Green's mother grabs her son without wiping the tears from his smooth brown face, pulls him off the field, and incarcerates him in the passenger seat of her car.

"Pay attention! Pay attention!" head coach Andre "Dre" Greene shouts to his squad, most of whom have turned from the action on the field to watch the fracas. "Keep your head in the game, y'all! We still playing a game!"

Not for long. Only four minutes later a second fight erupts. The mothers of Tony Brown and Darrell "Dee" Samuel, both running backs, have been arguing throughout the game about their sons' respective playing time. Both kids' teachers filed "unacceptable" progress reports earlier in the week, forcing the coach to bench the boys for at least part of the game. Yet (and apparently by accident) Dre put one of the boys into the game earlier than he was supposed to, and tempers flared.

"The mother of Tony starts ragging on Dee, saying he only has one finger," imparts defensive-back coach Tommy Streeter. (Nine-year-old Dee was born with a malformed left hand.) "You don't ever be saying that!" warns Streeter. "Not to a kid, and especially not to his mother. That's why they scrapped."

Two county police cruisers arrive after the second fight has died down. The officers stroll among the remaining participants of both altercations, calmly asking questions. When the game ends anticlimactically in another Bulls victory, no one cheers.

"We're 4–0, but I tell you, this has been the hardest season of my life," grumbles Dre's brother Darrell Greene, the team's offensive coordinator. "It's the worst season, so hard, so difficult. I mean, man, this team can go to the Super Bowl! If they just stay focused, they can *go*."

The National Football League's annual Super Bowl has become an unofficial American holiday, watched by nearly 130 million people nationwide. But in terms of pure passion, the Super Bowl of the Greater Miami Pop Warner football league may eclipse its grown-up counterpart. Nearly 6,500 people turned out for the two days of last year's championships, held in Liberty City's Curtis Park. That's 6,500 people to watch kids as young as six (and as Lilliputian as 65 pounds) play football.

When Darrell Greene says that "the Super Bowl is what it's all about," he's not referring to the professional game. "When I was a kid playing Optimists, we won a championship in 1975," Greene recalls. "I'll never forget that banquet afterward, how good we all felt from moving toward a goal and accomplishing it together. I want these kids to understand that feeling."

To win the Super Bowl in Miami–Dade County is to beat the best

young teams in the nation. The local Pop Warner leagues (also
known as Optimist football, after the charity that sponsors several
teams) are the breeding grounds for the county's superlative high
school teams; local high schools have won four of the past six Class
6A state championships. In turn, many of the county's top high
school players stay in-state to play for America's best college programs: the University of Miami, Florida State, and the University of
Florida have won five of the past ten national championships.

"The success of the University of Miami a few years ago inspired
a lot more inner-city kids to play Optimist football, which has really
improved the overall quality of football in Dade County," affirms
Billy Rolle, head football coach at Northwestern High, the 1995
Class 6A state champs. "Our high school teams are some of the best
in the country, and I think that's due in large part to the strength of
our Optimists."

The Boys and Girls Clubs' Daron Chiverton, commissioner of
Gwen Cherry's football program, believes football is ideally suited
for the kids who grow up in and around the Scott Homes. "Football is the most natural for them," says Chiverton. "Basketball puts
limits on their aggression; baseball puts limits on their aggression.
In football they had better well be aggressive. And with the background of these kids, where these kids come from, aggression
comes naturally."

Danny Dye, who coaches a 65-pound team and is the stepfather
of the 80s' quarterback, offers another theory about why football
dominates Miami's inner city. "I could sum that up in a couple of
words: everybody wants to see their kid play in the NFL."

Indeed, despite brutally long odds, several parents who stalk the
sidelines on game days see football as a legitimate career option for
their progeny. The Boston-based Center for the Study of Sport and
Society reports that only one in one hundred high school football
and basketball players will earn a college scholarship and only one
in ten thousand will play pro sports. Yet a few who have beaten
those odds came from this very neighborhood; Miami Dolphins
wide receiver Brett Perriman and New York Jets linebacker Marvin
Jones both played for Northwestern in the late eighties. Coach
Streeter, a former Northwestern linebacker, played college ball for
the University of Colorado and professionally in the Canadian
Football League. Such anecdotal evidence is hard for some parents

to ignore. "It's realistic!" imparts Tim Torrence, a coach of the 105s and father of a linebacker who plays for the 80s.

"Somebody a long time ago came to the idea that this — football — was the very best way to show that we could make it out, that we could rise above the slave mentality, segregation, and really be what we want to be," theorizes Carlos Guy, an aide to County Commissioner James Burke and the uncle of a boy on the 65s. "With the generations that passed since then, over time, things have gotten stronger and stronger. It's not a *part* of the culture now. It *is* the culture."

And the culture reveals itself at the Super Bowl. Speedy wide receiver Sammie Bush played in last year's Super Bowl for one of the Liberty City Warriors' 65-pound teams. Now with the Bulls, he dreams of making it back. "We was 10–0," he says of last year's final against the Northwest Boys Club Falcons. Time was running out as Liberty City marched toward the end zone in pursuit of a game-tying touchdown. "The clock was ticking, and the crowd was chanting 'three . . . two . . . one,' when their team intercepted the ball," Sammie remembers wistfully. "I hope to meet them this year in the Super Bowl. It'll be exciting to see them try to beat the Bulls."

Noon is the scheduled kickoff for today's home game against the Inner City Jaguars, based in M. Athalie Range Park across from Edison High School. At close to two o'clock, players and coaches still laze under a shade tree near the field, wondering where their opponents are. Eventually, and reluctantly, Charlie Brown calls the game. "All right, those niggas be scared of us. They forfeit," announces Coach Dre, prompting his players to cheer. "Listen, listen!" he instructs, hushing the celebration. "This don't mean we're off the hook. We don't want to win this way."

Even as Dre speaks, a yellow school bus rolls across the grass and comes to a stop near the football field. Teams of turquoise Jaguars spill out the door and onto the field. Inner City has arrived. "All right, it's showtime!" Coach Streeter shouts. "Get hyped, y'all!"

Nine-year-old Greg Finnie, sporting a Nike headband, Nike wristbands, and Nike cleats, leaps up to lead the cheers. "Everybody ready to throw down?" he hollers. "Yes we are!" the team shouts back. "Breakdown!" The Bulls peel off a series of rhythmic chants. "Bulls, Bulls, Bulls, no limit Bulls! . . . Undefeated, undefeated,

undefeated! Can't be beaten, can't be beaten, can't be beaten! . . . Blue get ready to roll! Gold get ready to roll! . . ." They stomp their feet and slap twice on their thigh pads. "Blue and gold, rolling to the Super Bowl!"

Under Coach Dre's command, the players drop to one knee to say a prayer. The younger Richard Dunn cranes his neck to catch the attention of his father, standing among the spectators. "This is the part I like best," confides the older Dunn, a minister. "It's holistic, you know?"

When the amens have been said, Coach Dre wraps up his pep talk. "They made us wait. Get mad," he orders. "What are you going to do?"

"Punch them in the mouth!" one boy shouts.

"That's not the answer I was looking for," Dre responds. "No, you-all saying the wrong thing. Teamwork. Play as a team. Teamwork. Let's go! Get mad!"

Through the Second World War and into the 1950s, Gwen Cherry Park was a rock pit. From about 1954, when Scott Homes was built, until 1963, the pit was filled with trash and construction debris. The county park opened in 1980, on top of the landfill. But county, state, and federal environmental officials have recently discovered high levels of lead and arsenic in the park's soil. Although the environmentalists insist there's no danger to the kids who play there, further soil and water testing is under way to determine whether the park qualifies as a Superfund site, making it eligible for federal clean-up money.

"The state and the feds — the big wheels — are all here," reports Charlie Brown at a town meeting called in early October to address the contamination. "If it was just the Metro-Dade Parks, maybe this could have been swept under the rug. But for the NFL to spend all that money to find this out, they're not going to be pleased. Not at all."

Brown is referring to the National Football League's Youth Education Town Center, a gleaming year-old complex constructed with a million-dollar grant the NFL awarded in 1995 in conjunction with Super Bowl XXIX. Besides a new football field and a 9,000-square-foot gym, the center offers two computer labs, tutoring, and arts-and-crafts classes. NationsBank, the Miami Dolphins, and other businesses covered the rest of the center's $3.1 million cost. The county maintains and protects the building, while the Boys and Girls Clubs provides the recreational programs.

"That center was the best thing to happen to this community, ever," states Danny Dye.

In the years before the YET center was built, Gwen Cherry youth football floundered. Coaches recall scrambling for cash to pay bus drivers to haul teams to away games. Although money had been set aside to purchase both practice and game uniforms, the game jerseys never appeared. Several coaches say the teams' former administrator Anthony Dawkins wore out his welcome in the community he served. "He was going to get himself hurt," asserts coach A. D. Williams, who has worked at the park for eight years. "I mean physically hurt. People were threatening him, driving by his house, accusing him of mismanaging the program and stealing funds. So he got out. He left before Charlie [Brown] and the other administrators asked him to leave."

Brown takes a diplomatic posture regarding his predecessor. "I commend Anthony Dawkins for coming in and trying to make it work," he offers calmly. "But with the Boys and Girls Clubs running the program, it gets a different respect. We came in with a forty-year history of being involved with youth. He was a single venture. Things just didn't work out for him. He wasn't prepared.

Dawkins admits he transferred money from one account to another, in violation of standard bookkeeping practices. And without a staff, he could provide only so much service. But he didn't break any laws and all the money went to the kids. "It was inexperience," he says. "Yes, I shouldn't have bought T-shirts for the kids with money set aside to pay the refs. Yes, it was run inefficiently. If I had been doing this for forty years [like the Boys and Girls Clubs], I'd probably be doing it better."

The former administrator, who confirms that county police investigated him for embezzlement, points out that he was never charged with any crime. "Do you think if I took government money I'd still be walking around free?" he asks. His problems with the community, Dawkins theorizes, stem from the community itself. "I am a local boy," he argues. "Too local. I grew up in the Scott projects. The people there would see me get a grant from the county and they'd say, 'Why should he have the opportunity?'"

The Boys and Girls Clubs took over the football program in

August 1996. One young player showed up for the first practice with a loaded pistol. At the second practice, when a coach scolded one of his players, a gang of young men watching from the sidelines stormed the field and physically attacked him. The park adopted the colors and nickname of the champion Northwestern Bulls. Not one Gwen Cherry team made the playoffs.

This year coaches and parents sport yellow T-shirts emblazoned with the team's new slogan: "From the bottom to the top, don't miss the climb, Gwen Cherry football."

Now, as the 80s prepare to storm the field after finishing their breakdowns, Charlie Brown pulls Coach Dre aside. Even though the Jaguars are here, the referees have already left. It's too late now to get a new crew, so Inner City must — officially, this time — forfeit. The Jaguars head coach explains that his administrator misread the schedule and wrote down the wrong starting time for the game. The administrator: Anthony Dawkins.

The play is a halfback pass. Keith Holmes is in at quarterback, Frankie Adams at halfback. For this practice drill, there are no defenders. "Hut one, hut two," barks Keith. "Hike!" As two wide receivers sprint down the sideline, Keith drops back two steps, turns, and hands the ball to the tiny halfback. Frankie carries it 5 yards toward the sideline, plants his foot, cocks his right arm, and throws.

"*WHOOOOooooooooooeeee!*" A whistle erupts in unison from three teenage spectators as the ball sails over their heads, the *WHOOOO* commencing the moment the ball leaves Frankie's fingertips, the last of the *eeee*s sounding as the tight spiral lands perfectly in Sammie Bush's arms, 45 yards down the field. "That git can *throw!*"

It's an amazing sight, Frankie throwing a football. It doesn't seem physically possible that a boy only 43 inches tall, encumbered by shoulder and elbow pads and a helmet looking as big as an apple crate, can chuck a ball so far. Yet he does, every time, effortlessly. Not only can he throw the ball, he can also kick accurate field goals of 35 yards, making him — at age 10 — the only kicker in the entire park. Thanks to Frankie, the Bulls are the only team in their league that regularly kicks for an extra 2 points after touchdowns (which owing to their difficulty at this level are worth twice as much as a running play).

But it's the throwing that dazzles the sideline gits at this practice, one of the few that Frankie attends. When asked why Frankie isn't the team's regular quarterback, defensive coordinator Anthony Snelling twirls a finger around his ear. "That boy be messed up in the head," Snelling declares. "He's got all the talent in the world, *all* the talent in the *world,* yet he'd rather play on the train tracks with his boys than play with the real men over here. Ain't that right, Frankie?"

Frankie finds himself in constant trouble at school, where he often fails to complete his homework and acts up in class. "He's screwing up," declares Coach Streeter, who frequently visits his players' schools to check on their academic progress. Frankie's file at Lillie C. Evans Elementary is crammed with disciplinary reports. One of his fifth-grade teachers tells Streeter that it's the boy's boundless energy that gets him into so much trouble. He's a good-humored, smart kid, reports the teacher, but he needs to be less disruptive in the classroom.

Three out of every four children in the Scott Homes are raised by a single parent, usually a mother, says the Boys and Girls Clubs' Daron Chiverton. He believes that age eleven is the cutoff, the time when kids choose to work within the system or to reject it. This dismal vision, that Frankie is on the cusp of doom at age ten, is shared by many Bulls coaches.

"Society says you're a man when you turn eighteen," observes defensive line coach Gary Robinson. "But in real life, rites of passage come much earlier than eighteen. Especially for some of the kids in the Scott Homes. Many of them are the man of the house at age twelve or thirteen. Their parents might be at work, so they have to work in the house helping to raise their brothers and sisters. And some of them can't handle that."

Robinson scans the practice field, where Frankie continues to uncork bombs. "Hopefully none of them will fail in life, but if I had to tell you realistically, and generously, only maybe 30 percent will turn out to be full successes. The other 70 percent? Realistically? Forget about it."

Despite his talents, Frankie plays sparingly on game days. With the exception of kickoffs and extra points, he whiles away most quarters on the bench, absently flipping his kicking tee. In close games Coach Dre itches to insert his secret weapon to drop one of those bombs on the other team's unsuspecting defense. Sometimes he gets to, when Frankie has shown up for practice and stayed out of trouble in school. Usually he does not. "My wife [a teacher at Frankie's school] comes home every day telling me, 'Ain't no way that boy should be playing this Saturday. Ain't no way!'"

Frankie says he learned how to throw and kick by watching his three older brothers. "I was good at kicking kickballs, but I didn't know how to kick a football. I kept kicking from the top of the ball, but my brother Cecil taught me to kick from the bottom," he says, punctuating this recollection by spitting on the ground.

When asked what his favorite food is, Frankie unspools a verbal list that embraces the entire nutritional pyramid. "I like macaroni, chicken, rice, spinach, carrots, potato salad, hot dogs, cupcakes, hamburgers," he says, taking more than two minutes to end on crabcakes, which he apologizes for not putting first. He wishes he could have $5,000 to buy his mama a house and a pool and a car. "I'd buy myself a little fish, and I'd build a pond with big fishing poles." He also wishes he lived in Heaven.

Why isn't he playing quarterback? "'Cause Coach won't let me play," he responds, spitting again. Is it because of his schoolwork? No response. Why is he struggling so much in school? If the question makes Frankie uncomfortable, he tries not to show it. Instead he snakes his pink tongue around the rim of a can of strawberry soda, spitting out what he finds. His eyes fix on a man diving into a Dumpster in search of aluminum. Absently he rubs the shredded skin of his index finger into one of several infected, nickel-size scabs on his shins. When he realizes that an answer is expected, he continues to poke at his wounds. Eventually he just shrugs.

The Bulls squeak past South Miami 8–0, on a touchdown and Frankie's extra two points. Six games into the season, the team is undefeated, and the dream of a berth in the playoffs is inching closer to being a reality. All that stands in the team's way is next week's road trip to Goulds, which is also undefeated. "Coach told us whoever wins the Goulds game is going to the Super Bowl," relays linebacker Vincent Powell as he dons his helmet before practice.

Most of the spectators at the practices are women — mothers, usually, though a few men do drive up to the field to lean against their car doors and watch a son or nephew scrimmage. In greeting one another, the men invariably employ the same salutation: *coach.* "That's a thing that we do in this culture," explains Carlos Guy. "Whenever a man out here sees another man, and they don't know each other, they call each other 'coach.' It's a sign of respect for what they are doing out here, even if they aren't actually coaching."

Watching a practice, when all the Bulls' age groups share the same big field, is like watching a three-dimensional growth chart. The 65-pound 6-year-olds are so diminutive they look like a helmet with two cleats beneath it. The 80s are taller (if that's the right word), and appear more stable; their heads fit better into their helmets. The 110s are lanky, with long shins and athletic gaits. The 140s, growing into their adult bodies, are nothing less than smaller versions of the pros.

After stretching and running sprints as a team, the 80s split up for positional work. While Darrell Greene and his brother run the offense through a new pass play, Gary Robinson teaches the linebackers how to sack, and Coach A.D. puts the offensive line through a blocking drill. "That's the definition of insanity," A.D. instructs a lineman who has dressed for practice in a Dallas Cowboys jersey. "You're doing exactly the same thing but expecting a different outcome. You got to crack it back, then come with some force. Some force! Crack it back, lose those zombie arms! Come on, man, you got to crack him!"

Like all the coaches, A.D. is out here Tuesday through Friday from 5:00 to 8:00 P.M. Like all the coaches, he has kids of his own waiting for him to trudge home worn-out from his volunteerism. And like all the coaches, he logs the hours in order to repay the debt he feels he owes the game.

"My friends and I were tight," the coach imparts during a short break. "We'd be together from as soon as we got up in the morning until we came home at night and went to sleep. We were *tight*, you know. So many of them grew up to be messed up with drugs and in jail and all sorts of problems, I look at them and I realize how lucky I was to be involved in Optimist football. If you can look at yourself, and at how you grew up to not be a total failure, it makes you want to give something back."

Dre, the 80s' head coach, puts in his three hours of practice before working the night shift at a Burger King warehouse, his job for the past decade. Gary Robinson replaces broken windshields for Charlie's Auto Glass. None of the coaches are paid for their time. All spend their own money on gas, on food after games, on team sleepovers and Halloween parties, and on the eight-dollar black neckrolls awarded each Thursday to the best defensive player from the previous game.

"These coaches are the best teachers these kids have," notes Carlos Guy. "Until they are 6, they're growing up with their mamas. They're waiting to find out what they're supposed to do as men. No one around them can show them, and the mamas know they can't show them, and the boys sure as hell can't know it. So they come out here and they see the coaches and they learn how to be men."

Gits who've dropped out of football still swing through the park on mountain bikes to scout for talent. Mothers sit in lawn chairs beneath the trees, idly chatting while they wait for practice to end. Across the park echoes a smack of plastic on plastic. "Tough!" someone cries out. "Oh baby, good hit!"

"Lil'" Tim Torrence stands on a steel scale in a storage room at Goulds Park, hoping to make weight. Though a 10-year-old might play on a team with kids who are 12 if he's heavy enough, far more common is the phenomenon of "making weight" — shedding pounds to play against younger kids. Under the careful watch of his father, 9-year-old Tim maintains a strict diet.

"When they come home for dinner, I feed them a tuna salad and some water," the father elaborates as his son steps off the scale, having made weight. "that will fill them up and they'll get tired. They'll go to sleep. In the morning I give them breakfast. They need that, and then they'll burn it off anyway during the day. One of my boys, I'm telling you, he lost nine pounds."

During the first half of the Goulds game, the Bulls offense bogs down, blowing several gimmick plays. Frankie is in, but his halfback pass fails twice and he's sacked by the Goulds defense. Reverses, in which the halfback hands off the ball to a wide receiver, gain little. At the end of the first quarter the game is scoreless.

Goulds threatens early in the second quarter, breaking off a fourth-down run for 40 yards to the Bulls' 1-yard line. But penalties and the Bulls' inspired defense keep the Rams out of the end zone and force a turnover on downs. Still scoreless at the end of the first half.

"Let's play authenticity football," Darrell Greene urges at half-time. "This is just like the playoffs. This is when the big-time players step up. If you want to make a name for yourself in Optimist football, now is the time to do it."

The Bulls catch a break on a fluke at the start of the second half. Frankie's kickoff travels only twelve yards, transforming it into a de facto onside kick, which the Bulls manage to recover. Once again Darrell Greene calls for a trick play, but this time it works: quarterback Keith Holmes fakes a handoff to his halfback, then hides the ball in his midsection before taking the defense by surprise. He throws 25 yards downfield to a wide-open Sammie Bush, who is brought down at the 7-yard line, not by a tackler from the opposing team but by an equipment failure of sorts. "I would have made a touchdown," Sammie later reports, "but my pants were all baggy. I had to stop to pull them up." Two plays later the Bulls score on a straightforward running play. Frankie's kick sails true for the extra two points, giving the team an 8–0 lead.

But as the Bulls offense continues to sputter into the fourth quarter, Goulds finally begins to click. The Rams' halfback gains good ground outside, and as the clock winds down his coaches keep calling for halfback sweeps, a strategy that pays off in a Rams touchdown with only twelve seconds remaining. Dre, Darrell, and Streeter muffle their curses while the parents let the profanity fly. Tie score, pending the point-after kick.

At this level of football, where it's against the rules to rush the kicker, distraction is the Bulls' only weapon. The defensive line commences jumping jacks. Sammie, at free safety, stares down the kicker, hoping to unnerve him. From the Bulls bleachers, parents chant, "Miss it! Miss it!"

The snap sails over the holder's head. Fetching the ball and running back to his place, the holder sets it down. The kicker hesitates, crossing fingers on both hands and clenching his eyes tight as if in prayer. "Please," he begs as he finally approaches the ball. His toe strikes the pigskin awkwardly, causing it to wobble wide left.

Bulls win.

The offense, the coaching staff, all the mothers, and everyone else in blue and yellow storms the field. "Yeah! Yeah! Yeah!" A.D. roars, flexing his muscles like a bodybuilder. Bulls players race to meet their coaches, hollering their own squeaky cheers. "I felt like I'd been touched by an angel!" cries an ecstatic Sammie. "It felt so good I jumped in the air higher than I've ever jumped in my life!"

Coaches hug players, players hug their mothers, mothers hug the coaches, cheerleaders frantically wave their pompons. The celebration subsides only for the handshakes at midfield. Cheerleaders on the right, players on the left, both teams march single-file toward the opposite sideline. Triumphant Bulls slap hands with sobbing Rams. Coach Streeter commands his team to gather at the end zone to usher in the next weight division by forming a human chute for the 90-pounders to run through. Coach Dre, chugging a can of orange soda, hovers around midfield, looking for more people to embrace.

"We're going to go all the way!" someone shouts. "We going all . . . the . . . way!"

After the Goulds game, Frankie misses every practice. As punishment he sits on the bench while the Bulls trounce West Kendall, 26–0. A week later he's still sitting as Scott Lake, from north of the Palmetto Expressway, is blown out 36–0. Coach Dre lets him kick off and convert extra points, but that's it.

Linda Adams, Frankie's mother, says her boy missed the practices because he was in trouble at school.

In the regular-season finale, Frankie doesn't play a down as the team loses its first game, to the Northwest Boys Club, a league power. He doesn't even get in to attempt an extra point because the Bulls never score. "Keep your heads up and feel good about Gwen Cherry Park," Dre orders after the 26–0 drubbing. "It ain't nothing but one loss, baby. We're 9–1, we'll see them again." Despite the upbeat words, tears stream down the faces of tackle Lawrence Hook and several of his teammates.

The loss means little: with nine wins the Bulls had secured home-field advantage for the playoffs even before the kickoff. Still, Dre pulls Frankie aside afterward. "This is the playoffs now, Frankie. Do or die," says the head coach, grasping his kicker by the shoulders. "I need you to show up for practices this week. We need you in there at tight end. Can you show up for me? Can you do that for me, Frankie?" Frankie stares blankly at Dre, nodding slightly.

Frankie does not show up for a single practice in preparation for the first playoff game, against defending champion Liberty City. Coaches Dre, Streeter, and A.D. all pay separate visits to Frankie's row in Scott Homes to try to persuade his mother that practice is the best place for him to be. Sometimes she says Frankie is sick, other times that he's being punished for poor behavior in school. "She says that," spits Darrell Greene, "then we see him outside playing on the street. Man, I give up on Frankie."

At practice the Friday before the first round of playoffs, Dre cannot mask his disappointment at Frankie's absence. He recalls how he first saw the boy back in August, playing on the railroad tracks while the team practiced. Not knowing anything about Frankie's talents, the coach persuaded him to join the team and paid the entrance fee out of his own pocket. "Frankie breaks my heart," Dre laments, watching his offense run through a drill. "Every season I try to get through to all my players. But Frankie, I just can't get through to him. I tried to work with him. I tried to talk to him. But I can't break through."

Frankie doesn't show up for the contest against Liberty City, his first game-day absence all year. Before the coin toss, Dre gives the kicking duties to Ant Henderson, a wiry 9-year-old. To everyone's surprise, Ant converts after a Bulls touchdown, providing the winning margin in a close 8–6 game.

Needing just one more victory to reach the championship game, Gwen Cherry finally feels the loss of its regular kicker. This past Saturday morning, on a field slick with drizzle, Ant returns a punt 60 yards to give the Bulls a 6–0 first-quarter lead over the visiting Kendall Hammocks Chiefs. But his 2-point attempt sails wide left, and the missed conversion proves costly when Kendall scores its own touchdown minutes later and amazingly makes the kick, taking a lead it will carry into the last minute of the game.

Down by 2 and out of timeouts, Gwen Cherry manages to move the ball 70 yards to the Chiefs' 4-yard line. After Keith Holmes attempts a futile quarterback sneak up the middle, Dre frantically calls for a running play with less than ten seconds remaining.

Keith takes the snap and turns to hand off to Sammie Bush, but there's a miscommunication and the ball falls to the ground. As time expires, players on both teams scramble to recover the fumble, which squirts into the end zone. Somehow, amid the tangle of legs and shoulder pads, Sammie spies the bouncing pigskin and falls on top of it.

"Everyone on both teams was just standing there looking at him," Coach Dre will later recall. "Everybody was quiet. Finally, after maybe ten seconds, the ref threw up his hands."

Touchdown: Bulls win, 12–8.

Sammie, mobbed by frenzied Bulls, breaks into tears. Dre and A.D. leap onto the pile. As Charlie Brown tries in vain to keep fans from hopping the fence to join the fray, the Kendall Hammocks players slump off the field dragging their helmets on the grass. The 80s remain in the end zone to bring in the 110s, who are about to face Liberty City. Clapping, laughing, still crying with joy, the Bulls break it down. Blue and gold, rolling to the Super Bowl.

PAT FORDE

Fallen Star "Goose" Ligon Is Looking for a Miracle

FROM THE LOUISVILLE COURIER-JOURNAL

GOOSE LIGON IS BROKE AND GOING BLIND. His glaucoma-ravaged eyes watch life fade to black from a bench in a bleak Louisville housing project, where he talks a lot about miracles.

He crosses the long legs that used to glide gracefully across Freedom Hall. His socks sag around his ankles and his left big toe pokes through a hole in his battered hightop Nikes.

The fanny pack around his waist holds a pack of Kools and a pair of gloves. Goose wears the gloves to mow grass around the Iroquois Homes project, charging a dollar or two per yard to supplement his disability checks.

When he's done mowing he retires to the bench in front of the community center. He sits and smokes, and searches with clouded vision for a divine bailout.

"I just hope for some kind of miracle to get out of this death zone." Cigarette smoke streams out the right side of his mouth, where a set of molars used to be.

This death zone is where 53-year-old Goose landed after a quarter-century skid from sporting fame to society's fringe.

A generation ago, James "Goose" Ligon was the running, rebounding fan favorite for the Kentucky Colonels. His luminous smile, expansive personality and nickname (bestowed by a sports writer when he was a teen-ager) made him popular beyond his talents. He latched onto seven years of pro basketball glory with the same tenacity he pulled down thousands of rebounds.

He was a big-league player when Louisville was a big-league town. Those days were the apex of a mythic life littered with stories, scandalous and sad, hilarious and horrifying. In those days Goose was golden, emancipated from a past he portrays through police beatings, prison time and a near-lynching at the hands of white vigilantes. And when those days were over, Goose tumbled back down the mountain and crashed into a cocaine addiction that cost him everything but his family and his sanity.

His most valuable memorabilia from those days — uniforms, red-white-and-blue balls, and warmups — are all gone. But even as his glory years recede into history, people warmly recognize him almost every day as an Original Colonel.

"It makes me feel like I must have done *something* good, for people to remember me," Goose says. "But people stop me and I get nervous. 'Goose, what you been doing?'"

"Everyone has their own way of doing things. And mine has always been the hard way."

Now, from his spot on the bench, Goose once again hears the echoes of those golden years — stirring up the old feelings, jarring loose the old memories. Three decades after its birth and twenty-two years after its death, the American Basketball Association is throwing a three-day reunion party this week in Indianapolis.

But after the party's over his future is the same. Goose is broke and going blind — with a wife, an 8-year-old son, and 5-year-old daughter to clothe and feed. "Unless a miracle happens," he says.

He puffs more smoke into the stagnant air. There are no miracles happening today on the bench in Iroquois Homes.

The street sign in the housing project says Oneida Avenue. But the gang-bangers call it Crenshaw Boulevard — named after the main drag in South-Central Los Angeles, part of which has fallen under the criminal hegemony of the Crips and Bloods.

"I was out here one day with all red on," Goose Ligon says from his bench. "Some Crips came by and said, 'Goose, you better not have that red on next time we come back. We'll have to do something about it.' It's ridiculous.

"All these guys are walking around with 9 millimeters in their pockets. Every night you hear shooting down here — until the police started walking through here nine deep. I think that was the best thing they've ever done here.

"I just don't understand why young kids want to die. You're 19, 20 years old. You ain't even done no *livin.'"*

Goose Ligon did a whole lot of livin' as a young man, Most of it hard.

The noose was around his neck before he knew what was happening.

Black of night in Kokomo, Indiana, the town that would drive out AIDS victim Ryan White a quarter-century later. Rosa Parks and Martin Luther King and civil rights marchers were beginning to transform the nation, but the black of night in many small towns still belonged to the hateful.

As Goose tells it, he had just squeezed out of the white girl's bedroom window and started walking when a man asked him for a light. He obliged without thinking.

"By the time I lit the lighter, I saw it was the father of one of the other girls I'd been seeing," he says. "By then, people were coming from everywhere."

Quickly he was thrown into the back seat of a car with a rope constricting his neck. The men hissed their homicidal itinerary: he was being driven out of town to be tarred, feathered, and hanged.

For once, being the star basketball player at Kokomo High School wasn't going to save him.

The son of a steelworker who died of tuberculosis when Goose was in fifth grade, he grew up a pauper king: so poor that he had to wrap wire around his crumbling shoes, but so gifted athletically that the 6,800 fans who packed Memorial Gymnasium were eager to help him out.

On weekends he earned cash — and broke rules — by playing semipro ball in Michigan under an assumed name. ("Norvell Brown," he says. "I even wore glasses.") But during the season boosters always made sure he had enough to eat.

And in the classroom he says he coasted through without taking exams — simply signing his name at the top and turning them in blank.

Who was going to flunk the Golden Goose?

"I took maybe — *maybe* — three tests in high school," he says.

But on this night, there was not classroom, and no sympathetic boosters in sight. This was the white end of Kokomo in the black of night, with Goose at the wrong end of a rope and begging for mercy.

He fathered a son at age 16 with a black girl, but most of his nocturnal wanderings were to the other side of town. That's where the police often found him and — depending on who is telling the story — dealt with him either savagely or humanely.

Ligon says there were several nights when the cops snatched him up after late-night trysts and drove him to a reservoir, where they beat him with rubber hoses.

"Hose doesn't leave marks," he explains.

Former chief of police Andy Castner laughed at the story. Several people who lived in Kokomo at the time described Castner and his cohorts as more friends to Ligon than antagonists, lending support when possible.

"Sometimes he'd be out a little late and I'd give him a ride home," says Castner, now president of the Kokomo city council. "I've never known Jim to have any trouble with policemen."

The police were unable to curtail Goose's tomcatting, whether by benign or malevolent means. So the local vigilantes decided to act — even if it meant jeopardizing the upcoming basketball season.

To reach their intended destination, the white men who grabbed Goose had to drive through Kokomo's black neighborhood. This was Goose's saving grace.

Stopped at a red light in front of a black nightclub, he snatched the coil of rope from the lap of the man next to him and leaped from the car, rolling away and screaming for help. Nobody in the car dared get out to give chase.

"If they had gone another way, I might not be here today," he says.

Castner says he'd never heard the lynching story before, but added, "He was very popular with the white girls at the time, so it's possible that might've happened."

Goose Ligon survived that night and went on to lead the Kokomo Wildkats to their first and only state title in 1961. The next year he finished his career as the school's all-time leading scorer with 1,900 points. That mark still stands.

Goose's rogue image in part prevented him from winning Indiana's Mr. Basketball award as a senior. But he made the Indiana All-Star team, and Kokomo High hung a picture of him in his All-Star uniform on the gym wall.

"He was probably the best high school basketball player Kokomo has ever had," says Ken "Red" Craig, an assistant principal and unofficial team manager at the time. "I haven't seen too many people who could measure up to the Goose — if he had good meals and those kinds of things."

But when Goose's high school career ended, so did his usefulness in Kokomo — even if he couldn't see it coming. Long before the onset of glaucoma, his vision was flawed.

"I thought I could keep on being Goose Ligon, the Golden Boy," he says. "I wasn't smart enough to understand that after I shot that last hoop, that was it."

It was less than a year after he shot that last hoop that his relations with a white girl became a crime.

U.S. marshals clanked cold bracelets on his wrists right there on the court, in the middle of a game, in December 1962 in some Oklahoma gym. Nineteen-year-old Goose Ligon was playing for the Harlem Magicians, a barnstorming team formed by former Globetrotter star Marques Haynes. He was arrested for statutory rape of a 13-year-old.

"Everyone started clapping and stuff," he says. "They thought it was part of the act." In a way it was — another tragicomic episode in James Ligon's mythic life.

He had never played college ball, joining the Magicians after an aborted matriculation to Tennessee A & I. And now the basketball hero was going to stand trial in his hometown for statutory rape. And as all the news reports made sure to point, she was a *white* 13-year-old.

Ligon was accused of having sex with the girl in late November, when the Magicians were performing in Kokomo. He says it was consensual, that he'd known the girl for some time, and that she even had spent the night at his family's home before.

But there would be no escaping this time. Goose was convicted on June 18, 1963, of a lesser charge of "assault and battery with intent to gratify sexual desires." He was sentenced to one to five years in the Indiana State Reformatory in Pendleton.

Goose spent the next three and a half years of his life as Prisoner No. 46142 — the star of the penitentiary basketball team, hating every minute of it.

"These kids who say they ain't afraid of going to prison? Ha. They ain't *been* to prison," Goose says from his bench.

When he was released from the joint he did not return to Kokomo. Resentment simmered — not only in Goose, but in many who knew him.

"There were five involved (in the statutory rape), but Jimmy's the only one who did time," Castner says. "To be honest, it kind of left a bitter taste in my mouth. He was at fault, but he wasn't the only one at fault. If he hadn't been a celebrity, he might not've gotten time out of it.

"While he was playing, he could do no wrong. But after he was done, people criticized him for doing the same things as when he was playing."

Ron Hughes was Goose's teammate at Kokomo. Today he is an insurance agent in town, and he speaks cautiously about Goose's fall from grace. But Hughes made it clear that he regrets how his former comrade was treated.

"I don't know any facts," Hughes said. "I just know that the times were pretty rough on blacks. I have my opinions, and they would all be on the positive side of Jim."

That was not the popular sentiment in Kokomo at the time.

When the trouble came down, they pulled Goose Ligon's All-Star picture off the gym wall.

When Goose walked free from prison, he walked straight back to basketball. It was all he'd ever done, all he'd ever thought of doing.

Just as he was working to get a tryout with a National Basketball Association team, the ABA sprang to life, and Goose decided to cast his lot with the Indiana Pacers.

Mike Storen was the general manager then. Goose says Storen told him, when he cut him, that his personal history made him a risk in his home state. He referred Goose to the Kentucky Colonels instead.

The year was 1967. Louisville has been Goose Ligon's home ever since.

He met with team owners Mamie and Joe Gregory and told them his story — the charge, the prison time, the whole deal. "They said no problem," Goose recalls. "They just wanted me to play ball."

Goose became one of the more colorful crystals in the kaleidoscope that was the ABA. He was a six-foot-seven battler who did all his work within ten feet of the basket, surviving on a soft hook shot and a hard edge. He averaged double figures in scoring for five seasons and always finished among the league leaders in rebounds, despite being outsized.

"He was kind of a Dennis Rodman of his time," says former *Courier-Journal* sports editor Dave Kindred, now a columnist with the *Atlanta Journal-Constitution*. "I hate to hang that on a guy, but that's kind of what it was. If he were playing today, that might be what he'd turn out to be; some kind of wild persona. He was a rebounder and a runner, a tireless runner. He loved to play."

He played well enough that Kokomo High decided to put Gooses' All-Star picture back on the gym wall. The winds of public opinion spun his weather vane back to the positive.

Goose was one of the Colonel's top attractions in those early days, his hard work blending well with a dynamic persona and fetching grin.

"The thing I'll always remember is that smile," said Lloyd Gardner, the Fairdale High School coach and former trainer for the Colonels.

Gardner recently watched an HBO special on the ABA days. In one video clip he could see a figure loping by in the background and knew, from the distinctive gait, that it was Goose. He spent much of his time in the background of the news footage, but he was an indispensable teammate to Dan Issel, Louie Dampier, Darel Carrier & Co.

Gardner remembers nursing Goose through six games of the 1971 ABA championship series against the Utah Stars with back spasms, only to have Goose's back give out in Game Seven. He played just a few minutes, and the Stars won the title.

"I remember that he was willing to do whatever it took to survive," Gardner said. "He was not going to give his place up without a fight. He played with a lot of pain that guys just don't do these days."

He had a high tolerance off the court as well. Goose says he saved the serious party binges for the off-season, but he hardly took a vow of sobriety and chastity between games.

There was, for instance, the Can Opener Story. One night Goose was pulled out of a "go-go club," as he called it, on Chestnut Street by one of the many women who rotated through his life. An argument erupted over whether he would return to the bar. The woman pulled out a stiletto and pressed it to Goose's neck. He escaped with a nearly severed left thumb that caused him to miss a few games.

Telling the real story about the injury was, obviously, out of the question. So the Colonels concocted a tale about Goose cutting his hand on a new can opener, which was a gift from teammate Wayne Chapman.

Everyone can chuckle about that story now. But not every day was a laughing matter with Goose.

"Jim seemed to have some demons he was fighting, and we didn't always see eye to eye," said the Colonels coach at the time, Gene Rhodes. "And that may be rather generous. I liked him, and in the best way I could — which wasn't always good — I tried to get him to do the best for himself. I think Jim couldn't quite see that it was all going to end one day."

No. Goose's troubled eyes rarely looked past the next game, the next girl, the next party. He was working for tip money (his richest contract with the Colonels paid $13,000 a year), but he was in heaven.

When heaven ended with a ruptured Achilles' tendon nineteen games into the 1973–74 season with the Virginia Squires, that was it. His life reverted to the only constants it has ever known: tumult and trauma.

From his bench, Goose Ligon watches a gray van carry two white men through Iroquois Homes.

"There go the narcs," he says.

You can tell?

He laughs.

"*Everyone* can tell."

A neighborhood with a bustling crack trade isn't the best address for a recovering addict. But in one of the many cruel paradoxes in Goose's life, it was the addiction that helped land him and his family in public housing.

Over the years it ate up large chunks of his pension from the ABA (a measly 12 grand in one lump sum, as Goose remembers it), and the down payment on a house. Income from the one steady job he held — twelve years cleaning and preparing buses for TARC — often went into his nose or veins as fast as it came in.

"Everything I had moneywise, it's all wasted," Goose says. "And now I'm in a place where I may never get out of. I feel like, in a sense, I put us here."

As his identity devolved from ballplayer to addict, Goose made three stays in drug-rehab centers. He spent most of his life after basketball ripped, and he looks it today.

"That drug done did damage to his body," says Jim's 83-year-old mother, Christine, who lives in Louisville. "I can only say this like an old country lady, but it just done did him in. He just don't seem like himself."

At on point Goose was so far gone that he and his friends had an agreement: you overdose, and the others dump your body in the nearest alley and scram. That way nobody is left with a corpse on their hands, facing a criminal charge.

"They told him one time at the clinic that if he didn't stop doing what he was doing, he wasn't going to make it," says Doris Ligon, Goose's wife of eleven years and companion of nineteen. "A lot of times I was scared to come home. I was afraid I was going to find him dead."

One day he and his junkie friends swaggered into the Cotter-Lang housing project with about $1,000. When the binge was over, he woke up in a garbage can, alone, and had to beg for a quarter to call home.

At least he knew Doris would answer the phone. Through all the lies ("He'd come home with no paycheck, tell me he got robbed") and heartache and ultimatums, she hasn't been able to turn her back on Jim Ligon.

He's not Goose to her. She never knew him as a ballplayer, and doesn't love him for his past.

"I always tell him he's like a bad penny," she says. "You try to throw him away and he won't stay away."

So they stay together, decorating their cramped apartment not with mementos of Goose's playing days (those are in a box in a closet) but family pictures. A sign on the wall says God Bless Our Pad.

Eight-year-old Eric and 5-year-old Mary dash in and out of the place. They are the reasons Goose gives for finally getting sober. "The only thing saving me is my children," he says.

They gave him back an identity: father.

His oldest son, Steven Purcell, is 37 and lives in Kokomo. He didn't return phone calls for this story. Goose wasn't much involved with him. He has his youngest kids, though, and a few other things besides. Here, at a brittle 53 years of age, he has the opportunity to flower anew amid the rubble of his life — as a father, son and citizen.

There remains a chance that when Goose Ligon's vision is gone for good and he's living in darkness, his mind's highlight reel will have something else to play beyond old basketball footage.

He calls his mother every night, right after the lottery drawing. After waiting on the bench in vain for that divine bailout, he goes inside to watch for a secular miracle.

When that fails, he picks up the phone.

"I do listen for his call," says Christine Ligon. "I love my son. A lot of his life I don't appreciate, the drugs and stuff, but I can't do nothing about it."

She is not the only person outside his home that Goose looks after. On weekends he and Doris help the Community Church of God put on "Super Saturday," an outreach program for at-risk children in Iroquois Homes.

The church feeds about one hundred kids every Saturday — more at the end of each month, when the government checks have all been spent — and teaches them about Jesus. Doris has a classroom, and Goose helps discipline unruly kids.

"They've been a blessing," says the church pastor, the Rev. Robert Davis. "He [Goose] has done things that robbed him of having things in life, but he acknowledges that. He can relate to the children."

He relates passionately to Eric and Mary. Much of his lawn-mowing money goes to them, in the form of trips to Dairy Queen or the pool. He recently scraped together enough cash to buy Mary a bike. And when she wrecked on it, gashing her chin, Goose was a wreck.

After five or six stitches were laced through Mary's chin, the nurse was telling Goose and his wife how to care for her at home.

Give her Children's Tylenol for the pain, they are told. Doris Ligon looks at her husband. He sighs and runs a twisted right hand across his face.

They have no Children's Tylenol.

They have no money to buy Children's Tylenol.

There are no miracles happening again today.

"I'll mow some grass," Goose Ligon says quietly. "I'll mow some grass."

TOM BOSWELL

Late Boomer

FROM THE WASHINGTON POST MAGAZINE

LAST NOVEMBER, baseball's best players gathered in Chavez Ravine in Los Angeles for a casual practice before leaving on their annual tour of Japan. Clumped in the outfield, Brady Anderson, Gary Sheffield, Juan Gonzalez and Steve Finley talked about this and that.

Sheffield fell quiet for a few seconds, simply looking at Anderson. "Man, *come here*," said Sheffield, grabbing the Orioles center fielder. "You gotta gimme some for that 50. God *damn*."

Then the high-fives began. That's the moment when Brady Anderson realized what he'd done. Even though the conversation had not been about him or even about home runs, his "50 jacks" hung in the air above his head like an enormous exclamation point.

This spring, everybody's got to give Brady some for that 50. He's now unique in the history of the game — the only player ever to have a 50-home-run season and a 50-stolen-base year, too. Not Willie Mays, Mickey Mantle, Jose Canseco, or Barry Bonds. But Brady Anderson.

A few weeks ago, Yankees shortstop Derek Jeter encountered Anderson near the batting cage. Jeter just started laughing. "Fifty homers and 110 RBI from a leadoff guy," was all he said. Then he walked away.

Anderson gets that treatment regularly. He's nonplused the whole baseball world, and everybody loves it. He's the good guy who's also a cool dude. He's the sex symbol who's also a workaholic. He's the breathtaking multisport athlete who also scuffled for years like some journeyman stiff. He's the underappreciated late bloomer, now 33, who's gotten better later than anybody ever. His career's been an impossible mission, but he's pulling it off.

Oh, yes, Anderson's got an attitude, a brain and a rhythm-and-blues soul. And right this minute he can't decide whether to play tennis with a touring pro, spar a few rounds with a heavyweight, run the 40-yard dash against a world-class sprinter or go on a date with a fashion model. Or maybe he'll just rollerblade in traffic.

Brady's not your father's center fielder. If you've got a little edge, you might even enjoy No. 9 of the Orioles more than the immortal No. 8. Recently, Anderson was talking to *his* father on the phone when Billy Ripken interrupted.

"Mr. B.A., I want to talk to you," said Cal Ripken's kid brother. "Your son is the greatest player I've ever seen. Good-bye."

With that, Billy walked away. You've just got to give it up for Brady.

One Phone Call Away from Japan

Maybe the bottom is the only place where you ever truly meet yourself. Perhaps bad luck puts you there. Maybe you fall there all by yourself. Or, if you're Brady Anderson, you wake up one day and have no clue how the devil you got down there in that pit. But you know you've got to get out.

Anderson can even name the day he hit rock bottom: August 20, 1991.

That's the day Orioles Manager Johnny Oates sent the outfielder down to Rochester. "It's not like I've blocked out that part of my life. But I prefer not to think about it. It's really hard for me to remember," says Anderson. "It's like it all happened to a different player, almost a different person."

Yeah, right. He still remembers every detail. For the fourth straight season, Brady had bombed out and ended up back in the bushes. The Orioles looked at the fleet, muscular 27-year-old and saw two things: one of the best all-around athletes in baseball. And one of the biggest flops. "Brady was one phone call away from Japan," says ex-Oriole Mike Flanagan.

"I was *trying* to go to Japan," says Anderson.

Desperation sometimes forces us into a Decision of Last Resort.

We commit, finally, to being who we really think we are. Damn what anybody else believes.

"I just want one favor from you," Anderson told Rochester Manager Greg Biagini. "I want to hit cleanup. I'm tried of this bunting bull. I'm not doing it anymore."

For years after they got him from Boston in a trade for starter Mike Boddicker, the Orioles had tried to turn him into a conventional leadoff hitter, the kind of guy who slaps the ball to the opposite field. Just days before Oates demoted him, with his average at .230, Anderson had straightened up his stance, grabbed a bigger bat, started to swing hard and, basically, decided that if his career was going to be a catastrophe, he'd flame out on his own terms.

The ignominious demotion steeled his resolve. Four years of perpetual humiliation gave birth to a ferociously determined player with so many superb skills that much of baseball still doesn't appreciate how great he has become over the past five seasons.

"From the day I was sent down, I've never swung a bat the same. I refused. It was just, 'O.K., enough of this. I'm going to play every day somewhere, maybe Japan. I don't care. Swing hard all the time. I don't care. I'm not going to bunt. I don't care.' Anyone who was going to come at me and tell me what to do now was going to do so at their own peril, as far as I was concerned."

For years Anderson had worried himself into a knot and hidden his many self-doubts. He'd tried to incorporate almost every piece of well-meaning advice, some of it idiotic. His parents had divorced early in his childhood, and he seemed to want approval from coaches and manager — like a good boy. He felt a child's guilt at failing the grown-ups. Teammates termed him "immature" but may not have known how accurate they were.

"Everybody was trying to help," Anderson says now. "It's not like the coaches got together and said, 'Let's really mess up Brady.'"

Finally, with his career disintegrating, he took responsibility for himself — like a grown man. "I rediscovered my stubbornness and my mean streak."

Anderson hit .385 at Rochester, then batted .385 in September in Baltimore, too. One late-season day, while running sprints in the outfield, he started to daydream.

"If I had my choice, would I rather have a ten-year career as a very solid, always-have-a-job player like Joe Orsulak? Or would I rather struggle terribly like I have been and turn into an All-Star player?" Anderson wondered.

"I had never even had a good year," he says now, laughing, "but I thought, 'I'd rather take the struggle and turn out to be an excellent or great player.' It's funny but that's what happened. Maybe it was better for me, not only in baseball terms, but in how I view life. I appreciate my success more now."

A couple of other epiphanies helped. In that off-season, Anderson went to the track for a workout. His legs were sore from weight-lifting. A world-class 60-meter man, Marty Krulee, was on the track, too. Anderson told a buddy, "I'm going to race him."

"You know he's going to beat you," said the friend.

"We'll see," said Anderson.

As friends watched in amazement, Anderson beat Krulee in the 40-yard dash three times out of four.

Anderson's years of baseball humiliation swirled in front of him. In his previous five attempts to crack the big leagues he'd hit .230, .198, .207, .231, and .230. He was a certified stiff. "I stood there thinking, 'I just beat a world-class sprinter. Man, what am I doing?'

"That was one of the happiest athletic accomplishments of my life," he says. Afterward, he'd look around the baseball field and say, "O.K., there are no better athletes out here."

"I always tried too hard," says Anderson now. "I didn't need people on me to practice more or think about hitting more. I just needed to break everything down to its simplest components and let my ability take over."

Finally, Anderson saw *Field of Dreams.*

"Burt Lancaster plays a character who only had one game in the big leagues and never got to bat," Brady says, reciting Lancaster's lines from memory. "He says, 'It was like coming this close to your dreams and watching them pass by you like a stranger in the crowd. We just don't know the most significant moments of our lives while they're happening. At the time, you think there'll be other days. I didn't realize that was the only day.'

"Obviously that line got to me. It kind of haunted me at the time. You have to constantly remind yourself: don't let too many days of your life slip by."

"Don't Worry — Brady's Learned How to Do It Now"

During his four dark years, nobody in baseball doubted Anderson more than Anderson. Now, everybody in baseball doubts Brady, except Brady.

Last season, Anderson tied the major league record with 11 home runs in April. In May, he reached 20 homers — just one less than his career best for a season. The sport was in shock. No player — no player *ever* — had improved his power so dramatically at the advanced baseball age of 32. When would Brady crash? The assumption then, and now, is that it's a question of when, not if.

The smart money assumes Brady will revert to the mean. Over the past five years, he's hit 112 homers. So, put him down for 22 this year, right?

The Orioles are so sure of this eventuality that they're gambling millions of dollars on it. Early this spring they refused to negotiate in earnest with Anderson, who will be a free agent after this season. To take those 50 homers seriously would mean an annual salary somewhere in Barry Bonds territory. Anderson and Bonds — who is six months younger and just signed for $22 million for two years — even have the same agent.

The Orioles have probably miscalculated badly. And it will probably cost them dearly — either in salary to Anderson or, worse, in his loss to another team. If the Orioles want the proper scouting report on Brady, they should talk to his girlfriend, Ingrid. She's been ahead of the curve on this one all along.

"Last spring, Ingrid was talking to my dad's wife," Anderson recalls. "I had twenty homers at the time. My stepmom was saying, 'Oh, my God, how long can this go on?'"

Anderson was especially interested in Ingrid's response because, in his view, she is his one pure, uncontaminated observer. That's to say, she's from Belgium and is still pretty clueless about baseball. Brady's confidence in Ingrid's perception was only strengthened recently when he overhead her describing his life's work thusly: "My boyfriend hits a ball with a stick."

Here is how she responded to his stepmother's worries last May. "Ingrid said, 'Don't worry. It'll go on. Brady's learned how to do it now.'"

Sitting in a spring-training dugout, Anderson can't stop laughing at this memory. He says the words over and over: "No, it's O.K. He knows how to do it now."

"But in a way, she's right."

The old Brady might have worried himself back to earth. But that guy is long dead. The new Brady is his own man. The Orioles made him that way. They accidentally toughened him up with failure until he found his baseball backbone. With Anderson now in his tenth season as an Oriole, the people who run the team should know who they're dealing with, but, amazingly, they barely have a clue.

"When you are told you are not a power hitter, over and over, maybe you start to believe it a little bit yourself," Anderson says. "Last year, I just refused. And I'm not going to believe it ever again."

Coaches had always told him a leadoff man shouldn't strike out 100 times a year. Finally, he learned to ignore them. "I'll take a player who walks 100 times and strikes out 100 times any day over one that walks 50 times and strikes out 50 times. There's no comparison." Anderson has a head for stats. Some coaches don't.

One former Orioles coach told him that leadoff men were "sacrificial lambs" who had a duty to take as many pitches as possible so other hitters could study the pitcher. "I was pretty much finished with that theory as soon as I heard it. That was about the last I was going to listen to anything he had to say . . . There's one thing I know. I'm adamant. Nobody will tell me otherwise. You don't walk by taking on 2–0. You get walks by knocking 2–0 pitches off the outfield wall. Pitchers are intelligent. They walk the hitters they fear."

Other geniuses told Anderson to study tapes of himself. Another disaster. "I do things by feel," he says. "I *know* what I'm doing wrong. Watching myself just messes me up. I think, 'Oh, I didn't know my elbow was *there.*'"

At the plate, Anderson doesn't think about his own swing. It's not that pretty, he says. Instead, he has a vivid image of Seattle's Edgar Martinez drilling an inside fastball down the line for a double several years ago. Tough pitch. Calm, quick, late swing. Perfect balance. Head on the ball. Gorgeous high follow-through. A piece of art. You see, *Edgar Martinez* really hit those 50 homers.

"Last spring," Brady says, "when I had twenty homers, I started analyzing it, saying. 'Twenty! That's pretty good.' I started slapping singles to left. Then I thought, 'What am I doing? I'm hitting home runs. And I'm not going to stop hitting 'em. And that's it.' I hit one out that day. And I didn't stop after that."

"The thing I liked most about last season was my [month-by-month] home-run count: 11-9-7-6-8-9. It went from the highest to the lowest, then back *up*. People were saying, 'Anderson's home-run totals have declined each month — as expected.' Well, they didn't decline the last two months."

So put Brady down for 30 to 45 homers this season, not 15 to 30. And put down the Orioles as dopes if they don't sign him. "I want to stay in Baltimore," says Anderson, who claims he'd bargain off multiyear stats, not just mega-'96.

Perhaps the Orioles' real worry should be that Anderson might get *better* — not at hitting home runs, presumably, but as a total player.

"It's hard for people to grasp that I'm improving a lot later in my career than almost anyone else. But that runs in my family." Anderson's sprint times are the same as when he was 22. In high school, he couldn't dunk. By the time he left college, he could — occasionally. Now, he's throwin' 'em down.

Before the '96 season, Anderson's vision tested at a phenomenal 20/12, better than ever before. "What do you expect? Brady lives on carrot juice," says Mike Flanagan. This spring, he tested at a truly eye-popping 20/10. Objects appear as large and clear to him at 20 feet as they do to an average person at 10 feet.

"Basically that's what Ted Williams had," says Anderson. "I was impressed."

Maybe Anderson's eyes are the reason he claims he has reduced hitting to "see the ball and hit the ball." It helps if you're seeing a bigger ball.

Only one person in the Orioles' brass thinks that Anderson's new power may be permanent. That's manager Davey Johnson, who greets Anderson by saying: "Sign, O.K.? Just sign. Pleeeease."

"How do I know he'll keep hitting homers?" says Johnson. "Because if I could do it, Brady can. He's a lot stronger and better than I was."

After eight seasons as a 10-homer-a-year Oriole, Johnson went to the National League and set the league record for homers by a second baseman with 43. Injuries drove him out of the majors but, in Japan, he hit 39 more homers in 660 at-bats. As Ingrid might say, once you learn how, it's O.K.

"His confidence in me meant a lot," says Anderson. "I'd look in the dugout for the bunt sign with two guys on and he's yelling, 'Come on, Brady, drive 'em in.' Or you look for the take sign on 2–0 and *it's not there.* You think, 'All right! This guy's behind me. He knows what I can do.'"

A ballplayer with a bit of a chip on his shoulder is hard to stop. And Brady's been ripped as a flop or seriously underrated for his entire big league career.

"It's nice I only hit nineteen homers at Camden Yards last year," he says. "They can't say my fifty were a product of playing at a short ballpark. I hit home runs before the [All-Star] break, after the break. They can't say I tricked 'em the first half. Nothing. I never stopped hitting 'em from the first week on.

"I hit home runs in the home-run-hitting contest in Japan. I hit two in the MTV softball game." By now he's laughing at himself. "Of course, I sucked in the Pepsi softball game."

Some players' motivation is dampened by a monster season. Anderson's seems redoubled. He only knows one speed — pedal to the metal. It's a scary style. That goofy MTV softball game included obstacles in the outfield. Brady sprinted after one ball, dove, and made a wonderful sliding catch. Of course, he also forgot that there was a covered wagon in the outfield. He barely missed it.

"He could have killed himself. My heart was in my mouth," says one Orioles official. "Brady is definitely different."

"My Next Project Is Speed Skating"

One night Anderson and Ripken, who are close friends, both had terrible games. Near midnight in the clubhouse, Brady found Cal running on a treadmill set at 8 mph. "What are you trying to do?" he asked.

"Commit suicide," Ripken said.

"Me, too," said Anderson, who was on his way to take a 180-degree sauna.

One hour later, after Anderson had left his self-imposed hell, Ripken was staggering off the treadmill. "Did it work for you?" said Anderson.

"Nope," said Ripken.

"Me neither," said Anderson. "Jesus, do we have to play again tomorrow?"

Now, when Anderson sees Ripken in the weight room after a bad game, he'll ask, 'Suicide attempt?' Usually, Ripken will answer, 'Nah, not tonight.'"

The intensity of both men, however, borders on the perverse. They are driven by a motivation so pure, so unquenchable, that it's inexplicable to them — let alone to ordinary folks. Before asking whether the body-building, cross-training Anderson is a bit of a narcissist, toss a tad of masochist into the equation, too.

"I only see what he does in the clubhouse," says pitcher Mike Mussina. "But apparently, Brady works out *all the time.*"

Anderson is definitely the Extreme Outfielder. His idea of true accomplishment is to run mountains until "I can't walk. I can't get up off the ground. It really feels like I'm going to die. You think, 'Tomorrow, stop a little sooner, I don't ever want to feel this bad again in my life.' The next day, you try again."

Last winter, when others might have taken their 50 homers on the banquet trail, Anderson did not take a vacation. The day after the season ended, he rowed and played three hours of tennis. Later, he went to Lake Tahoe for fifteen days to train at high altitude and add bulk — always a problem for a six-foot-one guy who weighed 145 pounds in high school and still — at close to 200 pounds — has almost no body fat. "I pigged out. Filet mignons three times a day," he says. Yet he ran and rowed so much he *lost* five pounds.

Anderson doesn't deny that — by other people's lights — he takes exercise to excess. "Basically, I have no life." he said once. That, however, was mumbled sardonically on a hot summer day. Now it's spring again. And work is joy.

"My ultimate day would be to go to the track, run, lift weights, throw the shot around. Eat. Go back to the gym and lift. Then maybe play basketball or tennis later in the day. To me that's fun. There's nothing like it. Your body produces endorphins when you work out like that. You become addicted to it, like any other drug," he says.

"Here's my thing. This afternoon, I'm going water-skiing. As a kid, I surfed, skateboarded and played ice hockey. I still rollerblade. My next project is speed skating. That may be the toughest [cardiovascular] sport."

"In some ways baseball suits me," he says. "But in some ways it definitely doesn't. You're not put in enough positions to show off your athletic ability. You don't get many chances to make great catches. You don't even have to be in good shape to be a great hitter. Though it's an incredibly difficult skill. Sometimes you like sports where you have to reach way down inside. Like watching [Pete] Sampras in the U.S. Open when he was vomiting on the court. You're not put in that situation often in baseball."

Perhaps this explains why, one off-season, Anderson worked with 1972 Olympic boxing medalist Jesse Valdez for weeks, then flew to Louisiana to spar with a pro. For many years he's trained with world-class sprinters and decathletes, like Steve Odgers. In season, he's played tennis with Andre Agassi. Anderson serves at more than 100 mph.

Last fall he and Roberto Alomar played with U.S. Federation Cup champions Monica Seles and Mary Joe Fernandez in a charity event. On the final point of the final game, with a side bet at stake, he aced Seles.

"A lot of people talk about what they would do if they played other sports. I like to go find out for myself. When somebody asks me, 'How would you do, Brady, if you practiced every day for a year against Monica Seles?' I don't have to speculate. I know. She would kill me, 6–0, 6–0, till the end of time."

When he gets older, will the fun stop?

"Not unless they start refusing to play with me."

Perhaps it's odd to think of a 50-home-run center fielder being the heir to Paul Gallico and George Plimpton, writers who became famous for attempting high-level games in which they were inevitably punched, tackled or humiliated. But it's not really such a stretch.

Brady knows that his drive mystifies many people. The day he tangled with that heavyweight, he was sick with the flu. "When it came time to box, I'd gone all that way, so I said, 'I'm going to do it.' My friend was like, 'Why are you doing this in the first place? And why are you doing it when you are this sick?'

"I said, 'I want to see what it's like.'"

To grasp Anderson, you have to understand that he was an economics major at the University of California at Irvine. Both his parents have master's degrees. One is a financial planner, the other an insurance underwriter. His stepbrother is a freshman at Dartmouth. In his family, intelligence and curiosity are the norm.

But perhaps the key to Brady, his main spring, is the purity of his love of sports. He's only part baseball player. One game can't contain him or define him. But he's all athlete. He was walking on his hands by age 3. If a freak accident in some other game costs him a $20 million contract, so be it.

He gets so much joy from off-season sports, in part because "my performance isn't evaluated. It's not under the microscope. I'm just doing it."

When he was a child, Anderson's favorite thing in the world was to put stickum on his hands and catch a football. His grandfather threw pass patterns. Down and in, down and out, bottom hook, banana, post. His ultimate goal was to make a diving catch. Because it felt good. That was it.

"I never thought, 'If I keep doing this, I'll become a great receiver.'"

During the Super Bowl, Brady would wail at his father, "Dad, what are you doing? We could be outside playing *catch*."

In college, Anderson had friends who'd spend hours lobbing baseballs over the wall for him "just because it felt good to stick your cleat into a fence and go lie four feet over it and make a great catch. It was just pure fun . . . One of the best things about being an athlete is your life can revolve around it."

That worries the Orioles every day. It's a big world. What's their center fielder *doing* out there? Davey Johnson already goes into the fetal position when you mention Brady rollerblading through traffic to get to Camden Yards.

Chill, Davey. It could be worse. Brady doesn't skydive or bungee-jump.

Yet.

"Cal is cautious. I'm not," says Anderson, laughing. "He'd buy water-skiing instruction manuals and watch those water-skiing tapes. I was on the water the first day."

When Other People Believe in You

Anderson is still close to both of his parents, who have remained friends. Because they've both been in his life continuously, their divorce — which came when he was 3 — does not strike him as particularly traumatic. Nonetheless, he was raised mainly by his father, Jerry. And that has made a difference.

"He changed jobs, changed his whole career pattern so he could raise me. I didn't figure it out until ten years ago," said Anderson last summer. "When he had difficult times, he didn't want it to affect anybody else. He got through it himself. He was an admirable man to me. Sometimes he doesn't know how good a father I think he was."

To this day, Anderson is deeply concerned that he earn the respect of the people he holds in esteem. He never operates from the assumption that he will be loved unconditionally, simply for being himself. Rather he drives himself to prove his worth, especially in his own eyes. He always has to earn love, even self-love. Sound like a boy raised by a man?

"Some people need to be pushed because they're lazy. That's the last thing I need. I'm on myself all the time," he says. "When other people believe in you, that means a lot to me . . . Davey complimented me in the press for being a hard-nosed player. You play hard for yourself, but if you've got somebody like that behind you, you don't want to let him down."

Anderson has a severe depression in the top of his right thigh, big enough for your thumb. It's the result of playing with a torn quad muscle for more than two months last season. Anderson would say, "I can go out there." Johnson would answer, "Just don't run too hard. Don't blow it out in center field."

"Just the fact that he wanted me in the lineup so badly, I had to go out there," says Anderson, who also played through what his doctors diagnosed as appendicitis, and — astonishingly — proved them wrong.

The irony of Anderson's career is that — because he has been known to wear Luke Perry–style sideburns and has a kind of swaggering hipster presence — he's assumed to be some southern California playboy who's laid-back and barely cares. "I don't know how Brady's *perceived*," says Ripken, sarcastically, "but he's one of the most competitive people I've ever met."

We often say of others what we really believe about ourselves. Anderson takes great pride in what he sees as his similarities of temperament with Ripken. And his view of Vanilla Cal has a very sharp edge.

"Cal has a mean streak that people don't know about," he says. "I've never thought of him as a 'nice guy.'" He then recalls an incident when Ripken was beaned in a game against Oakland. Later in the inning, Ripken knocked A's catcher Terry Steinbach out of the game, with a forearm to the head on a tag play at home plate.

"Cal did it with a vengeance, too. He got hit. He thought it was on purpose. And I guarantee you he couldn't wait to get a shot at Steinbach. He took him *out*. There was nothing dirty about it. Steinbach blocked the plate. But it was a vicious, vicious collision. Cal hit Steinbach so hard that, when he got back to the dugout, the marks from the catchers mask were imprinted on his arm."

Ripken may have this leatherneck attitude upon occasion. But Anderson has it in every at-bat. He stands on top of the plate, like Frank Robinson and Don Baylor, ignoring danger, challenging the pitcher. Last year he was hit by pitches 22 times, leading the league. In the last five years, he's been hit 61 times. He hasn't rubbed yet.

"Like any hitter who stands on the plate, Brady *wants* you to pitch him inside," says Johnson. "He'll get drilled some, but he'll hurt you more."

"I'll compete," says Anderson. "If I have to be mean to do it, I don't care. It has nothing to do with my personality after the competition is over."

That off-field personality is one of baseballs's delights. "Let's talk about one of my favorite people," beams the old-school Johnson. "Brady's a jewel."

Both teammates and opponents gravitate to Anderson. He's always at the center of pregame banter. The printed page can't capture his droll wise-up delivery or his comic timing. He makes ballplayers laugh, and that's a tough audience. For years, nothing has been deemed cool among the Orioles unless Brady has given it the nod. His uniform is as tight as paint and his hat always seems cocked forward rakishly. He once pulled a potential home run out of the stands, then acted like he hadn't caught the ball for what seemed like five seconds before casually lobbing it back to the infield. "He's more likely to set a trend than follow one," says Ripken.

"Fame?" says Anderson. "It's nice." So that cosmic subject is settled.

What about autographs? "Away from the park, I'm always flattered."

See, everything doesn't have to be tough. Albert Belle may be miserable, but Brady is having a ball.

To an unusual degree, Anderson seems colorblind. In a sport where blacks, Latinos and whites tend to separate, Anderson mixes with everybody and everybody mixes with him. The first veteran to befriend him in his Red Sox rookie days was Lee Smith. "People saw me with Big Lee and they'd say, 'What the hell is going on?' Lee'd say, 'Hey, Shorty, where we going?'"

Former teammates Mark McLemore and Mike Devereaux once told Brady he was "the coolest white guy they ever saw catch a fly ball. I'd be lying if I didn't say I took special pride in that."

Because Anderson instinctively likes people, including some who probably don't deserve it, people naturally like him. For example, it's rare to find anybody who makes a project out of rehabilitating Barry Bonds. Yet, in interviews for this article, Anderson spoke more passionately about Bond's lack of recognition than he did in making any case for himself.

"Bonds gets screwed yearly. He should have *five* MVP awards by now," says Anderson, who has an encyclopedic memory for baseball facts and stats. "Nobody can compete with what he's doing. It bugs me that people don't know how good he really is . . . The level he's been playing at, it's almost like Willie Mays is the poor man's Barry Bonds.

"Barry tells me his goal is 500 homers and 500 steals. He's gotten to the point where he's so frustrated he doesn't care about any award that has to be voted on — even the Hall of Fame. Now there's a guy you should do an article on. Go down and sit with him and tell him I told him not to be a [several expletives deleted]. Really get the good side out of him, which is not easy to do.

"He likes to keep that wall up. It's almost like he wants to be criticized for being an idiot. But that's not what he is. He's very generous. He's one of the most loyal guys. He's a student of the game. Sometimes I see how he acts around other people and I say, 'Come on, Barry.'"

On the Japan trip, Anderson and Ripken were ragging on Mariners superstar rookie Alex Rodriguez. Seeing Rodriguez talking to

Bonds, Ripken said, "Want some good advice, Alex? Listen to what
Barry says and do the opposite. *That's* good advice."

"Yeah, that's right. Don't do anything that I do," said Bonds.

"Barry, why don't you take heed of the advice you're giving
Alex?" said Anderson.

"It's too late for me, man. It doesn't matter," said Bonds.

That sad scene haunts Anderson. "Barry knows. He really does
know."

Not Like People Think

Late one night while writing this story, I went to a convenience
store in a rural Maryland town, looking for a sugar fix. In a scene
worthy of *Nighthawks at the Diner*, only three people were in the
store. Two of them were talking baseball. One of them was a woman
named Sandy Taylor. I overhead her say, "I've met Brady Anderson
about thirty-five times."

"What's he like?" I asked.

"Not like people think," she said.

Years ago, Sandy Taylor sent Anderson a letter, asking him to
write a birthday note to her sister Bonnie. Sandy described her
sister and what a big fan she was, especially of Brady's. Anderson
not only wrote to Bonnie but composed a whole letter, weaving in
some of the details he'd learned from Sandy.

Bonnie was sure the letter was a fake. So was their mother. Brady
Anderson could not possibly have invested that much effort in a
stranger.

Months later, Sandy took her mother and sister to see Anderson
after an Orioles game. Before she could introduce her sister Anderson said, "Is this Bonnie?"

Luckily, none of the women fainted.

Baseball has world-class athletes with monstrous power, track-
man speed and acrobatic gloves. Some of them pose bare-chested
for posters and feel at home on MTV. But they tend to be jerks.
They abuse women or chase down trick-or-treaters in trucks or spit
in umpires' faces. They scream obscenities on national TV, carry
guns or drive 120 mph. They're sexy. But, as a group, they're also
idiots.

Baseball has its exemplary citizens, too, like Ripken, Frank

Thomas, and Greg Maddux. They've got the work ethic, the respect for fans, the play-every-day grit and a feeling for the game's history. They're the steak. But where's the sizzle?

Then there's Brady. He's medium-rare and hot off the grill.

He's been to the bottom and he's climbed to the top. His natural manner, that of a cool but genuinely nice guy who happens to be a star, is finally coming through. His ego's under control, but with those fifty homers on his baseball card, he can relax just a bit more. This spring, he's been a little funnier, a little looser. But he hasn't gone over the edge into self-absorbed Bondsitis. So people enjoy Brady's glory.

The clubhouse razzing is constant.

"I missed your guest shot on *Sabrina.*"

"Good," says Brady. "I'm not terribly disappointed you missed it."

"What? Mr. 90210 is not a future actor?"

"I had trouble playing myself."

"How's the contract coming?"

"Mussina and I come as a package deal now. Actually, it's a three-way deal. Cal's in it, too. We just haven't told him yet."

Mike Flanagan wanders past Anderson's locker. The story comes up of how Flanagan and Scott McGregor negotiated in tandem when they were free agents long ago. But Flanagan and McGregor agreed to take *lower* contracts so the small-market Orioles could afford to re-sign everybody and remain a pennant contender.

"Really? Quite a team, those guys," says Brady. "That wasn't what Moose and I had in mind."

"You live the perfect life — for a 16-year-old," says a married man, feigning disgust.

"Come on. Be fair, dud," says Brady. "Could we move that up to 21?"

Come on. Be fair. What does Brady Anderson lack?

Will baseball ever forget the awful first impression he made? Will the game finally, before he bursts his appendix, see him for what he has become?

Any day now, Anderson could dive head-first into a covered wagon or start worrying about another 50-homer season until he goes into a four-year slump.

Something else is possible, however. Something that almost nobody in baseball sees as a possibility: that 1996 was not a fluke at all.

Can Brady keep it up? You could certainly say he has a fifty-fifty chance.

SCOTT RAAB

The Hit King

FROM GQ

IF YOU GREW UP IN CLEVELAND, rooting ten, twenty, thirty years
for what was then the most drab and futile team in baseball, you
loathed Pete Rose for at least three reasons. You despised him for
his skill and for his frenzy to win. You scorned him for being born,
reared and revered in Cincinnati, a fussy, gooberous river burg,
half Kraut, half hillbilly, buried so far downstate that it essentially
was, and is, the capital of north Kentucky. Above all you hated him
for July 14, 1970, when he scored the winning run in that year's
All-Star Game by maiming the Tribe's finest rookie in decades, a
toothy, well-muscled 23-year-old catcher named Ray Fosse. Fosse
was planted a stride or two up the third-base line, blocking the
plate; Rose wracked him knee to shoulder at full speed. Bruised,
Rose missed three games. Fosse dislocated his entire career.

I didn't care that this was not a cheap shot, that it was just the way
the game is played. I didn't care that Rose and Fosse had huddled
at Rose's home the night before — the game was in Cincy that year
— talking baseball until 3 A.M., or that they kept in touch for years
thereafter. I watched season after season as Ray Fosse fought to find
his stroke, fought and failed, while Rose and his team became the
Big Red Machine. I never forgave Pete Rose.

I never forgave Pete Rose, but on August 1, 1978, I discovered
that I had ceased merely to loathe him. Having hit safely in forty-
four games straight — second only to DiMaggio's untouchable
fifty-six in 1941 — Rose went hitless that summer night. Feeling
strangely bereft, I opened *The Baseball Encyclopedia* to DiMaggio's
name and saw that in '41 he had been 26, in the heart of his glory.

Rose was already a wondrous, ageless 37, and I understood then that this brick-bodied motherfucker would dog me forever. Without quite knowing it, I had come to regard him with that same mixture of emotion inspired in cave dwellers by earthquake and eclipse: terror, awe, powerlessness, and surrender. Beyond explanation or entreaty, he simply *was* and always would be. Even when he stopped playing, in 1986 — he was the Reds' player-manager then — Rose refused to officially retire, and I fully expected him to climb out of the dugout at any moment, bat in hand.

He never did. In 1989 Rose was tossed out on his ear, eighty-sixed like a drunk who had pissed on the jukebox. I took no pleasure from it, not even relief; whether he bet illegally or bet on baseball or bet on his own team, he was railroaded, denied due process in a vermin-infested, star-chamber investigation. I felt only wariness, certain he would sue and come back, until the almighty IRS, a force beyond even nature, pinched him for failing to report racetrack winnings and income from memorabilia sales. Pete Rose was finally done for. Before his sentencing, he read a statement asking for the court's mercy — he'd paid the government, plus penalties and interest — his voice choked and quaking, too shamed to lift his head from the page. The judge, a Reds fan, gave him five months, plus a $50,000 fine to cover the cost of his upkeep in the federal prison in — I scarcely could believe it — Marion, Illinois. Ray Fosse's hometown.

If you're a Cleveland Indians fan, that's how it goes: no justice, only irony.

"Lemme tell ya, I love Joe DiMaggio," Pete Rose says, chugging coffee at four in the afternoon. We're at a table near the back bar of the Pete Rose Ballpark Cafe. He's 56, rock hard and proud of it. His jeans are light blue and jock tight; his white ribbed cotton pullover is tucked in at the waist; he has a thick gold chain around one wrist and a battered Rolex around the other. His hair is short, receding — he keeps a ball cap on his head — and bottle-brown. His pugish brow and nose have thickened; the whole face has grown a bit heavier, more coarse; but his eyes, flat brown, still burn, and his voice is the same tough-guy bark. "I went to Vietnam in 1967 just so I could meet Joe DiMaggio. They asked me to go on a goodwill trip. Joe and me went south; the other three guys went north. We had to carry cards that said we were colonels, because if we got captured and we didn't have a card, we'd be considered spies. I was in awe of this guy. I mean, this guy was one of my heroes. I couldn't believe I'm ridin' in helicopters with *Joe DiMaggio*."

I try to picture them — the 26-year-old hick, crew-cut and knot-faced, five whole seasons in the Bigs under his belt, and the Yankee Clipper, 53 then, an authentic pinstriped deity, silvering, aquiline, regal — squatting flank to flank in a Huey, skimming treetops, skirting enemy fire, Colonel Charlie Hustle's incessant chatter *ack-ack*ing above the roar of the chopper and the bullets' whine and the Phrygian silence of Colonel Joltin' Joe.

Then Pete Rose says this: "I gave Joe DiMaggio a shower one night. I gotta be the only guy in the world ever to give Joe DiMaggio a shower."

Say WHAT? It is as if an unearthed Hemingway letter recounted a lazy afternoon in Paris when Papa gave Scott Fitzgerald a foot rub.

"We're down in the Mekong Delta. And it's . . . it's . . . it's a *jungle*. It's *hot*. I mean, it's so *goddamn* hot ya can't sleep. All you can hear goin' off is *boom-BOOM, boom-boom-BOOM*. It's a *war* out there. And we're tryin' to sleep. And Joe says, 'I can't sleep.' He says, 'I gotta take a shower.'"

Just then a paunchy white-haired man in a beige zippered jacket wanders over to the table, clutching a photo. Rose takes it from him without a glance, signs it, and hands it back. "Thanks, buddy," Rose says.

The man stands gaping at the glossy in his hands, perplexed. "What's that number there, uh, forty-two fifty-six?" he asks finally.

"That's my prison number," says Rose, poker-faced. Then he returns to the Mekong. "The way you take a shower, you got this big bamboo thing up here, like a pocket." Rose cups his thick, square hands, lifting his forearms above his head. They are massive, tight as tree trunks, covered with dark hair. "You gotta get up on a chair, and you gotta feed the water. Then you pull a string, and the water comes through. So I'm the feeder; Joe's takin' the shower. I'm up on the thing feedin' the water, and he's takin' a shower. *Joe DiMaggio*."

Rose grins like a schoolboy. He pushes his cap, black leather with a gator-skin bill, back on his head and clasps his hands behind his neck. A large gold pin dangles from the center of the crown of the cap, formed of two letters: HK, for "Hit King." I eye those oaken arms and see Ray Fosse somersaulting backward and coming to rest facedown in the dirt, his left shoulder torn from its socket.

"Joe was the most humble guy I ever seen. We got to sit in a meeting of fighter pilots who were goin' on a mission over North Vietnam. Now you imagine Joe DiMaggio walkin' in. 'Hi, I'm Joe DiMaggio, old broken-down ballplayer,' he used to say. And Joe goes up, and he gets the chalk, and — you know the bombs on the fighter planes? Joe writes 'Fuck Ho' on one. And this one guy came back [after the mission] and told Joe, 'I got an ammunition dump with that thing.' Joe was happy as he could be. '*Fuck Ho*,'" Rose repeats, snorting at the memory, shaking his head with delight.

Truly, it is almost more exquisite than I can bear to hear Rose tell about the great DiMaggio in Vietnam. Just then, though, something happens to Pete Rose, something visible and ugly. His face, from brow to chin, turns hard; his eyes go cold; his lips, shrunk to a miser's frown, barely part as he speaks. "*Joe DiMaggio* don't sell bats," he says, biting off the name. "They're forty-nine ninety-five. That's $4,995. Joe thinks everybody's tryin' to fuck him."

Ray Fosse hit .307 in 1970, .307 with good power, and never again came close. He played out his enfeebled string, built a pension, found a broadcast job. DiMaggio, wealthy and still worshiped, is an ice-hearted, reclusive old man. Something worse happened to Pete Rose. Something odd and slow and subtle, something that swallowed him up and took him drifting down into nothingness, into a pale nearly beyond remembrance. Go figure. Had Rose simply croaked or grown doddering, we might have pondered how this brash hayseed colossus bestrode and embodied, like Elvis or Ali, an entire era, spoke with his rough art to the soul of a nation. Instead people hear the name, pause, and say, "Oh, sure. Hasn't he got a restaurant somewhere?"

The Pete Rose Ballpark Cafe looks like any other edifice in Boca Raton, Florida, which is to say that it has a blank exterior of pinkish tan stucco. To find it, you should know that it is joined to the side of a tannish pink Holiday Inn, whose clover green marquee is one of a very few clues that the entire length of Glades Road from the freeway to the turnpike is not simply a palm-dotted, lizard-infested, pinkish tan strip mall erected to service the needs of an army of frosted-blonde women wielding scarlet talons, silver Lexi, and platinum Visas.

You may be tempted to order the Hall of Fame Chicken Scallopini. Don't. Irony is no substitute for flair in the kitchen. Stick with a burger.

Your chef is Dave Rose, Pete's younger brother. Except for Dave's stringy, shoulder-length hair, the basketball-sized gut beneath his grease-spattered apron, and the slack derangement of his eyes, he and Pete look much alike. Something happened to Dave Rose, too: Vietnam. He didn't go with DiMaggio.

The staff wear tags with their hometowns printed under their names. Everyone is young, trim, female, and from New York or New Jersey. Pete's customers are more typical Boca dwellers: fat old men from New York or New Jersey. Pete's afternoon routine is coffee, the sports page, and banter with the staff about fellatio technique, but today he's also doing business with Marty. Hoarse, fat, and fiftyish, Marty hails from Boca via New York's Upper West Side. His business is marketing sports memorabilia.

"I'm gonna throw out a name," Marty says, "a very, very dear friend of mine. I've got very few friends. Marv Shapiro. *Dr.* Marv Shapiro."

"Marv Shapiro," Rose says. "I don't know who that is."

"Marv Shapiro is an ear, nose, and throat guy. He has, and I've seen it, your jersey from when you broke Cobb's record."

Rose shakes his head.

"No?" Marty rasps, his eyes wide. "He swears he paid you twenty-five grand for it. No?"

"I said I was gonna use three jerseys," says Rose. "I only used one. I used that one right over there. Marge Schott's got one. I gave one to Barry Halpern for that Ty Cobb bust up there. Did he say he got it from me?"

"Yeah, and he's not a bullshitter. Great guy. Tremendous guy. Very successful guy."

"He might be a great guy," Rose tells Marty, "but he's a goddamn liar."

Marty sighs, crestfallen, searching for the right tone, the right words. When he speaks, his voice is heavy with sorrow. "The fraud that is running rampant in this business is perpetuated daily," he says.

While I wonder if Marge Schott and Barry Halpern know that Rose snookered them — an unworn game jersey is not a game jersey — Marty recovers nicely. "My idea," he tells Rose, "is to put out something that *you* authorize. I'll do all the promoting. I'll go to every show. It won't interfere with you at all. To me it would be a *privilege* to work with you."

Rose sips the coffee. "I think you could really sell bats with 'Charlie Hustle,'" he muses. "I've never signed 'Charlie Hustle' on a bat."

Marty beams at me, radiant, and begins squeaking with joy. "*Ooooh,* that coy little, sly little fox. He's Charlie Hustle? They call me '*Marty* Hustle.' *Ooooh.* When — not if — he gets put into the Hall of Fame? Right to the moon. He knows it, too. *Ooooh,* is he good. And he's young; he could be signing for the next thirty years."

At the Pete Rose Ballpark Cafe Gift Shop, a signed copy of the black Mizuno that Rose used in the later years of his career goes for only $250. For $75 less, you can get a copy of his old Louisville Slugger. Take it from Pete, though: "I wouldn't even look at that Louisville. I broke the record with a black Mizuno."

The record. Rose mentions it often, just as he adds it as a coda to his signature: "4256," more career hits than anyone in the history of baseball. He harps on this because he knows that despite "4256" he never reached the Yahwehvian stature of Mays and Mantle and, yes, DiMaggio; unbeloved, he was not even, like the demigods Clemente and Kaline, much admired. Not only did Rose lack the supple arrogance of grace, the titanic strength and propulsive speed, even the innocent exuberance of an aw-shucks kid — he had none of the stuff that drops jaws and warms hearts — but also, and crucially, the little boy inside Pete Rose came off as a runtish bully, the outer man as an imperious lout.

What made Rose a great player was an invincible physique coupled with a monomaniacal fervor unseen since the demise of the baseball god most closely linked to him, the shiv-wielding madman whose record Rose chased for twenty-three years: Ty Cobb. Rose grew so obsessed with Cobb that he named his second son, Tyler, for him, and on the night Rose broke the record in 1985, he saw Cobb above the stadium lights, sitting in the clouds. Dead since 1961, Cobb has no bats to hawk, but a huge copper bust of him sits rooted upon a waist-high railing just past the Ballpark Cafe's host-ess station, where the Georgia Peach glares out from eternal captiv-ity into the café's enormous, glassed-in game room. Like Rose, Cobb departed the game not long after he was investigated by the league for wagering on the team he played for and managed. No finding was announced; he simply retired and was in the first group of players voted into baseball's Hall of Fame at its inception in 1936.

Something far worse happened to Pete Rose. The agreement reached in 1989 with Commissioner Bartlett Giamatti — six months of inquisition had yielded a 2,000-page report based mainly upon the sworn word of two felons — stated plainly that there was *no* finding that Rose had bet on baseball games and that he could seek reinstatement in a year without prejudice. But at Giamatti's press conference announcing the agreement, he was asked if he thought that Rose had bet on baseball. "Personally," Giamatti replied, "yes."

Rose, gagged by edict of the commissioner throughout the entire ordeal, unable to defend himself, forbidden to question his accus-ers, saw this on television in his lawyer's office in Cincinnati and nearly shat his pants. He had spent a million and a half in lawyers' fees negotiating the agreement Giamatti had just trashed the day after it was signed. The IRS was sniffing at his spoor. His career was kaput; his endorsements were gone. He was fucked, and he knew it.

Something worse than all of that — something closely resem-bling justice — happened to Bart Giamatti, ex-president of Yale, wooed from the Ivy League to reign over baseball, qualified for the job only by having had the sort of love affair with the game unique to fey, pristine intellectuals. "Reconfigure your life," the commis-sioner told Rose at their last meeting, sending Rose out from the only life he had ever known. Then, after his press conference, Giamatti repaired to Martha's Vineyard for a week of rest and recovery, nodded off in a hammock, and never woke up.

Rose has yet to apply for reinstatement. Giamatti was replaced by his pudgy steward, Fay Vincent, whom Rose blames for keeping him off the Hall of Fame ballot. "That lying son of a bitch," Rose calls him. Vincent was ousted by a club owners' uprising in 1992; the chair has been empty ever since, the game itself nearly consumed by its cannibal kings. Meanwhile, Rose wanders through his horse-hide diaspora, Kafka in cleats. He may buy a ticket to see a game, but visiting old mates in the broadcast booth is off-limits. When a Cincinnati bakery designed a poster to commemorate the Big Red Machine's last championship, baseball informed it that an action photo of Rose was verboten. A group pose including him was okey-dokey.

I phoned the offices of Major League Baseball to ask what happened and what might happen to Pete Rose; my calls were not returned. I phoned Rose's former lawyer, who negotiated the Giamatti agreement; he had his secretary call back to say that he wasn't interested in talking. I also tried Rose's current attorney. He rang back and answered all my questions, each with the same words: "No comment."

I ask Rose what Bart Giamatti had meant by telling him to reconfigure his life.

"He never said. I assume that means be very selective of the people that I'm hangin' around with, and no more illegal gambling." He still bets, he says, but only at the track. He lives in Boca; his second wife, Carol, and their two children live in Los Angeles. Rose says he gets out to see them as often as he can. "I talk to my kids every day," he says in an aggrieved tone, as if he feels accused of yet another crime. "You have to do what you have to do."

Weeknights he does the syndicated, two-hour "Pete Rose Show" from a radio studio adjacent to the kitchen. Rose's on-air partner — Rose is neither glib nor focused enough to work alone — joins in on a phone hookup from Vegas. There is much talk of point spreads and odds, and a total of three phone calls are taken during the entire show. Through the Plexiglas window, customers gape and take snapshots of Rose yapping into the mike. In the booth, I can smell the potatoes frying, then hot cheese, as brother Dave weaves his culinary magic.

During one five-minute break for ads and a news update, Rose signs five dozen baseballs. While a producer and Rose's fan-club president open the boxes for him, he autographs the sixty balls in four and one-half minutes, digitally timed.

"I can't read this one," the producer says, winking at me.

"They're all the same," says Rose, pen gripped tightly, hunched in concentration, unsmiling, not looking up. After signing each ball with a smooth stroke that seems to be one careful, continuous motion, he rolls it away, down the table, toward me. The tail of each final *e* in *Pete* lifts to cross the *t* before it. Each curlicued *R* flows into the combined *os* in an almost floral kiss. He's absolutely right: they are all the same.

Late January in West Texas beneath a warm, high, blue noon sky, and the place is blasted, bleak. It's the land, skillet flat and dust brown, punctured by bobbing, creaking, sucking metal; it's the enormous, yellowing Space for Rent placards pleading from every oil tower and the ground-floor windows of every bank and most of the other buildings on the twenty-mile stretch from downtown Midland to the Ector County Coliseum in Odessa; it's the late-morning Saturday caravan of pickups moving sluglike down the road, each with its own wizened, check-shirted driver, lip bulging with either a pinch of snuff or a mouth tumor, each with his ten-gallon hat pulled down to his furled eyebrows. One weekend a month, sometimes more, Pete Rose hits the road for a card show. Today he's here.

Except that it turns out to be a boat show, not a card show, and the Ector County Coliseum is not a coliseum at all but a beehive of separate metal outbuildings surrounded by a chain-link fence. The main edifice, which might pass for a coliseum to people whose entire lives are spent dangling from oil rigs, is filled with gap-toothed salesmen fondly stroking big-ticket water vessels that seem exactly as useful here in the Permian Basin as a Psalter in hell.

Chaperoned by two skinny Odessa cops, his eyes shaded by the bill of his "Hit King" cap, shod in off-white ostrich-skin half boots and sporting a diamond-dusted Piaget on his meaty wrist, Rose sits behind a long table on a small wooden stage in Barn G. Behind him hangs a huge poster, blue with silver stars and marked with the cramped John Hancock of Dallas Cowboys defensive-tackle emeritus Jethro Pugh, yesterday's big draw. Ed "Too Tall" Jones was scheduled earlier this morning, but he didn't show. Former Cowboys safety Cliff Harris is due in two hours.

Rose is not grinning. "You don't have one guy charging money for an autograph and two or three other guys signing for free," he crabs. "I'm not used to doing shows where I don't sell out. The only way you don't sell me out is if you fuck it up."

The West Texas Marine Dealers Association has indeed fucked it up. It has paid Rose $18,000 for 1,000 autographs — below his standard twenty grand but enough to get him here — and it's charging the public only fifteen bucks per signature, five less, Rose says, than his own floor. So it has guaranteed itself a $3,000 loss, minimum, undercut the value of the only meal ticket Pete Rose has left, and just for humiliation's sake, it is trotting out these retired Dallas Cowboys — each of whom, however obscure, is the local equivalent of the Lubavitcher rebbe — into the same barn where the "Hit King" is enthroned.

About fifty people wait behind a roped-off set of stairs for Rose to begin signing; in addition to the $5 admission fee at the main building, they've forked over the extra $15 at a small booth marked by a spray of balloons near the entrance and received a hand-numbered slip of paper good for one Pete Rose autograph. First in line is a woman cradling the generic bat she has brought for a colleague dying of cancer. Rose's policy is name only, no personalization, but he adds "To Don, Good Luck" above his signature. He offers the boys his hand to squeeze, calls all the men "buddy" and lets folks snap his photo as they please. He seems downright cheerful now, until he realizes that the policeman flanking him isn't collecting the $15 slips.

"You gotta keep the tickets, buddy," Rose instructs in deliberately calm, measured tones, as if speaking to a toddler, "or they'll get back in line again."

The officer peers at him with knitted brow and vacant eyes. "Oh, *raaht*," he says, finally, flushing. "*Raaahht.*"

With the first rush of business over, Rose is alone onstage with two hours left to sit, visited occasionally by a few treasure hunters and, just as often, by men his age or older, their faces weather-lined and boyishly shy, who want only to shake his hand and speak their awkward piece.

"When you gonna make your comeback?" asks one, a rangy gent in newly pressed Levi's.

"This *is* my comeback." Rose, seeing nothing to sign, looks down at the table.

"But when they gon' putcha in the Hall of Fame, Pete?"

"I'm waitin'."

"Well, we are, too."

"It's not up to me," Rose reminds him.

"Yeah, ah know." Like Rose, he has nowhere to go, nothing to do. Later he will climb behind the wheel of his pickup and plod home. For now he is content to stand a spell in front of Pete Rose and shift his cud from cheek to cheek. Rose fiddles with his pens, lining them up on the table, capping and uncapping them.

"Well, so long, Pete," the guy says after a long silence, "jest ain't a Hall of Fame 'thout *you* innit." He heads slowly toward the stairs.

Rose turns to me. "People receive me, don't they?" he asks. He sounds tired, plaintive. I have no idea what he means.

"People receive me, don't they?" he repeats.

"Yes, I suppose they do."

"Not only here, but where you been. They recognize me."

They do the only justice left to him now, these old men who share the obliquity of their love in return for the singles and doubles he stroked back in 1965. Sitting in a tin shed with his silly cap, his $40,000 watch and gold bracelet, his police armada, his plane ticket back to Boca in his leather satchel, he can't grasp the irony, although his eyes betray the sadness of it. What happened to Pete Rose his 4,256 hits can't undo; they can't slake his naked craving for assurance, not only that he still exists but that he will never *not* exist. Whatever befell him, I can imagine nothing worse: to grow old 2,500 miles from wife and children, hungry for the passing love of strangers.

With an hour to go, he has signed exactly 227 autographs, and a marine dealers' rep starts to haul up cases of balls and stacks of pictures for him to ink. They have paid him his fee, and, by God, they are going to get their 1,000 Pete Rose signatures.

Studio City, California. Here Pete's wife, Carol, lives with 12-year-old Tyler and 7-year-old Cara. It is a fine house on a high-priced hill two turns off Ventura Boulevard, but nothing grand. The living room is enormous and completely devoid of furnishings. There is a pool out back, of course: this is L.A., where everyone outside of Compton and Pacoima has a pool out back. The most impressive thing about the Rose home is its landlord, Alex Trebek, who lives next door. When something breaks, Alex comes over in work clothes and a *Jeopardy!* cap to fix it himself. Pete says Alex Trebek's mother also lives on the block, in the house on the other side of Alex.

A Duraflame log crackles in the family-room fireplace, wrapper and all, while two cats sleep nearby. When I ask the cats' names, Rose has no idea. There is also a dog underfoot, named Jake, who belongs to Alex Trebek but who likes to hang at the Roses. Jake, small and dirty white, looks ready to bite when I reach to pet him, but Carol Rose tells me that something happened to Jake, some sort of nervous condition, that has forced his jaws into a perpetual gape, baring his filthy teeth in a caricature of ferocity.

We are gathered before a sixty-inch television to view tapes of the golden-tressed Cara, a fetching and adorable survivor of the Jon-Benet Ramsey pageant circuit. Cara is a pro now: guest shots on *Ellen,* an Amtrak commercial, agent, acting coach, voice coach, fax machine on the kitchen counter to receive her scripts. She sits next to me on the ivory leather couch as we watch footage of her as a rouged and lipsticked 4-year-old Miss Tiny Tots contestant, slowly, slowly, slowly doing full splits in her silver spangles and white leotard. Her lush chestnut tresses frame a small, satin apple of a face; she has a sweet, easy smile and dewy, knowing angel's eyes. She is, in short, terrifying. She is not jailbait; she is castration bait, Depo-Provera bait, short-eyes-gets-eviscerated-in-the-shower bait.

Snub-nosed, spike-haired Tyler also acts, and he plays catcher on his Little League team. He has a ring from Cooperstown, where his team won some kind of tournament. "He beat me there," Pete says. "Can you believe that?" He sounds more miffed than proud.

As for Carol, she is tawny haired and leather booted, her spandex workout clothes packed top and bottom by the hand of God himself. *She* doesn't scare me; I am drinking her in and wondering what happened to Pete Rose that makes him want to live 2,500 miles away in Boca Raton.

After the children go to bed, Pete inserts a tape of himself on *Larry King Live.* It is every bit as incisive and interesting as any of Larry King's oeuvre. In the final segment, Tyler and Cara appear at Pete's side, which, he tells me now, was the whole point of his appearance. "That helps me," he says, "when people see my kids, how talented they are and how down-to-earth they are and how nice they are. And how confident they are."

They are all that and more, and I silently forecast harrowing futures for them both. What happened to Pete Rose — his life and dreams, his present and future, all mortgaged to the past — is happening to his children, who haven't lived his cursed, infamous life yet are the means of its redemption in his eyes. Like most of us, he does not, *cannot*, see the brutal, common imprisonment of legacy. His own father was a bank clerk who played semipro football into his forties and drove Pete to focus every fiber of self on making the major leagues. Pete's own first-born son, Pete Junior, 27, has labored in the minor leagues for the past nine seasons in four different organizations without giving anyone reason to offer him a single at-bat in the majors. What happens to us, all of us, is, first of all, what happened to our fathers.

He bet, bet big, bet often, bet illegally, partnered with steroid-crazed gym rats, coke dealers, and ratfuck scum. Down $34,000 on college hoops in the winter of '86, he left town on business; his runner switched bookies while Rose was away. A snafu ensued over the debt and its payoff, followed by a rebuffed blackmail threat directed at Rose — and that, according to Rose, is how the whole thing blew up. A runner took his tale — that Rose had bet on baseball, on his own team — to *Sports Illustrated* and to a new scholar-commissioner who wanted to earn his spurs.

Rose says he never bet on baseball — not on the Reds, not on any team. Did he? I don't fucking know; no one will ever know. Which is why he must be presumed innocent until proved otherwise in a court of law where his accusers aren't also his judge and jury; precisely why he has no burden of proof to meet. Rose could have taken another route, tested Giamatti's mettle and the strength of his case and the power of his office; instead he signed the agreement. It was all he could hope for, he says now: no finding that he bet on the game and a shot at reinstatement.

"Three days later, the son of a bitch dies," Rose growls. "The son of a bitch dies, and everybody forgets all about the agreement."

Even if you don't believe him, don't love baseball, don't like Pete Rose, it's a sour thing to hear him say that he goes to Cooperstown each summer on the weekend of induction to sign autographs for the pilgrims on Friday and Saturday and skips town before the ceremonies on Sunday. Even if you don't believe in justice, it's agony to hear him tell about the halfway house — he spent three months there after the five in Marion — where he bunked with paroled rapists and murderers and found himself taunted and pushed around, even by the house staff. They even stole his clothes.

"I kept my mouth shut," he says, each word a drop of lye. "I didn't complain. I didn't bitch. But I shouldn'ta went. It was wrong."

It *was* wrong, what happened to Pete Rose. But there is no justice, only irony. Which brings us, finally, to what happened to young Fosse.

"I started to go headfirst," Rose begins, rising from his chair, coming at me, big and fit and strong, the cask of his chest and his arms hewn of oak, "but he had home plate blocked. So I'm comin' in from third base, and this is home plate, and I'm comin' this way, and he's standin' like this" — he turns and crouches, Fosse now, waiting for the throw, his legs astride the base line. "Now why in the *hell* am I gonna slide into home plate? My knee hit his shoulder, here. If I go headfirst, I'm gonna break both my collarbones. People don't know that. All they know is they think I ruined his career."

Ach. Something happened to Pete Rose, a man as hard as a spear of boned ash: he gambled and lost, came to bat more often than anyone in baseball history, and never once connected with another human being. He has a restaurant somewhere.

DAVID REMNICK

Kid Dynamite Blows Up

FROM THE NEW YORKER

THE CONVENTIONS OF THE RING demand that a fighter in training become a monk. For months at a time, he hardens his body on
roadwork and beefsteak, and practices an enforced loneliness —
even (tradition has it) sexual loneliness — the better to focus the
mind on war. Mike Tyson's monastery in the Nevada desert is a
mansion next door to Wayne Newton's mansion, and it could be
said to lack the usual austerity. There is a chandelier worthy of Cap
d'Antibes. There is a painting on silk of Diana Ross. There are
books, magazines, a big television, leather couches. But the diversions are not what they could be. When Tyson is not preparing for
fights, he keeps lions and tigers around as pets and wrestles with
them. "Sometimes I go swimming with the tiger," he told a visitor.
"But, personally, I'm a lion man. Lions are very obedient, like
dogs." Tyson was keeping his pets elsewhere, though. He has estates
in Ohio, in Connecticut, and off a fairway on the Congressional
Country Club, in Bethesda, Maryland. The big cats are most often
in Ohio. The Nevada mansion is surrounded by life-size statues of
warrior heroes whom Tyson has read about and come to revere:
Genghis Kahn, Toussaint-L'Ouverture, Alexander the Great, Hannibal. "Hannibal was very courageous," Tyson said. "He rode ele-
phants through Cartilage." In a week's time, Tyson himself would
be going through cartilage, too.

After spending three years in an Indiana prison for raping a
teenager named Desiree Washington, Tyson went back to fighting
in 1995. He denied to the end that he had ever raped anyone, but
he said he was a better man now. Tyson converted to Islam —

indeed, the bumper sticker on his Bentley reads "I ♥ Allah" — and he told his visitors in jail that he had spent his time studying the Koran, Machiavelli, Voltaire, Dumas, the lives of Meyer Lansky and Bugsy Siegel, "and a lot of Communist literature." He ordered up icons for his shoulders, a diptych tattoo: Arthur Ashe on one side, Mao Zedong on the other. He declared himself ready to regain his place in boxing. He would reclaim not only his title but also his image of invincibility. Iron Mike. Kid Dynamite. Once more, he would be the fighter who had expressed only disappointment after a knockout of one Jesse Ferguson, saying, "I wanted to hit him one more time in the nose so that bone could go up into his brain."

But after easily dispatching a collection of tomato cans who provided a warmup drill worth tens of millions of dollars, Tyson finally met a real fighter, if not a great one, named Evander Holyfield, who backed him down and beat him up. Holyfield took Tyson's title last November, in one of the cleverest displays of boxing guile since February, 1964, when Muhammad Ali, then Cassius Clay, stunned another invincible — Tyson's fistic precursor, Sonny Liston. Liston, like Tyson, had grown up in an environment of crime and never left it; Liston had done time for armed robbery, he mugged people, he beat up a cop, he broke heads for the Mob. And, like Tyson, he was considered a killer in the ring, unbeatable. Against Clay, Liston had been favored so strongly that the lead boxing writer for the *Times* skipped the fight and left it to a rookie in the office, Robert Lipsyte. But Clay, with his magnificent speed, dodged Liston's plodding bombs and bloodied the big man's eye. Liston quit on his stool, claiming a sore shoulder. Against Holyfield, Tyson had been similarly unmasked. "He's like any bully," said Gil Clancy, one of the game's legendary trainers. "Once Tyson saw his own blood, he backed down." The referee stopped the beating in the eleventh round. When it was over, Tyson was in such a daze that he turned to one of his handlers and asked, "What round did I knock him out in?"

The rematch with Holyfield would be worth 30 million dollars to Tyson, 35 million to Holyfield. The fight's promoter, Don King, whose good word, of course, is all one ever needs, promised record receipts for the live gate and pay-per-view television: "A hundred and fifty million, maybe two hundred million. After all, we got three billion people in Red China alone!" Whatever. If Tyson won, he would regain not only his championship but also his place as "the baddest man on the planet." Holyfield would be remembered as a fighter who on a given night had risen above himself and then, in the rematch, fell to earth.

After coming out of jail, Tyson showed signs of domestic stability. In April, he married a doctor named Monica Turner. (Turner's first husband was sentenced to ten years in prison on a cocaine-dealing charge.) Tyson and Turner have one child; another is due this summer. Until now, marriage had been a miserable topic for Tyson. His first wife, the television star Robin Givens, was famously manipulative. She had been a Sarah Lawrence girl and, even in public, treated Tyson with an airy condescension. There were, in some cynical corners, suspicions that Givens had actually married for money. Tyson was not slow to express his annoyance. The former light-heavyweight champion José Torres once asked Tyson what the best blow he had ever thrown was. "Man, I'll never forget that punch," Tyson said. "It was when I fought with Robin in Steve's apartment. She really offended me and I went *bam*, and she flew backward, hitting every fucking wall in the apartment." The marriage ended in divorce.

Unlike Givens, Turner has, for the most part, stayed out of her husband's business affairs and out of camera range, and there have been no reports of fights, physical or otherwise. Turner mainly stayed away from Las Vegas. Tyson's most frequent visitors to his desert house were the members of his entourage, each in his own way a sterling influence: Don King, a former numbers runner from Cleveland who once stomped a man to death in a dispute over six hundred dollars and then became the greatest (and most bloviated) carnival barker since Barnum; Tyson's co-managers, Rory Holloway, an old friend, and John Horne, a failed standup comic from Albany who specializes in yelling at reporters; Tyson's trainer, Richie Giachetti, a street guy from Cleveland who worked with Larry Holmes; and a self-described "master motivator" named Steve (Crocodile) Fitch, who admits that "in another life" he spent five years in jail for manslaughter. ("But I didn't do it," he told me. "A complete setup.") Crocodile proved to be a prophetic character. During the week leading up to the fight, he could be seen in fatigues and wraparound shades, all the while screaming his sugges-

tive war cries: "It's time for ultimate battle! Ultimate battle! Time to
bite! Time to bite!"

Tyson avoided the press — especially the print press. Horne and
Holloway had done a good job of convincing him that the papers
were filled with nothing but lies, that the New York reporters on the
boxing beat — Michael Katz, of the *News,* Wallace Matthews, of the
Post — were out to get them. Early in the morning, before the sun
was high, Tyson ran along the empty desert roads. Then he sparred
in the gym. His workouts were closed. For recreation, he watched
one gangster movie after another, sometimes through the night.
He is partial to James Cagney, Edward G. Robinson, and John Gar-
field. He can recite whole scenes of *Raging Bull, On the Waterfront,*
and — his favorite — *The Harder They Fall.*

Tyson would have preferred to be alone — or, at least, alone with
his entourage and his movies — but Don King knew that in order
to rouse pay-per-view orders the goat had to be fed. Tyson would
not allow interviews at his house, but five days before the fight he
agreed to go out to King's place to meet with a group of writers.
And so on an afternoon of long shadows and hundred-degree heat
a couple of white vans pulled out of the driveway of the MGM
Grand Hotel, away from the new family-friendly downtown, away
from the Brooklyn Bridge and the black glass pyramid of Cheops,
away from the palace of the Caesars and the Folies Bergere, out
of earshot, finally, of the unending music of the city, the air-
conditioned hum and the mad electronic ringing of a thousand
acres of slot machines and the slushy spill of silver coins pouring
into curved silver trays. Don King does not live on the Strip. He
lives out where it is quiet, at the outermost edge of the city, where
the desert resumes.

In all honesty, no one would ride to the edge of the desert to talk
with Evander Holyfield. No one much cared about Holyfield. He
was likable enough. But he was dull copy. He hadn't raped anyone.
He hadn't been to jail. He talked about Jesus Christ all the time and
literally sang gospel music while hitting the heavy bag. He seemed
like a good fellow, but what story did he offer? He talked in the
polite clichés of doing my best, having faith in my abilities and in
the will of God — but what did he mean? Heavyweight-champion-
ship fights, from the days of John L. Sullivan onward, are stories,

morality plays, and this story, regardless of its end, was all about Tyson. This was a war between middle-class aspiration and ghetto insolence, gospel and rap. Without Tyson there was no sense of danger, no interest, no hundred million dollars.

"People are full of shit. They want to see something dark," Tyson's former trainer Teddy Atlas told me. "People want to feel close to it and in on it, but, of course, only from the distance of their suburban homes. They want to have the benefit of comfort, security, safety, respect, and at the same time the privilege of watching something out of control — even promote it being out of control — as long as we can be secure that we're not accountable for it. With Tyson, the dark thing was always the anticipation that someone was going to get knocked out. The whole Kid Dynamite thing. But we wanted to believe that the monster was also a nice kid. We wanted to believe that Mike Tyson was an American story: the kid who grows up in the horrible ghetto and then converts that dark power into a good cause, into boxing. But then the story takes a turn. The dark side overwhelms him. He's cynical, he's out of control. And now the story is even better. It's like a double feature now, like you're getting *Heidi* and *Godzilla* at the same time."

King's minions wanted the reporters to understand that this was a special invitation — a very rare one, these days. The whole charade seemed absurd to the reporters who had been around boxing for a while. Until not so long ago, fighters before a big bout were available athletes, the least guarded of men. Like sultans, they often used to greet their visitors propped upon a few pillows in bed; reporters would sit perched at the edge of the bed or hard on the floor, notebooks out, ready to catch pearls. Archie Moore, the great light heavyweight, could unburden himself of a monologue worthy of Molly Bloom or the Duke of Gloucester. Boxers were free of the solemn self-importance of modern athletes in the team sports. They liked having people around. In the moments before fighting for the championship, Floyd Patterson napped in his dressing room, and a few writers were allowed to stay around, close enough to register the movement under the champion's eyelids, the timbre of his snore. Patterson would describe his dreams, the depths of his fear. He talked and talked, one of the great analysands of the prize ring.

Tyson used to be like that. When he was coming up as a fighter, and even as a young champion, he loved to talk to the press, tell his story. He was immensely aware of himself as the star of an ongoing Cagney movie. Some writers even saw a sweetness in him, the yearning for love and a home. Certainly it was a life beyond the imagination of the middle-class reporters who came calling. He was the kid from Amboy Street in Brooklyn's Brownsville, an especially vicious and hopeless delinquent. When he was six, his idea of a prank was to slit his big brother's arm with a razor while he slept. His father was nowhere in evidence, his mother was overwhelmed by poverty. Tyson idolized the pimps and the thieves in the neighborhood, and by the time he was 10 he was mugging old ladies and shooting into crowds for kicks. As he told his story, he could sense the titillation in the writer, and more details would pour out: "I'd shoot real close to them, skin them or something, make them take off their pants and then go run in the streets." After he had racked up dozens of arrests and was sent off to reform school, Cus D'Amato, an old and eccentric trainer who had settled upstate, along the Hudson, took him in. D'Amato was a kindly paranoiac. When he was still working out of the Gramercy Gym, in Manhattan, he used to sleep in the back with nothing to keep him company but a shotgun and a dog. To his fighters, he was a kind of Father Divine, at once inspiring and full of righteous gas. He preached the value of terror, the way that all fighters faced fear and the good ones learned to harness it, to make it their friend. He was an ascetic. Money, he said, "was something to throw off the back of trains." Writers loved D'Amato, the way any writer would have loved, say, Moll Flanders had she been presented, whole, in real life, and available for quotation.

Tyson represented D'Amato's wish on dying — the chance, after Patterson and José Torres, to have a third world champion. As if to satisfy every convention of the boxing movie, D'Amato "adopted" Tyson, became his legal guardian, but he died a year before his "son" won the crown. On winning the title, Tyson wept. If only Cus had seen it, he said, if only Cus were here. It was over the top, even for Hollywood, but not for the conventions of the boxing story.

Tyson was also good copy partly because he was brutal and unabashed about being so. Unlike Ali, whose helium rants usually had more to do with camp comedy or the prophecies of Elijah Muhammad than with the violence of his profession, Tyson was blunt, clinical. He knew he had been trained to hurt other men, and he saw no good reason to deflect attention from that. He was in the beating business and he had never acquired the tact or the reflexes to say he didn't enjoy it. In his comically high voice, he spoke of throwing punches with "bad intentions to vital areas," of blows to the heart, to the kidneys, to the liver, and the pleasure he took in delivering them. He talked of his yearning to break an opponent's eardrum, to shatter his will, to make him "cry like a woman."

At the same time, Tyson was self-aware, almost academic in his regard for boxing. In a time when most baseball players hardly know the name Jackie Robinson, Tyson grew obsessed not just with all the obvious contemporaries and near-contemporaries but also with Harry Greb and Kid Chocolate, with Willie Pep and Stanley Ketchel. The writers ate that up. With boxing under attack as crippling, as atavistic and cruel, his talk made them feel that their subject was important, somehow — not merely a skein of beatings in the parking lots of betting parlors but a matter of aesthetics and history. Tyson spent hundreds of hours watching old fights, and from those films he not only learned the details of his craft but also assumed certain traits of favored precursors. He cut his hair to resemble Jack Dempsey's. He took to wearing bulky button-up sweaters because he had seen such sweaters on some of the old fighters in the old newsreels. And so, while Tyson's story was not Ali's, while he lacked that level of wit, physical improvisation, and epic, his story was a good one, good enough for half a dozen biographies, good enough, certainly, to make him the best-paid athlete in history.

We drove out Flamingo Road, past the plastic-surgery parlors, past all the clip joints and software palaces that look as if they were built last week. We arrived at a "gated community," the sort of high-security mansion neighborhoods that you see now in every city where there is sun and money and heightened fear of larceny. We rang the buzzer and the gates swung open. Don King's house is Spanish-style, perhaps — a riot of white stucco. There were Range Rovers and BMWs parked outside and an enormous satellite dish parked on the roof. We walked up the front steps and were greeted by a portrait of Don King. The real thing was in the kitchen.

"Welcome! Welcome to my home!" he boomed. King invited us in for an early dinner. He had ordered out from Popeyes.

King is the evil genius of boxing, the latest in a long line. His electrified hair is merely a way to use "personality" to hide his substance. In his way, he is even more powerful than the so-called Octopus Inc., of the 1950s — James Norris's corrupt International Boxing Club. Tyson, like so many boxers, cannot bear King. He does not especially trust King. But he does business with King, because King is the singular presence in big-time boxing. They make a lot of money together, and so Tyson is as indulgent of King's conniving as King is of Tyson's tantrums. There is no profit in judgment.

In the kitchen, King was telling me that three billion people would watch the fight. The key was penetration, he said — that is, how many people would sign up for the fifty-dollar fee and order the fight on pay-per-view. "If we get 10 percent of the universe, then we'll be fine," he added. He never quite explained what that meant. He knew I would not bother to ask. "Mike generates more capital than anyone in the history of the world. Why do they want to destroy him, the goose that laid the golden egg?"

After a long wait, Tyson showed up. He took his place on a white leather couch. As he waited for the first question, he assumed the expression of a man who has eaten a bad egg and is waiting to be sick. One by one the questions came, and Tyson answered them in a way designed to make the questioner feel like an idiot. Yes, he felt good. No, he wouldn't make the same mistakes again against Holyfield. Yes, he expected to win. But, no, it wouldn't change his life if he lost. "The way my deals are set up, I'm pretty much set." At times, he spoke as a man obsessed less with a fight than with the rational distribution of his mutual funds.

To be with Tyson even for just a couple of hours is to witness the power of a ghetto kid's fatalism. He has, his accountants would attest, all he could ever want. He will never — or should never — end up like Joe Louis, coked up on the casino floor and working as a greeter. And yet he is forever saying "My life is over" and "I am taking the blows for my children." He has a boundless sense of self-drama, of the dark future. Even here, surrounded by his co-managers Rory Holloway and John Horne, he said he had no friends, he trusted no one. And who could doubt him?

"We have to trust, but people by nature are not to be trusted," Tyson said. "That's just the way it is. I got a Machiavellian effect as far as that's concerned. I'm not a philosopher, I'm not Machiavelli in that respect, but you can't be a person always willing to do good in an environment where people are always willing to do bad. You know what I mean?

"I have no friends, man. When I got out of prison, all my old friends, they had to go. If you don't have a purpose in my life, man, you have to go. . . . Why would you want someone around in your life if they have no purpose? Just to have a pal or a buddy? I got a wife. My wife can be my pal and buddy. I'm not trying to be cold, but it's something I picked up. . . . If I'm gonna get screwed, I'm not gonna get screwed over by the people that screwed me before. I'm gonna get screwed by the *new* people.

"I've been taken advantage of all my life. I've been used, I've been dehumanized, I've been humiliated, and I've been betrayed. That's basically the outcome of my life, and I'm kind of bitter, kind of angry at certain people about it. . . . Everyone in boxing makes out well except for the fighter. He's the only one who suffers, basically. He's the only one who's on Skid Row. He's the only one who loses his mind. He sometimes goes insane, he sometimes goes on the bottle, because it's a highly intensive, pressure sport, and a lot of people lose it. There's so much you can take and then you break."

In an effort to lighten Tyson's mood and, not incidentally, the mood of this sorry conversation, some of the writers started asking about a subject close to his heart: his new family. For a few moments, he was as fuzzy as a character in *thirtysomething*.

"That's all I have, my children," he said. "Wives are known to run off and fall in love with other people, because they are human, even die. But you have to take care of children. . . . The way I see it is that every fight I have is for their future. Every fight. Every fight is a different future for my children." Tyson said that he played games with his kids, ate ice cream with them. "They love *Barney*," he said. "I *hate Barney*.

"I have a stepdaughter and one day she was crying and she says, 'Mama, Jane don't want to play with me today.' And I burst out, 'She doesn't want to play with you? Then fuck her!' My wife didn't like that too much. But we're different people. She studied psychology and believes in working on a kid's mind. I believe in being strict — if you get out of line, you're getting hit! They're too young for that now, but I'm a strong believer in that. I think kids should learn discipline. If they get out of line, they should learn discipline. At what age? I don't know. Ten years old?

"See, I've been beaten all my life. My kids have parents, one's a doctor, a bright woman, and a father who's a . . . a father who's rich. I had an alcoholic and a pimp for parents. So they're gonna have a great life, if they don't turn out to be bad children. . . . I just don't want them out on the street, because these hustlers, they can be very exciting, people gravitate to them. I survived it, but they may not be lucky enough to survive. All my real friends are in prison or dead. The ones still out are so messed up on drugs they don't know their own name."

It was as if Tyson knew something that no one else knew — not his accountants, not his managers. He was convinced of his own wretched end. Nothing, save the well-being of his kids, would please him. Last summer, Tyson threw himself a million-dollar three-day-long thirtieth-birthday party at his estate in Farmington, Connecticut. There were magnums of Cristal, and cigars rolled specially for the occasion. Tyson handed out BMWs and Range Rovers to six of his flunkies. And yet he had an awful time. "I don't know half the people here," he said as he wandered his many acres. "This isn't what I wanted."

Horne and Holloway may know nothing about boxing, but they have been expert at feeding Tyson's sense of persecution. "Nobody's on our side," Tyson told us as his co-managers nodded like proud puppeteers. "The courts are against us, the corporations are against us, the news reporters are against us, the papers — your bosses — are against us. We have nobody on our side, and we're still fighting and we're still doing well. If we had you guys on our side, we'd be a phenomenon!"

From the back of the room, King yelled, "If you would just print the truth! You write what people throw out to you as a smoke screen!"

"The fact is, they call us monsters, that we're inhuman, they want people to be afraid of us," Tyson said. (In fact, Tyson has always cultivated that image. He once told his former friend José Torres, "I like to hurt women when I make love to them. I like to hear them scream with pain, to see them bleed. It gives me pleasure.")

"Who do you mean?" one of the reporters said. "Who's calling you monsters?"

"You. Not you individually, but reporters," Tyson said. "They write that we're monsters, that we're hideous, that we commit heinous crimes."

"Let's take the Newfield book, for example," said King, referring to Jack Newfield's scrupulous biography of him. "The Newfield book is all lies, and yet everyone uses it as the defining factor on me! Everything in there is a lie! So a guy who's a good writer knows how to *speculize* and *dramatize* those lies! You know what I mean?"

"They hope it leads to you being incarcerated," said Horne, who was standing at Tyson's shoulder.

"Look," Tyson said. "Don is still a fool to have you over to his house and talk to you. He had to beg me to come over here and talk to you, because of what you guys write about me. The people that know me, love me, they read this. It feels like shit.

"And this guy, knowing you guys ain't gonna give him no justice, he still, stupidly, has you guys in his house talking to you, knowing you'll write it was a good fight and then try to put his ass in jail. They're gonna write some madman tales, how he robbed this guy and killed this other guy. I don't know. I wasn't there when he killed the guy, but, shit, if a guy got killed he was probably doing something he wasn't supposed to be doing. You know what I mean? I'm a strong believer in that. Not in a drive-by shooting, but very few people get killed for no reason, from where I come from."

King was delighted by this moving show of support. "Just watch me prove that he attacked me," he said. "All I want is fair play! I'm still crazy enough to love America!"

We, the Americans, must have been moved to the core. There was a long silence. A European writer shyly turned to Tyson and said, "Mike, with all of that said, why don't you come out more and go on Larry King again, and go on David Letterman and set the record straight?"

Tyson's eyes narrowed. He flapped his hand in disgust. "Ah, fuck y'all. Fuck y'all," he said. "I don't have to suck your dick to justify me being a good guy. Listen, man, I'm a man! I don't go begging someone to love me."

"It's not begging," the European ventured. "It's—"

"Yes, it is!" Tyson said. "You see O. J. Simpson, he's going around all the time trying to prove his innocence. By court of law, he's innocent. Maybe common sense tells you he's not, but in a court of law he's innocent. I'm not going to go around saying, 'Well, I've done this or this for this organization.' The hell with that, man."

Now Horne started egging Tyson on. "When the intention is to destroy you from the beginning, you can't get no level playing field to set the record straight," Horne said. "Let me say one thing. All of us live different lives. None of y'all have lived the lives that we have. We have different perceptions of things. . . . You guys go into back rooms, you conference about everything, you help each other out, to destroy somebody who is the only reason you are all out here. No other fighter takes you out of the country, no other fighter makes your jobs so interesting."

Finally, Tyson had the presence of mind to wave Horne off, to settle King down. All he really wanted us to know was that he was unknowable. He had probably given more interviews, in his time, than Dora ever gave to Freud, but it didn't matter. "Look," he said. "I'm harder on myself than the goddam reporters. But they don't know me well enough to write what I'm about, that I'm a monster, that I'm this or that. No one knows me. . . . I'd like to be written up like the old-timers. There's no doubt about it, I'm a wild man. I've had my share of the good times. but that's just part of the business, that's just who Mike is. I work hard, I live hard, I play hard, I die hard."

Like mediocre fiction, fights for the heavyweight championship of the world are invariably freighted with the solemnity of deeper meanings. It is not enough that one man shock another man's brain and send him reeling. There must be politics, too — or, at least, great lumps of symbol, historical subplots, metaphysical frosting. In team sports — in football, baseball, basketball — there are individual stars, there are rivalries, but, finally, the athletics is the thing. A team athlete's talent is usually the mastery of some peculiar and relatively recent invention: kicking a pig's bladder through a set of posts, swinging a stick of polished ash, tossing a ball through an iron hoop. Boxing is ancient, simple, lonely. There is hardly any artifice at all. Padded gloves and the gauze and tape underneath do little to protect the fighters; they merely prevent broken hands, and allow for more punching, more pain. Boxers go into the ring alone, nearly naked, and they succeed or fail on the basis of the most elementary criteria: their ability to give and receive pain, their will to endure their own fear. Since character — the will of a person stretched to extremes — is so obviously at the center of boxing, there is an undeniable urge to know the fighters, to derive some meaning from the conflict of those characters.

John L. Sullivan's triumphs were triumphs of the working class, the immigrant wave, "the people." Joe Louis fought the moral war over German fascism — fascism coming in the bruised and prostrate person of Max Schmeling. Most of all, the fights have come to be parables tinctured with the issues and conflicts of race. Indeed, some of the first boxing matches in America were held on plantations before the Civil War. White slave owners (the promoters) set up fights between their chattel. The slaves were often commanded to fight to the death. Was it such a great leap from there to the M-G-M Grand? "If [the heavyweights] become champions they begin to have inner lives like Hemingway or Dostoyevsky, Tolstoy or Faulkner, Joyce or Melville or Conrad or Lawrence or Proust," Norman Mailer wrote twenty-six years ago in *Life*.

> Dempsey was alone and Tunney could never explain himself and Sharkey could never believe himself nor Schmeling nor Braddock, and Carnera was sad and Baer an indecipherable clown; great heavyweights like Louis had the loneliness of the ages in their silence, and men like Marciano were mystified by a power which seemed to have been granted them. With the advent, however, of the great modern Black heavyweights, Patterson, Liston, then Clay and Frazier, perhaps the loneliness gave way to what it had been protecting itself against — a surrealistic situation unstable beyond belief. Being a Black heavyweight champion in the second half of the twentieth century (with Black revolutions opening all over the world) was now not unlike being Jack Johnson, Malcolm X, and Frank Costello all in one.

Black fighters found themselves fighting intricate wars over racial types, over shifting notions of masculinity, decency, and class. In 1962, with the endorsements of President Kennedy and the National Association for the Advancement of Colored People, Floyd Patterson fought in the name of the black middle class and white liberals against Liston, the gruff ex-con, who represented, as Amiri Baraka (then Le-Roi Jones) put it, "the big black Negro in every white man's hallway, waiting to do him in." But Patterson was not physically equal to his preposterous moral task. Liston flattened him in the first round. So shamed was Patterson that he fled

Comiskey Park disguised in a fake beard and mustache and drove all night back to New York. He had not merely been defeated. He had let down the race, he had not fulfilled his meaning, his role in the story.

It is hard to imagine today the sense of disappointment in Patterson's loss. A columnist for the *Los Angeles Times* wrote that having Liston as champion "is like finding a live bat on a string under your Christmas tree." Some papers felt free to refer to Liston as a "jungle beast," a "gorilla." Only Murray Kempton, writing in the *Post*, was able to find an arch note of optimism in Liston's ascent. "The Negro heavyweights, as Negroes tend to do, have usually given that sense of being men above their calling," Kempton wrote. "Floyd Patterson sounded like a Freedom Rider. We return to reality with Liston. We have at last a heavyweight champion on the moral level of the men who own him. This is the source of horror which Liston has aroused; he is boxing's perfect symbol. He tells us the truth about it. The heavyweight championship is, after all, a fairly squalid office."

Liston tried desperately to please. He promised to be a good champion, to emulate Joe Louis. He explained that he had been one of twenty-five children in rural Arkansas, that he was illiterate, abused by a violent father. He apologized for his "terrible mistakes." But the country seemed not to accept the apologies; it was hard for whites and blacks alike to countenance a man who, when asked why he would not join in the civil rights marches in the South, had answered, "I ain't got no dog-proof ass." People only laughed when Liston started associating with priests. After Cassius Clay beat Liston in Miami — and then, as Muhammad Ali, beat him again — his story took a tragic course. Liston retired to Las Vegas, where he fought a little, hung out with gangsters like Ash Resnick, and in 1971 died with a needle in his arm. The funeral procession went down the Strip. For a few minutes, people came out of the casinos, squinting in the sun and saying farewell to Liston. The Ink Spots sang "Sunny."

For a long time, especially since coming home from prison, Tyson has seen himself in Liston. Watching films of Liston working out to the old James Brown rendition of "Night Train," he said, was "orgasmic."

"Sonny Liston, I identify with him the most," he said. "That may sound morbid and grim, but I pretty much identify with that life. He wanted people to respect him or love him, but it never happened. You can't make people respect and love you by craving it. You've got to *demand* it.

"People may not have liked him because of his background, but the people who got to know him as an intimate person have a totally different opinion. He had a wife. I'm sure she didn't think he was a piece of garbage. . . . Everyone respected Sonny Liston's ability. The point is respecting him as a man. No one can second-guess my ability, either. But I'm going to be respected. I demand that. You have no choice. You couldn't be in my presence if you didn't."

A few weeks before the fight, I went up to Michigan to see Liston's conqueror. Muhammad Ali lives on a manicured farm in a small town near the Indiana border called Berrien Springs. It was obvious to everyone who saw him tremble as he ignited the Olympic torch in Atlanta that Parkinson's disease has all but silenced Ali and forced him to wear a grim mask on what had been the century's most sparkling face. But out of the way of television cameras, which make him nervous and even more rigid than usual, Ali can show delight. He is especially delighted to watch himself when his body was fluid and his voice the most widely recognized in the world. We spent the better part of an afternoon watching videotapes of his fights, the early fights with Liston and then the first bout against Patterson. Ali leaned back and smiled as he watched himself, in black and white, dissect Liston, duck his blows, and sting him with jabs until Liston looked very slow and very sad.

"Ah, Sonny," Ali said. "The big ugly bear!"

Now Liston was quitting. He sat slumped on his stool. Now Ali's younger self was standing at the ropes, hysterical in his triumph, shouting down at the reporters who had dismissed him as a loudmouth and a fake, "Eat your words! Eat your words! I am the greatest!"

"They all thought I'd lose," Ali said. "Thought he'd tear me up."

After a while, I asked Ali about Tyson and whether he compared to Liston.

"Liston was faster than Tyson, but came straight ahead," he said. His voice was whispery, almost all breath.

"Could Tyson have beaten you?" I asked.

"Don't make me laugh," Ali said, and he was laughing. "Tyson don't have it. He don't *have* it." For a second, I wondered what "it" was, but then The Greatest made it clear. He pointed to his head.

About a week later, I took the ferry to Staten Island to visit Teddy Atlas, who had trained Tyson when he was learning to fight in Cus D'Amato's gym. Atlas is one of boxing's most appealing characters, the son of a doctor who used to treat patients in the ghetto for a couple of dollars. He was rebellious, a street kid who learned to box. A knife fight on Rikers Island left him with a scar on his face that runs from his hairline to his jawline. When Atlas was barely twenty, D'Amato taught him how to train fighters and then entrusted him with Tyson. Atlas last taught Tyson the catechism according to D'Amato, the peekaboo style of holding the gloves up near the face, the need to overcome the fear inside. During one amateur fight, Tyson told Atlas between rounds that his hand was broken and he couldn't go on, but Atlas knew it was just fear, the fear of disgrace, and he pushed Tyson back out into the ring and to a victory.

Atlas, however, grew disillusioned as he saw D'Amato indulge Tyson in one ugly incident after another. Tyson harassed girls in school, beat other kids up, threatened teachers, and D'Amato nearly always found a way to make it good with the school, with the police. He would have his champion, one way or another. He was not raising a son, after all. He was raising a fighter. But in 1982, when Tyson molested Atlas's adolescent sister-in-law, Atlas lost it. He held a gun to Tyson's head and threatened him. D'Amato never punished Tyson. He did, however, get rid of Atlas.

Tyson's co-manager John Horne had told me that "the only difference between Mike Tyson and Michael Jordan is Mr. and Mrs. Jordan." But Atlas thought that was too simple, too easy on Tyson. When I asked him if he had overreacted when he held the gun to Tyson's head, he said, "This was a kid who did not hesitate to tear out the soul of another human being. He completely violated other people. And then he just moved on.

"Mike is very selfish. He was bred to be selfish. I remember sitting in the kitchen once at Cus's place and there were two plates of spaghetti, one for Mike and one for some other kid, another fighter, who hadn't sat down yet. Tyson went to take the other kids' food, too, and Camille" — D'Amato's companion — "said, 'Mike, no, don't take it.' But Cus said, 'No, go ahead, take it. You're gonna be the next champion of the world. Eat it.' Tyson was just fifteen or sixteen, and it was the wrong lesson. Listen, there are plenty of kids from Brownsville with that background and some of them are great people, people who find something in themselves to trigger a sense of accountability, the sense that someone else in the universe matters."

Atlas said Tyson was a fighter who depended solely on fast hands and the image of extreme violence. Nearly all his opponents were beaten before they ever got in the ring. Tyson never fought a truly great heavyweight (as Tunney fought Dempsey, as Ali fought Joe Frazier), and on the two occasions when an opponent stood up to him he lost: first to Buster Douglas in Tokyo in 1990, and then to Holyfield last November.

"You can lie to yourself in the ring in a hundred different ways," Atlas said. "You can quit by degrees. You can stop punching with the idea, crazy as it sounds, that the other guy will stop if you do. Then you can make excuses to yourself, and the people around you will echo the excuses, and everything will seem to be all right. You can even foul and then claim you would have won, given the chance. Remember, this is a kid who used to hide between the walls of condemned buildings to make sure he wouldn't get beaten up. When you live like that, you learn to lie, to coax people that you are the toughest — you learn to scare people, to manipulate them. And when you can't do it you're lost.

"When I see Tyson, I see a guy who's scared, a guy who can't do it on the up and up. In his world, he was never allowed to be scared, or even honest, and so he is neither of those things. He is lost. When Tyson is alone with himself, I don't know if he believes there is one single person around him who is there because of his merits as a person. I don't even know that the women would be around without his ability to raise money. He'd have to show something independent of the ring and of his ability to send people on two-hundred-thousand-dollar shopping sprees."

On the day of the fight, I wandered the Strip. Earlier in the week, the casinos in hotels like the MGM Grand, New York New York, and

Excalibur — the new family-friendly places — had been jammed with middle-class parents pushing strollers past the blackjack tables at midnight. Las Vegas is a better deal than Disney World. In Las Vegas, you can get a cheap hotel room, visit the Sphinx (at the Luxor), have your picture taken with a stuffed movie character, induce nausea on the rides, and be in the pool by lunchtime. But at the end of the week (when my room rate shot up from 79 dollars per night to $399) all the strollers were gone. The planes out at McCarran International Airport disgorged high rollers from New York, Tokyo, Taipei, and Beijing, athletes and gang-bangers, movie stars in Armani and hoochie girls in Moschino. The mind reeled — and the neck swiveled — at the effect of health clubs and silicone on the American form at century's end. All that hard work and earnest surgery. From the looks of the women at the luggage belts, there could not have been a single hooker left in the greater Los Angeles area. They had all flown in for the fight.

At the instigation of my friend Michael Wilbon, a sports columnist for the *Washington Post,* I spent the afternoon roaming the most expensive stores in town. Fight day, Wilbon instructed me, is a big shopping day, and many of the key stores — Neiman Marcus, Versace, Escada, Gucci, Armani — signed up extra seamstresses and tailors to get things ready for the evening. You don't buy a three-thousand-dollar suit and then not wear it to the main event. Even if you didn't have tickets — and that meant the vast majority who had "come in for the fight" — you showed up in the casinos looking dowdy at your peril.

At Neiman Marcus, I watched Louis Farrakhan take the Italian boutique by storm. While half a dozen of his bodyguards assumed positions near the ties and the shirt racks, the minister tried on a fine pair of mustard-colored slacks. Zegna is evidently one of his favorite designers. I watched him try on slacks for the better part of half an hour. When I asked one of his guards whether it might be possible to interview him, the guard took off his sunglasses and blinked. I took this to mean no.

The Forum Shops at Caesars Palace proved to be a nice place to hang out, too. The ceilings are painted like a cerulean sky with perfect Biblical clouds, and there is a fountain outside the Versace store that is better than the Trevi Fountain in Rome in that the Las Vegas Rome is air-conditioned.

Versace seemed to be the appointed headquarters of Tyson fans, and even Tyson himself. Before the first Holyfield fight, the managers shut down the store for Tyson. "He bought real good," a manager told me, but he declined to be more specific. The mythical figure among the boxing writers was that Tyson dropped a hundred and fifty thousand there last time. While I was fingering a blouse worth more than a decent used car, a guy with some major forearms and a purposeful stare came in: Tyson's bodyguard. Even if one did not know him by his face, there were hints: a "Team Tyson" tattoo on his arm and a "Team Tyson Rules" bomber jacket. The manager spotted him and raced over to serve. He actually rubbed his palms. Within seconds, the bodyguard was handed a suit bag. "Mike says thanks," the bodyguard said. He used his phone to order "immediate pickup" and walked out.

The fight crowd was not always thus. In the films of the big fights of the fifties and sixties, you can see that the ringside seats were taken up mainly by boxy white men in boxy blue suits — Mob guys, like Blinky Palerno and Frank Carbo, or, on a slightly higher plane, Rat Pack members. When Ali returned from exile in 1971 to fight Jerry Quarry in Atlanta, the fight crowd changed: suddenly, there were blacks at ringside. They held the same reputable and disreputable jobs as their white predecessors, but the plumage was different. The style of the hustler had shifted from Carbo's dour wool (he was known as Mr. Gray) to the iridescent suits of his black inheritors. It was as if a row of sparrows had flown the wire, to be replaced by a flock of cockatoos.

There were still plenty of white big shots around, plenty of pompadours and big-guy rings. One night at dinner at an Italian place, Trevesi, at the MGM Grand, a woman tossed her glass of wine at her big-guy boyfriend. Then she rose from her chair and, after a second of real consideration, took her glass and smashed it over the boyfriend's head. At which point there was blood on the boyfriend's skull and slivers of glass in the capellini of the woman at the next table. That would turn out to be the cleanest blow of the week.

It is customary at a big fight to surround the ring with press people, anonymous high rollers, and, most of all, "luminaries from the world of sports, politics, and the entertainment industry." In the press section, we were handed an alphabetized list of celebrities in attendance: Paul Anka, Patricia Arquette, Stephen Baldwin, Matthew Broderick, Albert Brooks, James Caan, John Cusack, Rodney Dangerfield, Lolita Davidovich, Ellen DeGeneres, Larry Flynt, Michael J. Fox, Cuba Gooding, Jr., etc. This, of course, was "subject to change," the King people warned us.

It is also customary at big fights to come late, to ignore the undercard. But I had seen about as many vermilion leather vests, chartreuse pants, and siliconed bodies as I wanted to see, and headed into the MGM Grand's arena. King had told everyone that the fight was "the greatest boxing event of all time." It was a wonder, then, why he put together one of the grimmest undercards of all time. The highlight was surely the one women's bout, which left the canvas spotted with bloody pools. The woman in the pink shorts, Christy Martin, won the match. She had acquired all the best habits of boxing. She taunted her opponent, Andrea DeShong, at the prefight press conference, by saying she was glad DeShong had finally worn a dress. "It's the first time I've seen you look respectable, like a woman," Martin said, thus proving her . . . manhood.

By eight-thirty, the seats were filled and the place buzzed, loud and nervous, a sound peculiar to the mass anticipation of violence, a more manic buzz than at a basketball playoff game or a political convention. Don King opened the proceedings by having the ring announcer tell us that the fight was dedicated to the memory of Dr. Betty Shabazz and to "the many, many innocent victims of crime and violence." We all stood, and the timekeeper sounded the bell ten times, boxing's equivalent of a twenty-one-gun salute.

Tyson, the challenger, came into the arena to the sound of gangsta rap. In the bowels of the arena, he had complained that he could hear Holyfield's music — electric Jesus music — and couldn't Holyfield turn it down? Tyson, as always, wore his warrior look: black trunks, black shoes, no socks. He came surrounded by Giachetti and Horne and Holloway and Crocodile and a dozen other men, all of them strung out on self-importance. They tried very hard to look dangerous.

Then Holyfield, with a far smaller entourage, came down the aisle toward the ring. He wore purple-and-white trunks with the logo "Phil 4:13" ("I can do all things through Christ which strengtheneth me"). While Tyson assumed his death mask, his intimidator's face, Holyfield was smiling. He mouthed the words to a gospel song that only he could hear. Tyson paced, and Holyfield stood in his corner, satisfied to jiggle the muscles in his arms and legs. One of his seconds massaged the ropes of muscle in his neck.

In the casino, Tyson was the favorite. You had to bet a hundred and eighty dollars on him to win a hundred. Those odds were based almost entirely on Tyson's Kid Dynamite reputation. Holyfield, however, was the pick on press row by a wide margin. And yet we knew why we were here. It was not to listen to Holyfield sing "Nearer My God to Thee."

Mills Lane, a bald and mumbly judge from Reno, was the referee. At the center of the ring, Lane reminded both fighters of their obligations to the law, to boxing, and to the Nevada State Athletic Commission, and both men nodded assent. They would, of course, not dream of trespass. So said their quick nods, the touch of the gloves.

At the opening bell, Tyson came out bobbing and weaving, but with a certain self-conscious air. He had lost the first fight not least because he had forgotten his old defensive moves. For months, Giachetti, his trainer, had been pleading with him to move his head, to jab, to forget about the one-punch knockout. But within half a minute Tyson was back to where he'd been before, throwing one huge hook at a time. Holyfield ducked the hooks easily and then held on, muscling Tyson around the ring. Last time, we had been amazed that Holyfield was stronger than Tyson, that he could push Tyson back on his heels, that he could grab Tyson's left arm in the clinches and save himself untold trauma to the kidneys and the temple. And now it was happening again. All the training, all the instructions were coming to nothing. Tyson could not intimidate Holyfield — he could not, as he had done to so many others before, terrify his man into dropping his guard, into committing a kind of boxing suicide. Holyfield had every intention of winning again, and he took the first round by controlling the pace and scoring big with two left hooks and then a right hand to Tyson's jaw.

Between rounds, as Tyson drank some water and spit in the bucket, Giachetti told him to take his time.

"Jab for the throat!" he said.

Tyson nodded, but who could tell what he was hearing — what inner voice?

In the second round, the pattern was much the same. Holyfield scored left hooks to the meat of Tyson's flank and shoved him around and back toward the ropes. Tyson jabbed occasionally, but more often he threw big, dramatic punches, and Holyfield smothered them, ducked them. Then came the crucial moment of the round — the moment that set off in Tyson some torrent of rage that would, in the end, botch the fight and possibly ruin his career. As the two men wrestled, Holyfield unintentionally rammed his skull into the sharp brow above Tyson's right eye. Within seconds, there were rivulets of blood running down the side of Tyson's face, and in the clinch he looked up at Lane and said, "He butted me." The physical side was bad enough: the gash was sure to bother Tyson throughout the fight. The blood would run in his eyes, and Holyfield, sensing his advantage, would work over the cut — punch at it, grind his head into it in the clinch — and win on a technical knockout. What was worse for Tyson was the tremendous fear the butt stirred up in him, the way the blunt pain on his brow summoned up the last fight, his humiliation. Last time, the two men had butted heads inside, two berserk rams, and Tyson had come away the injured one, dazed and bleeding. It was as if his nightmare had come true. It was all happening again. He was in the ring, bleeding, and facing an opponent who would not back down.

Lane warned both men against excessive "roughhousing" (imagine!), but he didn't deduct any penalty points. Now, in the clinch, Tyson grew more desperate. He shoved a forearm into Holyfield's throat. But his punches, his big punches, were still missing, and they were coming in single volleys rather than in combination. Again, Holyfield won the round because of his superior strength, his ability to waltz Tyson around the ring, and the efficiency of his blows. What he threw, for the most part, landed. All three judges scored the first two rounds for Holyfield, ten to nine.

After the bell, a plastic surgeon worked on Tyson's cut.

As the doctor held a compress to Tyson's brow, the fighter jerked back.

"Aaahhh!" Tyson moaned.

"I'm sorry," the doctor said.

Tyson was breathing hard now — harder than he should have been after six minutes in the ring and months of roadwork. He said nothing. He gave no hint to anyone that something was wrong — that something had "snapped," as he put it days later. Tyson got off his stool and waited for the bell. As the two fighters stood facing each other, Holyfield suddenly pointed to his mouth, reminding Tyson that his corner had not put in his mouthpiece. Tyson walked back to Giachetti and opened his jaws; Giachetti put the mouthpiece in.

At the bell for the third round, Tyson stalked forward, and it was clear that he was enraged, desperate to end the fight before his eye failed him. He was relatively controlled at first, throwing his first sharp hooks of the fight. Holyfield was standing up to the blows and was still moving forward, crowding Tyson, but he was suddenly no longer in command. For more than two minutes of fighting, Tyson showed that he was capable of reviving his old style. Now his punches came in combinations. He kept his head moving, side to side, up and down, making it impossible for Holyfield to flick the jab at his gash. In the clinches, however, Holyfield was still in control. He seemed to be telling Tyson that, while he could win the round, he could not win the fight, and Tyson seemed to see the sense in that. And with about forty seconds left in the round, as Holyfield was steering him around the center of the ring, Tyson suddenly spit out his mouthpiece and started gnawing on Holyfield's right ear. For a second, Holyfield seemed not to feel this lunatic attack, but then the sting hit him. He backed away, jumping up and down, pointing to his ear and the blood that now bathed it. At the same time, Tyson turned his head at an angle and spit out a half-inch chunk of ear. Lane called a time-out. Holyfield headed for his corner. Tyson chased him down and shoved him. Holyfield seemed almost to ham it up, to bounce crazily on the ropes, as if to highlight the madness of it all.

Don Turner, Holyfield's trainer, told his man to keep cool, to think about Jesus, just stay calm.

Lane said to a Nevada State Athletic Commission official at ringside that he was ready to disqualify Tyson — and he certainly would have been within his rights to do so — but first he invited the ring doctor, Flip Homansky, onto the canvas to have a look at Holyfield's ear. Homansky gravely inspected the ear and, presumably in the interests of Nevada and boxing's good name, pronounced Holyfield able to continue. Lane went to both corners and explained to the assembled handlers what had happened. He told Giachetti that Tyson "bit him on the ear."

"No, I didn't," Tyson said.

"Bullshit," Lane replied. He had already examined the ear, the teeth marks. "I thought my ear had fallen off!" Holyfield said later. "Blood was all over!" Lane deducted two points from Tyson — one for the bite, one for the shove — and, or so he claimed in a post-fight interview, warned Tyson that if he did it again the fight was over.

The time-out had lasted more than two minutes, long enough for the crowd to see replays of the incident on the big screens around the arena and start booing, enough time for Tyson to decide if he had "snapped" or would do it again, and more than enough time for the jokes to begin sweeping through the press section: "Tyson's a chomp," "He's Hannibal Lecter," "a lobe blow," "pay per chew," "If you can't beat 'em, eat 'em." There would be a hundred of them.

Finally, Lane cleared the ring and resumed what little was left of the third round. The crowd, which had been fickle, swerving between chants first for Holyfield, then for Tyson, was now greatly affronted. They booed wildly. We were, of course, all prepared to see one fighter deliver a subconcussive blow to the other's brain, but a bite on the ear was beyond imagining. We were offended, disgusted, perhaps even a little thrilled. Boxing is a blood sport. Now there was blood.

Holyfield was intent on following his corner's plea to keep his cool. He marched in and connected with a stiff hook to Tyson's face. His message was delivered thus: you can do what you want, you can foul, you can threaten, you can even quit, but you will not intimidate me.

The fighters clinched again. There were about twenty seconds left in the round. And, incredibly, Tyson once more nuzzled his way into Holyfield's sweaty neck, almost tenderly, purposefully, as if he were snuffling for truffles. He found the left ear and bit. Once more, Holyfield did his jumping dance of rage and pain. The bell sounded.

Tyson's handlers now wore guilty looks; their eyes shifted. They knew what was coming.

Holyfield was not quite so sure. "Put my mouthpiece in," he told his cornermen. "I'm gonna knock him out."

But Lane could not let this go on: "One bite is bad enough. Two bites is the end of the search."

"I had to do some thinking," Lane said, reasonably, later on. "I thought about it and thought about it, and decided it was the right thing to do. Let the chips fall where they may." Tyson was disqualified. Holyfield was declared winner and "still heavyweight champion of the world." Subsequently, Tyson said that he had been forced to retaliate for the butt in the second round. After all, he said righteously, "This is my career. . . . I've got children to raise."

In the mayhem that followed Lane's announcement — Tyson still going berserk in the ring, pushing at the police, and then fans raining down ice cubes and curses as he headed for the locker room — in all that, one bit of business was almost forgotten. A hotel employee named Mitch Libonati found the chunk of ear that belonged to Evander Holyfield. He found it on the ring mat, wrapped it in a rubber glove, and delivered it to the champion's locker room.

"At first, they looked at me like I was pulling a prank, but I told them I had a piece of Evander's ear, and I thought he would want it," Libonati said. "It wasn't really bloody, actually. It was like a piece of sausage."

After leaving the arena and the press tent, I walked through the MGM Grand casino toward the elevators. I wanted to drop off some things in my room before heading back out to the Strip. How could one miss the victory parties? But just as I was passing some slot machines I saw a stampede of twenty or thirty people running straight at me. There were screams: "Get down!" and "There's shooting!" and "They got guns!" I had already seen some fistfights between Tyson's fans and Holyfield's fans. It was not beyond reckoning that some of the visitors could be armed. I dived behind a bank of slot machines, feeling at once terrified and ridiculous.

"Keep down!"

"Ya hear the shots!"

People were face down on the carpet, ducking under blackjack tables, roulette tables. And then it was quiet. No shots — not that we could hear, anyway. It seemed safe to walk to the elevators.

But then, as the doors opened, more people started dashing around, ducking behind slot machines and into the elevators. I went up to the fourteenth floor and then went back down in a service elevator. I had to get to the bank of elevators that would get

me to the twenty-fifth floor. As I was getting out of the service
elevator, Jesse Jackson and a team of police were getting in.

"It's sad. The whole thing is sad," Jackson said. "That's the one
word I can think of to describe it. It's a tragedy that no one can
explain. As far as Tyson is concerned, I guess the butting trig-
gered something in him. I focus on him and what's going on in his
head. And now this. They're out there shooting with Uzis, these
bad boys."

It was never entirely clear whether there had been any shooting.
I doubt it. But the Nevada Highway Patrol did shut down the Strip
from Tropicana Avenue to Koval Lane. No one wanted a repeat of
the action after the Tyson–Seldon fight last September, when the
rap star Tupac Shakur was shot to death in a car.

The rumors of Uzi fire did little to help the gambling receipts at
the MGM Grand, but elsewhere on the Strip the high rollers were
happy. We had all been witness to a spectacle — to the unraveling
of Mike Tyson. In the days to come, he would apologize. He would
reach out "to the medical professionals for help." But who now
cared about him? In the ring, at his moment of greatest pressure,
he had lost everything: he had proved himself to be what in gentler
times would have been called a bum. Biting is certainly not un-
heard of in boxing — Holyfield himself once bit Jakey Winters in
an amateur bout when he was eighteen — yet Tyson had done it
not once but twice, in a championship fight seen by "three billion
people," or however many Don King had managed to attract. The
abysmal and lonely end that he had seemed to predict for himself
had come so soon.

"It's over," he said in the locker room. "I know it's over. My career
is over."

No one had envisioned this end more clearly than Tyson himself.
On the day before the fight, he had gone out to a cemetery near
the airport and laid a bouquet of flowers on the grave of Sonny
Liston. The music ahead for Tyson would be not rap but something
more mournful. "Someday they're gonna write a blues song just for
fighters," his role model, Liston, once said. "It'll be for slow guitar,
soft trumpet, and a bell."

Betrayal of Trust

FROM WOMEN/SPORT

THE START FOR ALL THREE GIRLS was innocent enough. A heady compliment. A promise of extra coaching attention. Soon enough, Rick Butler, their coach at Sports Performance Volleyball club in West Chicago, would follow that with an invitation to talk again — this time alone. Then Butler would profess his affection to the teenager. Each recalls how her breath caught in her throat. Butler would say she was a special talent and he could help make her athletic dreams come true. He could get her a college scholarship, a spot on the national team, perhaps even a shot at the Olympics. All she needed to do was put her unquestioned trust in him. As if to underscore what he said, he might fix the girl with a long look. Or gently set his hands upon hers.

That is how all three, now women in their 20s and 30s, describe their experiences with Butler. They were 15 or 16 years old when he began making advances, they say, and they recall being confused — simultaneously bothered yet flattered by the attention of their coach. They all badly wanted that shimmering volleyball future they say he held out before them.

By the time the youngest of the three, Julie Bremner, joined the program in 1984, when she was 15, the pattern was well established, according to the other two women. Butler was an unabashed martinet in the gym. But in private, with the girls he identified as rising stars and then isolated, he showed a more subtly manipulative side, all three women say. Bremner recalls Butler treating her to dinner at McDonald's and asking her if she was prepared to give her heart and soul to him. "I found out later he gave the same speech to the girl he slept with before me — only at a Burger King," Bremner says. Soon, according to Bremner, she had another heart-to-heart with Butler after he called her over to an empty corner of the gym one day before practice. She says Butler wondered aloud if he would reach his lofty goals in volleyball. He spoke of how he was afraid he would spend the rest of his life by himself, how no one loved him. Soon, she says, he was asking if she had a boy-friend, and what did they do when they were alone together? "I was a virgin," Bremner says. "I told Rick again and again, I didn't believe in premarital sex." As Bremner describes it, people were filtering into the gym by now, and as she and Butler stood to go, he asked for a hug. "I thought, No big deal, O.K. But he held me close to him and whispered, 'Oh, Julie. You always know exactly what I need.'"

Butler soon made stronger advances toward her, Bremner says in affidavits and interviews. She played setter, volleyball's version of quarterback, and strategy sessions were part of the job. On a March 1987 team trip to Japan, she says, Butler called her to his room one night to talk about the upcoming matches. Bremner says she arrived to find Butler alone, wearing a bathrobe and sitting on a Japanese floor mat. As she recalls it, Butler said, "Sit here," and patted the mat beside him. Bremner sat down. "No, sit closer," Butler said. Bremner did. "All of a sudden he leaned over and kissed me — he forced his tongue in my mouth and put his hand up my shirt and fondled me," she says. Bremner recalls being "frozen with fear." She says she left quickly and cried herself to sleep. "I didn't know what to do. You have to understand: I trusted him completely. More than anyone in the world."

She says she spoke of this to no one. Nonetheless, about two weeks later, Bremner says, Butler told her "people are starting to talk" and said they should meet somewhere away from the gym. Bremner says she suggested a restaurant, but Butler said no, they needed privacy. She says he named a hotel. "As an adult I know how stupid it sounds now," Bremner says. "But he promised me we were just going to talk volleyball." Bremner was 17 and Butler was 32. She says in a written statement to USA Volleyball, the federation that governs the sport in the United States, that almost immediately after she walked inside the hotel room Butler "started forcing himself on me. He pulled off my pants. . . . He held my arms and hands

down. . . . I pleaded with Butler to no avail. . . . He had sexual intercourse with me. . . . I bled. . . . It hurt worse than anything I had
ever felt."

Bremner, now 27, married and known as Julie Bremner Romias,
reported her experience in April 1994 to the Illinois Department
of Children and Family Services (DCFS), the state agency responsible for investigating child abuse. Since Bremner's call set the DCFS
case in motion, Butler also has been investigated for sexual misconduct by the DuPage County state's attorney's office and USA Volleyball. After an investigation and two closed hearings, the DCFS cate-
gorized Butler as "indicated for risk of harm," meaning that the
agency found what it calls "credible" evidence that the sexual allegations against Butler are true. Although Butler could have appealed the DCFS finding in court, he did not.

Butler fared no better with USA Volleyball. After three highly
charged 1995 hearings before the federation's Great Lakes regional board, its national ethics and eligibility committee and its
national executive committee, Butler was 0 for 3. In November
1995, the executive committee unanimously upheld a recommen-
dation to revoke Butler's membership for a minimum of five years
and banned him for life from coaching junior age (under 18) girls.

Butler challenged his expulsion in a Chicago circuit court and
won a short-lived reprieve on a procedural point: Judge Michael
Getty, explaining his January 1996 decision, said he was not ruling
on the veracity of the sexual allegations but on whether USA Volleyball had relied on "impermissibly vague" rules in ousting Butler.
USA Volleyball challenged Getty's ruling and won a reversal last
November. Butler has appealed to the Illinois Supreme Court and
is waiting to hear if his case will be heard.

In the meantime, the DuPage County state's attorney's office
began a criminal investigation of Butler but has not found any
accuser whose case falls within Illinois's statute of limitations for sex
offenses. "Just say our investigation remains open," prosecutor Michael Wolfe says.

Through it all, Butler — who cofounded Sports Performance in
1982 and runs it with his wife of three years, Cheryl — remains in
the gym. He continues to coach his elite 18-and-under girls' team.
He continues to tout the runaway success of his program: Since

Sports Performance's inception, its teams have won 22 national titles and, according to Butler, the 174 female graduates of the 18-and-under teams have received approximately $12 million worth of full-ride college scholarships. A handful of players, including Bremner, have played for U.S. national teams or turned pro. The most famous is Nancy Reno, a 1986 Olympian in beach volleyball. Reno says she is no fan of Butler's, and she decries how some high-ranking USA Volleyball officials (notably Jim Coleman, general manager of the men's and women's national teams, whose eldest daughter, Kim, played for Butler in the early 1980s — "I think he's a superb coach," Coleman says) still support Butler as a candidate for national or Olympic coaching positions. "It's appalling to me," Reno says. "Whether he can teach a woman to pass a volleyball . . . I'm sorry, but that's not the issue. It's sexual abuse. And it's wrong. It's wrong."

Although the number of athletes who are abused or exploited by coaches has never been quantified, the research on sexual abuse in general is voluminous and sobering. A 1986 American Medical Association study found that one in four girls (and one in eight boys) is sexually molested before the age of 18. Stephen Bavolek, a clinical psychologist and the executive director of the National Institute for Child Centered Coaching, in Park City, Utah, says many experts believe that sexual abuse in sports — like sexual abuse in society — goes well beyond isolated incidents. "This is a social problem deserving national attention," Bavolek says.

In many ways sports are an ideal setting for abusers. Experts say sexual predators typically seek the trust of both the parents and the child before beginning the abuse, so the child will be afraid to complain. In instances of same-sex abuse — like the recent case in which Canadian junior hockey coach Graham James admitted molesting NHL player Sheldon Kennedy and another boy when they were teenage members of his team — a child may keep quiet for fear of being called gay. Toss in the fact that sports create an emotional bond between player and coach, and the fact that coaches often spend large chunks of time alone with their athletes and, Bavolek says, "You have all the makings for an at-risk situation." There's a growing movement among sports organizations to establish explicit policies that prohibit coach-athlete sexual relationships, even when the age of consent is not an issue. The reasoning is the same as that prohibiting student-teacher relationships. "It's an abuse of power," says Gil Fried, assistant professor of sports and fitness administration at Houston.

In Chicago, Butler has continued to fight his expulsion despite a list of accusers — former players who say he had sex with or propositioned them while they were underage members of his club — that has expanded to at least six, including Bremner and the two other former players who came forward with her in 1994. (Both asked that their names not be used in print.) Like Bremner, the two other women provided statements to the DCFS and USA Volleyball alleging that Butler, as outlined in the first paragraphs of this story, had sexually exploited them when they were under 18 and still in his program. Each now says she reluctantly submitted to having sex with Butler at age 16 or 17 because she believed he controlled her future or because she felt helpless. None of the three women deny Butler's general assertion that they kept some contact with him — ranging from occasional phone calls, for two of them, to continued sexual relations — after they left his program. All of them say Butler solicited their trust by assuring them as teenagers that he loved them.

Butler says the charges are "stale" and insists he has done nothing wrong. He says he "dated" his three accusers, but only after each had left the program and turned 18. He characterizes the charges against him as a "witch hunt" masterminded by his former business partner and landlord, Sports Performance cofounder Kay Rogness, who helped Bremner contact the other two women and pushed USA Volleyball for Butler's expulsion, knowing that membership is a necessity for a coach to compete in sanctioned events like the national championships. Says the 56-year-old Rogness, "This isn't personal. It's the principle."

Butler has mounted a blitzkrieg defense. His coaching methods — based on intense discipline, constant drilling and the notion that girls should train as hard as boys — have helped make his $2-million-a-year organization what it is. He has marshaled scores of parents, players and business associates to deliver testimonials on his behalf at hearings and to proclaim publicly that they've never seen anything amiss in his program. They cite examples of girls whose lives have been set straight by playing at Sports Performance. They point to Rick and Cheryl's adoption of a former player's newborn baby in 1995, after the unmarried woman became pregnant at college. The arrangements went so well that Cheryl attended Lamaze classes with the birth mother.

Cheryl told USA Volleyball's executive committee that she has never felt there was "an ounce of truth" to the allegations against her husband. "If I had, I would never have married him, let alone adopt a child with him," she says.

Thirty-six months into his public ordeal, two questions hang over Butler's case: why did he wait eighteen months to abandon his initial answer that he "didn't recall" when his sexual relationships with each of his three sworn accusers began, then suddenly provide USA Volleyball with dates? And why would the women make up their excruciating stories?

In interviews with more than sixty former players, coaches, parents, law-enforcement authorities, and volleyball insiders, *Women/Sport* found numerous people who corroborated significant parts of the women's stories and much of the behavior the women ascribe to Butler. *Women/Sport* found five former Sports Performance players — including Bremner and the two others mentioned above — who say Butler had sex with them when they were teenage members of his program. A sixth former player told *Women/Sport* that Butler propositioned her in 1988, when she was 17.

Women/Sport also found instances in which Butler made contradictory or misleading statements and solicited narrowly worded testimonials that are notable for what they don't say. One example: in a two-paragraph statement that Butler asked a former player to submit to USA Volleyball, the woman said she had never been "molested or sexually abused by Rick Butler." What the statement failed to say was that in 1984, when she was a high school senior, she openly admitted having a sexual relationship with Butler while she played at Sports Performance, according to the DCFS testimony of two of her teammates. One of those teammates and Bremner told the DCFS that Butler admitted the relationship to each of them, in 1984 and 1987, respectively. Another former player, Karen Trebolo Weppner, a member of the '84 Sports Performance team, says, "I know there was definitely a physical relationship with Rick. She [the woman who wrote the statement] told me personally."

The woman, who asked *Women/Sport* to withhold her name, now denies that she and Butler had any sexual involvement before she left Sports Performance. Butler denies it as well. But both Butler and the woman admit to having had a sexual relationship when she went to play for Western Michigan in 1984. That same year, Butler accepted a job at Western Michigan as an assistant coach but left after one semester.

By 1990, Bremner says, she was beginning to let a few friends in on the humiliating details of her twenty-month sexual involvement with Butler, which ended in December 1988, when she was preparing to leave to train with the national team. Says Bremner, "He said, 'You're moving to California and you're going to move on with your life. I'm getting too old for you. The best thing for both of us is breaking up.'"

By 1991, Bremner was a sophomore at UCLA. Herb Summers, who had coached at Sports Performance during her senior year there and had since moved to California, stopped by the school one day to pay a visit and was stunned by the story Bremner told him. "I asked Julie how could I have missed it with her when I was right there," says Summers, who had been told by another Sports Performance player that she too had slept with Butler when she was 17. "When Julie explained some things to me, I understood."

Though Bremner was just 15 when she tried out for Sports Performance, Butler quickly pulled her up to train with his 18-and-under team, many of whose members were high school seniors. Encouraged by Butler's talk of her Olympic potential, Bremner says she was soon spending long hours in the gym, both to practice and to escape her parents' disintegrating marriage, which ended in divorce in 1988. "I started coming to practice right after school and I'd stay until 11:30 at night," Bremner says.

Butler has always demanded that his 18-and-under players forgo other sports and commit to training five days a week during the club season, which begins in January and ends with the Junior Olympics in July. In a typical season Butler's 18-and-under teams play 125 matches — "more than you play in a Big Ten career," he says. The elite players pay about $3,000 a year to travel the country competing for Sports Performance and to train at the program's Great Lakes Center, a 30,000-square-foot facility that Butler opened in 1991. Today nearly 200 girls and 50 boys, ages 11 to

18, play for Sports Performance. Even workouts are an impressive sight.

Five afternoons a week, dozens of girls fill the center's six indoor courts. Butler's 18-and-under teams train on the two courts in the newer wing of the gym. Among the perks the seniors enjoy is a separate locker room with each girl's name above her cubicle. The courts in the new wing are painted a shimmering red with white lines and a blue border. A sign on one wall proclaims OUR ONLY OPPONENT IS PERFECTION.

Practice on this January day will run three hours, and it's soon clear why Butler's players are renowned for technical excellence: only thirty minutes will be devoted to scrimmaging. The 18-and-under girls are wearing form-fitting red shorts and blue long-sleeve shirts that read IF IT'S TOO TOUGH FOR YOU IT'S JUST RIGHT FOR ME. They punctuate their work with high-fives and loud chatter. They seem to be having great fun.

"Playing at Sports Performance is the best experience I could've had," says setter Laura Abbinante, 21, a former Wisconsin star who was back at the club training this spring. Outside hitter Nicole Kacor, 17, says "I came to Sports Performance because it's intense. I know this is the best program in the nation and the best place for me."

Butler, a wiry man with receding black hair, presides over practice with an air of efficiency. His eyes are intense, his jaw firmly set. One of his heroes is Indiana's dictatorial basketball coach, Bobby Knight. In past interviews Butler has described himself as "serious as a heart attack" and as an unapologetic "hard-ass." Cognizant of Japan's Olympic success in women's volleyball, he traveled there in 1983 to study the highly regimented methods of Japanese clubs. "I remember sitting on the floor for two weeks," Butler says, "and I took ninety pages of notes."

But there was no time to lose. He had fallen into volleyball belatedly, and quite by mistake. In 1973, at 17, Butler married his girlfriend and they had a son. Butler was divorced by 1975, and later that year his 2-year-old boy drowned in eight inches of bathtub water while his ex-wife's husband babysat the toddler. Police in Eugene, Oregon, initially misclassified the death as an accident, then reopened the case in 1995 and pursued it as a homicide; his ex-wife's husband, Steve Hinkle, pleaded guilty to manslaughter. The police inquiry increased the burden on Butler at about the same time the USA Volleyball inquiry against him was accelerating and his mother was dying. Butler says these pressures prevented him from providing specific answers and dates to USA Volleyball.

Butler graduated in 1979 from the University of Redlands, in southern California, where he played defensive back and majored in history. He went to Chicago, where he landed a strength-coaching job at Bob Gajda's Sports Fitness Institute in suburban Glen Ellyn.

One of his coworkers there was Rogness. At Gajda's suggestion, she and Butler organized a girls' volleyball team in 1980 and enlisted Jerry Angle, then head coach at Northwestern University, as coach. Butler coached the team in a couple of tournaments in 1981 and succeeded Angle when Angle departed in 1982. That year, Butler and Rogness broke away from Gajda's Institute and made the volleyball club their full-time vocation, incorporating the business under the name Sports Performance Volleyball Inc. Rogness ran the office and often worked the bench as Butler's assistant. Though Sports Performance is not for profit, another Butler-owned company, GLV Inc., is a for-profit entity. It runs Sports Performance's lucrative camps and coaching seminars. It also produces instructional videos, which Butler claims are among the best-selling in the country, with total sales of 3,000 to 4,000 copies a year.

Parents and players who came to Sports Performance in the 1990s may not recognize the harsh atmosphere that Butler's players from 1980 to '89 describe. Parents whose daughters were in the program a decade ago say they had little idea what was going on inside the closed practices that Butler held then and still insists upon. Nor did the daughters always tell their parents exactly how Butler was pushing them to their stunning success — let alone which players Butler seemed to fancy. "The subject [of relationships between coach and player] was just too, too scary to touch," Reno says. "At that point as a kid your whole past, all the work you've put in, your scholarship — it all seems on the line." And so? "So you shut up," says Reno.

"You shut up," says Disa Johnson, a member of the 1984 elite team.

"You didn't talk about it," Weppner says.

Some of the '80s players who don't accuse Butler of sexual abuse nonetheless describe him as a frightening and paradoxical figure. On the rare occasions he passed out compliments, he could make their day. But mostly they depict him as a volatile taskmaster who cultivated a climate of fear and unpredictability and insisted on exercising control over their lives.

Butler says he has mellowed some over the years but admits that a decade ago it was nothing for him to sling a rack of balls across the gym. He has always had strict rules: no makeup, no nail polish, all shirttails tucked in. On one occasion a girl who forgot to remove her nail polish was ordered to scrape it off with a key. When Weppner skipped a practice to go to her senior prom, her father, Phil, says, "Butler just quit playing her."

He was fond of what he called "team-building" regimens, such as no-sugar diets. Until three or four years ago, he held mandatory weigh-ins before every practice, and some girls took laxatives or vomited to make weight. Jeane Erlenborn, who played for Butler from 1984 to '88, says, "There would be girls throwing up in the bathroom before practice." Several former players say that most of the girls on the team stopped menstruating. Butler says he was never made aware of any of those health concerns but he has since changed to weekly weigh-ins. "In the eighties nobody knew about eating disorders; nobody knew about nutrition," he says.

All of Butler's rules were explained as being for the good of the team and the program — just part of the pursuit of excellence. Loyalty was emphasized. Team captains were expected to report everything to Butler or risk censure. In the gym he exerted absolute authority and he countenanced no talking back.

"He drove that into our heads," says Johnson, now the women's volleyball coach at Missouri. "You either fit into his system his way or you were done. And that's just how it was. We were trained not to question him on anything." And if someone did? "There'd be a major, major penalty," Johnson says.

The penalty might be some lung-searing wind sprints or a grueling distance run before practice. Sometimes it would be verbal — a lacerating comment, a five-minute dressing-down, a sexually inappropriate remark. Jenni McGregor, an outside hitter who went by the nickname Fred, says, "I hit the ball really hard. I dove to the floor hard. I remember Rick walking behind me at practice one day and loudly telling an assistant coach, 'Boy, Fred does everything hard. She's gonna kill the first guy she sleeps with or marries.'"

For Reno — who played for Butler from 1980 to '84 and says, "I feel like a survivor of Sports Performance, not a graduate" — the nadir was an '84 incident that three teammates also mentioned in interviews: a "pit" drill that Butler angrily ordered during a team trip to Japan.

The player in the drill has to return shots hit by a coach and get a certain number of them in a row into the air. A miss means she must begin counting again. "The coach can make it as hard as he wants to," Reno says. "This time, Rick just made it ridiculous. It was a total power trip for him. Imagine, all these Japanese coaches in the gym have stopped to watch. All your teammates are standing to the side watching. And Rick just drove this poor girl to exhaustion. He fired balls at her and it got to the point where she could hardly get up. She was breaking down physically and starting to cry, and all the rest of us were almost crying and pleading with him, 'Isn't that enough? Please, can't you please just let her go?' But he kept it up. And he drove her so far into exhaustion she wet her pants in front of everybody."

Players say experiences like that left them both appalled and transformed. "I was scared to death of him and I worshiped the ground he walked on at the same time," says Erlenborn. When a rumor got around that one or two girls had seen Butler kissing a teammate in a car outside the club gym in 1984, three former players say, Butler called a closed-door team meeting and ranted at his quaking team. Reno says, "He basically told us, 'None of you saw what you say you just saw.' He was telling us, Don't believe what your own eyes may see."

McGregor says, "He did a good job of affecting our self-confidence. We didn't even trust ourselves or our own thoughts. He would tell you that if he did not really work you hard, you would know he did not care about you as a player. So at 15 and 16 we came to associate the two: when I'm beating on you, that's a good thing. It was like he was saying if he didn't abuse you, he didn't really care."

Bremner would go on to great things after her time at Sports Performance. She was named 1987 national high school co-player of the year and accepted a full scholarship to Notre Dame. Unhappy there, she left after a semester to train with the national team in 1989 before transferring to UCLA. She led the Bruins to the 1991 NCAA championship and was named All-America in 1993. She's now a third-year student in UCLA's school of medicine. Her life appears to be a roaring success.

Yet shortly after becoming engaged to Brian Romias in December 1993, Bremner decided to enter therapy. She says she couldn't put the emotional fallout from the alleged rape by Butler out of her mind and "I was worried that unless I worked through it, I was going to have problems in my marriage."

Within a few sessions she began telling her therapist details, which she recounted in her affidavits. In those statements, Bremner described not just the alleged rape, but also how Butler pressured her to have anal intercourse, how he pushed her head down on his lap in his car "so I would be forced to perform oral sex," and how he rented pornographic movies and "made me watch him masturbate while he watched the people have all kinds of sex." She says he told her that he'd had sex with underage players before. Bremner says she told no one as it was happening because "I felt no one would believe me." When Bremner filed her April 1994 DCFS report, investigators asked if she knew of other victims. She called Rogness. On Bremner's behalf, Rogness called the two other women who came forward.

The older of the two is now 32 and, like Bremner, married. The woman says, "My biggest memory of being a little girl is I wanted to be the best volleyball player in the world." It was a personal triumph when, in the summer of 1981, she was asked to join a Sports Performance team that was traveling to Montreal via Michigan and New York. She was 16, embarking on her first trip away from her family, and she was thrilled.

When Butler held an optional practice during a stopover at Western Michigan, the 16-year-old eagerly set out to work on her spiking, disregarding a suggestion Butler made about hitting the ball off a setting device. In a statement to USA Volleyball, the woman writes that at the end of practice Butler called her over and screamed, "What the hell is wrong with you? Jesus f— Christ!" She says he told her he was putting her on the next bus home. When she began crying he relented but made her ride in the equipment station wagon, not the team van, for the twelve-hour drive to Syracuse University.

Once there, she says, Butler called her to an empty lounge in the dorm where they were staying. "He apologized and said he had to do that to make me a better player," she says. "I needed to obey his coaching to be the best." Then, she says, Butler grabbed her and kissed her: "I had no idea he was going to do that, or why."

A few weeks later Butler, then 26, invited her to his home to talk about her athletic progress, the woman says in her written statement submitted to USA Volleyball. To her surprise, she says, his roommate was gone. She remembers they ate Chinese food and made small talk about her upcoming year in high school and her game. "Then he stood up, took my hand and led me to his bedroom and undressed me," she says. "He had sexual intercourse with me. . . . I felt there was no way to stop it. . . . It was painful."

She alleges that over the next two years Butler kept initiating sex with her — in his car, at her father's home, in a train bathroom on a team trip to Germany. She says when she was around friends she started to feel that "I didn't fit in. I had this huge secret. It took me ten years before I could tell anybody. You feel so alone. When your girlfriends are there talking about their first kisses, what was I supposed to say — 'Oh, I had sex with my coach in the backseat of his car?' Along the way it bothered me. I'd say, 'I'm so young.' He'd say, 'Don't think about our ages.'"

When the woman left for college in 1983, she says, she broke off the sexual relationship. By then Butler had moved on, according to the third of his accusers, who played at Sports Performance from 1983 to '85. Upon trying out at 15, this woman, too, had immediate success: Butler pulled her up to an elite squad for a 1983 team trip to California.

Like Bremner, the woman was a setter upon whom Butler lavished private coaching. She writes in a detailed report to USA Volleyball that in the fall of 1983, when she was 16 and Butler was 28, Butler offered to help her with a school paper on Vietnam. She says he invited her to his house and her parents let her go, assuming Rogness, then Butler's landlord, would be there. But again, according to the woman, Butler was home alone. She says that they went out for pizza and that, while they were at the restaurant, Butler told her "he had these overpowering feelings for me that he just couldn't control." According to the woman's statement, once she and Butler returned to his house, "He backed me against a wall, kissed me, fondled me, and then had intercourse with me. I was scared to death — scared to tell him no, scared I'd get pregnant, scared my parents would find out and what they would think of me." She says she had never had sex before and that she told no one about the incident.

Butler admits having had sex with the woman, but says it was not until 1985, and that their relationship continued until December 1990. By then, she was a student at an out-of-state college. Today she's 29 and happily married, with two kids. But she says, "It took me a long time to realize love does not equal sex, love is not perversion, love is not control. I had no other experiences that would tell me differently."

The woman says she decided to join Bremner before the DCFS because "I didn't want this to happen to anyone ever again." As the investigation opened, the three women began a series of tearful telephone calls to one another, and they were stunned at what they learned.

"I literally got chills," says Butler's 32-year-old accuser. "I just remember being on the phone and saying, 'Oh, my God! Oh, my God! He did that to me, he did that to me too!' We figured out he probably made us watch the same porn movies. We found he'd used the same language with all of us."

Butler does not deny having had sex with all three women but insists the relationships were consensual and took place when they were of age and out of his program. He questions why, if anything improper happened, the women waited so long to come forward. He argues that their continued contact with him or the club after they left for college shatters their credibility.

Experts say that victims of sexual abuse are often slow to report such incidents, especially if an authority figure is involved or if they know their assailant. "For young people, especially, there can be difficulty defining what an abuse experience is when the sexual abuse isn't, say, an attack on the street by a stranger," says Sharon Lamb, an associate professor of psychology at St. Michael's College in Vermont and the author of *The Trouble with Blame: Victims, Perpetrators, and Responsibility.* "With someone you know, small, exploitative things often happen first and the girl or woman may give the perpetrator the benefit of the doubt. By the time larger things happen, the victim feels complicit in it even though it's not her fault."

During the early days of his disciplinary proceedings before USA Volleyball, Butler was not only defensive but also angry. He couldn't believe the association would sanction its most successful junior coach. Before the ethics and eligibility committee in July 1995, he spoke of how successful his business was and painted an ominous picture of how damaging his expulsion would be to him and to volleyball in general, saying, "The last thing this sport needs is a scandal." He ricocheted from point to point — at one juncture daring the panel to investigate his current program: "I've got 160 girls, take every one of them, put them on a polygraph, do something, do something." Then, when he was asked directly if he recalled when his sexual relations with his former players began, Butler responded: "I don't recall . . . I can't recall."

At his last-chance hearing before the federation's executive committee three months later, Butler was suddenly able to give the exact dates on which he'd first had sex with each accuser. However, in his first interview with *Women/Sport* on January 29, he came without the transcript from that hearing and was back to being unable to recall.

When USA Volleyball announced the expulsion of Butler — its first member ever ousted for sexual misconduct — he moved to civil court and won his stay from Judge Getty. But he didn't fare so well at his November 1996 appeal hearing before a trio of judges. At that hearing, Butler's attorney, Jerome Wiener, advanced Butler's argument that the federation had no rule prohibiting coaches from having sex with athletes and, anyway, such activity might have been acceptable in the 1980s, before "times changed." At that point Judge Sheila O'Brien interrupted. "Excuse me, sir," O'Brien said. "But we are talking about rape. These girls were underage. Two of the incidents involved force. You would have to be retarded to think that there was nothing wrong with this conduct." The judges' decision went against Butler, 3–0.

Yet he remains in the gym.

Butler says he has never shown players pornography or talked to them explicitly about sex. Erlenborn is among those who say he is lying. "I was almost one of his victims," she says. "In '88, when I was

17 and about three weeks away from leaving the program, he called me at home and asked me to meet him at the Sybaris, this sex hotel in the [Chicago] area that advertised mirrors on the ceilings, triple-X movies, heart-shaped beds. He pressured me to go. He told me, 'C'mon, I promise you'll have a good time.' He promised me he'd be very 'discreet.'" Butler says, "There's not one ounce of truth to that."

He also disputes the former player who says they first had sex in 1983, when she was 16 and accepted help on a paper about Vietnam. He insists they first had sex in December 1985. But she has handwritten letters from Butler that begin in 1983, when she was 16. In January 1985, when she was 17 and he was coaching at Western Michigan, he wrote, "I think I've loved you from that first day in Burger King when I asked for your heart and soul. . . ." In letters dated January 11 and May 8, 1985, he compares their relationship to *The Thorn Birds,* a novel about the forbidden love between a young girl and her priest. Butler wrote, "I'm scared to death of losing you. . . . We have the most special relationship that I have ever known. . . . I've seen you go from someone who was totally dependent on me to someone who I could sit and talk with for hours and never think about you only being 17."

As many of his lines of defense have crumbled, Butler has increasingly blamed his accusers — and Rogness — for his predicament. He says they are jealous or scorned women who coveted him. Butler rhetorically asks, "Is it any coincidence that I get married in January of 1994 and all of a sudden this starts ninety days later?" Rogness insists she began her lengthy disentanglement from Sports Performance and its spin-off business in 1986, when she learned of Butler's sexual liaisons with players. Butler says Rogness left because they had deep disagreements about the direction of the business plus a personal relationship gone sour.

Through all the charges and countercharges, Butler has enjoyed phenomenal parental support. Chicago home builder Bill Kennedy, perhaps Butler's biggest booster and the father of Kelly, who played at Sports Performance from 1992 to '95 and is now playing at Wisconsin, tells *Women/Sport,* "When I was 23 I was in love with a 16-year-old girl. It was more than a passing relationship. So I know it can happen."

Many other parents concede they weren't around when Butler's accusers were, or that they never have seen anything amiss. Dale Davis had two daughters in the program from 1989 to '95, and he says they found it "wonderful." He believes Rogness is jealous, saying "the business did not take off until Kay Rogness left" and "Rogness was the first one to call the DCFS and start this whole thing. Rick did tell me that."

When told that Rogness was not the first to call the DCFS — that Bremner called the agency after her California therapist said that if Bremner did not report the sexual allegations, the therapist would be required to by law, because Butler works with minors — Davis pauses. Then he says, "My mouth is literally open. This is the first time I've ever heard this."

One of the other thunderclaps in this case came when Bremner's younger sister Bonnie decided to stay at Sports Performance after Julie came forward with her accusations. Bonnie, now 19 and a freshman setter for Penn State, was only 9 or 10 when the alleged abuse of her sister took place, and she admits her memory of that time is dim. "I love my sister," Bonnie says, "but I was in that program since sixth grade and I just can't believe Rick is capable of something like rape." Joy Dooley, the Bremner girls' mother, says she has had to battle that same incredulity.

"I support Julie," Dooley says, "but I understand Bonnie. Years ago, I was sticking up for Rick. I had had him in our house for dinner. I was on the booster club. I stood up and defended him at meetings when people grumbled about his closed practices. Now I realize by trusting him implicitly, it was like giving him indiscriminate permission to do whatever he was doing. I beat myself up a lot about that."

USA Volleyball has spent more than $140,000 in legal expenses on this case. It refused to blink when Butler filed a $1 million wrongful expulsion suit against the federation last year. Although USA Volleyball has banned Butler for life from coaching junior girls at tournaments or camps it sanctions, he is free to run his own programs. If no new charges surface in five years, he can be reinstated and back on the fast track for senior national team jobs.

As the third anniversary of Bremner's initial call to the DCFS approaches, she and the two other players say they're committed to seeing the case through. All three still have good and bad days. But they all say there was something cathartic about that July 1995 USA Volleyball ethics and eligibility hearing — the only time they have confronted Butler face-to-face.

His eldest accuser says, "I was so afraid, I insisted on sitting right next to the door. I was terrified. But I started to get braver, and it was because Rick started to confront us. And I started to get angry. When you're reading the transcript you can't tell, but I had a choked voice. When I started talking I was very scared. But by the end of my statement, I am *strong.* I am adamant. It was like I just got this power or strength, like, I can do this! It was my chance to say, 'You did do this! You know you did it! And how dare you say you didn't. How dare you.'"

STEVE MARANTZ

A Man's Appreciation for Women Athletes

FROM THE SPORTING NEWS

MEN LOVE WOMEN ATHLETES. As a man I state this with a strictly honorable intention. We love their grit, courage, savvy, finesse, strength, discipline, and determination. When they win we love their exuberance; when they lose we love their disappointment. We love their innocence within a jaded male sports culture. We love their health, grace, self-assurance, and clear-eyed beauty. They don't care if we love them. Even their indifference is beguiling.

Audience figures make a dry beginning to a romance; nonetheless they describe a snowballing phenomenon:

• Male viewership increased 11 percent for the Atlanta Olympics — with NBC's prime time weighted to women's events — over the Barcelona Games in 1992.

• Attendance at NCAA Division I women's basketball last season was 4.16 million — up from 1.15 million in 1981–82 — with men filling just less than half the seats.

• An ongoing ABC Sports series on women athletes — *Passion to Play* — is watched by as many men ages 18 to 34 as women.

• Male viewers of women's college basketball and women's pro golf on ESPN comprise 10 percent more of the total audience than five years ago.

We celebrate thee, O high priestesses of liniment and tape. Yet lest anybody take our affection for granted, remember that only twenty-five years ago men were depicted as chauvinists resisting athletic opportunity for schoolgirls. In fact, many men did not take women seriously as athletes. Women athletes were stigmatized as unfeminine and possibly gay. Aside from a few high-profile Olympians, golfers, and tennis players, most women athletes occupied a dim nether world. The greatest female hoopster of the 1950s and '60s, Nera White, played most of her adult career in high school gyms.

Proponents hoped Title IX — mandating equal athletic resources for women — would liberate women to grunt and sweat as freely as men. But the 1972 law had an unforeseen effect. It liberated men to appreciate the athleticism of women.

Our appreciation only occasionally detours into sexism. Women athletes have egalitarian appeal. Sure, some are conventionally sexy, but that isn't the point. A woman athlete is appealing not because of how she looks but because of how she performs.

"You can luck your way into being beautiful and you can luck your way into being rich, but you have to earn an Olympic medal," says Bart Conner, a former Olympic gymnast and the husband of the Romanian gymnastics legend Nadia Comaneci.

Sport is a meritocracy. Women athletes appeal to men because they work hard. They combine form with function.

Swimsuit models, on the other hand, appeal to men because they appear never to work. They have no function other than to shill. They are limp fantasies. How does one practice being a fantasy? Pout in the mirror? Laze languidly beside a swimming pool? Apply eyeliner? As fantasies go they are a thin gruel, too wholesome for pornography, too quaint for fashion. Men who indulge a fantasy of swimsuit models, of perfect beauty, inert and compliant, entertain a hollow and boring delusion.

If sex appeal enters marginally into the equation of women athletes and male fans, then it is positive sign. Men who find women athletes sexy are more apt to accept women in all of their dimensions. Athletic women sweat, blow snot from their noses, grunt, and lose their tempers. That is sport. Real women athletes eat quiche, and they might bake it. Men who love women athletes by definition embrace a fullness of behavior ultimately healthy to both genders.

Now when I see Sheryl Swoopes drive to the bucket, Mia Hamm split a defense, Dot Richardson turn on a fastball, Karolyn Kirby spike a winner, or Kiana pumping iron, I know I am a lucky man. I am witnessing a great flowering that uplifts my gender as well as theirs.

Women athletes appeal to male macho. They are tough, as personified by Kerri Strug's Olympian pain tolerance. Germany's Uta Pipig, winner of the 1996 Boston Marathon, was menstruating during the race, and ran the last several miles cramping while blood ran down her legs. She finished in 2:27:12 and was hospitalized. Public reaction was split. Men were impressed; women were angry. Women fans appreciated neither administration of it.

"Men are attracted to the toughness of women athletes, perhaps because it goes against stereotype," suggests Conner. "With many men there is a curiosity about women athletes. They have a mystique. We find that very attractive.

"I know from being married to a famous woman athlete, if you tell her, 'You can't do that,' just consider it done. I believe that was part of her hunger and drive as a young lady."

Women athletes transcend feminine stereotypes to attain a sort of "toughness" equality. UConn women's basketball coach Geno Auriemma has an effective method for enlivening a lethargic practice. He tells his players they are "playing like girls."

"Obviously you are dealing with a different gender, but athletically I've chosen not to treat them differently," says Auriemma, who has coached high school boys. "I don't buy the idea to coach them like women. You treat them like women, but you coach them like players."

For a long time men viewed women athletes as less rugged. With few exceptions, women's basketball until 1970 was six-on-six, with four women anchored to either the offensive or defensive end. Women were believed too delicate for the court game.

Title IX allowed for notions of female delicacy to be dispelled. Women athletes gradually gained toughness credentials, a dramatic watershed being the 1982 Hawaii Ironman Triathlon, in which Julie Moss crawled the last couple hundred yards to the finish line. The scene repeated in 1995 when seven-time winner Paula Newby-Frazier collapsed near to the finish, lay on the ground for twenty minutes, and crawled across the finish line.

Last summer Colorado Sliver Bullets outfielder Angie Marsetta was hit five times by opposing male pitchers. On the fifth she charged the mound. Another player, Stacey Sunny, was hit in the face with a fastball. She was back in the lineup after missing one game.

Post–Title IX thinking goes a step further. If women athletes attain the toughness of male athletes despite rewarding women of conventional femininity, then perhaps they are innately more tough.

"Toughness isn't gender-specific," Conner says. "It seems athletes in general are good at coping with obstacles and challenges. Perhaps people who aren't able to cope with monstrous challenges get weeded out. Maybe the women athletes we celebrate achieve what they do because they have something internally. I am a big believer in environment; some things can be learned. But not everything."

Which goes to Conner's point about mystique. The toughness of male athletes may start with cultural expectations. The toughness of women athletes must come from within. Men are intrigued.

At least one man at the Summer Olympics did not miss a women's event. He watched women's gymnastics, swimming, and track — events men traditionally watch. But he also watched women's volleyball, soccer, softball, and basketball — events men traditionally ignore. That man, NBC broadcaster Bob Costas, sees the '96 Olympics as a watershed for women athletes.

"While the popularity of gymnastics and figure skating remains way up there, the stuff moving up on the rail is team sports," Costas says. "Where a generation ago there was almost no interest in team sports, not only on the part of men but women as well, there is an explosion of interest and participation."

In the aftermath of Atlanta, the American Basketball League is in its first season, with attendance averaging 3,000 to 5,000, slightly ahead of projections. A second women's pro league, the WNBA, begins its ten-week season June 21. Women's Professional Fastpitch, a six-team pro league, is lauching in June in the Southeast. A group including national team coach Tony DiCicco is planning a women's soccer tour next fall, laying a foundation for a pro league.

Recently I watched the star of the Swampscott (Massachusetts) High girls basketball team become the first girl in school history to reach the 1,000-point plateau. When senior Katelyn Leonard tossed in her historic basket, the crowded gym erupted. Half and possibly more of the audience was male.

Here's why men are watching women's team sports and why viewership will increase: law. Simply, the effect of twenty-five years of Title IX. A 1995 study showed 39 percent of high school athletes were girls, compared with 7 percent in 1971–72. Boys have grown up playing basketball, baseball, soccer, hockey, and football with girls or at least sharing gyms and fields. They have grown up with an institutionalized message of tolerance and respect.

"The Title IX generation is growing up," says Lydia Stephans, ABC Sports vice president of programming and a former Olympic speedskater. "Boys are growing up with an appreciation of what girls can do. They realize there's a different skill level, but there's an appreciation for who girls are."

Accessibility. Women perform at levels accessible to men. When men watch Jen Rizzotti of the New England Blizzard drive to the hoop they think, "I can do that" or "I used to be able to do that." When men watch Michael Jordan soar above the rim they think, "What planet is he from?"

Men long have appreciated women's tennis and golf because of the accessibility factor. Now it applies to team sports.

"A lot of guys who go to [NBA] games are living a fantasy," Auriemma says. "They are seeing things they couldn't possibly ever do. It's entertainment, but I'm not sure it's even basketball anymore.

"But they come to our games and appreciate the way kids play because that was how they played. The game was played below the rim, where you couldn't break a man down and get a shot. You had to work together to get things done. Not to say that one game is better than the other."

O.K., we'll say it. The women's game is more thoughtful, rhythmic, and intricate. It is devoid of freakishness. It feels like the crisp, stylish men's game John Wooden coached thirty years ago.

"The essence is more movement and grace than bodies banging into each other," Auriemma says.

"At the Olympics," Costas says, "women's basketball was much more interesting to watch."

Accessibility applies to other team sports. Men know they can't sneak a fastball past Junior Griffey. But past Olympic shortstop Dot Richardson, maybe. Women's soccer and volleyball appear to be played on mortal levels.

Respect. The alter ego of accessibility. I might take Lisa Leslie to the hoop, but I expect to eat leather. I might bump Michelle Akers off the soccer ball, but I know she would run me into the ground. Men know they are looking at superior athletes.

"There is a realization women are just as serious," says Lesley Visser, ABC and ESPN commentator. "Women lift weights and are committed to nutrition. Look at Jackie Joyner-Kersee. No man ever trained harder. Men look at her and say, 'Whew! That is an athlete.'"

Innocence. Money hasn't corrupted women's team sports. There is a perception that women play for the joy of competition, since financial incentives still are limited (ABL salaries average $70,000). Absence of money has as a corollary the absence of jerks. Women's team sports have not produced counterparts to Albert Belle, Bryan Cox, Dennis Rodman, Barry Bonds, Tie Domi, and Jeff George.

"When you see Dot Richardson, a terrific softball player, go off to her [medical] residency, that makes people feel good about sports," Costas says. "Part pure sports."

This may be a stretch, but I think innocence is seen in the emotional quality of women athletes. Women athletes don't spike the ball, taunt opponents, confront officials, harangue fans, or do victory dances. They tend to display sportsmanship and humility. Though some male athletes have a quality of feminine emotion — Cal Ripken, Emmitt Smith, Ray Bourque — no women athletes are so self-involved and narcissistic as to display the extremes of male emotion.

All of this could change in a flash, of course, if professional opportunities become lucrative.

Alternative. Men's games are priced for corporate writeoffs. A decent NBA seat costs $40. A good ABL seat is $10.

Beyond expense is excellence. People want to see the best of something. The University of Connecticut women's basketball team is undefeated and ranked number one. The men's team, which suffered the indignity of two players drawing suspensions for taking airplane tickets from an agent, was 14–9 going into last Monday's game against Syracuse.

"People in Connecticut are starved for a winner," UConn fan Tom Kelley says. "Where else are we going to see one?"

Fathers. Men are fathers of daughters. Fathers want positive role models for daughters. Let's assume a 15-year-old girl is more fascinated with celebrities than the school nurse. Which celebrity provides a better example: a model, actress, rock star, or athlete? Models vamp on catwalks. Actresses work in mindless sitcoms. Rock stars puncture their arms. The choice is an easy one. Fathers want daughters to have healthy incentives and opportunities.

Curiosity. Men wonder about the upper limit of women's athletic ability. Learning curves are steep. Can they reach parity with the top men?

The Colorado Silver Bullets, the first professional women's baseball team to play against men, are on ongoing experiment. Players had experience in softball but not baseball. The transition has been painstaking and revealing. The Bullets won 6 games in 1994, their first season, 12 in their second, and 25 in their third season. Skills are markedly improved.

"The work ethic is the highest level I've ever seen," says manager Phil Niekro, the Hall of Fame knuckleballer. "When you coach them you've got their full attention. They want to stay out all day long. When you're teaching them something they've never been taught but they've wanted since they were little girls, you're really teaching. If men had the desire, guts, and determination to play the game like these women do, I don't think there'd be too many problems in the game."

The Bullets play against semipro, college, and minor league men. Niekro believes a woman eventually will break into the minor leagues and major leagues. The pioneer probably will not make it on power hitting, but on defense or a specialty pitch, such as the knuckleball Niekro threw.

"It won't be our players," Niekro says. "It will be the little girls buying gloves now, going to cages, getting lessons, learning how to turn a double play. Give them high school experience and four years of college experience. By the time they're 19 they'll be much more polished than the players we have."

Victim identification. In a curious turn, white men identify with women and minorities. White males are ridiculed and villainized in popular culture. Watch prime-time TV for an evening — white males beat up spouses and children, lay off workers, drive drunkenly, cheat on wives, practice incompetent law and medicine, and subvert law enforcement. And those are just the comedies.

The point being: as a result of pop culture — TV, magazines, music, literature — white males suffer the same low self-esteem women and minorities have suffered for years. Equality is a wonderful thing. Now white males feel badly enough about themselves to cheer for women and minority athletes.

What about men who hate women athletes? Barb Kowal, UConn's associate director of communications, wants to know what those men have to say. I tell her I haven't found any. She snorts.

Kowal: "They're out there, believe me."

Me: "Where?"

Kowal: "Look around, you'll find them."

Me: "They must be at that mythical country roadhouse where sexiest guys go."

Kowal: "It's not so mythical."

Me: "Who are these haters?"

Kowal: "I would say he's the guy who religiously reads *USA Today* and watches *SportsCenter,* who follows all the sports and knows all the point spreads and who participates in or has participated in a sport."

Me: "He sounds pretty busy. Why would he care about women's sports?"

Kowal: "I think he thinks they take attention away."

For journalistic balance, I undertake a nationwide search for men who hate women athletes. In my mind's eye I find them at Lyle's, a whiskey-drenched roadhouse outside of Borger, Texas. Vern and Earl, middle-aged truckers with squinty eyes and orb-shaped bellies, lay it out plain.

"Cain't stand them women athletes," Vern says. "Get too much attention."

"Woman's supposed to smell good," Earl says. "Not stink like a man."

"Give a woman a basketball, next thing she's wearin' the pants in the house," Vern says.

"Women ain't built for sports," Earl says. "Built for love."

"If God wanted women to play sports He woulda give them slime-ball agents," Vern says. "Like He did men."

"Title IX is a communist conspiracy," Earl says.

"The Cold War is over," I say.

"Not for me, it ain't," Earl says.

There you have it — men who hate women athletes. As I leave Lyle's roadhouse, Vern and Earl spike Lone Star longnecks with testosterone. I grab the bottles, drain them over Vern and Earl's balding heads, and head back toward civilization.

Some men fall in between love and hate. These men are casual fans for whom women athletes inspire admiration but not passion. They perceive a lower level of intensity, aggressiveness, and, ultimately, competitiveness.

"Just once, I'd like to see Kara Wolters dunk," says Paul Adamowich, a 37-year-old fan from New Britain, Connecticut. "I don't know why she's holding back."

Wolters is Connecticut's six-foot-seven senior center. Adamowich has come to the dome in Storrs, Connecticut, to see her against Boston College.

"Would that make the game better?"

"Definitely," he says. "More exciting."

Wolters is chatting with reporters after Connecticut's victory. She is open and affable. Wolters tells me she notices more men in the seats than even three years ago when she was a freshman. Most encouraging, she says, is that men now watch women without comparing them with men. About 45 percent of her letters comes from boys and men. Most want autographs; some ask for a date.

I tell her about Adamowich. She isn't surprised.

"That's my number-one request from men," Wolters says. "There are only a few women doing it — Lisa Leslie, Charlotte Smith. I don't know. It's kind of a macho thing."

"Are you tempted?"

She stifles a giggle.

"I don't know. I've got so many things to work on."

Her dark eyes are dancing.

"Yeah, I'm tempted. Maybe this summer."

Meanwhile, men continue to appreciate women's individual sports. Our passion for gymnastics is stoked by Kerri Strug, an iron maiden, and for figure skating by Ekaterina Gordeeva, a grieving widow. The emergence of Martina Hingis, 16, as a rival to Steffi Graf, could bring us back to tennis.

Some world-class women are less publicized. For years I have watched a woman run the streets of Swampscott and Marblehead, Massachusetts, lightly bounding as though free of gravity. Marty

Geissler, 34, ran for Boston University and once tried out for the U.S. Olympic team in the 10K.

Today she makes a living as a personal trainer, and in her spare time she runs, bicycles, sailboards, snowboards, and rollerblades. Last summer she heard about an event called the duathlon, a combination bicycle and running race. In her first duathlon — a 5K run followed by a 20-mile bike followed by a 5K run — she finished second, in 1 hour 28 minutes. It qualified her for the World Championship last September in Italy. Geissler won her age group and finished second overall.

"Here's the difference between women and men," Geissler is saying. "I can invite five women friends to go mountain biking on a weekend, and none of them will do it. I can call five guys, and they all show up. Sports is their way of spending time together. It bothers me that more women aren't doing this."

We are at her training studio at a Marblehead health club. Geissler is tanned from a week of snowboarding, dressed in a nylon warmup, blond hair tied behind her head.

"Men always ask me why more women aren't doing biking or snowboarding," she goes on. "I don't know, unless it's cultural. It may be the way women are brought up with a lot of fears. My father is an athlete. He brought me and my brother up to be the best at whatever sport we tried. Sex wasn't an issue."

Single, childless, and self-supporting, Geissler is free to indulge her athleticism. She runs 7 to 8 miles five days a week and lifts weights three days. Depending on her mood, she might substitute running with biking, rollerblading, or sailboarding.

Last summer on a whim she joined an all-male club of elite road cyclists. She was received coolly — not because she is a woman but because she was an unproven newcomer. On her first 38-mile ride she was "dropped" eating dust five miles behind. Geissler's competitive instinct flared.

"By the third week I was staying with them," she says. "By the end of the summer I was up in front, taking poles."

Acceptance came with performance.

"At the beginning nobody would talk to me. By the end of the summer they were waiting for me. They wouldn't start without me."

Geissler noticed another change. Not only were the men nicer to her, but they were nicer to one another, too.

"At the beginning they were all business," she says. "But I'm not like that. I like to talk and joke. I complimented them — that's a female thing. By the end they were all joking and laughing."

Men have many fantasies, after all. Yes, men want to meet a Victoria's Secret model. But what does a man say to a Victoria's Secret model when at last talk cannot be avoided? "Excuse me, dear, is your gold silky teddy available in all sizes?" After the last flicker of candlelight and the last drop of champagne, silence would be deafening.

No such problem with women athletes. Men relate to women athletes because they are not fantasies. They are women men might take to a sports bar on a Sunday afternoon. They might drink beer and watch games, banter and elbow and cut up. If we complain about the "bump" rule, or make reference to Tiny Archibald, they would know what and who we mean. If we need someone to explain a balk, they would be there for us.

With Kara Wolters, a man could discuss screens, zone traps, and weakside rotation. She could share the secret of her off-season conditioning and, in an intimate moment, name her all-time women's five. Here, Kara, have another nonalcoholic beer. Tell us how you would defense Teresa Edwards. Don't stop.

"There's the old stereotype of a guy sitting on a couch watching football and his girlfriend can't wait for the season to end," says Dodgers third baseman Todd Zeile, husband of former Olympic gymnast Julianne McNamara. "A lot of guys feel that women who are athletes appreciate sports and relate better to their interests.

"On a personal note, I have found it's a lot easier to relate to Julianne. Coming up through the minors, spending time away from home, the work ethic — she understands all that. Her supportiveness has made a big difference in my career."

Track and conditioning coach Bob Kersee, husband of Olympic track star Jackie Joyner-Kersee, says he dated nonathletes before marrying twelve years ago.

"Some women didn't understand the frustration I went through when losing or the dedication it takes to organize a practice," Kersee says. "The difference with Jackie is she understands what I go through as a coach."

O.K., so men love the way women athletes compete. They are tough and disciplined. Others love them — and even marry them

— for perceived compatibility. They keep us company, on television and at arenas.

Perhaps there's another reason. Could the feeling men have for women athletes have less to do with gender and more to do with sport?

"Mia Hamm, who dives for every soccer ball, is very feminine off the field," Lydia Stephans says. "But when she plays, she's a competitor. She's genderless."

At a pure level, athletes are gender-, color-, and caste-neutral. In sport every athlete is every fan, and vice versa. Women athletes are us. We love them as we love ourselves.

SUSAN STERLING

The Soccer Parents

FROM THE NORTH AMERICAN REVIEW

THE SOCCER PARENTS ARE UNHAPPY. It's a Saturday afternoon in late October, the playoffs for the State Cup, northern division, and our team is losing. Well, not losing exactly — it's a scoreless game — but the girls need to win. And they can't score; they can't finish it off. "Let's go, girls!" the soccer parents shout, and "Come on, girls, let's get a goal!" and "Let's go, Blue!" This is meant to be encouragement, but anyone can hear we are really irritated because the girls can't score.

And we want them to score. We need them to score because they are more experienced than the other team and should be winning by now. And last weekend? At the start of the playoffs, they lost when they could have tied. It had rained the night before and the girls were slipping around on the muddy field, and then a fullback on our team kicked the ball into our goal. The ball went off her cleat and past our goalie, giving our opponents the winning score. A pall fell over all of us watching from the sidelines. We can't kick it in the other goal, but we can kick it in our goal! No one said that out loud, of course. We all murmured, "That's O.K.," but we couldn't believe it, because that's the kind of thing the girls used to do four and five years ago, when they were six years old and just starting soccer, before they'd had soccer camps and uniforms and expensive team jackets. The girl who kicked it into our goal cried, and the goalie cried, and the other girls ran up and comforted them. Several girls put their arms around the goalie and said, "That's O.K.," and then the coaches said the girls had to get on with the game, mistakes happen, but it was the end of the second half, and we all knew what that goal meant. It meant we might not go to the finals for the State Cup.

So this afternoon the October sky is pale, but the field is dry. It's the second weekend of the playoffs, and the game is well into the second half, with no score. It's what we hoped for last weekend, but this weekend if the girls only tie they might not make the finals for the State Cup. And so we're not happy, we parents, hunched on the sidelines, watching our daughters out there on the field. We listen to the referees' whistles and the girls' shouts and the smack of cleats against leather, and we look up at the bare trees beyond the field, and we're tense and anxious, though we're trying not to show it, because we have spent all fall out here, giving up our weekends to watch the girls play, to encourage them on with "Let's go, Blue!"

And if they're not winning, some parents murmur, then it must be because they're not trying hard enough. And if you look out on the field, where our girls are chasing after the ball and stumbling and picking themselves up, all dirty and sweaty, you know they could be running faster, because sometimes the girls on the other team get to the ball first. ("But then, again, what does it matter," one of the fathers mutters, "because even when our girls get the ball and bring it down the field, they can't score! We're dominating this game, we've already had twenty shots at goal, so who knows what the hell's happening out there?") He believes — many of the parents believe — the problem is one of desire. We never mention any names, of course, because everyone wants to be friendly and supportive. No one would ask a particular girl's parents if they send her outside with her ball after supper, if they are instilling a fighting spirit. But a few parents wonder, among themselves, why that girl is starting when she keeps losing the ball. And some parents suspect that it's politics, since the coaches' daughters play the entire game, and that's politics, too. "Hearts are being broken out there on the field," confides one mother, "but I won't second-guess the coaches. I know my role is to encourage." So she yells, "Come on, girls, get the ball!" but of course she notices — we all notice — which girl looks dreamily toward the woods for a moment, as if she were thinking of her cat, or does a little skip when she should be racing toward the goal. Or that girl who runs her hand through her hair at a critical moment when she should be paying attention to the ball (and why doesn't she put her heart into the game?). And today it seems the whole team's not paying attention. Not even the girl who cried because she missed two penalty kicks. ("And they had two penalty kicks, did you see that, and they couldn't even get those in, my God!" complains another father.)

So the soccer parents pace along the sidelines and mutter to each other and look worried — even those of us who tend to be quiet during the games pace and look worried. And if there are some who are not happy with this parental scene, we don't mention it to each other because that would be disloyal. That would look as if we didn't have the right spirit to pass on to our daughters. Maybe we don't, or maybe I don't, because sometimes I find myself perversely hoping the other team will get a goal, just to show up the soccer parents, just to spite them — as if I weren't one, too, as if my daughter weren't on the team, and I didn't want her to get a goal, or at least an assist, and be a star player.

And she's not a star. She's an 11-year-old girl who plays the piano and violin and is a good mimic and mathematician and likes *sea-Quest* and *Star Trek* and watching *Lamb Chop's Play-Along* when she's home sick from school. She's not a star at all, though she plays her position well and can pass, which is why she was chosen for this team. What she likes best is being with the other girls, but she wishes they didn't play soccer every weekend. It's too much soccer for her — she knows her feelings about this — and she tells me, when I talk of my friends' daughter, who at seventeen was on a girls' soccer team that won the Nationals in Minneapolis, that I have told her about this girl three times, and she is not going to be like that, and I say I know, and I do know. So why do I keep talking about the daughter of my friends, who is a soccer star?

And sometimes I know (days later, because I have no perspective on the game at all when I'm watching) the problem for us, as parents, has to do with our not getting enough love, years ago, and not feeling like stars ourselves. And now we have daughters who have a chance to do what we couldn't — we mothers, anyway — when no one took girls' sports seriously and/or noticed much if a girl handled a ball well. Because of that, I suspect, we mothers are worse with tone. Both mothers and fathers stand on the side-lines and yell encouragement and mutter, "They aren't trying hard enough, they don't want it enough, they aren't hungry." The fathers shake their heads in disbelief and huddle in little groups, discussing strategy — but those are their little girls, after all, and many of them have sons. It's still more important for boys to be good at sports, they think, though it isn't fashionable to say this out loud anymore.

So it's the mothers who really can't stand it when the ball goes wide of the net yet another time. It's the mothers, mostly, who shout from the sidelines, "You need to run faster, girls! You aren't running fast enough!" The girls are racing down the field now, passing the ball, and they're panting and their faces are red and their knees hurt, because someone has knocked them down or they've tripped, and their elbows are bleeding, and they're only 10 and 11 years old. We barely notice their falls, though, or if we do, we think they just have to try harder not to trip — they have to run harder. They have to run, and run, and keep running, and we'll encourage them. "Come on, girls! Run! We need a goal!" the soccer parents shout, as if the girls hadn't noticed, as if they didn't know they need to get a goal to win. "Run!"

And because we believe they simply need to be tougher, we never worry that maybe someday the girls will hear us so well that they'll keep on running — past the goal posts, past the school buildings, past the playing fields and the river and the woods, past the golf course and far away from our town. They'll keep on running, and trying harder, only they won't be wearing yellow shorts and blue shirts anymore, and they won't be passing a soccer ball. They'll be running and running, farther and farther away, and we'll hope desperately that they aren't alone, that they are happy even though we never hear from them, because how could they have thought they had failed us? They're out in the world and running, and they still hear our anxious voices, urging them on, telling them they aren't trying hard enough.

They don't come back. We never see them again. Yet sometimes, years later, when we're very quiet, we imagine we hear them again, just outside the windows, in the fields behind the school. It's summer and they're all together, and they've taken off their cleats and are playing barefoot in the grass. They're just running around, laughing and kicking the ball to each other, the way they did when they were small, but they know more tricks now and they like that. They can dribble and pass and head the ball, and they can fake each other out and do perfect throw-ins. They're quick — quicker even than their older brothers — and they're excited, because they're 10 and 11 years old and they're together again and they're happy — you can hear it in their voices as they call out to each other. They feel wonderfully strong, and they like their bodies, which can do so many things, and they're proud of themselves. "Look!" they call out (and we hope they're calling to us, but we're not certain). "Look at us! We're good at this, you know?"

Biographical Notes

Tom Boswell was guest editor of *The Best American Sports Writing 1994*. He covers baseball for the *Washington Post* and is a frequent commentator on National Public Radio.

Robert Cole is professor of English and director of journalism at the College of New Jersey. He was CASE New Jersey Professor of the Year in 1992 and received a Lifetime Achievement Award from the New Jersey Press Association in 1994.

David James Duncan is the author of two novels, *The Brothers K* and *The River Why*, and a collection of nonfiction and stories, *River Teeth*.

David Ferrell, a father of two, has been a feature writer at the *Los Angles Times* for the past fourteen years, where he was part of the news team that won Pulitzer Prizes for their coverage of the 1992 Los Angeles riots and the 1994 Northridge earthquake. He is currently at work on a novel entitled *Screwball*, a baseball black comedy.

David Finkel is a staff writer for the *Washington Post Magazine*.

Since 1992, Pat Forde has been a columnist for the *Louisville Courier-Journal*. A graduate of the University of Missouri, he played high school football for Gary Barnett. He was also a contributor to *The Best American Sports Writing 1996*.

Tad Friend is a contributing editor to *Outside* and a staff writer at *The New Yorker*.

Tony Hendra's profile of bullfighter Francisco Rivera Ordonez appeared in *The Best American Sports Writing 1997*. He is a contributor to numerous national publications and the coauthor with Ron Shelton of the screenplay for the 1996 film *The Great White Hype*.

JOHNETTE HOWARD is a senior writer for *Women/Sport* and *Sports Illustrated*. She began her career with the *Detroit News* and later wrote for the *National Sports Daily*. Her profile of the hockey player Joe Kocur appeared in the inaugural edition of *The Best American Sports Writing*.

THOMAS KOROSEC is a staff writer for the *Dallas Observer*.

TIM LAYDEN has been a senior writer for *Sports Illustrated* since 1994. A graduate of Williams College, Layden previously wriote for the *Albany Times Union* and *New York Newsday*.

STEVE MARANTZ wrote for the *Trenton Times*, the *Kansas City Star*, and the *Boston Globe* before joining the *Sporting News* in 1994. He lives in Swampscott, Massachusetts.

BRUCE MCCALL is a frequent contributor to many publications, including *Esquire*, *The New Yorker*, and *Outside*. His most recent book is *Thin Ice: Coming of Age in Canada*.

J. R. MOEHRINGER is a staff writer for the *Los Angeles Times*.

LESTER MUNSON is associate editor for *Women/Sport* and *Sports Illustrated*. He regularly appears on the popular television program *Sportswriters on TV*.

CHARLES P. PIERCE appears with Bill Littlefield on the National Public Radio program *Only a Game*. A former columnist for the *Boston Herald* and writer at-large for *GQ*, he is a contributing editor for *Esquire*.

ROBERT ANDREW POWELL has been a staff writer at the weekly *Miami New Times* since 1995. He is a graduate of Ripon College in Wisconsin and Northwestern University in his native Illinois.

SCOTT RAAB is a writer-at-large for *GQ*. He is a graduate of Cleveland State University and the University of Iowa. His work has appeared in a wide variety of national publications.

ELWOOD REID's first novel, *If I Don't Six*, was recently published by Doubleday.

DAVID REMNICK's story on Mike Tyson marks his third appearance in *The Best American Sports Writing*. A graduate of Princeton, he became the editor of *The New Yorker* in July 1998. His book *Lenin's Tomb: The Last Days of the Soviet Empire* won a Pulitzer Prize in 1993.

The story "Planet Venus" represents LINDA ROBERTSON's fourth appearance in *The Best American Sports Writing*. She has been with the *Miami*

Herald since 1983 and is the former president of the Association for Women in Sports Media.

JOHN SEABROOK, a writer for *The New Yorker,* is the author of *Deeper: My Two-Year Odyssey In Cyberspace.*

GARY SMITH is a senior writer for *Sports Illustrated* and a past winner of the National Magazine Award for feature writing.

A native of Hartford, Connecticut, SUSAN STERLING lives in Maine and teaches at Colby College. Her essays and stories have appeared in the *Christian Science Monitor* and other publications.

RICK TELANDER is a graduate of Northwestern, where he played football. He is currently a columnist for the *Chicago Sun-Times* and is a special contributor to *Sports Illustrated.* He is the author of five books, among them the basketball classic *Heaven Is a Playground.*

Notable Sports Writing of 1997

SELECTED BY GLENN STOUT

Soccer Soul. *Northeast,* November 2, 1997

WILLIAM TAPPLY
Murphy Was One of Us. *American Angler,* September/October 1997

STEVE WALBURN
Lord of the Ring. *Atlanta,* July 1997
MICHAEL WEINREB
Glimpse of the Tiger. *Akron Beacon Journal,* June 1, 1997
TIM WENDEL
A Full Count on Cuba. *USA Today*

Baseball Weekly, January 29–February 4, 1997
DAN WETZEL
Hot and Cold. *Basketball Times,* April 1, 1997
PETE WILLIAMS
Pumped! *USA Today Baseball Weekly,* May 7–13, 1997
ROBERT WOLONSKY
Wrestling with Tragedy. *Dallas Observer,* November 20–26, 1997
MARK WUKAS
Running with Ghosts. *Sport Literate,* Spring 1997